I0761751

Lean Cat, Savage Cat

ALSO BY LAUREN J. JOSEPH

At Certain Points We Touch

Lean Cat, Savage Cat

A NOVEL

Lauren J. Joseph

CATAPULT
NEW YORK

LEAN CAT, SAVAGE CAT

This is a work of fiction. All of the characters, organizations, and events portrayed in this novel are either products of the author's imagination or used fictitiously.

First Catapult edition: 2026

ISBN: 978-1-64622-328-2

Library of Congress Control Number: 2025944596

Jacket design by Sarah Brody
Jacket images: dust particles © Shutterstock / Brocreative; eyes © Shutterstock / Jlmrtz Photo

Catapult
New York, NY
books.catapult.co

Printed in the United States of America

1 3 5 7 9 10 8 6 4 2

This book is dedicated to the Sacred Heart and Felix,
who give my life its meaning

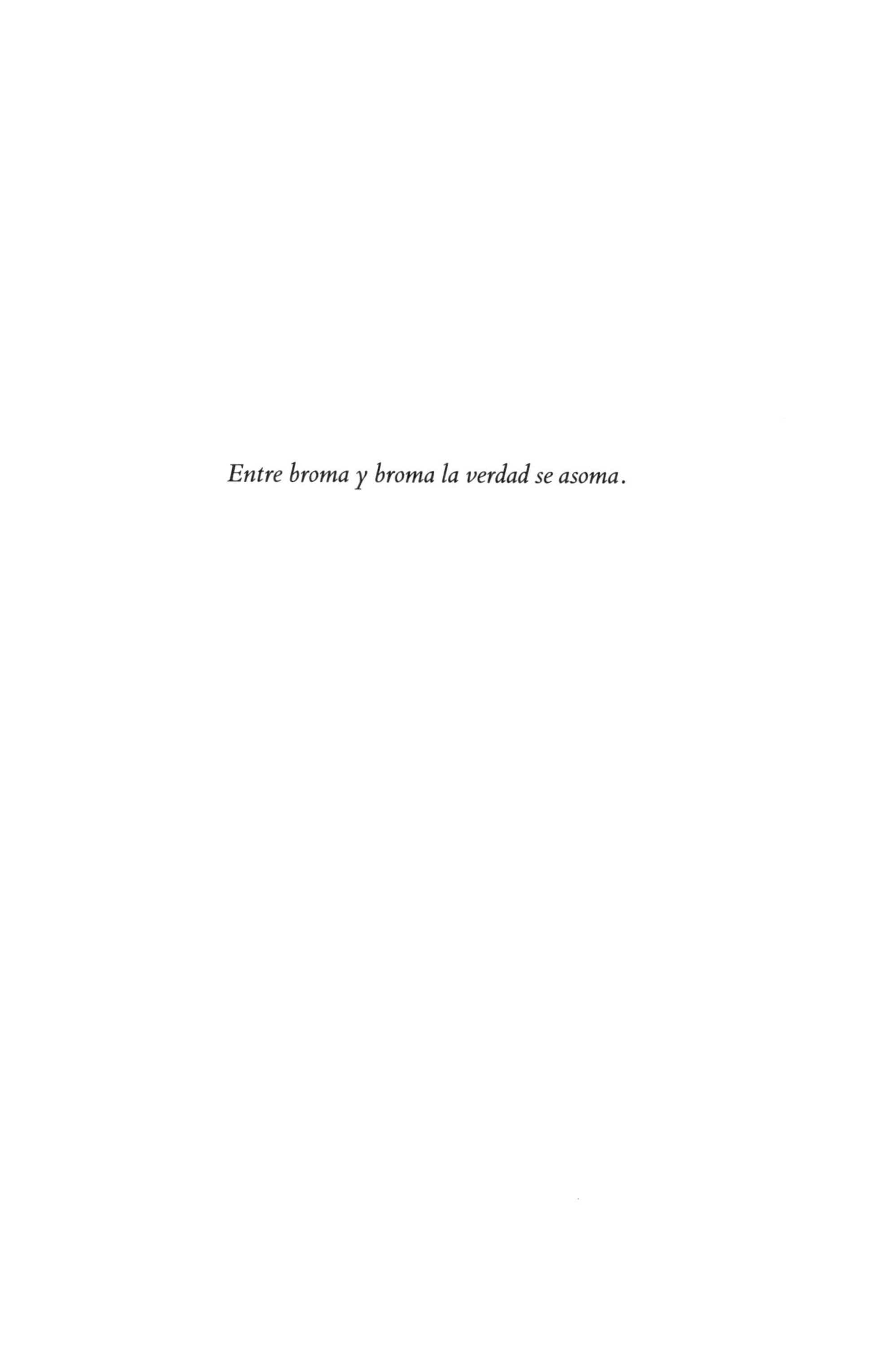

Entre broma y broma la verdad se asoma.

PART ONE

Night and Her Children

I

On the night my life changed forever, I laddered my tights quite dramatically. I snagged them on a splinter of wood which nicked the flesh below, drawing a queer little squiggle of blood to the surface. Any other time I would've taken myself straight home, disgraced and fearful of what the ladder augured, but I was feeling zesty that evening and thoroughly unwilling to forfeit my two free glasses of plonk.

I was giving a reading, from behind a heavily embroidered curtain of my own design, at the Art Workers' Guild in Bloomsbury. I'd been invited by a former classmate at Central Saint Martins to perform as part of a happening. We were celebrating the launch of a new book of photography, *Modernist Writers and Their Influence on Interior Design,* something like that. He worked in PR now. He wasn't offering a fee but there would be drinks and a chance to network afterwards, and I accepted because I thought it would be good to have something else to do with the evening other than lurk in my room, re-reading rejection emails from PhD programmes and googling 'One breast bigger than other – normal?'

From behind my tapestry I read out a story about a young girl who meets David Bowie in the supermarket. It was September and still far too hot. My words tumbled down a brass megaphone which I found at a flea market in Berlin, it poked out towards the audience through an embellished slash in the fabric and carried my text to them. I told my friend in PR, 'I see this piece as being the concrete manifestation of the artist's desire to be at once seen by everyone, and simultaneously invisible.' I fiddled with the strap of my one good black frock so that it lay flat. 'Obscured,' I said, 'obliterated by the artwork.'

'Sure, yeah,' he said, 'these are the big ideas we're working with here, so do whatever. As long as you don't break anything, or like, *lick* anything.'

I blushed.

These sequestered readings had become my signature you might say; the Bowie story, though, was new. I had been working at it on and off all year but I hadn't yet shared it with anyone, so I was nervous and excited, like on a first date. Previously I might've shown parts of it to my housemates (we were all friends from art school) but they had collectively decided to *give me some space.* I had imagined that living with them would be liberal and generative only they were upset, they *said,* because I was financially reckless and incapable of respecting boundaries. I found their hostility pathetic and transparent. A strained 'Hello' in the kitchen was all I got, a brisk 'See you' on their way out if I was lucky. *And these are supposed to be the brightest artistic minds of the new century*, I said to myself, *sad.*

Truly I only went to Saint Martins because I couldn't function in the real world. I had tried, I'd even had a job at a call centre for six weeks after I finished high school, only they fired me because I climbed out of the bathroom window in the middle of a shift and didn't return for two days. I'm sure I didn't understand what going to art school even meant, any more than I understood what going to heaven meant, or going to Disneyland. I simply felt that I was called to do something important with my life, even if no one else around me recognised my vocation, but then they do say Catherine of Siena's stigmata were only visible to the saint herself, at least until after her death. My aunt told me that. She became a nun in later life, because she wanted to follow her personal calling without being further subject to the facile will of the world. I thought that was very noble, and I might've taken holy orders myself only I knew too well that though I could manage the vows of poverty and obedience, chastity would defeat me, and so I chose Central Saint Martins, which is where I learned to sew.

I made the decorative screen for my readings there as part of my MA project: it earned me a very good grade. I hand-stitched all 10,000 words of my thesis onto a damson velvet drape, in thread I had dyed the very same shade as the cloth, rendering the text almost imperceptible, available only to haptic readings. It took me nearly six months to stitch this erudite tapestry, but I thought that what I had created was quite honestly transcendent. Nigella Lawson came to the private view of our graduate show, and said it looked like something she'd hang in her own sitting room. Moreover I loved the silent, meditative quality of the work that went into it the embroidery, work that made me all but forget myself, made me think of my aunt in the convent, copying out great tracts of *The Interior Castle*.

Before I left for the happening I phoned my mother; she likes to be kept up to date with developments in my career. She said she'd spent a lot of time attuning with the Archangel Gabriel recently, so she wasn't at all surprised to hear about it. 'Now, Gabriel is never wrong,' she said, 'he's God's *purest* messenger. *He* looks a bit like David Bowie actually, funny eyes like. Anyways, he told me something very, *very* exciting was going to happen for you.' She said I should meditate on the image of a brilliant white diamond for clarity of communication; I assured her that I absolutely would.

We performed in a room rather verbosely named The Hall. It was Edwardian and casually intimidating, terracotta walls and a salon hang, countless portraits of stately old fellows in three-quarter profile, oils in gilt frames dangling on brass chains, the secular saints and former masters of the Art Workers' Guild. Above the fireplace hung a whopping great painting of three men sat around a table, looking like bank managers or the signatories of a peace treaty, notable names scribbled in tiny golden font on more and more and more mahogany running the full ambit. Life-size bronze busts of poets and carpenters were set into the untroubled plasterwork above our heads, a table of antique oak loaded with white wine, and red wine, and pasteurised orange juice the same colour as the walls, and a hundred or so dishwasher-safe glasses. There were two other performers: a Taiwanese live artist called Lan who had stitched himself into an armchair, with just a cut-out for his dick, and Mad Pete, another old friend from school, who moulded the shapes he saw on shroom trips out of hot pink modelling clay in real time. The three of us presented concurrently; no one was watching.

It was after I finished reading, once I'd taken my tapestry down, that I noticed the ladder in my tights. I didn't sweat it though, in fact I thought the rip added a note of danger and glamour to the look, it brought to mind Jackie Curtis slashing at her Halston gown with hairdressing scissors. I tucked my megaphone under my arm and set about uncorking a cheap Chilean red with my front door key. The bar was unattended. A very energetic lady in late middle age swooped down on me, she looked like a stork in suede kitten heels. 'Was that you behind there?' she enquired. 'You clever thing! We weren't sure if it was a recording or not, but it was you, wasn't it?'

I said, 'Yes, yes it was. I was *activating* the work.'

'Oh aren't you marvellous?' she seized me by the shoulders. 'And just look at you. All grown up!'

I didn't know who she was. My puzzlement must have been apparent enough because she explained, delicately, 'It's Margaret, darling. Margaret Campbell-Bannerman.'

'I'm sorry,' I said, 'but I don't think that I am who you think I am.'

She insisted that I was, and that she had visited my brother and me with her little son Eddy, *practically every weekend* when they were still living in Suffolk. I continued poking at the wine bottle and said that seemed very unlikely. My father ran a small business in Manchester manufacturing paper party plates, so unless she'd spent her Saturdays driving up to Alderley Edge and her Sundays watching re-runs of *Poirot,* she clearly had the wrong person. 'Besides,' I said, 'I'm an only child.'

This confusion was evidently hilarious to her, she was already three sheets to the wind. She waved over her husband, hooting, 'Archie, dear, Archie!' and insisted I retell it from the top, for his benefit. Archie chuckled and Margaret said, 'Isn't that just too much?' He agreed that it was and she clapped her hands. 'Now let's go get a real drink!'

So I was led out of The Hall, curtain draped over my arm like an opera cloak, acutely aware that in this light the assembled company finally saw me, and I beamed. My friend in PR looked on astounded, mouthing, '*What the fuck?*' I bade him 'Goodnight,' through my megaphone, as I sailed by on the arm of Margaret Campbell-Bannerman, whoever she might have been. 'We're heading over to the Groucho, darling,' she said, 'because, well, what else can one do on a Tuesday?'

2

When you are young and unsophisticated even the most extraordinary events don't really seem all that curious, you simply imagine that this is how it is, how the world works, and as you aren't prepared for any of it, not for the filing of taxes, nor the negotiations with irascible student finance officers over unpaid fees, nor the sharing of a cigarette with a supermodel in an electricity cupboard, it all gurgles together like radio programming in a foreign language. None of it makes sense, but you are sure that to someone smarter, it would. Clever old Violette Le Duc said, '*Ignorance is also a perpetual promise.*' I scribbled that down on a serviette somewhere.

If I can remember entering the Groucho so very clearly, that's because it was a moment well illuminated. Flash bulbs lit it up, and so the scene is still cloudless in my mind. There was a gaggle of press photographers idling outside when we arrived, smoking, joking, chatting amongst themselves. They surged at the club door as it opened outwards, startling some poor sozzled so-and-so in blue jeans and a blazer as he was leaving. A crush of camera flashes around the entrance then peeling away despondently only once they realised that they were bum-rushing a nobody.

'I wonder who they're for?' said Margaret. 'They seem ravenous tonight.'

The hostess asked me if I'd like to check anything into the cloakroom. I gave her my tapestry which she registered as an evening wrap, but she wouldn't accept the megaphone. 'Sorry, no,' she said, 'we can't take hats, we just don't have the space.' I carried it about with me all evening.

Margaret led us to the bar upstairs. It was turquoise, very crowded, dressed like an airport lounge, fun furnishings and globe light fixtures, expensive handbags propped up on velvet pouffes whilst their owners swigged and scrolled. I had always imagined that wealthy, urbane people whiled away their evenings with martinis in tuxedos, feeding little bits of cake to very small dogs, but that may well be because I'd read too much Nancy Mitford at an impressionable age. I was honestly a little disappointed.

Margaret handed me a celery sour, Archie raised his in a toast, we three clinked glasses and she said, 'To your great success with that gorgeous curtain!'

'Actually,' I began, 'It's an embroidered facade, a *site*, which I use to activate . . .'

But she was elsewhere. She smiled at me gratuitously. 'Excuse me a moment, I *must* say hello to Charlotte Graff. I had no idea she was back.'

She disappeared into the crush of deluxe hair extensions, sheepish television personalities, and the twenty-something daughters of Britpop stars. Naturally Archie shuffled off in her wake. I was left to sip at my drink alone, awkward and embarrassed, my right eyelid starting to spasm. The gin, the juice and all the sugar sloshed rudely in my stomach; I was suddenly very aware that I hadn't eaten since breakfast. I could've slipped away quietly now, only something made me stay. The bartender, very good-looking, fine gold ring through his left ear, Italian maybe, was staring at me with an expression of fair intensity. ''Scuse me,' he said, his breath warm with aniseed.

I answered very sweetly, 'Yes?' and inclined myself towards him.

'Will you move that?' he said with a smile as fake as the Getty kouros. He was pointing to my megaphone. 'I cannot have it on the countertop.'

'Of course,' I said, pink and uncomfortable. I picked up the wretched thing with a small apologetic smile and swung it right into the ribs of the drinker now standing next to me at the bar. He was my height and about as slim, I hadn't seen him arrive. Honestly, I couldn't have hit him all that hard, still he spun with shock and glared. 'Can't you see that I am standing here?'

'I'm sorry,' I squeaked, 'I didn't mean to – did I hurt you?'

'No.' He glowered. 'But watch what you are doing please!'

'I'm sorry,' I repeated. 'The celery sour, it went straight to my head; I think I drank it a bit too quickly.' My eyelid was twitching wildly now and the man I had struck was grimacing in response. 'I'm sorry.' I said it again.

'It is fine,' he said, cooler but no kinder.

'Honestly,' I exhorted, 'I'm not usually like this.'

'It is *fine*,' he said, 'really.'

He spoke in slow, stressed syllables, a look of rigid politeness rising in place of the previous annoyance; he was mastering himself. I could see that he was struggling to be less terse: 'No harm done,' he said, though more to calm himself than comfort me.

Then, the wildest thing: he lit a cigarette, it was bright pink. Impossibly, he was smoking, indoors, at the Groucho, as if it were the most natural thing in the world, and the bartender took no notice. *Must be German*, I thought, *Germans never pay attention to the smoking ban*. I wanted to ask, but it seemed rude, and so a clumsy cotton-wool hush hung between us.

Through the brume he exhaled, his eyes glimmered a strange gold-green, almost reptilian, the heavy lids made his gaze seem wilfully provocative. He was drinking alone too, a highball, I think. He chewed idly on a curl of lemon peel in between drags on his pink smoke. I felt compelled to talk more to him. I asked him if he had the time and immediately flushed with shyness – of course I would come out with a pick-up line from a black-and-white movie. How stupid I was.

'It is almost ten-thirty,' he said without referring to a timepiece, then he cracked a grin, crocodile-like, as if to say that he were onto me. I returned the smile nervously and thanked him; he bowed to me from the waist, like a Regency gentleman on the ballroom floor, not a little sardonic.

From the off he engendered the most uncanny feeling in me, as though I were looking at a long-forgotten dizygotic twin. He was handsome yes, but his masculinity was tempered by a girlishness, a certain soft butch quality. He wore a midnight blue velvet smoking jacket; he was Katharine Hepburn dressed as a boy, Marlene Dietrich in a tux, Ingrid Bergman in Joan of Arc drag, I couldn't quite bring him into focus. He reminded me somehow of another boy whom I'd loved and lost, I wanted to touch him, I wanted to say, *Don't you know me?* but I knew that this would be ridiculous. Worse, I felt his attention starting to turn from me, felt something crumple up in my breast, I ran again through the available options for small talk, looking for something decorous, desperate to make further conversation: 'Nice shoes!' I said.

His black-heeled boots were of a matte leather with a split toe like a goat's hoof. With more total attention I found them to be quite horrible, but I'd committed to the compliment now, and he looked flattered.

'Yes?' he said. 'You like them? Margiela.' He was smiling again; indeed he seemed to glow a little.

They were obviously very expensive shoes, so I replied, 'Oh really?' skating on the thin ice of my simplicity. 'Well, they're very, ah, handsome.'

He regarded me with a new curiosity now, my face, my hair, my dress from under those sleepy lids of his, slowly, blatantly invasive. I began to colour, then almost cringe under his assessment. 'And this,' he said, extending two fingers and stroking my shoulder, 'is a beautiful gown.'

I'm often paralysed in situations like this by an attack of the demure. I wanted to say something dirty like 'You should see how good it would look on your bedroom floor,' some saucy Mae West wisecrack, but what spilled out of me was 'Gosh isn't this place fun? So full of ah, all sorts of people!'

'Oh?' he said, unruffled. 'This is your first time here tonight?' with that strange syntax of his, backwards or strangely dated, I couldn't tell. 'You know of course, they are all Masons.' He spoke with surety and consideration, as if to enforce elegant vowels on a brusquer tongue; I didn't know what it was he meant, so I just smiled and accepted his offer of another drink.

'Cheers,' he raised his glass to mine, 'good health.'

A hidden chorus of well-wishers sang 'Happy Birthday' to an unseen guest, a woman doused in Green Irish Tweed wafted by on her way to the bathroom, Margaret did not return. My new friend said, 'I am Alexander,' and I shivered, that name always has an effect on me.

'Charli,' I replied, 'pleased to meet you.'

We drank and we talked, he was very funny, he told me he was a musician and asked me what I did. I said 'Guess,' and he chanced, 'Painter?' I straightened him out. 'No but sometimes I wish that I were, *I envy the painter's lifestyle*. Virginia Woolf said something like that, somewhere. I forget. I'm a little drunk.'

He tried again. 'So then you are a writer?'

'In a way,' I said, 'I suppose. I'm trying to find a PhD supervisor. I want to write my doctoral thesis on Romy Haag, the disco singer. You know her? She dated David Bowie in the seventies, she's fabulous, she's my hero.'

He nodded casually. 'Yes, I know her. She lives in Berlin.'

'Oh!' I said. 'So you *are* German?'

He shook his head. 'No, I am not. But I feel like I could have been – in another life. I do have a house there though, it is very big.'

I chose to gloss over this detail. 'I like it there,' I said. 'It feels just like the recent past, you can't pay for anything with a credit card and everything closes on a Sunday.' I had often fantasised about following my heroes to Berlin and leaving my own dreary life behind for good. I sighed. 'It's just so dreamy.'

I told him that I had friends in the capital, a couple of artists who shared a studio at the back of a fried chicken shop in Neukölln. I had spent just time enough there to still feel green about the city, to think of it as a sort of urban Arcadia, all cheap rents and casual sex, contrasting graphically and favourably with my life in London, which only made me feel entombed. The booze was beginning to make me feel heavy, woozy, a little morose and moony. I sighed again, and concluded the lecture on my discontents saying, 'God, I wish I could go back there right now.'

'So why don't you?' he asked, as if it were the simplest thing in the world.

I shrugged. 'Oh, you know,' unable to conjure up a single reason why.

He lit another fag, this one pastel yellow. 'Sobranie?' he said, and gestured towards me with his cigarette case, offering me one. I shook my head and declined; still nobody challenged him, I began to think he must be a big shot in *the business*. He smoked so beautifully, really he did, it put me in mind of watching Julianne Moore on the big screen, bopping about her ashtray to 'Green Onions', I could have watched him exhale streams of blue smoke through those fine flared nostrils forever. I said, 'You know *a lot* of people say *Moby Dick* is America's greatest contribution to world culture but in my opinion, it's cinema.'

He told me about some of his own particular interests, Arthur Russell, art deco and astral projection. I imagined his life to be romantic, robust, full of lascivious self-discovery, disco music and equinoctial revelations; truly he seemed illuminated with a dreamlike quality, opaque yet immaterial, an aura that was the product, I was sure, of wild swimming and close reads of the *Cipher Manuscripts* in equal measure. I was also somewhat intimidated by him, there was something cruel in his charisma, a queen regnant; in his smile I saw Marlon Brando putting out his cigarettes on James Dean's forearms. Serpentine and saturnine, that's how he struck me that first evening, though I suppose, from this point in time, I might be inclined to ascribe the more psychedelic aspects of our meeting to Mad Pete's mushrooms, which I had been microdosing all week.

'For my mental health,' I said, 'I've been under rather a lot of stress, you see. My doctor said I really shouldn't risk another episode.'

'Ha!' he scoffed. 'Psychiatrists. They know nothing, they are all frauds.' The sentiment lit him up with a sudden indignation. 'They tried to convince *me* that I had a narcissistic personality disorder. Pathetic!' he scowled. 'A scam.' He flushed a little, a single glistening bead of sweat breaking on his pristine hairline. I wanted to know how it would taste.

The bar was muddy with echoed conversation, the countertop was slightly tacky to the touch, across the room somebody shrieked, 'Oh my God, Francesca! No way!' I said, 'Sometimes, I feel so out of place. Do you know what I mean? *I'm alive now, yes, but I would have rather been born at some other time. I never liked this present age.*' I hiccupped and finished my citation. 'That's Petrarch. Paraphrased.'

'Petrarch?' he laughed. 'You *are* a strange soul, Charli. Let us have another drink.'

I protested, 'No really, I don't think I should. I skipped dinner and . . .'

'Please,' he beamed, 'don't worry.' He gave a little three-finger gesture, like a papal benediction, to the bartender, who nodded and started to mix another round. 'The old gentleman you arrived with left the tab open.'

A figure sailed over Alexander's shoulder into my eyeline, a woman vibrating with self-possession, like a Christmas tree on December the twenty-fourth. She wore a turban with a constellation of pom-poms orbiting it, and a leopard print jumpsuit. I didn't immediately recognise her but I gasped when I realised who it was. I hadn't seen her since that awkward incident with the envelopes at the ICA. 'Sophia?' She looked renovated, pristine. I stood up and called her name louder, unsteady on my feet, 'Sophia, hi!' but she didn't hear me and so I sat back down, abashed.

Alexander rested his drink on a coaster. 'You know her?'

I said, 'What?' desperate to save some face. 'Oh Sophia? Yeah, sure. We've known each other forever, she was in the year above me at Saint Martins.'

He rolled his indolent eyes. '*So* original. An art school pop star. Don't they know inspiration must come from life?'

I wanted him to like me, more and more. I sipped at my sour and lowered my voice. 'Of course, she didn't graduate.' I wanted to impress him with my wickedness, I looked about and over my shoulder conspiratorially. 'She got kicked out. For posting porn to the course email list. It was a total scandal.'

'Is that so?' he sniggered. 'Miss Milquetoast herself.' The shimmer of venom in his eyes made me feel a little guilty for tattling.

I backpedalled. 'I mean, it wasn't hardcore porn, it was cartoon porn. *The Simpsons*, I think. Pictures of Marge sitting on

Krusty the Clown's face, and Homer getting fucked by Ned Flanders,' I explained. 'I thought it was quite funny.'

He grinned at me wolfishly over the rim of his glass, really I was only making it worse but still I prattled on, paying for my indiscretion. I said, 'Everyone goes a bit mad in art school, don't they? I once got a two-week suspension for licking a marble sculpture on a class trip to Apsley House. Canova's *Napoleon as Mars the Peacemaker*, in fact.'

'Ah-ha,' he cocked one corrupt eyebrow, 'and where exactly did you lick him?'

I coloured, remembering the taste, like dirty chalk, the ruckled edges of the fig leaf; I felt him in my head, following my thoughts, and I had to I look away.

I have always been drawn to the worst kind of man, I'm masochistic like that. I've always dreamt of giving myself over to someone I know to be more than capable, ready even, to crush me like an empty can of Coke, a man like Napoleon, a man who would face no retribution for his actions. I suppose in a way I was hoping that if I could hand myself over to someone who was primed to destroy me then it would save me the bother of having to do it myself.

Across the crowded room Sophia posed for pictures with a group of girls who were bobbing about behind her like Juvédermed cherubs. Alexander watched her with an intensity that flecked me with jealousy. 'She's very famous now, you know,' he said, his 'V' wobbling towards a 'W'. '*Very* famous.'

I cast my eyes down into my drink, diffident. 'So I've read.'

When Sophia first started gigging she had me and Mad Pete splash about on-stage in buckets of milk whilst she sang old jazz songs in a cocktail dress and a suffragette's sash which read: *Yes, all women!* I'm sure she'd explained what it all meant but I was honestly only in it for the drinks tickets. I said, 'Last time I saw her she was singing Ella Fitzgerald for an A&R man who was checking his tweets throughout, and now . . .'

'And now,' he repeated, and mimed an explosion with his delicate hands. 'Showbiz,' he said, 'hype, to justify product.'

'Product?' I sniffed. 'Is *art* a product?'

'Oh lover,' he said, 'it's *all* product.'

A page from the Saint Martins alumni magazine came to mind, congratulating a pair of sculptors turned pig farmers who had won a big contract supplying sausages to Fortnum & Mason. When I first saw it I'd felt sad and snobbish, which was ungenerous, but now I only thought, *swineherds, sculptors, pop stars, new wave, no-wave, nu-rave, same difference, man.*

'Were you very close friends?' He was prying. As I was coming to discover, he was fascinated by this kind of intrigue.

'God no,' I said, slugging back the end of my drink, 'just pigs who shared a sty.'

He laughed, and I was pleased, it pealed out of him like the striking of a temple bell. The booze was making me mischievous, and he was egging me on. He snorted, 'You are a very indiscreet girl, did you know that?'

Giggling now and quite drunk, I slurred on, 'You know, once, *once* she had me and this queen called Tina, whom I despise, by the way . . .'

'Whom?' he repeated, teasing me, taunting me, pressing his knees closer to mine.

'Yes, *whom* I despise,' I continued. 'Well, Sophia had us perform at a show of hers for like fifty quid, and then at the end of the night, her manager, or whoever he was, handed us our money because Sophia was *far* too busy to do it herself of course. And get this! My cash came in an envelope marked *Red Dress Tranny*. Can you imagine?'

I thought what I was telling him was just another funny story about my now-famous friend, but the joke did not land. His face soured and he crinkled up his nose at the word, sucked in his breath between his teeth. 'Ohhhh,' he said. 'So much for *all women*.' He sat up very straight, shook his head and tut-tutted. I felt like I'd put my foot through a rotten floorboard: sometimes a joke can reveal a bruise too unsightly. 'I've never told anyone that,' I said. 'Yeah. That hurt my feelings.'

The bar was less busy now, and the space around us made the stillness between us abruptly sombre. He reached to rest a gentle hand on my shoulder and I closed my eyes, a surprising rush of relief from articulating such a slight to a stranger in a bar, it felt like making confession, like that old Judy Collins song. I don't think I've ever really mastered the art of expressing my emotions appropriately.

He said, 'Do not worry over this,' and stroked my hair back off my shoulder, 'she has three good songs in her, I guarantee. After that – car commercials.'

I giggled again and he lit another cigarette, took a long deep drag.

'I'm sorry,' I said, 'booze always makes me a little silly.'

He exhaled and he held my gaze, narrowing those queer, languid eyes of his, daring me to break off. *Shades of Napoleon here*, I thought, *yes. Crush me like a Coke can, lover, lead me into that life, romantic, robust, full of lascivious self-discovery, which I have imagined for you*. The seductive quality I thought I had seen in him resurfaced, a sense of trepidation too. I shuddered, some erotic chill running wild along my spine, the ghost of desire conjured up by this coquetry. I had to make it clear that I was his match. *Alright then*, I said to myself, *if that's how you want it*, and I leant forward to let him kiss me.

The bartender cleared his throat, rather theatrically, 'Ahem!' ruining the scene and, unbidden, placed a glass of champagne in front of me.

'No, no,' I said, frustrated by his tactlessness, 'I didn't order that. And I do not need it.'

He shrugged and signalled with his thumb like a hitchhiker across the room. 'Lady over there sent it.' He spoke to me without making eye contact.

It was Mrs Campbell-Bannerman, she was saluting me with her flute, waving me over.

'Oh fuck,' I muttered through teeth pressed into a rictus grin, 'Margaret. Of course.'

Alexander regarded me sidelong but intrigued. 'You really know a lot of very interesting people,' he said. 'For somebody who was never here before.'

'Long story,' I sighed. I watched Margaret, her arms flailing above her head as though flagging down a taxi in a storm. 'I really should go and say hello. God knows how much we've run up on her tab.'

'Sure,' he smiled. 'Say hi from me.'

I stood up and fixed my hemline, straightened my runaway bra strap. 'I'll be back in a minute or two, I promise. I'll tell her I have court in the morning.' I knocked the fizz back in one go and kissed him on the cheek. 'Watch this for me?' I said and handed him my megaphone.

He dropped his cigarette butt into the last trickle of amber at the bottom of his highball glass. 'Sure thing, lover, no problem.'

3

Lying, unable to hazard more than a guess as to how long I have been enjoying this chemically induced repose. Coughing causes flashes of mysterious, extended pain. Under virulently starched sheets, asparagus green, thin like paper towels, waking up and tasting blood in the back of my throat, touching my face, pawing at the bandaging: Oh, I finally got my nose job.

My left arm does not behave as I believe it should, it is dragging, heavy over the sheets as though through water, plastered I see, scrawled – with a message of best wishes perhaps. I can't decipher it, can't make the words make sense, gute Besserung. *Should I be wearing glasses? Ah, no, it's German.*

The nurse at the end of my bed has woken me with her scuttling, she is scowling softly, she is stern like a Mother Superior, but she is illuminated with love. There are a lot of drugs in my system. My mouth is dry, it is so dry, and I'm asking, 'Why am I here?' but she cannot answer. Her lips are pursing, she is regarding me over the rim of her spectacles, over the lip of a chart, shaking her head, she is griping, also in German (did she sign my cast?).

'Kein Englisch.' This splinter of her machine-gun mutterings I can comprehend.

I am formulating a slow and stumbling response; when I reach out I find fragments of language. 'Warum, ah, warum bist ich hier?' The nurse is regarding me with sympathy, no, it's exhaustion, folding her arms over her scrubs. 'Noch mal?' I am blank, I am without understanding, I am groggy and grasping for the words I don't understand.

'Auto-un-fall. Verstehst du?' She is speaking slower and louder, as one must when faced with a foreigner. 'Auto-un-fall. Auto-UN-fall.' She is miming a collision with her fists.

I was in a fight? I must've been pretty wasted. It seems out of character, running from the police, flashes of Polly with blood on her hands, 'Kampfen?' coming out of my mouth, the briefest somniloquy (where was I storing that word?). But no, the nurse is shaking her head, thumb and middle finger pressed to her temples, 'Kampfen? Nein. Nein, autounfall ist . . .' and trailing off now, she's flailing through all the crappy American movies she's ever seen looking for the word, and I'm thinking, What is the name of that film, where the soldier wakes up after the war and everyone thinks he's a hero, but he's actually an enemy combatant?

'Car crash,' sounds like a sneeze. 'Car crash, yes. You are car crash.' The nurse looks triumphant and departs.

I am car crash, Alex was driving us home, that's where it ends. Alex was driving us home then, memory redacted. Alex was driving us home and now I wake up here, and where is he, since I am in this room alone? The indignity of being car crash.

I quiz myself: who is the president of the United States? What was the name of your childhood best friend? How many full-length albums has David Bowie made? I want to see what's still in there. Barack Obama, Mr Froggy, twenty-six, not including soundtracks. Good! I am car crash but I am not amnesiac no, it's all still there, more or less. Tossed like a pasta dish maybe, doll parts jumbled, and though I couldn't write the lyrics out for you (I have a broken arm!), believe me, lover, I know all the words to this song. A stage, a train, a painter's studio, blackout, ten Ziggy Stardusts, someone threw up on my shoes, me and Finley are at a graveside, Alex was driving us home. When I close my eyes I can hear the melody playing backwards, the lyrics are in me as yet unborn, I'm just waiting now, waiting for the cue light, waiting for that voice in my headphones to tell me that they'll drop me in at the top with a count of six. Static. 'To sing you must first open your mouth.' Henry Miller said that.

4

Margaret was holding sway over a cluster of blonde ladies all of whom looked to share an aesthetician. She said, 'I was just telling the girls about your fabulous curtain.'

'Actually,' I began again, 'it's a site. It's an activation of . . .' The canvas on the wall behind her, a grid of painted dots, popped and oscillated; activated by my four celery sours, it foregrounded her like a theatre flat. I was unsure how long I would last. 'Oh blah blah blah,' I sighed, nobody was listening.

Margaret said, 'I told you she was marvellous,' and *the girls* all chimed in merry agreement, raising glasses and threatening me with studio visits. I was too tired and too tipsy to really follow along. I just smiled affably and said things like 'Quite,' and 'Oh really?' and 'How interesting,' things I'd seen the Queen say to staggered commoners at train stations and flower shows, so as to seem present but still august. I regretted accepting that last drink.

Apropos of the dots one of Margaret's friends said, 'You know, he's our neighbour in Ilfracombe?' and another asked, 'Who's that then, Damien Hirst?'

Her pal nodded sagaciously. '*Apparently* the dots represent the underlying unease of daily life,' she said, 'though I always thought they looked rather like wrapping paper.'

Margaret lowered her voice. 'Archie says he saw him pissing in a sink here once.' She cast a glance at her husband, sceptical. 'But between you and I, I think that's just a story he read in a magazine.'

I wanted to extricate myself only Margaret had attached herself to me now, looping her arm through mine. I threw a look over my shoulder to Alexander, begging for some chivalry, or a timely excuse, but he simply shrugged, and so I returned to sipping at my champagne, agreeably taciturn, only realising once I'd hit the bottom that it was in fact Margaret's drink.

At some point Sophia sauntered past and Mrs Campbell-Bannerman grabbed at her, like a cuttlefish feeding on a crab. 'Here you are, my darling girl. I was looking for you all evening!' Margaret was doubly delighted to learn that we two knew each other, it seemed to prove her instincts about me correct. 'Small world,' she said, 'small, small beautiful world.'

Sophia was more measured, and aware that in the far corner of the drowsy room, people were nudging their dates and conjecturing; she made sure to give them her good side. 'Charli, babes,' she said, 'it's been so long, how've you been?'

Now, I'm usually a very self-effacing sort of person but that night I was overbalanced with desire and alcohol and I started in on an extended soliloquy detailing my recent successes, personal and professional, the fantastic response to my reading at the Art Workers' Guild, the sexy fella I'd met at the bar and the outline of my PhD thesis. Margaret wandered away before I was halfway through, but I wasn't put off. I said, 'I've pretty much secured the funding now,' and smiled broadly. 'Several supervisors were keen to take me on, it's been quite a tough decision. But in the end, I think I've picked the winning horse out of the hat, if you know what I mean?'

'Babes,' Sophia squeezed my hand and whispered into my ear, 'you're sort of slurring. Do you want a line of coke? Sober you up a bit.'

When Margaret returned she had my megaphone in her hand. 'You naughty thing,' she chided. 'Tony was very cross! Said he'd asked you to move it several times.'

'Honestly!' I took it from her quickly, drunkenly, said, 'I didn't just leave it there! I asked my, ah, friend at the bar to look after it.'

She shrugged. 'Well, there's no one there now.'

I looked and saw for myself: the countertop was empty, Alexander was gone. 'Fuck,' I sighed, 'I was counting on him for a ride home.'

'I can drop you off in the cab,' offered Sophia, 'if you're still up in the same place?'

'Yes,' I said, 'I am. Thanks.' I felt rather despondent.

'What are friends for?' She grinned, giving the full luminous effect of her generosity and her expensive dental work to the last few hangers-on.

I said goodbye to Margaret; she made a big show of it, making me promise that I'd call in on her for lunch the next week. Of course I never saw her again. Sophia sluiced on some lip gloss, and I cast about the bar one last time, but no sign of my man. 'OK,' I said. 'Let's go.'

As we came down the stairs Sophia picked up speed and increased in stature, back straight, shoulders down, the golden thread up through the crown of the head. At the door the hostess helped her slip into a cloak trimmed with red cockerel feathers, two uniformed club giants stepped forward and said, 'Goodnight, Miss Hope,' then they threw open the doors and we stepped out into a night sky fully irradiated by camera flashes. Photographers jumped up and down, jostling each other and yelling, 'Sophia, looking lovely! Give us a smile!'

I staggered embarrassed through the scrum. I could hardly see and didn't know which way to look, but Sophia, already amphibious in this new atmosphere, was sovereign. One of the doormen cleared a path through the photographers and moved to open the taxicab door, I followed close behind him and slipped straight inside, Sophia did not. She stayed on the pavement throwing wild Carmen Miranda poses and beaming gleefully at the cameras, as if all of her dreams had come true, as if she'd won the lottery, I suppose in a way she had. Even though there were no more than eight or ten of them there, their constant weaving and bobbing and calling out made it seem like Sophia was enveloped in a huge seething jelly, a gelatinous mass of yells and flashes and clicks. At some point she produced a bag of popcorn and started to throw it up in the air towards them. They delighted in the absurdity of all this.

'Eh?' The driver turned to look over his shoulder at me. 'Is she famous or something?'

When she climbed into the car, her heart was beating so fast I could hear it through her catsuit and feathers. The paparazzi were crowding the cab and shooting through the windows.

'Where to then, love?' the cabbie asked, blithe.

'Just drive,' she said, smiling and waving like the Queen coming up on a pill. 'If I tell you where to go, they'll follow.'

The driver started his engine and beeped his horn to clear the photographers, we moved off. I looked back to see if indeed they would follow, but they were already lowering their lenses.

5

Sophia told the driver that we were going to Hampstead via Green Lanes. I was grateful for the lift. She said, 'But do you mind if we make a stop at the Brick Lane Beigel shop first? *I'm dying* for a hot salt beef.'

I groaned, I wanted to be home so badly. I said, 'Maybe I *should* do a line after all?' because although I know that coke inevitably turns me into the worst version of myself, I really was that tired.

Sophia smiled. 'Sure, babes.' Amenable and calm, she rummaged about in her bra and pulled out a baggie.

It was awkward, trying to cut it and line it up and snort it in the back of a moving cab, not least because the driver was observing the whole thing in the rear-view mirror, but I'd had enough practice to manage it. I set it all up on my knee like a pro, hunched myself over Sophia's Chanel compact and jammed a fiver up my nose. An image rushing up, a page from one of my dad's eighties pornos, of some college twink in tube socks trying to suck himself off.

It was only once I had hoovered the crystals up my nose that I felt something was wrong – there was no numbness, nor did I feel electrified. I faltered, 'I don't think that was coke.'

'Oh yeah, sorry.' Sophia blushed. 'Might've been ket actually.'

On the radio we heard the news, someone had firebombed Apsley House. 'That's the Duke of Wellington's pile,' the cabbie said, 'bet it was an inside job.'

'Insurance fraud,' Sophia said definitively.

The driver agreed. 'Had a tax bill they couldn't pay, most likely.'

I thought of our class trip, the tapestries, the curtains. 'But,' I spluttered, 'the upholstery *alone* is priceless, the artworks, the . . .'

'Wouldn't put anything past that lot,' sneered the driver, 'I've had them all in the back there, and let me tell you, some of the things I've heard . . .'

'That's crazy,' I began again, 'that's just crazy.' But a strange slippery feeling was coming over me and I couldn't venture any further thought.

'Crazy, is it?' said the driver, laughing. 'You think the bloody aristocracy aren't capable of *that*?'

He started to recount a historical theory of how Elizabeth I was an imposter, switched at birth, his voice dropping lower and slower with each word, telling us that the Virgin Queen was in fact a peasant's child. 'Why do you think she never married or had kids, then eh?'

'Because she was a feminist,' Sophia declaimed.

'No!' the driver groaned. 'Because she was a man!'

I was heavy, sliding slightly in my seat, trying to piece another sentence together, but the words were rolling away from me like pearls from a broken string. 'The upholstery,' I said. 'The upholstery alone . . .' There was a ringing in my ears, a white noise, and I slumped back, not in a faint, but as though I had huffed a load of gas and air, my body lettuce-like.

Sophia squabbled on playfully with the driver in wordless brass gargles, trombones and mewlings passing between them like all the adult voices in Charlie Brown's world. As she spoke I saw her words come spooling out of her mouth, reams of metallic tape, the magnetic ribbons from inside a classic rock cassette unwinding on the breeze. Then subtitles of sudden concern – *Are you OK, babes? Charli? Are you OK?* – and I floated up out of myself entirely. I saw the red digits on the meter turn over monstrously slow, then stop, and I thought to myself, *Oh! Well, I guess I'm dying!* though I was honestly quite at peace with that.

I watched the geometry of the cab fragment at neon right angles, saw myself looking down on myself almost beatifically, followed myself down a long, muddy path and into a wardrobe where I felt closely confined but unafraid, as on some level I recognised that I was recalling all of this from the pages of *The Life of Saint Teresa of Ávila by Herself.* I saw Alexander's lips smoking and Mrs Campbell-Bannerman twirling naked for the paparazzi, I saw Sophia's hand in front of my face, now fingers now talons now bones, saw waves in the sky and a pair of yellow lizard eyes staring back at me in the rear-view mirror.

I remember Sophia shaking me, feeling for my pulse, and I remember looking up through the cab's panoramic roof and out at the endless night, the reflected flames of the Apsley House fire colouring the glass. I was wondering, *Has heaven always been so far away?* I couldn't speak, I couldn't move anything besides my eyes, but I guess Sophia was confident that it would pass. I saw her intertitles flash up in cursive: 'She'll be fine, mate, honestly,' and the driver's reply, 'If she pukes it's a hundred and fifty quid.'

Their speech came back slow and slanted, as though they were talking over an analogue phone line, rasping against a background thick with hiss. Occasionally the voices distorted back into the lilac static again, so that I lost parts of the conversation, and I only really knew I was still with them in the cab because Sophia intermittently pressed the back of her hand to my forehead. I heard the driver say, 'Oh yeah, he was the family arsonist before anyone even *heard* of the Bee Gees. Set fire to all the billboards in Charlton, didn't he?'

Since neither of us responded the cabbie gave us a world-class orchestral arrangement on how the world really worked. AIDS was a hoax designed to depopulate the West, he said, Paul McCartney had been killed in a car crash and replaced by a look-alike, Hillary Clinton drank the blood of little children, and the CIA smuggled all the highest-ranking Nazis to Argentina on a Type VIIC U-boat. Show business, politics, finance – it all functioned for the benefit of the New World Order, nothing was as it seemed and the Vatican ran the whole thing, all the evidence was right in front of you if only anyone'd bother to look.

'I know for a fact that Hitler was running a casino in Rio de Janeiro until the 1970s,' he said, 'bloke high up in the Navy told me that. Had him in my cab about a month ago, hand to God.'

I remember thinking, *Life has brought me here for a reason*, I was smiling on the inside, *into this very cab, into this catatonic state, and for a purpose*. Solidity was returning to my body, but slowly. I could feel myself breathing again, hear the air heave in and out of my chest, I was bobbing on a new wave of understanding. In my miasma I felt it, I knew it, I knew that this man had all the answers, I understood that I had to come here to ask him the question. I fought to the surface of my consciousness, swam against the waves of the sky, slapped myself hard in the astral face, wrenched my body awake as though from a nightmare, with a shout, 'Is the King still in Graceland?' I tried to sit up, overbalanced and almost fell out of my seat, steadying myself and shouting once again, 'Is Elvis alive?'

Sophia looked alarmed at this outburst of gibberish, she rested her hands on my shoulders and said, 'Shh, now, shh. Come on, it's OK.'

I recognised that I was drenched in drool, though thankfully not vomit, that I had been screaming way louder than I had realised and perhaps for longer than I knew. I was embarrassing myself and my friend and so, disgraced, I let my now rigid body flop right back against the leather, in an attitude of feigned lucidity. 'I just don't feel good,' I mumbled meekly. I wanted to combust, like an anti-war activist, a Tibetan monk, like that Hitchcock actor who set himself on fire protesting outside the tax office in Sweden. I had the keenest craving for a cigarette, patted my pocket as if I would find a pack, and realised with no small shock that firstly, I don't smoke and secondly, I had left my tapestry behind at the Groucho.

Sophia turned the cab around and dropped me back a few blocks away from the club, she didn't want to get too close on account of the press. 'It'd ruin the optics,' she said, 'and it was such a great night.'

6

Remembering is always a ridiculous ordeal, but there's nothing else for it when the nurse says I can't watch television. Creaking fuzz and slipped digits, I'm narrativising now. This little room is the limit of my existence, with apologies to Wittgenstein, I am in the kingdom of the nurse. She is sizing me up like she might devour me, she is a horrible spider, and she never goes off duty, or if she does, she shares her face with a colleague. She is telling me I am too empfindlich (which either means sensitive or lazy) for television and I'm thinking, Either way rude, either way true, *and I almost wish she would. If I am not watching reality TV dubbed into a language I barely understand, then what is the point of hospitalisation?*

Something in the IV drip is making me irritable, or maybe the withdrawal from it, from whatever had me so blissfully asleep. I am car crash, I am bored and irked and soggy and sore, visions of that dreadful girl with white dreads (what was her name?) calling from a musty corner of the past, she's telling me that pain is a good thing because it connects us to our bodies.

There is a man staring in through the little window in the door at me, the nurse is unaware of him, she is peeling me a tangerine. She has beautifully manicured eyebrows like Audrey Hepburn in The Nun's Story, *playing a little sister nursing in the Congo; the man at the window has a small, mean face, he is no Peter Finch. I am free associating the teal of the bed sheets with the turquoise logo on the hockey jersey of the poet who went down on me at Bad Kissingen. The water was turquoise too, he said it was because of all the copper in the thermal springs, he had a face moulded like a boy band singer.*

A tap on the glass and the nurse is withdrawing towards the window. She sees the face in the door for the first time, catches the trespasser, she is rising to find out what it is he wants, she is taking my tangerine with her! I'm whimpering in disappointment, saying, 'Moment, bitte!' but the nurse is retreating backwards somewhere saintly and I'm gasping to express my needs. Distracted by the visitation, she is not comprehending me, she isn't offering me what I'm pining for, rather she is on autopilot fulfilling another request. She is releasing more nebulous sedatives into my arm, she is sailing away with my tangerine, skimming across the floor, gliding by the grace of Ginger Rogers, down along the runway and taxiing upwards, a sea plane taking off from a loch.

Here comes the television static, snow on the screen, chartreuse green, nauseating really, my head swelling up like a balloon that surely must pop, prankish pins and needles in my feet and hands and again I'm giggling. That old devil-dull ache in my head has gone, and my broken arm has ascended to heaven on wings of a dove, and if now I cannot feel my pain does that mean I no longer have a body?

7

It must've been close to 2 a.m. when I toddled back down Dean Street alone, clutching my slingbacks and my megaphone and jonesing for a fag. I saw a triptych of truckers huddled in a circle beside their vans, laughing amongst themselves whilst supermarket workers unloaded crates of canned goods into a Tesco Express. They were bunched around a phone, sharing some meme or viral video, I asked if anyone had a spare smoke. They looked at me uncomprehending, then back and forth between themselves, talking in a language I did not understand. I mimed smoking and one of them piped up cheerfully, 'Ah – papieros!'

'Yes,' I nodded. 'Papieros!'

He shook his head, looking deeply regretful. 'Nie. I am only vape.'

At the Groucho they could not locate my tapestry. At first it seemed simply a question of categorisation, since it had entered the cloakroom as an *evening wrap* and such items were hung on a different rack. But no, even after fifteen minutes of poking about back there, the hostess couldn't find it. 'I don't think I can handle this,' I told her as calmly as I could, 'I think I'm going to faint.'

I stayed upright but must've really looked all in because the concierge took pity on me and allowed me to call my mother from the phone at the front desk. Quite what I expected her to do about any of this I don't know – it was 2 in the morning and she was 200 miles away. It didn't occur to me that it was far too late to call until after the phone had begun to ring.

I apologised straight off, said, 'I'm sorry, I didn't think about the time. I can call you back tomorrow,' but she wasn't at all fussed. She was watching a livestream of Daphne Culver's *Conversations with Angels* – tonight they were making an invocation to Archangel Uriel for true inner wisdom. 'She goes live on YouTube every Tuesday at six p.m. California time,' my mother told me. 'So I was up anyways, watching that.' She said, '*Meeting your celestial self* really is a fantastic course of study, you know. I don't see why you won't try it.'

I explained it all to her, the whole sorry story: the mix-ups, the loss of my tapestry, my life's work. She was definitely listening, but she'd turned Daphne up a bit in the background, so as not to miss any incoming messages. The late-night prattlings of your apostate daughter fall pale, I suppose, when you're waiting on a call from the other side. I must've started crying at some point because the Groucho staff all started to whisper and the doorman offered me a Kleenex.

'You never have been very good at letting go, love,' my mother laughed softly, 'you always want to hold on to what's gone. You get that from your father, he's a beggar for it an' all.' In the background one of the dogs barked at a passerby and my mother called for quiet. 'Now, *some* people might say that this is an *opportunity*. A chance to heal the psychic wound caused by traumatic loss in your past.' She said, 'We're all gonna have to you know, love. If we want to evolve spiritually.'

The hostess took down my contact details and promised to be in touch if my evening wrap turned up, then graciously conveyed me to the door with an airlock smile; it was closing time and I wasn't signed in by a member. Outside it was threatening to rain but the press were gone. I contemplated just slumping down in the doorway for the night, only the security guard was fixing me with a look that said, *It's two-thirty in the morning, bitch. Don't try my patience.*

The sky loomed an unkind purple, the journey home was going to be arduous. I knew there was definitely a night bus to Green Lanes, only I couldn't remember where to catch it from. I admit that at that moment, I regretted having nailed my phone to the wall at home. Tiny tears of rain began to freckle my skin, and a man in a Fred Flintstone costume shouted, 'Oi oi! Get your tits out,' from the back of a rickshaw. I was hitting my head against a *No Parking* sign, slowly and rather melodramatically, muttering, 'Fuck fuck fuck,' when Alexander came gliding out of the club.

Some meetings are purely coincidental, others are happy accidents, and some can only be described as fated, don't you think? He observed me for a moment, through a glazed silence, then lit his cigarette. I came to a halt and said, 'Alex, hi. I thought you'd already left.'

'I didn't,' he shook his head, indifferent, 'but you did.'

I gave a demure little giggle, hopeful that he was only play-acting, gestured to his candy-coloured Sobranie and asked, 'Can you spare one?'

'Oh?' He affected a mock incredulity. 'I thought you did not smoke?'

'It's been a long night,' I said.

He took the case from his pocket and a cigarette from the case, his brilliant golden lighter produced an inch-long flame. His fag was pink, mine was acid green, iridescent and noxious, like inhaling hot ash, it tasted like poison and clawed at my throat.

'My God!' I hacked. 'How do you smoke these? They're awful.'

'Practice,' he said and cracked the briefest smile.

On a nicotine rush I explained the evening's many hiccups to him, hoping he would accept the implied apology. It came out sounding screwball, mistaken identities and a taxi ride to nowhere. 'I just wanted it to be clear, that I hadn't ditched you,' I said. 'Not intentionally anyway. I think you're very handsome actually.'

'And you are a very charming girl, Charli,' he took a second to find the right words, 'only a little erratic.'

I blushed. 'Yes well, *charm is the great English blight*. So Evelyn Waugh said.'

Alexander looked at me blankly. 'And who is she please? Another of David Bowie's girlfriends?'

'Yes,' I said, because I couldn't see the use in correcting him, 'that's right.'

The rain had petered out, the clouds had called it a night, the street was slick with vomit and broken glass. I wished to God that Alexander would seize me and take me far away. He looked off over my shoulder into the mid-distance, pulled on the dog-end of his cigarette; a new thought arrived. 'You really should come to Berlin with me,' he said, 'I think it would suit you very well.' He spoke as if in response to my own thoughts. 'You have often fantasised of following your heroes there. So why not?'

'Well, there's my PhD,' I started, 'my roommates, my ah, life.'

He unnerved me, he was so still, implacable, steely; my mind dragged up an old TV interview with Debbie Harry telling the story of her narrow escape from Ted Bundy's pickup truck. I shivered, he crushed his cigarette with the heel of his boot and said, 'Excuses.'

I laughed at him which seemed stupid, dangerous even. 'You're cute, Alex,' I said. 'You are. But we barely know each other.'

'And so?' he shrugged. 'New friends can often have a better time together than old friends.'

This line was familiar to me, and I asked if he was quoting from something, maybe in translation, *Faust* perhaps, but he said that no, it was just a picture that came to him. He told me not to change the subject – his offer was legitimate.

I was sceptical. I said, 'And what would I do with myself when we got there exactly?'

'Whatever you want,' he said. Something immoral played in the corners of his mouth and caused his lips to pull back into a radiant snarl. He was toying with me again, but I didn't rise to it.

'What I *want*,' I began, 'is to start on my doctoral thesis and –'

'No, no,' he interrupted me again. 'Excuse me please, but you don't. Not really.'

He aggravated me, sure, but he excited me too, I pushed back. 'You seem to be very sure of what I want.' I was burning with a lewd curiosity about this man; I really knew nothing about him.

'I am,' he said archly, 'surer than you.'

'Whatever,' I flicked the butt of my cigarette into the gutter, 'I know what I want.'

'Oh yes?' he said, locking me with that demoniacal gaze of his, daring me to go further. 'And what is that?'

I returned a stare as intense and invasive as his and took a step closer. 'I want you to take me home,' I said, 'right now.'

He was silent for just a beat. I thought I had taken him by surprise, confounded him, but in truth I had shocked only myself with this outburst. He was not for a second rattled, he just said, 'Well, now we are getting somewhere.'

He kissed me, and I knew that this was what he had been waiting for, biding his time. In the long slow excursions he made with his tongue I felt him slacken not with relief, but with satisfaction, victory. He had me where he wanted me and I had done all of the work myself – I had handed myself over complete.

He raked his fingers backwards through his hair. 'This way,' he said, 'my car is parked a few streets over.'

He strode ahead with purpose and I followed barefoot behind, avoiding the broken bottles, fag ends and chicken boxes which littered the pavement in disconcerting quantities. He had parked on West Street, outside the Saint Martin's Theatre where *The Mousetrap* plays in perpetuity. I hurried alongside him in nervous silence. The pavements were still busy, muscle twinks in promo T-shirts and trolleyed tourists staggering up and down Old Compton Street looking for somewhere to end the night, bouncers squaring up to small-time dealers, and rough sleepers begging for loose change. Alexander cut through them all like a knife.

We skimmed the lip of Chinatown, *Lotus Garden*, *Cantonese Wok*, *Good Times*, passing through the glow of all that golden signage until we reached his ride, a square, black Mercedes Benz. I was dazzled by the sheer size of the thing – it looked ancient, like something a Soviet dictator would be driven around in, it made me instantly horny. A warden had left a ticket on the windscreen, Alexander tore it off and threw it in the street. I did wonder, for a second, if he should be driving, but then I declined to care. *Ho-hum,* I said to myself, *It's his car. I'm sure he has insurance.* I fiddled with the hole in my tights.

He took out his keys. 'I won her in a game of poker,' he confessed with an awkward pride, 'the top comes down but there is no GPS.'

'Don't worry,' I said, 'I know the way.'

The next morning, in a state of some degradation, I crawled from underneath him and out to the newsagent for a litre bottle of Coke. I was wearing the clothes I hadn't slept in, swaying on the shop floor and clutching the soda as if my life depended on it. The woman in front of me in the queue looked me over askance, muttering to herself as she plonked two tins of cat food, a microwavable burger and a bottle of luminous orange juice onto the countertop. 'Fags and the paper,' she said, 'same as usual.' The newsagent passed her a packet of Marlboro Red and the *Daily Mirror*; he let the newspaper flop flat on the counter as he rung up her shopping, the red headline screaming up at me, *Flamin' 'ell!*

The paper had run a picture of the fire at Apsley House on the front page, there in the top-left corner, a short block of text below it which I was in no condition to decipher. Another, larger picture filled the right-hand side of the page, a vertical portrait of Sophia, striking her sex kitten poses in the street outside the Groucho. Given the schizophrenic combination of images, it was hard to tell which of the two photos the headline referred to. *Flamin' 'ell!* I thought, *Maybe both?* Looking over the shoulder of the disgruntled shopper in front, skimming the *Mirror* for a clue, I recognised with a shock that I was in there too, visible a pace behind Sophia, looking bombed and open-mouthed, gorgonised by the paparazzi flashbulbs, bold print below reading, POP STAR SOPHIA HOPE PARTIES WITH GENDER-BENDING PAL!

The strip lights, the shame, the smell of stale Pot Noodles, the intoxicants leaving my system, I was red-faced and staring hard at the floor, the woman in front of me harrumphed, 'Ack! The state of it!' I felt crushed, quite humiliated, *This can't be my life,* I said to myself again and again, *This cannot be my* life.

I scurried home, chased by the image on that drug-fucked front page, flinching at every ray of unseasonable sunlight, sequestering myself in my bedroom, chugging half the bottle of cola straight off, waking Alexander with my caffeinated anxiety. 'If the offer still stands,' I said, 'I think I would like to come with you to Berlin after all.'

'Sure thing, lover,' he said, 'I am driving back there this evening.' He yawned. 'But can you tell me please why there is a mobile phone nailed into your wall?'

8

We kept all the money for our household bills in a Garfield biscuit barrel on top of the fridge. At the end of the month one of us would take the cash to the post office and pay it in, council tax, electricity, gas. On the morning I left for Berlin, there was close to 300 quid in dirty, unguarded banknotes stashed in there – it was providence. Alexander said that since I was leaving London with only a single suitcase it was fair enough to take the cash. My roommates could sell the rest of my belongings after I'd gone, he calculated that they'd probably even make a profit. I admired that about him, his entrepreneurial spirit; he saw where opportunity lay and encouraged me to be bold in seizing it. Besides, I had offered to pay for the petrol.

I grabbed at whatever seemed most indispensable and stuffed it into my case, took a few aspirin for my headache and wrote to the friends I had in Berlin to let them know that I was headed their way. I was hoping they would let me crash in their atelier, if they hadn't been kicked out yet – their set-up seemed perpetually frangible. Alexander had been expertly vague about his own living situation: he hadn't offered, I hadn't asked. I suspected he had a lover tucked away in his big house already. I expected to be just one of many in fact and the thought stung, so I wanted to let him know that he wasn't my only option either. I told him that I'd probably be staying with my friend Finley for a while. 'He's a really great painter,' I said, in an offhand manner, 'and he has a beautiful cock.'

Alexander was flat on his back on the floor, sunglasses on, smoking and soaking up the meagre sunlight as it filtered into my room. He said, 'You mean the American boy with the gap in his teeth? Yes, he is very cute. Is he a painter? I did not know.'

One square of sun fell through a greasy windowpane right onto his face, he looked like an optical illusion. I said, 'Yes, that's him. He paints all the saints in orthopaedic shoes, and ghosts shagging bishops and whatnot, he's really *out there*. I think he's a true visionary. You know him?'

'Oh yes,' he snickered, 'I know him.'

We waited until the house was quiet, until I was sure everyone was either at the library or at work, then we bundled out of there with the cash, my case and a carton of oat milk that I didn't want to waste. I didn't leave a note, they'd figure it out themselves soon enough, but I did pop the DVD of *What Ever Happened to Baby Jane?*, which I'd borrowed from Mary next door, back through her letterbox.

Alex told me that it could take up to sixteen hours to get to Berlin by car. I was quite content with that, because I still had an M on my passport, and while they barely looked at it at Calais, at Heathrow that incongruous character always caused no end of confusion and harassment. 'That's perfect for me,' I said, 'I hate flying. Something David Bowie and I have in common – he crosses the Atlantic by ship you know? Much better for the environment too.'

'That depends on the ship,' Alex said.

Our course skirted the north of France, cut through Belgium and the Netherlands and then on into Germany. Notwithstanding my initial fascination with the endless strange sausage restaurants all along the Autobahn, it was a remarkably colourless route, just toll booths and tarmac for hour after hour. Every so often the radio station would pass into another indecipherable language, that was the only way of marking the distance travelled. The sun was setting by the time we got to Ghent, and by Antwerp it was pitch black.

There was no Bluetooth or CD player in the car, only an old tape deck, and over and over again we played a Mary J. Blige cassette, which I found at one of the numberless service stations we stopped in at. We drank Coke, smoked Sobranies and stared ahead at the unchanging asphalt landscape, picked out before us by the beam of the car's headlights. It excited me to imagine what people thought when they saw the two of us, cruising down the motorway in that hulking Mercedes. I could see on their faces just how amazed they were by its great spectral glamour.

Perhaps it was the sleep deprivation, or the promise of everything Berlin held, or maybe Mary J. Blige inspired it, I can't say, but the voyage definitely had a romantic flavour. Often when I looked over at Alexander I saw that he was already looking back at me, he had the most beautiful eyelashes. Oncoming traffic threw light then shadow on him, light then shadow, he flickered in the driver's seat, Apollo becoming Dionysus, the headlights hitting him then receding into antiquity. The night, thick as marble all around us, the complementary vibrations of his body, my body and the full-figured car, the biscuit tin of stolen money sitting there on the backseat, it all made me feel so lawless and sexy and free. I knew he was with me, following these Bonnie and Clyde scenarios; from the off we could communicate like fungi. Somewhere between Essen and Dortmund he said, 'I am going to pull over at the next lay-by, and I am going to make you cum.'

The car was almost as long as a hearse but he handled it effortlessly, tucking us in amongst a row of heavy goods vehicles neatly, dragging on a cigarette as he looked over his shoulder to reverse. After the last toke he flicked the butt out of the open window and said, 'Hitch up your skirt,' so I did.

His tone was neutral, still forceful; I didn't ever question his intent, that was part of the pleasure, the complete surrender and the feeling I often had with him, that I had ceased to exist, as a subject possessed of personhood anyway. 'Now take down your panties,' he said, and again I did as I was instructed.

I felt extremely embarrassed sitting there in his car exposed from the waist down, but the sound of his breathing, quickening with excitement, which he tried to disguise with slow controlled swallows, was turning me on, and that was patently clear. I started getting hard and he grinned, taking on a tone of mockery and chastisement. He said, 'Oh, Charli, this is not what I would expect from a nice girl like you. Aren't you ashamed of yourself? Taking out your cock in public and showing it off like this?'

I felt my face flush scarlet, instinctively I moved to cover myself but he reached out and caught my hand with his, growling low, 'Don't touch it. I didn't say you could touch it.' I gasped, nodded in compliance and withdrew my attempts at decency, my modesty in tatters. 'Good girl,' he said, 'hands above your head.' I obeyed and he turned my face from side to side with his slender fingers, assessing me. 'You know,' he whispered, 'you have the most perfect skull.'

In the low light of the lay-by those queer eyes of his glimmered green like a predator's, and I was aware that some of the trucks around us and facing us had men sitting up in their cabs. With his left hand Alexander pinned my wrists together against the headrest so that I was as defenseless as a holy martyr, and with his right he groped my breasts through my blouse, almost savagely. No, he was not gentle, he made me squirm in my seat, then he glossed his right palm with spit and said, 'So, you've been fucking your friend Finley as well, have you?'

I bowed my head, nervous, whimpering, alive to his power, and he began stroking the shaft of my cock with his firm slick hand. 'Tell me then,' he said slow and deliberate, 'tell me what a bad girl you have been.'

I stammered through how I'd met Finley at Polly's place, how we'd hit it off and he'd kissed me in her kitchen, but Alex was impatient and pressed me to cut to the chase. 'I want to hear how he fucks you,' he said. He spoke to me in a tone so laced with cruelty, he was like a high-school bully, and I couldn't get enough of it, I poured it all out. I told him how Finley had led me into Polly's bathroom, locked the door and unzipped his pants, told him how I'd immediately pulled up my dress, let him fuck me from behind against the bathtub, and as I spoke my breath grew shallow and quick. All the time Alex kept that stroking motion going, brisk and measured, along the length of my dick. He said, 'You let this strange guy fuck you on the bathroom floor? You are a real slut, you know that?' I nodded *yes* emphatically *yes* but it wasn't enough. He seized my face, gripped it hard, and hissed, 'Say it,' his spit flecked my face. I knew to keep my hands where they were and I knew the words to use now, 'Yes,' I said, 'I'm a slut, I am a real slut.'

He grinned wider, 'I am glad you can admit this,' and issued a ridiculing little snicker, his even pearly teeth glinting in the darkness, the heat of his breath licking my face. I was by now writhing under his grip and so he reached back to secure my hands away from where I most wanted to run them. I bucked in ecstasy, in frustration, and he glowered. 'You're not going to cum are you? You are not going to cum all over yourself are you, Charli?' I tried to hold back but he went harder and faster until I was panting like a dog, losing control, spinning out, only conscious of the moans hammering in my head, ringing in my ears, and the wave of intense, debilitating pleasure rushing through my body.

I came hard and loud, felt surge after surge of cum spurt and land, hot and thick on my stomach and on my thighs, and as I boiled over, I saw two hauliers staring down from their trucks, watching me. Alex held me there in that position, on show until my spasming subsided, hands above my head, forcing up within me an awareness of my arrant depravity, unable to cover myself. He assessed me with quiet satisfaction and tsk-tsked, 'Oh dear. Look at the mess you have made.' He ran two fingers through the goo pooled in my belly button and regarded its consistency for a second or so before he licked them clean.

I started to tidy myself up, to put myself together, silently, feeling sheepish, exhausted, a little shaken even, as the world came back into focus. I thought I recognised one of the truckers as the guy who had offered to share his vape pen with me the night before, though from this distance, of course, it was impossible to tell. I pulled up my knickers and rolled down my skirt; Alex took a swig from the now warm oat milk and pulled a face, passed the carton to me, lit another cigarette.

'We should go,' he said, yawning, 'it is getting really late.'

When I was a kid I read an interview with Kylie in *Sugar* or *Just 17* or some other teen tabloid, in which she spoke about how her ex-boyfriend, Michael Hutchence, had taught her sex. Alexander did that for me. I was hardly a virgin before I met him; I'd had plenty of unsatisfying hook-ups and a handful of messy relationships, though the more memorable fucks had come about more by good luck than by good design. I had always known what excited me sexually, ever since I was nine or ten, only I hadn't known how to express it. I thought it was a challenge enough for any sexual partner to go to bed with a girl with a dick without asking that they choke me too. So I simply made myself amenable to the desires of whomever I might be fooling around with. I would never have asked any of them for anything, I was afraid I would push their tolerance too far. But you see, with Alex I didn't have to say a thing. He had read me at a glance, seen me for what I was, licked his lips and set to work.

Once I was finished dressing he started the engine and said, 'Ready to go?' I gave a little *yup* of confirmation and fastened my seat belt. He laced the steering wheel between his hands and heaved it to the right to pull us off and out of the lay-by. I pressed play on the car stereo, the cassette wound on in silence for a few seconds whilst the old tape deck warmed up. In the stillness Alexander sighed very deeply and said, 'Fuck, Charli, that was really hot.'

'Yeah,' I said. 'Really.'

Then the music came on comically abrupt and we both laughed aloud, merging with the Autobahn, driving on to Berlin.

PART TWO

Proportioned to the Groove

I

Alexander dropped me off outside City Chicken, with a kiss on the cheek and a simple 'We will see us soon.' I didn't feel completely out of my depth yet, but I was beginning to realise what a potentially lunatic move I'd made. Night's sky was already in rags, the hem of her beautiful indigo gown torn and scorched by dawn's smutty fingers. On the breeze I caught the sound of laughter, inhuman like a saxophone wail. I had arrived without knowing if my friends would be around or amenable to this unannounced imposition, but as is often the case, when something has to work out, when there is simply no other alternative, it did.

I pressed the buzzer and waited in the courtyard at the back of the chicken shop, staring up at the studio window. I saw that there were lights on, rang and rang again, intoned *Please be in, please be in* over and over until Polly flung open the window and shrieked, 'Charli, you mad bitch! What the hell are you doing here?'

She threw her arms open to me and brought me up the three flights of concrete stairs, unhindered by her stilettos. We lugged my case through the wasteland of what had once been an industrial mirror workshop, a rusted, haunted space. I could hear music playing, some sort of chill-out come-down soundscape rolling along the corridor – this seemed fitting given it was 5 a.m.

'Were you having a party?' I asked.

'Yes,' she said, 'we were celebrating.'

The landlord was trying to evict everyone from their ateliers and turn the building into apartments, but he had been unable to secure the necessary permissions and so the artists lived on to paint another day. The whole building had come out to whoop it up. Polly and Finley's studio had been the epicentre of the action; the place was awash with beer bottles and makeshift ashtrays, discarded wigs, plastic bags, hummus and gleaned chicken bones dished up on paper plates. In the middle of it all was a huge white cake, frosted in blue with a message of defiance or congratulations, I couldn't quite make it out, because someone had apparently walked through it and tracked butter icing across the floor and down the hall towards the bathroom.

A boy I recognised from a previous visit sat slumped against the radiator, one hand in his pants, the other gripping a bottle of Sterni, fruitlessly trying to fight off sleep. Finley had already succumbed and was crashed out on his mattress in the corner, sprawled flat and naked snoring alongside someone in a ski mask and Thai boxing shorts. Polly was the last one standing. Perhaps still a little high, she had set about cleaning the place, and was sweeping the worst of the trash into a neat little heap. She hadn't changed out of her python print minidress though, didn't so much as slip off her shoes. She held fast by a mid-century playbook which said that a woman's sense of self-respect came from pristine presentation; she may have been skirting puddles of puke in an old German factory but she was dressed for cocktails in Coconut Grove.

In the past when we'd been out together, people who saw that I was trans presumed Polly was too, I suppose because she matched the stereotype of how trans women dress better than I do. Once, some drunk at Kumpelnest suggested that I wear something similar to her, if I wanted to people to think of me as a *real woman*. I was visibly hurt and Polly slapped his face. 'What would you know about *real* women?' she yelled, jabbing her finger in his chest. 'As if any woman would look at you, du hässliches Schwein!'

Before Finley moved in Polly had run a sex shop from the atelier. The adventure had been a bust. She had been gifted a few thousand euros by her parents to help find her footing in Berlin, but she didn't know a thing about running a business. Really who in their right mind *would* start selling sex toys from the back of a chicken joint in Neukölln? Nobody ever bought anything, and the vibrators and edible panties all ended up in a big box somewhere, depreciating. A hip kid blogger wrote about it once and for a month or so the place received a steady trickle of expats and tourists, Yanks and Brits convinced that the shop was actually an art project. They thought Polly had set it up as a comment on late-stage capitalism and the exploitation of artists. 'On reflection,' she said, 'I suppose I should've played along, I could've been a successful installation artist by now.'

Polly was in the year above me, the same year as Sophia at Saint Martins, they hated each other. She painted big blocks of text over neon and verdant landscapes, deer grazing in fields of flowers with the words *Nothing Makes Sense Anymore* scrolling above their heads, big cats mid-pounce leaping through the legend *Time to Die, Bitch*. She met Finley when they were both exhibiting in a group show; he needed a live-work space and Polly offered him a corner of the shop since she wasn't exactly raking it in with sales. He took over one half of the space, tucked away for privacy behind a curtain of gauzy purple. I always felt like I was visiting a fortune teller on Blackpool promenade whenever I crossed over to see him.

He lived in the studio, illegally. His family were all fundamentalist opioid addicts back in Nevada, they did not care for contemporary art. He had inherited something of their belief system though: he was steadfast that his work was a calling and that the hardships he suffered to fulfil it were proof of concept, *thy will be done*. My mother would've said he was working with the angelic realms. He had an unshakeable sense of justice and a remarkable temper too.

Polly lived off-site; she shared a flat in Kreuzberg with a devious little twink she knew from Dublin. She had a very French surname, *Grainger*, but was Anglo-Irish. Finley had a very Irish surname, *Hagan*, but was American with Mexican grandparents. No two people were ever so simultaneously dissimilar and yet indistinguishable, and whatever mischief she might have been capable of without him was doubled by his presence. They would answer the door naked to curators and offer collectors dildos as free gifts with any purchase, their studio had a reputation for animated debauchery, an infantile depravity outstanding even in a city defined by it. I cherished every moment spent with them there.

Polly gathered up the empties and I recapped the last forty-eight hours for her, or rather I gave her the edited highlights, the scenes I thought would most appeal: Margaret mistaking me for a member of the family and the paparazzi swarming all over Sophia's taxi. Polly rolled her eyes at the mention of her name. 'Then the silly bitch gave me ketamine when I thought I was taking coke,' I said, 'I was in a K-hole for fuck knows how long.' Polly laughed as she laboured. I was too tired to pitch in but at least I could bring a little levity to her chores from the sidelines, like Raquel Welch in Vietnam, entertaining the troops in her go-go boots.

Gradually the studio grew to look a little less like the municipal tip. Polly dusted off her hands and sipped at the end of what I think was a gin and juice, she was quite surprised to learn that I had moved to Berlin permanently. I told her it was because I was finding London just too intense, I didn't mention Alexander, of course. I suppose I knew how she'd respond – I had made a fairly rash decision. Moreover I was still kidding myself that I hadn't come all this way for a man

I barely knew, that his presence in the city was just a happy coincidence.

The sky was by now the colour of lobster bisque and Polly said that she needed to go home to bed. I was also dazed and desperate for sleep. She belted herself into an old Armani overcoat which had once belonged to her mother. I stripped to my underwear and tied my hair up out of my face. A couple of lamps were still lit, giving off increasingly impotent brilliance; we circled the studio putting them all out, cautious of any forgotten chicken carcasses. I draped a blanket around the boy now sleeping against the radiator, he wasn't who I thought he was after all. Polly came over to kiss me goodnight. 'Right,' she said, 'herzlich wilkommen zurück in Berlin! Schlaff gut.' Then she sauntered out into the yolky light of the new day.

I slipped into Finley's bed and pressed up to him for warmth, the morning was still cool. He opened his sleepy, sticky eyes, confused. 'Charli?' he said.

'Hello, lover,' I replied.

'Girl, when did you get here?' he asked.

'Just now actually,' I replied, 'your friend Alexander drove me.'

He repeated, 'Alexander? The French guy, the sculptor?'

'No,' I whispered, not wanting to disturb the other sleeper. 'Well, I don't know, maybe he's French. He says you two know each other *intimately*,' and I imitated Alex's strange accent. 'We met at a bar last night.'

'What?' he mumbled, groggy with booze. 'You drove all the way here with some random guy? Girl, that's crazy.'

But I was too tired to even begin to explain. 'Shh,' I said, 'I'll tell you all about it in the morning.'

2

For a few weeks Finley and I shared everything: food, weed, boys, his mattress on the studio floor. I would often wake up before dawn to the sound of him talking aloud to his paintings in German, he said it helped him practice. I loved him for his fortitude, his unwarranted optimism, his incorruptible sense of purpose. He gave me my first paying gig in Berlin too, DJing at a Sunday night party called Piggy, which he threw at a sex club. I wasn't very good, but then nobody was there for the music.

When we were really hard-up Finley and I would take a shopping trolley out and collect glass bottles. Most incurred a *Pfand*, a deposit which you could claim back at the supermarket, as much as 25 cents. On Sunday mornings in fair weather we could make enough to buy a week's worth of groceries. Finley said there was true grace in poverty. He was the real deal, he wasn't masquerading, he didn't eat from dumpsters all through his twenties only to go on and buy an apartment for cash at age thirty when his father told him it was time to grow up and invest his capital. He lived in the studio because he had to, he collected trash in the street because he had to, and if he needed to give an old man a €50 hand job in the sauna to pay his half of the rent he would, because he had to. My own family were hardly aristocratic, but my father had been pretty canny with his wholesale operation and so I'd always been insulated from any real scarcity. I fantasised about them buying one of Finley's portraits and helping him out. My father might've paid a few hundred quid for a painting, actually, only my mother's tastes ran rather more towards Chagall prints from the Tate and stained-glass sun catchers.

I think I could have married Finley, only he wasn't available for that, not with me anyway, perhaps not with anyone – his heart would never let him be still. He fell in love and out of love again at a speed I found inconceivable; he was unreservedly passionate, he picked up boys everywhere. Sometimes he'd bring one home and the three of us would fall into bed together, sometimes he'd ask me to take a walk around the block, sometimes we'd cuddle up for warmth and find ourselves with our fingers in each other's arses idly, half-listening to NPR.

Occasionally we ran after the same object of desire and squabbled over him – we were like siblings really, sometimes we just did not want to share. Once a big handsome Dutchman whom we met while buying cigarettes decided he liked me more than Finley and Finley flipped. Men were the only thing we ever really fought about. He'd call me delusional and I'd call him hysterical, and though our stand-offs never lasted very long, they could be really intense. Thankfully I found a place of my own to rent before we ever actually came to blows.

I took a room in an apartment on Sanderstrasse, ten minutes from the studio, a few blocks away from Karstadt, the ailing department store they say was once the largest in Europe. I roomed with a psychiatry student called Carl who had papered the kitchen in old Mickey Mouse cartoon strips. He was unnecessarily handsome and almost always high, a small-time speed dealer. He always said he wasn't queer and if that's the case he was the only person I knew in Berlin who wasn't. He spoke English to an almost functional level, but as my German comprised little more than a few joke phrases I'd picked up from watching all those old sitcoms about Nazi incompetence, our conversations were always somewhat stilted. Still, he was patient with late rent, which was only fair I suppose, as he was charging me more than he was paying himself, and for a smaller room.

The walls were unpapered, plaster on show, and riddled with what looked like bullet holes. I had an old sofa upholstered in flocked grey tweed and a single bed with a fanciful metal frame. There was a Man Ray print on the wall and a deer skull over the door; the windows looked out onto a beautiful little garden in the Hoff, entry to which was forbidden to all by the Hausmeister's wife, who tended it weekly and watched over it tyrannically. It was in the back of the building, away from the street and quiet as the grave, so often I had to walk outside just to be assured that the apocalypse hadn't been and gone and left me behind. We had a brothel at one end of the road and a Greek restaurant at the other, and in the middle an art gallery run by two drag queens which became a sort of speakeasy at the weekend. There was a late-night shop too, a *Späti,* and a cafe called Kuchen Mafia. In the autumn I moved in there, the bus stop on the street corner had a huge poster up advertising the dates of some upcoming concerts to be given by Romy Haag. I bought two tickets – I thought it would be a great idea for a date – but Alexander vetoed it on account of the venue's lousy acoustics, so I never got to go.

I called him from the telephone kiosk in the Späti because I didn't have a working phone of my own, I called him and asked him to come over. Such an odd experience, stepping into one of the phone booths behind the stacks of beer bottles and peanut flips, closing the screen door to sit and make a call, as though the twenty-first century had never happened. They were just regular old plastic telephones, with a handset and cradle, no coin slot, you paid up at the counter which made it feel somehow illicit. Everyone else came in to call family in Nigeria or Turkey so the shopkeeper was always very suspicious of me, since the only other white people who used the booths went in there to shoot up.

'I found a place to live,' I spoke into the warm receiver, 'near Hermannplatz.'

Alexander replied quite casually, 'Very nice. Close to my gym. I will come by after my calisthenics class.'

He arrived late of course, though I still wasn't ready – Carl buzzed him in. He came straight down the corridor whilst I scrabbled to fix my hair and directly into my bedroom without having to call out or ask which room I was in, as if he had visited me many times before. Indeed it never seemed necessary for him to orientate himself in any space. I chalked this up to his catlike nature: every place I ever saw him in he seemed to own.

He brought me a gift-wrapped package in a Karstadt bag, festooned with ribbons and wrapped in pink paper patterned with little elephants wearing diapers, and swirling text that read, *Hurra ein Mädchen!* – gift wrap for a new baby girl.

'Here,' he explained, 'the reason why I am late.'

I took the bag and unwrapped the parcel: Egyptian cotton sheets, a set for a single bed. I asked how he knew I didn't have a double. 'Intuition,' he shrugged and lit a cigarette, 'these old buildings, they are much alike.'

He really was a mystery to me, an impossible natural phenomenon, like evaporation. Some rule of physics must be able explain him, I reasoned, but I myself could not. Besides, did I care to? No. I was quite content to bathe in ignorance, it was far less complicated that way, to submit to pleasure without meaning. I didn't need to spoil things by demanding an understanding, better to flow on into oblivion. I thought of wacky old Whitman scribbling on the back of an envelope, bowed before the suitability of the line. *Surely, whoever speaks to me in the right voice,* he wrote, *him or her I shall follow.* In reverence, I set about making up the bed.

Later, after we'd sunk a few Sternis and watched a YouTube documentary on alien abduction, Alexander told me to strip and I did. I undressed in front of him, dropped the dress I had only recently finished wriggling into, slipped out of my panties but remained in my bra, as instructed. Smoking, he sat back in the old armchair, like a puppeteer guiding me to nakedness, the crotch of his trousers grew visibly tight. 'Slowly,' he said, 'there is no hurry tonight.'

The only light in the room now came from a standing lamp in the corner which threw a bronze hue over us both. 'Turn around,' he said, and I did, feeling like a nymph on an Art Nouveau sundial. 'Show me your ass. Good,' he appraised me. 'Now come here.'

I was nervous, I could hear my roommate in the kitchen on the other side of the wall; there was no lock on my door. I moved towards him shyly, resisting the impulse to cover myself, not wanting to make him angry, my nipples hard and my dick harder. He reached out to stroke it, briefly, then instructed, 'Put it in my mouth.'

Men had wanted me to do this with me before of course, but usually they were drunk and they drooled a lot, and either choked or came on themselves after thirty seconds. But not Alex, he really was very talented. It wasn't a secret kink for him, the idea of sucking my dick, he said it excited him in just the same way that eating out some other girl's pussy did, he did it all and he did it well. He swallowed the whole length with gracious, languid ease, and squeezed my arse, forcing me deeper down his throat.

'Is that good?' he asked, knowing it was. 'You like that don't you?' he said, seeing that I did. I was never in control, he used me like a toy, I could only pant, 'Yes, Alex,' between snatched breaths, 'don't stop.'

With one hand he kept things steady, with the other he unbuttoned his shirt – he always wore shirts – he broke off just as my knees began to buckle. I thought I was surely going to cum all over that milky body of his, white on white on white, but he hadn't granted me that permission yet, so I held out hard against the feeling.

He stood to take off his pants, his cock was already glistening at the tip, a bead of viscid pre-cum dribbling. I reached for it but he batted me back, told me to keep my arms at my sides, took a length of pink gift-wrap ribbon and tied it around my throat, then he led me to the bed like a dog on a leash. There he kissed me, holding my jaw soberly, bringing his fingertips to my chin and manipulating my face, he stroked our dicks together, silken with spit and Cowper's fluid. I groaned under his grip, I writhed, again I reached to take hold of his cock but he knocked my hands away once more, grinning a little sadistically in the gloam. 'You really want it, don't you?'

'Yes,' I gasped, 'you know I do.'

'So.' He lay back on my ornately infantile bed with one arm behind his head and squeezed his cock at the base to make it throb. 'Say please,' he gibed, 'if you want it so badly.'

'Please,' I said, ashamed that Carl might hear.

'Please what?' he asked, words dripping with mockery. 'Say it louder.'

'Please give me your cock,' I said, and I felt like I could've cum just from touching it.

He beckoned me closer with his hand, lazily, and I crawled up to him and kissed him again, lay my body flat against his, whispered in his ear, 'Fuck me.' He used his slick and fluent fingers to open up my ass, my body put up no fight at all, it bloomed with the greatest willingness and welcomed his fingers in. He spat on his hand and slathered his cock in saliva, coating his shaft and then my hole, I was aching, I was ready. I knelt above him and he teased at my arse with the tip of his cock, brushing it against my most tender spot, over and over just to make me whimper, just to hear me beg, 'Please, Alex please.'

He slipped it inside me roughly and I yelled out loud, forgetting my roommate entirely. 'Ride it,' he said, and tucked both hands back behind his head.

I pulled myself up along and back down on his dick, I felt it stretch me almost to the point of pain each time I descended and took it deeper inside myself. I gripped his hips and let my head drop back, my hair spilling around my shoulders and my mouth falling open in one constant moan, until I was taking it so rhythmically, so organically that it almost required no effort. I realised how easily he had taken back control; he was holding me firmly at the hips and thrusting with a manic precision, hitting that original pleasure point, a look of pure determination on his face. I could feel just how close to the edge I was, I started to slam myself down harder on his girth, a rivulet of sweat running from my forehead and into my eye, wave after wave of gratification wracking me until I couldn't take it anymore, and I let out a deep, guttural groan, cumming hard, arcs of sperm splattering Alex's chin and chest. He pulled his cock out of my arse and jerked himself off for just a few seconds, then I felt his load shoot up my back and drizzle, cooling like frosting, trickling towards my contented hole.

When it was over he crossed the room to fetch his cigarette case and I saw, really for the first time, how skinny he was, wondered if the reason he was always so overdressed was so as to better shape himself into the form he wanted to present – Superman revealed as Clark Kent.

'Do you mind?' he asked as if remembering his manners, wiggling the cigarette between his extended peace fingers, though he was lighting up before I even answered. 'Want one?' I nodded, he tossed the case to me and returned to bed with two long strides.

We smoked in silence, I pulled the duvet up against myself, he stared off into the mid-distance; by the low light, up against the bare walls we must've looked like a Mark Morrisroe portrait. I pondered what the image might've been called, *Untitled (Alex and Charli in bed)* perhaps.

He wanted to watch one of those reality shows about rich housewives in America insulting each other over dinner and was disappointed that I didn't have a television. I felt the first flush of pique with him and asked if this was all he ever did with his time, fuck and watch this kind of junk. He told me that to him it was a goldmine of inspiration; 'I have written some of my best lyrics watching *this kind of junk*,' he said. This surprised me.

'It's funny.' I expressed blue smoke through my nose. 'I know almost nothing about you.'

'Oh, no,' he countered, 'I think you know a lot,' and he grinned again.

I put my cigarette out in a half-empty teacup, passed it to Alex so he could do the same. 'What's your name?' I asked. 'Your full name.'

'Alexander Matthias Geist,' he replied, 'but I never use my middle name.'

I smiled. 'Angenehm, Herr Alexander Geist.'

'Angenehm!' He laughed. 'Where did you learn that, Miss Charli Hughes?'

Careful not to betray my sense of surprise, I asked, 'How did you find out my name?'

'The internet,' he said. 'Heard about it?'

3

I've been trying to ask the nurse for a mirror, because I want to see my face, since I don't know how badly it is broken. Instead she has brought me a cup of scrambled eggs. It's not much to ask for really, a mirror, the possibility to inspect the bruising and welts of my poor visage. I feel like I've been asking the same question all afternoon, to no avail. I'll try again.

'Ich brauchst Spiegel,' I'm saying, 'Ich brauchst Spiegel.' I figure that if I just keep saying it over and over, again and again, eventually I'll make myself plain. 'Ich brauchst Spiegel.'

The nurse looks ready to snap, she is pointing to my cup of cold congealed eggs and spluttering, 'Komm schon, iss!' She is telling me to eat! Is this some sort of diversion tactic? Well, I won't be fooled. Even though I am very hungry now, I will refuse these eggs. 'Ich brauchst spiegel,' I'm saying, only much louder now, much, so let's call it shouting. I am car crash, I am hunger strike.

The man with the mean little face appears at the window again, attracted to the scene by my increasingly audible demands no doubt, and the nurse suddenly looks embarrassed. He has a notepad and pen and Ah-ha! *I'm beginning to understand it! He's a journalist! He's here to get the scoop on my relationship with Alexander, he's going to report everything he sees to the tabloids.*

The nurse knows that I know, she sees that I see, understands that I have the power now! Now I can disgrace her and the whole ramshackle institution, I can denounce them as abusers, withholders of basic commodities – in front of this greedy scribbler, I can expose their cruelties. What a nice splash that will make for the morning edition! Hospital investigated for torturing pop star's lover.

I'm giving the journalist my best side. 'Ich brauchst spiegel!' I am shouting again, I have my hand to my forehead. The nurse is gesturing wildly, quacking back at me, 'Wir haben keine Spiegeleier hier nur Rühreier!' and I simply flip over her psychotic fixation with eggs. I slap the cup out of her hands, it bounces back off the wall like a squash ball, spilling a parabola of scrambled eggs above our heads, a larger spread than I would have expected from such a modest portion, and the journalist outside is scrawling frantically in his notepad.

Furious, the nurse is leaving the room, and so for good measure I shout out 'Ich brauchst spiegel!' once more – it has quickly become my very own Carthago delenda est*! I treat myself to a little chuckle. Outside the journalist is all agog. 'Did you get all that?' I shout. I'd hate to send him home empty-handed, even hacks have to earn their crust, you know.*

4

When I told my mother that I was in Berlin she said it was a strange choice for a holiday; when I explained that I'd moved there she said, 'Well, what will I do with all your post?'

'Do I have a lot?' I asked. I'd called her from the phone in the Späti.

'Quite a bit, yeah,' she said, 'none of it's very interesting, though.' She sounded disappointed. 'Mainly letters about your overdraft. What are you doing with yourself in Berlin anyways?'

'Working on my doctoral thesis, of course,' I sulked. 'You never listen to anything I tell you.'

She said, 'Of course I listen love, it's just that you're always up to so much. I can't keep track. You're always here there and everywhere!' She laughed to herself and then took flight in another direction. 'Now *that's* what I was meaning to tell you!' she said. 'One of your housemates rang looking for you – she was fuming – calling you fit to burn she was! Said you'd done a runner. So *I* said you were unwell again and that you had to take some time out to get better. I told her that *she* needed to be more empathetic if she was going to be an artist. Low vibrational frequencies block the higher creative frequencies, as I don't need to tell *you*. Anyways, that changed her tune. She told me to pass on best wishes from everyone at the house and said you don't have to worry about the money or the damage to the wall. Nice girl really. They're not going to press charges.'

I said, 'Mother, you didn't have to lie to her.'

She was indignant. 'Well, how's she ever going to find out? And will you please stop calling me *Mother* like that? Makes me feel like an old woman.'

She told me that she was thinking of getting another dog and asked if I'd found a mass in English yet. She said that they'd discussed a portrait of the Virgin Mary made out of elephant shit in her divine art book group, which she personally found very powerful, even if Carol had called it *blasphemous* and *grotesque*. She was also very excited to tell me she'd heard Sophia on the radio and seen her on breakfast TV.

'I love that song of hers,' she said, and she started singing, '*I'm a sober party girl in a rock'n'roll world baby, yeah yeah yeah yeah yeah*. You know sometimes I feel a bit like that myself!'

I tried to remain polite. 'Mmmhmm. Yeah, she's really making a splash.' I was dying for a cigarette, thinking about Alexander. Why weren't his songs playing on the radio? Some of them were pretty good. *Product*, I thought, *it's all product*.

My mother said, 'Carol wasn't having it that you and Sophia were at university together so I showed her a picture on Facebook. She said "She's a crazy chick isn't she? And doesn't your Charli look like you, eh?"'

I replied, 'Oh really? That's nice.'

My mother continued, 'So I said, "Well, she's my one and only, is our Charli, and she always will be and nothing can change that, *nothing*."'

I was growing increasingly uncomfortable with the rising sea level of emotion here, I said, 'OK, *Mum*, I guess I should be going now,' but she didn't hear. I stressed, 'I *really* have to go now. I'm in a phone booth you see, and someone else needs to use it.'

'Ahhh,' she mewed, 'that's nice, isn't it? Dead old-fashioned like. Well, you take care of yourself love, alright? Have you been doing your affirmations? I want you to picture yourself surrounded by pure white light when you're feeling overwhelmed, OK? No more nonsense now.'

'Absolutely,' I said, 'I will absolutely do that.'

'Alright then,' she concluded, 'your dad says hi and so do the dogs. Isn't that right, eh? Isn't that right Julie, my big girl, Julie?'

'OK then,' I said, 'I'm going now, love you, talk soon,' and hung up.

I wanted to buy some champagne but the Späti only stocked Rotkäppchen: cheap, inelegant German sparkling wine. I grabbed a few bottles all the same – I was going over to Polly's that evening and didn't want to show up empty-handed. I would've gone to Karstadt to find something better, but Finley was picking me up at 8 p.m.

It was supposed to be a dinner party, only Polly didn't have a dining table or many chairs. Her guests always sat on the floor, on her bed, or on one of the pink hot seats left over from the sex shop, lurid PVC pouffes each with a plastic prick sticking straight up from the centre like the stamen on a lily, *for her pleasure*. She had a truly bourgeois horror of profligacy and only shopped at Aldi or the Turkish gidas – she had too much good sense to fritter away her money unnecessarily. Polly didn't spend her allowance on household niceties, she said, because *somehow* dishware etc always ended up broken. I should've asked my father to send her a box of paper plates, there were probably loads left over from the World Cup.

As it was there was only ever enough crockery for about 10 per cent of those invited: Polly owned maybe six plates. She was wildly optimistic with the invitations and inevitably her guests brought their friends, who at least brought bread and beer, though Polly wouldn't touch either since she lived in terror of refined carbs. She was, however, an excellent cook and would spend whole days preparing salads and chicken and roasted vegetables, baking fruit and whipping up alarming Victorian puddings like blancmange and lemon syllabub. She once served twenty people a raspberry trifle from a mop bucket, which was, she assured us, brand new.

Polly was throwing the party to welcome me to Berlin: it was my coming out ball, I remember thinking, *Everybody here looks like hell*, and being really into it. Everyone's clothes came second-hand from Humana, where a shirt cost €1.75, or else from cardboard boxes labelled *zu verschenken*. It was an irreconcilable mixture of off-brand sportswear, chintzy grandma knits, outdated evening clothes and Soviet-era fur coats. There were lots of Swedes there, several filmmakers and a surly moral philosophy student whose name I never knew. I recognised a few people from the studio, and a few more collected from parties: Polly's friend Suzanne, a guitarist from Russia, who was there killing time before a 6 a.m. flight to Lisbon, some off-duty drag queens from Schwuz and a poet with manga-red hair called West, on whom I had a longstanding crush. Ryan, Polly's journalist neighbour, brought a pair of American gay boys with him: they had chalk-white teeth and had dropped out of Stanford to sculpt and live in squalor. Finley brought a pharmacist he'd met at the sauna and Polly's roommate, Callum, invited both of his boyfriends. I would've invited Alex only I hadn't been able to reach him all week.

Guests crowded in doorways and squatted on the kitchen floor, sharing chopping boards repurposed as tableware, or eating with fingers directly from saucepans and baking trays. Everybody's sleeves were in everyone else's salad – no one ever stood on ceremony. Polly played Prince and the Revolution, Suede and Einstürzende Neubauten, more people arrived, we drank Sterni and cheap Sekt, ate mustard mashed potato out of a washing-up bowl. Suzanne took a lot of pictures on the awkward little analogue camera she always carried around with her. I never saw them, but I know one day

I'll find those photos in a coffee table book in my lawyer's office, twenty years from now when Berlin is as dull and expensive as Frankfurt and everybody needs reminding that it wasn't always so. *Nostalgia is a kind of death wish*, you know? I read that in a Virginia Woolf biography.

I had not been sleeping well since moving in with Carl; I was tired and the joints Callum and his boyfriends were passing around hadn't helped any, they'd only made me feel anxious about my situation. I sat myself on the floor. Ryan stepped over me on his way to the kitchen, he wasn't wearing any underwear, and I saw his big, pierced cock up the leg of his shorts. It startled me. West came and sat by me, he brought me a slice of the Streuselkuchen he'd made, asked me how I'd been since last summer, and I told him the tragic story of my tapestry. He said, 'Charli, that's so awful, I'm sorry,' wincing as though personally responsible. 'I wish I could've seen it; it sounds like a beautiful piece. Like an homage to *Façade*, maybe?'

'Yes,' I laughed, 'my Edith Sitwell tribute act.' Nobody else had ever made the connection. 'If you have a nice set of drapes and a spare half hour I could recreate it for you sometime.'

'OK, but,' he took a steadying sip of his Sterni, 'it'd be a terrible shame to hide that beautiful face away for so long.'

I blushed, and he offered me a swig of his beer. I took it, grateful to be able to cover my self-consciousness. His hair fell into his eyes and he swept it away with a gesture so gracious it had to have been practised. I could smell his cheap deodorant; it felt like we were high-school sweethearts for a moment. He told me that he worked at Pfeiffers, the cafe on the corner, and that he was organising a reading there next month – if I had anything new, I was welcome to share it. Then he sipped at his beer again and my lipstick transferred from the rim of the bottle onto his lips, tinting them pink and glossy in the middle as though we had been kissing.

The cork popped on a new bottle; a handful of mashed potato glanced off my shoulder. Polly called out, 'Sorry, Charli – wasn't aiming for you.' Finley stumbled through the crowd and came to join us on the floor, he had handed his pharmacist over to someone else's attention already. He was pretty drunk and beaming at West like a child's drawing of her mother; he took the beer from West's hand and sank it. I knew immediately where this was going and I excused myself. Two or three weeks earlier I might've been game, but something had changed for me, I couldn't quite summon up the appetite for either a quarrel or a three-way that evening.

'Stay,' said West, 'I want to hear about your plans.'

'I can't,' I sighed, 'I promised a friend I'd call tonight.'

He looked at the screen of his phone. 'Charli, it's after one.'

'I know,' I said. 'He's a real night owl.'

5

I blagged Alexander a gig at Finley's dance party by promising to DJ the late-late slot, Finley hated having to do it himself because it got in the way of the real action. He said there was nothing to it and I believed him; besides, everyone I knew in Berlin had been a DJ at some point, there were so many parties it was almost an obligation, like signing off the chore wheel in a house share. Polly was DJing too, just for the first few hours. She was using the pseudonym Fagatha Crusty, hoping to avoid another instance of her father googling *Polly Grainger Berlin* and finding pictures of his favourite daughter French-kissing bartenders in just her thigh-highs where studio portraits should have been.

I hadn't minted my own alias so Finley put me on the flyer as plain old Charli Hughes, my name right there, in significantly smaller letters than the evening's live act, *Disco Darling: Alexander Geist*. I gasped the first time I saw it printed like that. The flyer was a glossy pink oblong with text in a font that dripped, made to look as though the details were written in blood or cum. It said *Pork Out at Piggy! Sundays from 11 p.m.!* On the back there was a picture of Finley wearing a plastic snout and poking his head out from the middle of a row of anonymous bare arses. It was a beautiful picture actually, a sort of Avedon at the Factory moment, shot by a photographer Finley was fucking for a while. I kept one in a frame by my bed for a long time, until Alex knocked it off one night when we were fighting, and the glass cracked and the flyer tore.

He was going to meet us at the club later, insisting that he needed very specific conditions before a performance. I was a little crestfallen, but I understood. Polly came over for a drink and to sync playlists, she said that only one of us could play 'Monster Mash' otherwise it just wouldn't be funny. We knocked back a few shots of tequila in the kitchen and listened to some old Diana Ross B-sides while my roommate spooned Heringssalat onto rye bread and watched us, commenting warily, 'You very much go out.'

'It's research, Carl,' I said, 'for my PhD. Do you want to come?'

'I cannot,' he replied with a mournful shake of his head. 'I have no speed until the next week.' And he shuffled back to his room with his plate, to the one Pink Floyd album he played on a loop.

'He is such a Bette,' said Polly, 'so maudlin, so aloof.' She was reading a big book on the Hollywood feuds of Davis vs Crawford, and had become fixated on the idea that everyone in the world could be categorised as either a Bette or a Joan.

'He's not so bad,' I answered, 'we are being a little obnoxious.'

Fagatha was due to start spinning at 11 p.m., but Finley was still stapling up a Mylar curtain behind the DJ booth and eating a McVeggie sandwich when we arrived at 11.15; he hardly noticed that we were late and already drunk. The party happened at a cruise bar on Urbanstrasse, towards Kreuzberg, away from Neukölln, half a block down from Karstadt. I used to fantasise that there was a secret passage leading from the fine foods market in the department store's basement, running under the bank and the pet shop in between and opening into the darkroom. I thought that such a scenario was very pragmatic and honestly quite possible in a city as perverse and obscure as Berlin.

There was a small crowd gathered: at first it was just the men who came in every night for a drink at the bar and a wank on the way home, plus a bevy of skinny boys in black vests, kids who had heard about the party from friends who had passed through town, who wanted be in on the action. The two contingents rubbed shoulders awkwardly to begin with, only loosening up when the music came on and the drinks specials started.

The bar wasn't very big, it was really just a few stools dotted around a well-scuffed dance floor with a cigarette machine and a cardboard cutout of Cher for decoration. The DJ booth was flanked on one side by a pleather banquette which stood in for a green room backstage, and to which favoured guests were invited to slug a Sterni or snort a line off the cracked faux-marble table top. On the other side was the stage, an unhelpful, stubby little thing which sprouted a metal pole slap bang in its centre: a support beam for the floors above, and not a stripper pole, as the palms of many bashed-up drunks came to prove. The ceiling was a constellation of CDs some bright spark had glued up years ago by way of a rock-bottom renovation, so the whole place glowed with a weird emerald cast of reflected light, and when the party really got going the plastic discs all started to mist up with evaporating sweat; one or two had come loose and fallen, leaving puncture holes in the night sky.

In the corners of the room, mounted above head height, there were crappy little television sets, bolted down as if priceless, the screens forever playing the same loop of skin flicks from the 1980s and '90s. Vintage hunks fucked collegiate twinks in phoney bathrooms, construction workers groped their crotches, the occasional priest masturbated in a country field whilst conflicted seminarians watched in alarm from behind trees, esoteric oiled scenarios took place in bars which mirrored the very one we watched from; it was all the more mystifying for the fact that they played on soundlessly, banging mute for all eternity.

Slowly the bar filled. On Sundays it wasn't a men-only space, and after midnight a second wave of revellers arrived: hot dykes who liked to play rough, one or two trans girls with their sugar daddies and a few handsome boys on T. It was real low-rent decadence: no champagne, only Rotkäppchen over ice. Finley had thrown parties before, but this was his biggest success. Many famous people partied there – during the few years that Piggy ran, I saw everyone from aspiring arthouse directors to major Hollywood stars there, Turner Prize winners and Booker Prize winners, children of Beatles, Carnegie Hall headliners, junkies, working girls and faded DDR pin-ups bumping into world-renowned couturiers at the bar and spilling their Campari spritzes. Stars came, I think, because nobody fussed over them, nobody asked for a selfie or tried to press a screenplay on them. Celebrity was weaker currency there than just about anywhere else in the world, and of course if they should end the night wrist-deep in somebody's grandfather, discretion was largely assured.

Polly played an ungodly mix of early 2000s R and B, old gospel records, the electroclash classics that were starting to come back into vogue again, Madonna remixes and New Wave oddities, like an amped-up wedding DJ who knew how to read a room. She was really very good. People danced in harnesses and sports bras and Bikini Kill T-shirts cropped above the navel, in jockstraps and boots, and Finley ran about between songs, encouraging everyone to strip off further. Because it was such a small, jammed place it got very hot very quickly. Everyone smoked continuously all night, straights and joints and rollies, until the air turned blue with a constant fog and the animating vapour got in our hair and in our clothes and in our mouths and in our eyes, until it was fully inside of us and we exhaled a second-hand, third-hand haze.

Alexander was supposed to go on at 2 a.m., right after Polly's warm-up set, but by 1.45 a.m. he had yet to appear and Finley was starting to freak out. He'd been telling everyone who'd listen about this great new live act he'd booked, even though he'd never heard a single track of course. It must've been a quiet night in the city without much competition, because it was really, truly packed out. One of those strange coincidences, I guess, when cancellations in one part of town and poor promotion in another collaborate. Circumstances having herded a larger crowd than usual over to Piggy, it was uncomfortably busy. When I think back of course I know it can't have been more than 120 people, but it felt like the whole of Berlin was there, elbow to elbow, awash with sweat and spit and expectation, with Finley mouthing to me, 'Girl! What the fuck?'

When he finally did materialise, Alex sailed through the crowd like a ghost in a blue velvet blazer, and I had never seen anybody look so completely out of place. He handed Finley a CD over the lip of the booth and stepped up to the microphone stand on that unsound stage, dropped his shoulders, inhaled with theatrical intent and just waited. Polly faded out the final chorus of 'Young Americans' and Finley, drenched in salty relief, cupped his hands around his mouth to announce, 'I hope you piggy sluts are ready for this! Heeeeeeere's Alexander Geist!'

The crowd turned towards the stage, away from their conversations, away from the on-screen gooning, though still puffing on their fags, still sipping on their Moscow mules. They cheered, warm, if not wildly enthusiastic. The music came on, first through one decrepit speaker, then the other, a chugging electronic baseline somewhere between disco and show tune, and then his voice came over the sound system. 'Hello, lover,' he purred, 'I am Alexander Geist. You are beautiful!'

He was teetering right there on the edge of being ridiculous, but he seemed to know it, he flicked his eyes over the room as if sizing up conquests, and when he began to sing he had the entire room's attention. His voice was surprisingly low, not rasping, but rather crooning, and so incongruous with the situation. He threw the back of his hand up against his forehead like Garbo, as if to underline the sentiment. He sang these very sad lyrics about love and heartbreak and everything pop stars usually catalogue in their allotted three minutes thirty, only all the sorrow was set to a relentless, ecstatic score of synthesisers and arpeggiated violins. He had the most uncanny ability to make you feel like this was all for you, that regardless of how many other people were there, he only saw you.

His face was the perfect mask, impassive, shaded with slight contempt, but his eyes burned up with a bestial intensity, and when he fixed that gaze on you, you felt it. He pulled from a little repertoire of gestures, arching his left eyebrow, letting his head drop back over his shoulder, reaching an arm out to the crowd like a Mannerist painting, once running his hand over his crotch and squeezing, seemingly expressing genuine pleasure, thrilled by what he found, as if the junk belonged to somebody else. I wonder if you can visualise him now? Glowering and occasionally grinning into that green-blue atmosphere, princely over a crowd, most pleasantly surprised, who were snapping for posterity, dancing with grace and abandon, grinding closer together.

He lit a Sobranie at the end of the first song, smoked it throughout the second, crushed it under his heel midway through the third, and that was that. No encore, just three numbers showcasing a prowess and a charisma you would never expect to find on such a small stage. When the final track finished, he bowed from the waist. It was almost an open act of mockery, only the joke was lost in the drunken whooping, as was his whole self when he stepped down off the stage and into the crowd.

Finley said, 'Wow! Girl, that was actually really good!'

'I know, right?' I replied, vain with proximity. 'Did you doubt it?' I was already sure this would become an *I was there back when* moment, it felt mythic, I preened.

'No! Well, yeah,' he laughed, 'but congratulations girl, it was great!'

So, lustrous with embezzled glamour, I waited for Alex to re-emerge from the jam on the dance floor, sipping my vodka and cranberry juice through a straw so as not to smudge my lipstick, nervous. I wanted to tell him how good he was, but not too soon, wanted to flatter but not fawn. Finley picked up from where Polly left off, spinning Talking Heads then Karen Finley then some lo-fi LA synth pop from John Maus or Ariel Pink maybe, somebody said that the singer from SSION was doing booty bumps in the darkroom downstairs. Polly had herself entangled between two butches on the banquette. I danced about half-heartedly on my own, bopping beside the DJ booth smiling up at Finley, waiting for Alexander to finish glad-handing his new fans. I craved a fag, felt my self-assurance slowly fall away.

I don't know if it was impatience, arousal piqued and then dissipated, or plain jealousy, but I was increasingly put out, and after waiting close to twenty minutes I had become a little haughty with what I registered as rejection. I had lost sight of Alex whilst bumming a cigarette from Callum, it looked to me as though he'd cleared off the dance floor, I surmised that he'd split with an admirer. 'Bastard,' I muttered to myself. Of course, he didn't owe me anything: I wasn't his girlfriend, but all the same I might've appreciated five minutes of his time, a thank you. I saw myself as a sheet of newspaper that had caught around his ankle in the street, and I felt ashamed. Maybe this was just his way of showing me that he was still a free man.

I had stopped dancing now but the crowd bumped on around me still; I was too hot, naturally this was the one party West had skipped. No problem, there were other men to be had. I set my glass down and promised Finley, 'I'll be back in a minute,' walked to the staircase, towards the darkroom, flushed and trepidatious. Down there it would be cooler, damp and dark enough to lose myself. Sometimes Polly and I would descend together, sloshed and heckling the trade. In the past we'd been thrown out for interrupting the boys, for dubbing in a live soundtrack of moans and obscene grunting to their secret silent rutting, but in truth it scared me a little to go into that cold alien atmosphere alone. I felt a little shiver of angst as I thought of the silent antiquated pornos screening bright as karaoke tracks against the blackness of the vault, of the heavy slapping sounds, regular and metrical, like the moonlit ocean lapping at the shore, the only indication that anything down there lived at all. Two boys came up the stairs towards me, giggling behind their hands, they made me feel apish, unnerved. Still, I think I could've overcome this fear, only Alex caught me by the arm.

'Do not go down *there* Fräulein,' he said, 'it is not a suitable environment for a young lady . . .' He was grinning, feline, his jacket discarded.

I scowled, but I was relieved. 'I was looking for you.'

'I was in the bathroom,' he said. I was not entirely convinced by this. 'I have bought some speed. Perhaps you would like some.'

I sized him up, considered my options, the night ahead. 'Sure,' I said, 'I have to take over from Finley soon, and I'm flagging.'

I swallowed the wrap he offered with a mouthful of his vodka tonic. 'That is what I admire about you, Charli,' he said, 'you always live up to your responsibilities.' Then he took my hand and led me back to the dance floor.

6

When I woke up the next morning Alexander was gone, leaving just a few golden fag ends in the teacup on the table beside my bed. I looked at the alarm clock and saw that he had pressed a Post-it over its cheap plastic face, it said *Gerhard 8 p.m.* I read the note aloud a few times in his voice, puzzling it over, when I peeled it back, I saw that it was almost 3 p.m.

I have no idea how late we were out, though it must've been close to dawn when we finally crashed, because I remember that the birds were beginning to tweet in the Hoff.

Alex asked me what I'd thought of the show and I told him, 'You remind me of Bowie, actually. The way you sing.'

'That is a great, great compliment.' Alex accepted it with no false modesty. 'In a way I do see myself to be his final incarnation.'

We had found the remnants of a bottle of vodka in the fridge – my roommate's, I'm pretty sure – and finished it. We smoked – though I had been asked not to – inside the apartment. He asked me if I'd like to get involved and I said, 'Aren't we already involved?' He grinned and said, 'I mean professionally.'

He told me he felt very inspired by me, that I was something like a muse to him, and I was very flattered; he said that he wanted us to work together in some creative capacity. I was admittedly drifting a little in Berlin and Alexander thought it might be a good idea for me to have an organising principle, he could be very considerate like that. I said that yes, it might be amusing to work with him, if I could find the time. Privately I was thrilled to have been offered this expanded role in his life, though the capacity in which I might be of service remained unfixed. He fucked me and I went to bed feeling glutted and invulnerable, comprehensively shielded by pleasure and indulgence against all ills, though when I woke up, alone, I was served a swift reckoning.

I felt as though I had been kicked in the head by a horse, as though every last drop of moisture had been wrung from me, as though my stomach were full of very sour popping candy. I hauled myself out of bed and made my way, frail and nauseous, to the kitchen. Unexpectedly Carl was in there, reading at the table – usually he was out on weekdays, at lectures or in the library, so I hadn't bothered to dress. I came into the kitchen in just the T-shirt I slept in, a scruffy old number depicting a red-eyed Garfield in his pyjamas and night cap, clutching a steaming mug of java with the ineluctable catchphrase 'I hate Mondays' bubbling up out of his head. Thankfully it was slouchy and oversized so it reached to my knees.

My roommate looked up from his book and said there were messages from my mother on the answering machine. There was a pot of coffee on the table so I asked if I could have some and he nodded. 'You look really a lot like this cat right now,' he said.

'Thank you,' I smiled, the effort agonising, 'lots of people say that he's my doppelgänger.'

'This cat?' he asked, confused. 'Echt?'

'No,' I said, 'it's just a joke. I'm just being silly. Sorry, I have a terrible hangover.'

He considered this for a while and said slyly, 'Oh really? Was it so much fun?'

I clutched my head, 'Too much fun, in fact,' hoping he'd take a hint and let me be, but he didn't.

'And who are you taking to last night then?' he asked.

'No one,' I said, 'you wouldn't know him. I'm sorry, I have to go and lie back down now.'

Polly came over from the studio around six, she said we'd arranged it last night. She must've been up as late if not later than I had been, but she hardly looked any the worse for wear. Makeup done and hair blown out, she was doused in the heavy perfume – leather, birch, tobacco – which her mother gifted her each year and which she wore whenever she needed to pull herself together. Family legend had it that her Huguenot great-grandmother wore the same stuff all through the war, carrying coded messages for the French Resistance. Her mother kept the original glass bottle, with its last remaining drops sitting amber and putrefied, and brought it out to show guests after dinner, like the Bishop of Naples does, three times a year, with the blood of Saint Gennaro. Enrobed in fragrance and a silk scarf, she arrived as immaculate as the first snow of Christmas, it was only when she turned her head to look down and the light caught her in a certain pose that the deep grooves beneath her eyes were revealed.

'Your roommate is behaving very strangely,' she said, 'he asked me if I had any amphetamines.'

'Yeah,' I sighed, 'I'm late with the rent so you'll have to be nice to him.'

'In the soup again?' she asked.

'As *usual*,' I nodded, 'though I've had the most exciting premonition that it's all about to change.'

Polly admitted to a headache and I made her a cup of tea, it was late October and already the twilight was edging closer in. Polly was musing, she said, 'You could try burning green candles. They bring in prosperity. It's an old occult ritual.'

I frowned. 'Candles? Polly, really?'

She shrugged. 'Works for me.'

I wanted to take a moment to examine that statement, to suggest maybe it wasn't black magic that kept her afloat but rather the €1,000 her father mailed to her in a birthday card each month, but that seemed plain rude. And anyway, I liked her father, his distrust of the central banking system seemed a very smart attitude to take, knowing what I did about how heavily Lloyd's of London invested in technology to control the weather.

'I always think tinkering with the dark arts is very chic, very Bowie,' she said. 'Kether to Malkuth, silver to reflect, black to absorb and all that. You know, you've seen the documentaries.'

'I have,' I said, 'and more.'

I told her that I was quite certain I'd seen him once in the flesh, on a family holiday to London. He was all in denim, picking up a portion of shepherd's pie from the food hall in Harrods. When I told my mother she said that I was probably just overtired, that I'd most likely imagined it, and we went back to the hotel straight away so I didn't upset myself again. It was the second saddest day of my life but I hadn't ever given up hoping that we would cross paths again, eventually. I said, 'One day we'll meet and I'll introduce myself by saying, "Didn't I see you by the food-to-go counter at Harrods circa 1998?"' I laughed. 'I just know he'll crack up at that, at the lunacy of it all.'

Polly drained her cup. 'You know, when I was a teenager I wanted to go on *Stars in Their Eyes* and sing "Life on Mars"?' She was frowning. 'Only they wouldn't let me on because I was a girl. Isn't that silly?'

'And you would've made such a fab Ziggy too,' I said. 'I went to my grandparents' silver wedding anniversary as the Thin White Duke, did I ever tell you that? My auntie took up one of her old suits on the sewing machine for me.'

Polly looked at me askance. 'Isn't your aunt a nun, though?'

'No,' I said, 'she's a lesbian, my mother looked her up on Facebook. The whole thing was a lie my uncle made up after she left him for the woman next door.'

Polly took this in her stride, cupped the back of her hair to check it was still in good shape. She reflected, 'What's amazing is that he hasn't become a reactionary. His contemporaries are all tax evaders and transphobes now, aren't they? Just a bunch of old men advertising margarine on television and complaining about political correctness. It's sad really.'

I shrugged. 'It's the way of the world, Polly.'

We sat in stillness for a while quietly ruminating, and every so often I caught a snatch of 'Shine on You Crazy Diamond' from down the hall. Polly told me she had terrible cramps; I asked her if she wanted another pot of tea, or maybe some toast. I didn't really have anything else to offer.

'No,' she said, 'I'll wait for dinner. Speaking of, hadn't you better dress?'

Apparently Finley had invited us over to meet with his elderly gentleman friend, Gerhard, who was hosting a dinner at his place in Mitte to mark an acquisition or the anniversary of something, I wasn't sure. He had a great big apartment near the Konzerthaus which he had by all accounts made a palace of. Having never met the man I was touched to have been asked to join, even if I didn't remember having been invited.

'Well, you were extremely keen last night,' Polly said, 'you were beside yourself with excitement. So get your glad rags on, Finley says there'll be oysters.'

From the outside, Gerhard's building was as unassuming as any other *Altbau* in Berlin, white plaster, graffiti, Antifa stickers all over the door, but inside it was another world, cavernous and furnished with an artist's eye and a carpenter's hand. We were shown in by a young man, who looked to be an undergraduate. He wore service blacks, and a vigorous smile, he spoke English with a Hanoverian accent. 'This way please,' he said, 'I can take your coats. Herr Köhler is in the green room.'

Polly said it was awfully pretentious to name the rooms of your house. 'Only people with too much money do that,' she sallied, but personally I thought the whole set-up was marvellous. I had never seen such a beautiful home, very quiet and considered. There was a Persian rug in the hallway which Finley told us was 200 years old, and a wall of luminescent pale green plates on display in the dining room which seemed like they belonged in the V&A, if not on the table of a Song dynasty emperor. The whole place was smelted and timeless; I was amazed that someone as unremarkable as Gerhard lived there.

In the Green Room thirty or so people milled about holding glasses of champagne and plates of bread, pâté, cheese. Polly and I were most definitely underdressed. Finley was already half-cut, he came over in a dinner jacket I had never seen before and wrapped us up in a lusty hug which in such polite circumstances seemed a little much. 'You bitches made it,' he exclaimed, 'finally. Go get a drink.'

Myself, I felt a little cowed by the elegance of it all; under the duress of her menstrual cramps, Polly was likewise subdued. Timid like schoolgirls, we shuffled over the parquet to the bar where the toothsome waiter poured us each a glass of Pol Roger. The room was lit by candles, Bach played from a stereo system somewhere out of sight, a draught made the shadows on the wall jitter like dancers. A sophisticated older man appeared at my elbow. 'I see you're admiring the paintwork. You know they haven't produced this colour since the eighteenth century, because the pigments are traditionally quite toxic.'

I introduced myself, 'I'm Charli, this is Polly, how do you do? So nice of you to have us.'

'Oh, my dear, no,' he chuckled, 'no, no, no. I'm not *Gerhard*, I'm Hubert. I'm in the apartment above.'

'Excuse me,' I blushed, 'I just presumed. On account of the, ah, paintwork.'

'Yes,' he said, '*Churlish Green*. Magnificent by candlelight, isn't it? Only, my dear, if you've ever seen it in natural light,' and here he looked about himself slyly, 'it's *vile*.'

He delivered an impromptu lecture on the history of the house for us, how a group of gay pals had started squatting the building as the Soviet Union collapsed around them, then come to own it. Across the room I saw that Finley was climbing into the lap of his sugar daddy, the real Gerhard, a man of maybe eighty with a face like Edmund White's.

'And of course you must meet my boyfriend.' Hubert waved over a squat and sulky thirty-something. 'This is Jamie,' he said. 'Jamie, dear, this is –'

His boyfriend interrupted, 'Uh-huh, yeah I've met the paper-plate princess.'

Polly kissed him on both cheeks and said, 'Small world.'

He didn't respond to her greeting but rather said to me, 'Saw you at Piggy last night, getting pretty crazy. I guess you British girls *really* don't have any shame.' He grinned as if to say that he was only joking, but there was intentional malice in his tone.

'Ha ha,' I faked a little laugh, 'yeah, wow, that place is pretty wild.'

He barely waited for me to finish before he began again, 'I mean, like I kinda understand it. For sure it's not *my* vibe *personally* but like not *everyone* can find a guy in like, the regular way and I guess must be really hard for people like you. I bet it's like *impossible*.'

I bristled though I kept the smile on my face. 'I don't think I know what you mean.'

'You know,' he gave an exiguous grin, 'people who are, like, not one thing or the other.'

'Mmm-hmm,' I grimaced, 'yes, well, I'm going to get something to eat now. Excuse me.'

Polly came with me to the buffet table. She was silent so I pressed her, 'Who on earth is that pudgy cunt?' The word rang out wholly discordant in the room.

'Jamie?' she said. 'You've met him a hundred times. He can be a bit of an arse.'

I drew a blank.

Polly said, 'Honestly, Charli, what's wrong with you today? He used to date that poet you fancy, and he made that dreadful film about queer bebop artists. We saw it at the Berlinale. Ring any bells?'

'No.' I picked up a plate but nothing on the table appealed to me. 'Not really.'

Finley found us, he tottered over barefoot across the carpet, having kicked his lace-ups aside. He said, 'Girl, I hate those shoes, they make me feel like I'm going for a job interview.' I don't think that he'd had any sleep: he had that good-natured, upbeat energy that often comes on the other side of exhaustion, once you've pushed on through. Gerhard had taken him for a facial that afternoon, and he did look great, dewy and happy, his pupils were dark and wide like the embrasure between his two front teeth, which my mother always told me was a sign of good fortune.

The three of us stood about chewing sticks of celery and dissecting the party. Finley pointed out a seventy-something fashion designer, Germany's Vivienne Westwood, a Hohenzollern prince, and a handsome grey gentleman who owned a major car manufacturer. 'He runs a ring bringing boys over from Slovakia,' Finley said indifferently, 'that's how I know Gerhard. It's very high end.'

Polly wanted her crustaceans. She explained, 'It's always the way when I come on.' Finley nodded sympathetically, he said the rest of the seafood should be on its way out from the kitchen soon, and apologised that the caviar was just the cheap orange stuff, criticising Gerhard for having ordered it.

'He thinks people don't notice that shit,' he shrugged, 'but they do.'

Polly said she had a great recipe for lobster tails. This somehow led to a discussion of Salvador Dalí's lasting friendship with Princess Grace, and when I brought the actress and the surrealist together in my mind's eye, him handsome, swarthy and slightly crazed, her svelte and blonde and high-born, the picture I created was not wholly dissimilar to that of the two friends stood before me. If I placed one image over the other they popped stereoscopically. Finley said he'd seen *Hitler Masturbating* at the Dalí museum in Florida and told us that the painter had believed himself to be the reincarnation of his brother. Polly claimed that the princess's fatal car crash was a result of overpacking. 'My mother met her in the seventies,' she sighed, 'said she was an insatiable nymphomaniac.'

'Oh girl, me too,' said Finley and laughed.

Hubert joined us with a huge plate of potato salad in one hand and a tiny little cake fork in the other. He insisted that he never normally ate after 8 p.m. but that he'd had to try just the *smallest* mouthful of Kartoffelsalat: it was Gerhard's mother's own recipe and he remembered her with great fondness. Jamie was at his elbow, scowling, scrutinising me. The hateful, insistent glare he fixed on me gave me an awful, raw feeling, and the suggestion of a bad memory, necessarily repressed, burbled up in my stomach like gastroenteritis. He made me sweat.

I turned to Finley. 'I have the most terrible headache from last night,' I said, 'I think I should go home. We were out *way* too late.'

Finley frowned. 'Girl, you haven't even met Gerhard yet.'

'I know,' I said, 'I know, but he seems lovely. We can all get together for, ah, noodles sometime.'

Polly asked me if I needed her to come with me, but I declined. I set my plate down. 'No, no, stay and celebrate

Gerhard's birthday. Or retirement, or whatever it is. I'm going to take the train.'

'Well, make sure to take a look at the celadon pottery on your way out, won't you, my dear?' Hubert said, and I felt it was his attempt at an apology. 'The green plates on the dining room wall. Priceless you know, all stolen of course, but that's another story.'

Jamie smirked, he looked very pleased with himself, I could feel his eyeballs slashing into my back, following me all the way out of the room. I headed out into the hallway, asked the waiter for my coat, cursed myself, *I should've spat in his face, the miserable little bastard, I didn't even get my oysters.*

The doorbell rang and I opened it on impulse, almost without thinking. It was West clutching at a bottle of Rotkäppchen, his red hair now faded to a very flattering apricot. He beamed when he saw me.

'Charli,' he said, 'you aren't leaving already are you?'

'Yeah, well, I just bumped into *your* ex-boyfriend,' I growled, 'and that rather took the shine off my evening. Why is he such an arsehole? What have I ever done to him?'

'Well . . .' West began, squeamishly, 'might be because you . . .' but then the waiter came back with my coat and he went quiet.

I put my jacket on and West asked if he could walk me to the U-Bahn. I told him that I would prefer to be alone, that I had to be up early the next day anyway, I needed to get to the library to start in on my PhD research. He looked a little dejected and asked if he could get my number all the same, said he'd been hoping to run into me again. I explained that I didn't have a phone, that I hated the idea that they tracked you wherever you went, and anyway I didn't think I needed one. Did anybody, really?

'Yeah,' he nodded, 'that makes sense.' He scratched the back of his head and tried again. 'So is it just email for you? Or are you the girl keeping Deutsche Post in business? Is there any way of making contact with you? Crystal ball, Ouija board?'

I laughed. 'There is a phone in my roommate's room, but it's only supposed to be for emergencies. People call and leave messages on the machine, usually just my mother. He really doesn't like it though.'

He smiled. 'Sure, sure, I get it. Give me that then? I promise I won't abuse it.'

I scribbled the number down for him in biro on the back of a Piggy flyer. He looked genuinely delighted – if he'd tried to kiss me, I think I would've let him. I had half a mind to take him and his Rotkäppchen home with me after all, if only to spite Jamie, but something inside me, which spoke in the voice of Alexander, talked me out of it. I wondered where he was at that moment, if he was out on a balcony right now, smoking and thinking of me. It was a possibility, but then you never really know how much real estate you take up in someone else's imagination, do you?

'I'll call you,' West smirked again. 'In a few days. I'll play it cool, yeah? So you won't think I'm *that* interested.'

I ruffled his hair. 'You do that,' I said and kissed him on the forehead. 'Goodnight.'

7

There was a gold rush of talent in Berlin; if your favourite band weren't originally from the city, then they had moved there. On any given night of the week you could see a synth duo perform in a former public toilet, a girl with a guitar play a set in the bar of the Kurdish social club, a keyboard concerto given in a gallery by a musician wearing a rubber hippo head, a DJ set from a hyper-pop producer who, unbeknownst to anyone, was just a few years away from a Grammy nomination. Sometimes you'd find yourself standing at the bar with Gudrun Gut or Udo Kier, ordering the cheapest drink on the menu in some grubby Schöneberg hooker dive, wondering how this could possibly be real life. Other nights would take you through the window of the Volksbühne canteen and into the closing-night party of a show which had been so mauled by critics that the cast members had come to blows, brawling, launching bottles of sparkling water through the air and narrowly escaping a night in the slammer. The capital reverberated with a manic creativity; every week filmmakers shot their new shorts in supermarket car parks and painters, coming down hard from smack, threw themselves out in front of trains with almost the same frequency. Berlin was flammable with an immense possibility, and things could always go either way. Everyone I met there was on the precipice of a breakthrough or a breakdown.

For Alex it all unfurled just like a musical montage in a Judy Garland movie, or like that old pop song, *You're really hot and I'm very smart, we'll make tonnes of money . . .* He had something that people were drawn to, and luckily I was right there to help build the framework around him. I didn't really have any of the skills needed to support his development, but I was just stupid enough to believe I could learn and that he would love me for it. He told me once that, really, that's all success is, being just about stupid enough.

Some kids who had seen him at Piggy asked him to perform at their new party over near Alexanderplatz, in an old bar from the DDR days that had kept the Soviet theme, where he went over well with the hipsters, the tourists and the original drunks alike. He was also invited to sing on the main stage of a karaoke bar, where they had concerts from breakout acts every Wednesday night for a crowd of 200 or so regulars. Berlin's monthly gay rag asked to interview him, gaggles of androgynous twinks started to turn up at his shows; he was an instant success, just add hot water.

There came a steady stream of requests, all through the autumn and into the winter, for him to appear at parties, club nights, street festivals, and though there was never any serious money on the table, only ever €60 or €70 plus a few drink tokens, the promise was always there – that this gig could be the one that made him a star. Polly said Sinéad O'Connor started out singing 'Don't Cry for Me Argentina' in hotel function rooms, her mother had been there and seen it for herself. Even Madonna had been discovered in some shitty disco.

Alex performed at a few fundraisers for some of the remaining squats and co-ops, for film labs and anti-fascist language schools, always extremely overdressed in his blazer and tie, aware of how this positioned him, at an arthouse cinema before a screening of *The Talented Mr Ripley*, at several *vernissages*, at clubs with names like The Club and Le Chateau and El Lugar, and once at a second-hand book store, where the crowd spilled out of the door and the neighbours called the police. Promoters from out of town started to ask if he'd considered touring, journalists requested his images to slot into the art and culture sections, random strangers wanted to know if he was single, and if not, whether he was up for a fuck on the side. I know because I was the one answering all their emails.

Silver Future, a bar in Neukölln, offered him a residency every Sunday evening for a month on their little stage in the backroom, where he worked on his showmanship and whipped up a patter, introducing new songs each week; soon he had a very robust set. Each week his audience grew larger, until it filled both rooms and nobody could get to the bathroom or to the bar, and I had to escort him from the stage to the tiny dressing room we improvised in the stock cupboard. There amongst crates of beer, boxes of straws, drinks mats, paper towels and pallets of cranberry juice cartons he'd sit on an upturned rubbish bin, sweat running from his hairline down in between his brows, catching his breath over the hoots and cheers of his admirers outside. I'd say, 'Well, that was a success, right?' And he'd light a Sobranie and say, 'Maybe, maybe,' smiling furtively as if he were in on the truth behind some long-running rumour. He could be oddly coy like that.

December brought the strangest fusion of desolation and abandon to the city. Many people left to visit family for the holidays and everyone who remained took it upon themselves to celebrate twice as hard for those who were missing. We got a gig request for a club night called Cindy's House of Sin. At first I thought that it must be a joke, because who would ever choose a moniker like that for a dance party? It made the place sound like a massage parlour. It fell on the 27th or the 28th, I can't recall which, during that little no-man's-land between festivals into which Berliners packed as much excitement as possible, as if in fear that 1 January might mean the beginning of the end of the world.

We had been going hard ourselves since at least the 22nd, boozy dinners in the ritzy neighbourhoods of the West, Charlottenburg and Wilmersdorf, a screening of *It's a Wonderful Life* at a little picture house on Kastanienallee where we took shrooms and instantly regretted it, a Diamanda Galás concert at the Philharmonie where we levelled out, brandy and noodles at Monsieur Vuong where we were seated straight away and at a very nice table, on account of Alexander's growing profile. We spent a few cloudless nights cruising around the empty city in his Mercedes driving to Fehrbelliner Platz, the AVUS grandstand, and out as far as Olympiastadion because he wanted to see the Nazi-era buildings still standing. In truth I didn't want Alex to play the show at Cindy's because I was so enjoying having him to myself, but then he pointed out the €300 fee and I revised my opinion.

During the rest of the week, Cindy's House of Sin was a live music venue which hosted rockabilly acts. It was decorated in schlocky Wild West style, with mounted cow skulls on the walls and saloon doors between the rooms, all bathed in the sallow yellow light of fake flickering candles which gave it more the atmosphere of a funeral chapel than a cowboy honky-tonk. There were a couple of incongruous pinball machines and a very popular table football game, not quite in keeping with the Western stylings, jammed over by the bathrooms, and then the decor veered entirely off theme in the smoking lounge, where a gargantuan photograph of Saddam Hussein grinned down from behind the sticky leather sofas, and who can say why? Cindy's crowd comprised eighteen-year-old boys in white vests with cheap bleach jobs, fifty-something men in V-neck T-shirts and Ray Bans, and nobody in between, unless you included the hostess herself in your count. At first I thought I recognised her as a sister spirit but the party's promoter baulked at the idea. 'Cindy is not a transsexual,' he intoned, 'she is a gay man with tits.'

She wore a gold sequinned minidress and nude tights, glossy black shoes with high platform soles, a spike heel and an ankle strap, fingerless gloves, and what I guessed was a wig. Her makeup was none too subtle, purple eyes and heavy liner, fake lashes, blood-red lips, extreme contouring and, I presumed, some face tape under her wig line, one side pulled tighter than the other, dragging her left eyebrow higher than her right and giving her a permanently quizzical look. We sat with her for a few hours at the back of the club in a cage behind a velvet curtain, where touring bands locked up their kit. She was swarmed with boys in booty shorts offering her glasses of Sekt and cigarettes, begging her for attention; she referred to them only as 'my fans', batting them away like fruit flies when they became too demanding.

I fixed Alexander's face and tried to get him ready as best I could. Around us the boys all gossiped about a pair of drag queens who were suing each other over the right to use the name Gina Tonic professionally; both were claiming to be the original. The case was going all the way to the Federal Court, I think, someone said, but the conversation switched back and forth between English and German and it was hard for me to follow. I looked at Alex in the mirror and rolled my eyes to discreetly express an exhausted superciliousness. He stared back at me blankly as if this situation were of my own making.

Cindy suddenly blew her top. 'You know who is the real fucking Gina Tonic?' she bawled in outrage. 'Me! I was having this name at Romy Haag's club in the eighties. Everybody knows this!' The boys all shut themselves up pretty promptly – even Alexander looked thunderstruck. She spouted a litany of insults in all directions, decrying the whole world as full of idiots and traitors, she was absolutely inconsolable until a joint and a new glass of Sekt were passed her way. 'Die dummen Fotzen,' I think she said, 'They are thiefs,' but I might be misremembering. 'Who has speed?'

The music from the dance floor had somehow got worse in the time we had been back there; it poured in unwanted. One of Cindy's twinks tripped over another and upset my makeup bag, eyeliner pencils and tubes of lipstick went stuttering across the floor, bottles broke against the concrete, I did not have the power to clean it up. Cindy calmly stroked a stray hair from her face, smoothed out her sequins and took up a new pose as if going for another take. 'I also can play the trumpet,' she said, to no one in particular, 'and I am fabulous. I'm not just some old whore. I have so much skills.'

Her boys chorused in praise of her, insisting that she was legendary, incredible, an icon of Berlin, and I chimed in, 'Yeah, I DJ sometimes too. It's kinda my thing now.' I don't know why I said this because I had only ever played at Finley's parties, I suppose the drugs and the deranged atmosphere backstage made me feel like bathing myself in a little showbiz light too. 'I'm Charli Hughes,' I said. Just for a second, I wanted to have some standing in the room. 'Maybe you guys have heard of me?' They had not.

Things got woozy, a few of the boys took off their shirts and rubbed up on each other, a handful danced, badly. Cindy took out her compact and started to caress her own face saying, 'Cindy is beautiful, Cindy is gorgeous, Cindy does not need makeup!' over and over, repeating it like a charm into her tiny mirror. I couldn't say how long this went on for, only that the promoter rushed in at some point to tell us we were due on-stage and Cindy shouted, 'I said you two hours and do not be late!' She was panicked. 'Do you think I am joking or?'

On-stage she sang her big club hit, it went, '*Come into the house of sin, house of sin, house of sin. Sexy sexy disco disco, house of sin, house of sin.*' She croaked the lyrics of this horrible little ditty half-heartedly over a backing track which squelched along behind her like the opening credits from a kids' TV show, until at some point she simply grew bored and gave up. She threw the DJ a savage gesture of fingertips slashing back and forth across her throat, and the music came to a halt. The crowd whooped and she shaded her eyes against the spotlight, singling Alex out and dragging him on-stage with her for an awkward bout of air-kissing and a brief burst of camera flashes. The crowd cheered again and she asked them if anyone had poppers, took a hit of the proffered bottle and began jumping up and down on the stage, her big tits bouncing like pillows in a tumble dryer. Alexander looked out at the audience like a man marooned, he found me in the crowd with a look of despair, his face smeared in Cindy's lipstick, flexing his fingers the way he always did when he was losing his equilibrium.

'I have a very special guest here tonight – aus England!' Cindy shrieked. 'Ja, a real Britisher, like a David Bowie, here at my party!' and then she introduced Alexander to the crowd, by my name. The audience, oblivious, hooted all the same, and though Alexander's face fell to his feet, the first track had started to play and there was nothing for it but to sing.

8

Because of the increasing number of picture requests Alexander was receiving from nightlife journalists and music bloggers, I decided it was high time to get some new images made. Previously we'd been using a few very scrappy shots taken in a room at Tacheles, where Polly had been showing her paintings. The space was empty for half a day after the deinstallation, and we snuck in then.

In these pictures Alex is crouched on the floor resting his chin on his fist, shot from above, looking up into the lens like a villainous orphan, eyes ringed in malachite. The vibe is *dandified punk* maybe. These pictures had served us well but they'd been circulating for months already, so I asked Finley if he would shoot a few, since he had access to a pretty decent Canon. 'Sure,' he said, and suggested we take the pictures at the studio, where they had one whole wall of south-facing windows, which allowed the precious little light still available in Berlin at that time of year to pour right in.

With only a little persuasion, Polly had agreed to do Alexander's makeup. As a painter I figured she'd have more competence with the rouge and the blush than I, and moreover she had much better products. She said that she didn't want it to interfere with her studio practice though, she didn't want people to think she'd failed as a painter, so she requested that she be credited as Beauty by Trudy wherever relevant.

Alex was sceptical of the plan. I insisted, as his manager or creative consultant or whatever it was that I was, that we needed to do this, and so we fixed a date for the second week of January, once Polly and Finley had returned to the city from their respective familial enmeshments.

All told, Alex and I had spent a blissful winter break together watching children throw firecrackers in the Hoff and eating my roommate's salami. Carl was away with his family so we had the apartment to ourselves and made good use of it; fucking capaciously in his double bed and listening to his copy of *Wish You Were Here* over and over, smoking menthols for novelty, amusing ourselves, watching MGM comedies and improvising little skits in the style of Hepburn and Tracy, peeling clementines in the nude as the snow fell thick outside. Sitting up in bed Alex took my hand, traced a slender finger over my palm and pointed out how my heart line and my head line were merged into a single traverse crease.

'The simian line,' he said, 'you are a visionary, but you are volatile.'

'Is that so?' I asked.

'Yes,' he said, 'look, I have it too.' He placed his palm beside mine, and sure enough they lined up quite perfectly, like a fine figaro chain of gold had been laid across both of our palms.

My roommate's dealer came over on New Year's Day, paying a semi-frequent social call, and since Carl was not at home, Alex and I bought ourselves a little something special: half a gram of heroin. I had never smoked it before and was admittedly nervous, but Alexander regarded it as no big shakes. 'Going on holiday' is what he called it.

The following days turned to slush, it really was like taking a vacation: from my body, from my mind, from life entirely, really. There was no need to talk, no need to eat, we just lay sprawled out on Carl's bedroom floor, writhing naked against the cream sheepskin rug his family had made for him up on their farm, euphoria wracking us head to toe. The drug made me feel wildly horny, but Alex said he couldn't ever get hard on horse, so he made me a profile on Planet Romeo instead, and invited a ream of unknown men over. He positioned me in the hallway, where I waited stripped and on my knees, and he brought up these strangers one by one, or in pairs, standing off to the side and watching me like a pimp as I sucked their cocks and swallowed their sperm. I don't know how many men came by, I remember Alex had been marking a tally on my chest with an eyeliner pencil, only it must've washed away with sweat or rubbed off on the sheets, because when I woke up I was back in bed and Alexander was above me, fucking me, squeezing at my breasts, and the count was smeared and indecipherable.

We wrestled with ourselves, once the junk was all gone, see-sawing between immediately buying more and swearing to never touch the stuff again, an intense, circular logic, a debate which only found resolution with the earnest agreement that we'd only do it rarely, to mark special occasions, and only do it together, because who else had our backs, would make sure we were OK?

We showered together and ate the last of the salami with a little dark chocolate for breakfast, the two of us wrung out and stumbling around as we tried to dress, realising for the first time in days how cold it actually was. It was 5 or 6 January when he went home, I'm not sure which, but I know that by the time I bade goodbye to him the evening was already purple, it was hours after the sun had set. I think we knew we needed some time apart, and though I found it increasingly painful to be away from him I did not need to make my dependence so abundantly apparent.

I held off from speaking with him again until the day of the shoot. It was a show of sheer will, this refusal to ring him up as soon as he left, ask him to return. It was harder to resist calling him than it was fighting the urge to call

Carl's dealer again, but I succeeded on both fronts and I was proud, though I won't say sobering up was a walk in the park: I thought of him constantly. I was glad at least for the screen of my unfixed creative role in his career, it allowed me to tell myself that this was not an obsession but an artistic endeavour.

I bought a Mr Tom peanut brittle bar from the Späti, along with a pink cigarette lighter adorned with a photo of a man in a pink posing pouch, flexing. I called my mother from the booth. I just wanted a chat; I was lonely, and I wanted to tell her about Alexander, but she was peeved that I hadn't called her on Christmas Day and so she was sulking.

'You know how I feel about that name, Charli,' she said, 'I think it's unhealthy.'

She insisted that I needed to be wearing light, bright colours to keep my energetic channels open. 'That'll help your angel guide manifest a more suitable soul connection,' she said. 'Besides, you should be on the lookout for a Michael or a Raphael, I've told you that before. You're never going to heal the psychic wound otherwise.'

Perhaps I was misdirecting my emotions, magnified as they were by this week-long hangover, but I felt insulted. I lost my temper. '*You* should be on the lookout for something else to do with your time,' I sniped, 'cancel your bloody Daphne Culver dot com subscription already. That's what's really unhealthy here!' I hung up.

On the day of the shoot, I arrived at the studio forty minutes behind schedule, but neither Polly nor Finley seemed to care: they were already back on Berlin time. She had returned from Dublin with another bottle of Chanel Cuir de Russie, a pair of pavé earrings and a very chic new hairdo; he was back looking tanned from three weeks in California, and very lithe though jet-lagged – worry lines, like archer's bows, were starting to trouble the corners of his mouth. They were calmly tidying up the studio, clearing away the plates and paintbrushes which had been lying out since before Christmas. The radio was playing Billy Idol, they were talking between themselves about a new yoga-meditation class, assessing the likelihood that it was all bullshit.

'Suzanne *says* that she's experienced the point at which it all falls away,' Polly recounted, 'you know, where you're just so deep into it that you don't even think you exist anymore? I mean you don't even *think* at all, you just *are*.'

'That sounds nice,' I said, and Finley laughed: 'Girl, you *do not* need any new ways to zone out.'

Polly's nephew was now her niece, she came out while icing gingerbread men on Christmas Eve. Finley had been to a church service for the first time in five years, his brother had got clean and become a minister, extremely wholesome stuff. When I jokingly mentioned trying heroin for the first time they scolded me like disappointed parents. I think Polly may have actually tut-tutted. Finley looked personally insulted, and it was only later that I remembered how smack had killed his mother. Then I felt really awful.

'For fuck's sake, Charli,' Polly snapped, 'one has to draw the line somewhere.'

She was the only person I ever knew who used the singular pronoun 'one' without any irony, but only ever when she was angry enough to unwittingly let out a flash of her class.

I felt obliged to apologise, to explain myself. 'I know, it's stupid, I know,' I said, 'it was Alex's idea.'

Polly and Finley shared a look of disbelief, muttering about *reckless behaviour* and *manipulation* and saying that maybe Berlin wasn't any good for me, criticising the company I had chosen to keep, being expressly antagonistic towards Alexander. I wanted to stick up for him, honestly I did, only before I could find the words, I realised through some sort of sixth sense that he was in fact standing right behind me.

'Hello, lover,' he said. I had no idea of how long he'd been there.

'Hello, lover!' I repeated, shamefaced.

His eyebrow shot up gibingly and I stood grinning, extremely uncomfortable, with Polly and Finley staring on. 'Look!' I declared, rather redundantly. 'Alexander's here now!' Finley scowled, Polly insisted I call her Trudy for the rest of the day, a protest I suppose.

It was uncanny to encounter Alex in the daylight, he seemed to flinch from it like Nosferatu. His eyes looked red but perhaps he was, like Finley, simply tired. He took off his jacket and I sat him down in a chair at the table where Polly had spread out her makeup. She recoiled a little from him, I felt terribly awkward. I tried to usher in some calm, asking her how long she thought it would be before she was ready to begin. She started sharpening an eyebrow pencil and said, 'Ten minutes maybe?' but wouldn't meet my eye. She excused herself to briefly confer with Finley on the other side of the room.

Finley himself seemed very wary of Alexander, as if he now recognised something in him he hadn't seen before and perhaps, having only fumbled with him in darkrooms, he'd never taken his full measure. My friends whispered conspiratorially, and though they tried to be discreet about it, it was quite clear what they were turning over. I thought that they might fabricate some sort of excuse to cancel the shoot; when Finley finally strode over I thought it was surely to send Alex home. Instead he moved to take control of the situation with a composure which was almost patronising, telling us that we should get started already before we lost the light, that he didn't want to fuck about today because he'd given his time and didn't want it wasted.

Polly began the makeup as if against her will; she seemed to find the whole thing somewhat ridiculous now. When I squeezed in to make small aesthetic suggestions – 'A gloss lip,

I think, not matte,' or 'Actually Alexander suits quite a vibrant colour on the lid' – she furrowed her brow mockingly and said sardonically, 'Oh does he? Does he really?'

Alex barely spoke, he didn't even try to win them over, just sort of snickered inwardly, which made for a strained atmosphere. It was clear that my friends did not like him, at the same time I knew they felt bound to help me with him. Everyone was uneasy, and though I tried my best to smooth over the simmering contention with small talk, I failed. I cracked a joke about how one day we'd see these pictures on posters, defaced by teen socialists and junkies, but nobody laughed, not even Alex.

He wore a powder-blue ruffle frill tuxedo shirt and a pair of straight leg pegs which could only have come from the back of the wardrobe of some elderly Charlottenburg lover. His cologne sang of sex too. We had set it up so that he would stand in front of an exposed brick wall, a plain backdrop but one suggesting ruin and romance rather than warehouse living, the cigarettes he chain-smoked throughout adding an extra level of insolence. Finley shot him from a low angle so that he appeared to sneer down into the camera, haughty, cold, indifferent, cut through with a sadism which Finley seemed to steel himself against by talking about Alex rather than to him. 'Face to the left, eyes to me.' I started to wonder now what had really transpired here; I felt a little jealous even.

Alex didn't take to Finley's style of direction at all, he bristled, he started to act up with petulant little provocations. He flicked his cigarette butt to the floor and gave a nettling smirk, unbuttoned his shirt, squeezed his crotch and leered into the lens. Finley and Polly were striving not to react, and the more restraint they tried to show the more immoderate Alex became. It made for some great friction, it set sparks flying; I came to learn that just as speed makes a motorbike stable, Alexander really only solidified under pressure.

He may have been in a wicked mood, but we got some great pictures out of him: we had it in the bag within the hour, three or four strong shots which was all I needed. In the back of the camera they looked like Cosway miniatures portraits on ivory; on Finley's computer screen they glowed hieratic. Something transcendental came off them, like hot air veiling the horizon, the burning Sobranie the punctum.

Sometimes I think that the only way I ever really came to know Alexander was by looking at his picture. In real life he was always separated from me as if by a rood screen, but in images he was wholly present. When I saw these portraits I had the same feeling I'd had the first time my mother took me to buy a dress to wear to a family party, seeing myself in the changing room mirror, of recognising a friend from childhood all grown up. I loved them, just as I loved him. I told him that once, but I think he was asleep.

I said, 'The face is the mirror of the mind, and the eyes without speaking confess the secrets of the heart.' The assembled all looked blank, so I elucidated, 'St Jerome.'

'You really are quite mad, you know?' Polly sighed. 'Are we done?' She flounced off to the bathroom.

To keep from floating away I busied myself with packing up the various pins and powders which I'd brought along to try and be useful. Alex scuffed the flooring with the split toe of his boot, yawning. I asked if he was pleased with the images, he tugged on his bottom lip and shrugged, said he'd seen his face before. I showed him out because he seemed, if not exactly eager to leave, then bored, distracted. He walked out ahead of me without a thank you, without even saying goodbye. I told Finley I'd be back in a minute,

In the corridor, in a low voice so as not to attract more attention, I asked him what was wrong. He seemed hung up on something, he said, 'I do not think they liked me so much.'

'Well.' I was exasperated. 'You didn't really try with them.'

'They were rude,' he said.

'*You* were rude!' I replied tartly.

Alex stared off over my shoulder, away out of the window, and said, drolly, 'I am *so* sorry I do not have your beautiful English manners.' Outside the afternoon was dead and dying.

I couldn't understand why he was behaving like this – I thought the session had gone beautifully all things considered. I wondered if he'd called the dealer again, if he was on a comedown.

'And I am not,' he insisted, taking the words out of my mouth, 'hungover or anything like this. I am just curious about where you have been for this past week?' He pouted. 'I left messages for you.'

I explained that since Carl was away nobody ever checked the answerphone. 'I don't even know how to work it,' I said, 'and besides the only person who ever calls me is my mother.'

He suggested that it was time I got myself a phone or else, he threatened, he would take to turning up on my doorstep unannounced. 'It was unsettling,' he said, 'to be unable to reach you for so long.'

He had missed me. Silent disgrace accompanied this admission and I prickled with a sense of pride. Finally I had made my way under his skin.

'Did you think that I was avoiding you?' I taunted him, but gently. 'Playing around with my other toyboys? Think I'd got bored of you?'

He finally cracked a grin because he knew such an idea was ridiculous. 'Oh, Charli,' he said, 'you are such a silly girl sometimes.'

He kissed me for the first time that day, for the first time since he'd left me alone in my apartment picking at the casing of that hardened salami; he kissed me with passion along the length of my neck and I begged him, 'Let's go home.'

He stepped back from me, reluctantly, ran his eyes all over my body, quite lewd. 'I would love that,' he said, 'but unfortunately I have an appointment.'

He took my hand and kissed it, promised to come over that evening, then he slipped away towards the staircase. With just one quick glance over his shoulder, deeply carnal, he was gone.

I must've looked a little mischievous because when I went back into the studio Finley said, 'What were you whispering about out there, girl? What are you up to?'

'Oh nothing,' I replied shyly. 'Nothing, nothing.'

'So, are you back with us now?' he asked. 'Has Alexander left the building?'

'I get the feeling you don't like him much,' I said.

'Blessed Assurance' was playing from his laptop speakers. 'No,' he paused in thought, 'I just like you better.'

I felt flattered by the coquetry that lingered under his thick, bovine lashes. Alexander had stirred something up in him, but I also felt protective. I was enthralled by Alex and I wanted Finley to see that.

'It's amazing, isn't it?' I said. 'How he can just manifest like that? Don't you think? Friends of Marilyn Monroe said she could do it too,' I noted. 'They said she could just turn it on and become Marilyn. I guess it's what you call star quality.'

Finley looked at me with a certain scepticism. 'Uh-huh, right.'

Because we were all hungry but none of us had the necessary zest to go home and cook, we went out to a kebab shop someway down Oranienstrasse which none of us knew the name of. It was a place we often hid out in because it stayed open real late and the owner gave us fries for free whenever we ordered the soup. He looked like a doleful vampire, forever shut away from natural light in his fluorescent sepulchre, with a pronounced widow's peak and such an air of desolation that Polly had taken to calling him Count Chipula. Finley had said flat out that he'd fuck him, but Polly and I couldn't ever really decide if the Count was sexy or not. If she was feeling raucous, she would stick two chips under her top lip so they stuck out like fangs and cackle, 'I vant to suck your cock,' but not with any serious intent.

The TV was on very low, playing classic rock hits, Meatloaf and Genesis, that sort of thing. We sat and ate, stirring French fries through cooling soup, each of us a little lost in our own thoughts. Polly started talking about a new painting she had conceived of on the Ryanair flight back from Dublin, orcas breaking the surface of an inky black sea. 'It's not a nightscape,' she said, 'but there isn't any light.'

The two of them wanted to show their work in a joint exhibition at the little gallery run by drag queens on my street. They'd been trying to set up a meeting with the queen who organised the calendar, but she was very technophobic and would only discuss business in person. She also hated to be tied down by making appointments with anyone, which complicated things further. I'd met her and she really was impossible.

They went over the logistics of it all: how many works would they both hang, should they collaborate on a new piece, could they get Ryan to write about it for the magazine even though he was a music journalist? My input wasn't really needed. I threw in the odd 'uh-huh, cool' in the same way you might when a child of primary school age describes to you the plot of *The Little Mermaid*. I left that convivial mouth of mine running behind me there, on social autopilot, so that in my mind I might trip the light fantastic back towards that kiss in the corridor, the matrimonial quality of it. I thought of Alex fucking me in a stairwell at Christmas and how holy it felt, of suddenly becoming lucid in the supermarket at 7 a.m., deshabillé, and realising that people were staring at us, disgusted. I remembered saying to him 'Alex, everyone is looking,' and hearing his smart reply, 'Well, of course they are.' And now he was *unsettled* when he couldn't reach me. I had to admit that had thrilled me.

'Have you heard of the simian line?' I was speaking out loud before I realised what I was saying. Polly and Finley both looked at me blankly. I added, 'It's a palmistry thing, it's how you know you've found your soulmate.'

Finley shook his head; Polly said I looked a little strained. I blamed it on the city's lousy weather. 'How is anyone supposed to handle sunset at 3.30 p.m.?' She suggested I wake up with the sun, as if it were as simple as that. 'Try getting up at seven and going for a run. One never gets depressed if one follows the rhythm of the day,' she said.

9

They have changed my medication. I am suddenly alert to the fact because the doctor and nurse are moving around the room at once incredibly slowly and simultaneously in double time. It's like those scenes in Chungking Express *where the unnamed femme fatale in the blonde wig flees the mob through the streets of Hong Kong. One grows sensitive to these things. I'm pretty sure that dame smoked Sobranies too. The doctor speaks English, she tells me that my dosage of hydromorphone was way too high. She is friendly, she explains that although Spiegel does in fact mean mirror, Spiegelei means fried egg, hence the whole fandango with the nurse and the breakfast tray. Awfully embarrassing. She has asked me to refrain from throwing food from now on, and of course I have agreed; I'm rather abashed about the whole thing. This change of policy has been relayed to the nurse though frankly she remains highly sceptical of me, suspicious even.*

I ask the doctor for news about Alexander. I tell her that I don't understand why nobody will explain it to me, if he is OK. I can't possibly see why they would withhold information from me, unless, unless . . . and then I start crying again. Really it's more than crying, there's yet more screaming, I'm sorry to say. The journalist outside, taking down impressions the whole time, I'm honestly mortified. This is what finally shuts me up, the notion of him getting this particular humiliation down on his €2 notepad. The nurse whispers something to the doctor, who nods her head in agreement, and says, 'Ja es ist noch zu früh,' which I understand as 'it's still so early' so I ask, 'What do you mean so *early?'*

The doctor is startled by my comprehension and says, 'We think that it's still too soon for us to be talking about that with you.' She tells me that she isn't the right person anyway, that she's here to attend to my physical health, promises that when the time is right, she will find a suitable member of staff, a counsellor maybe, to talk it over with me, but not yet. Then I start crying again, and she asks if I am in pain, and even though it isn't the physical kind I say yes, and the nurse administers a little more and I fall backwards into the past.

10

We pulled up outside Arial Records the following Wednesday at 9.50 a.m. in Alex's old Mercedes. The morning was crisp and grey and cold. When we buzzed we were admitted into another entirely ordinary apartment building with a baby buggy in the hallway and a row of dented metal mailboxes on the wall, Art Nouveau tiling, still surprisingly beautiful. In Berlin it was quite usual for a business, say a dentist's office or a psychotherapist's practice, to be run from a residential building. I always found that touch of the Old World somehow very human, demotic notes about refuse collection and lost keys dotting the walls.

I didn't really know what to expect, though in my mind I must've pictured a man in a navy suit and a silk tie when thinking of a *record label executive*, some cartoon fat cat, potentially smoking a cigar at a big shiny desk. Moritz, however, was a slim thirty-something in a white sweatshirt, jeans and pleasantly grimy New Balance running shoes. His office looked like a junk shop, he had heavy eyes and a big nose which I thought made him terribly attractive. He himself was evidently very taken with Alexander, because although he wore a wedding ring and had a picture of his wife and child pinned on the noticeboard amidst favoured party flyers and gig tickets, I caught him casting glances that could only be described as pornographic over Alex whenever he thought we were busy looking at the paperwork he had placed before us. Moritz had seen him perform at, of all places, Cindy's

House of Sin. He said that he had recognised Alex's talent immediately.

'I think you really have something,' he rapped a pencil on his desk, 'I honestly do. So. I wanna ask: how would you like to start your recording career here, with us? Just putting it out there.'

He explained his vision: to get Alexander on-stage with bigger acts, put a band together for him, press a single on vinyl in the spring, arrange his publishing rights, finance his first music video and monetise his profile, a most extraordinary offer.

'This place might not seem like much,' Moritz said, 'but we've had some real success stories come through. We're long-term thinkers, you see, big picture guys.'

He dug through the piles of magazines bookmarked with old press releases and the heaps of snarled cables which filled the place to bursting. Striking gold, he tossed us a CD. 'You know these guys, right? The Mud Club Kidz? Well, we discovered them.'

Two anime-adjacent figures in PVC pants and mesh shirts lazed on the cover of the compact disc. Alexander feigned an unearthly enthusiasm, he whistled through his teeth, a one-note trill of wonder; it was clear to me that he had no idea what he was supposed to be looking at.

Moritz winked. 'Awesome, no?'

'So awesome,' said Alex.

'Geist?' Moritz mused. 'That's not your real name, right?'

Alex shook his head. 'No,' he answered, 'it's just something a little kid told to me in the street. "Hallo, Geist!" he said, and I thought it was much better than my own family name.'

'Well, it's great,' Moritz beamed. 'It works beautifully, it's great. Don't change it, OK? Don't change a thing. Sign here and here. Shall we make a toast?'

And it happened just like that, in a shared office space with a dead rubber plant in one corner and a big green medicine ball in the other. Moritz signed his copy of the paperwork, Alex autographed his; by 11 a.m. we had a deal, by noon we were good and drunk, knocking back two bottles of conspicuously expensive champagne from a stash in the mini fridge. Moritz explained all the ins and outs of the music industry in between swigs of fizz. It was all very interesting stuff, and I did try to tuck away the relevant details – lots of talk of *innovation market modelling* and *brand liability negation* which might've seemed intimidating, threatening even, if only it weren't for how handsome Moritz looked bandying it about. He was like a substitute teacher who brought a new allure to double physics; I could have stayed all day drinking and laughing and barely comprehending the situation, only he had a lunch meeting. With someone at Warners, I think he said. 'We work closely with the big boys,' he smiled, 'very closely. Who we watch, they watch.'

In the hallway he swept out his foot to prop open the door with a battement frappé and a kettlebell. He hugged us tightly to his chest, his stubble grazing my cheek, the sweet smell of metabolised fizz on his breath, the slightest stink of sweat rising from his armpits. I wanted nothing more than for him and Alex to bend me over and take turns. With promises of *more to come*, he waved us off. He shot Alexander another quick, sly wink which made me flex with the most arousing jealousy.

Drunk, we left the car outside Moritz's building and staggered to Rote, the one bar in Kreuzberg that never closed, a place where nobody thought anything of you rolling in steaming at any such hour, since the staff and all the regulars were long past telling the time. It was a lot like a casino in there, they still allowed you to smoke which was a thrill, plus they also served sausage around the clock, boiled orange bratwursts with phosphorescent yellow mustard and hard rolls, on which we gorged, Alex hiccuping with delight that this was really happening. Too loudly and too frequently he whooped, 'I am a pop star! I am a real pop star!' rattling the bartender's cage, chuckling maniacally.

The truly committed alcoholics scowled and muttered. I'm pretty sure one of them called us *Schwuchteln*, but what did we care? We pounded the bar and ordered shots of Schnapps, insisting that we be allowed to try some of those funny old herbal liquors in the ancient bottles they kept stashed behind the plush leprechaun dolls and the goofy troll figurines, cackling and spluttering so violently with the acetone taste of them that one of the meagre grey lushes asked the bartender to turn the music up to mask our squawks. Eventually it was the juvenile noodlings of AC/DC, more so than the fetid stench of the place or the oncoming waves of nausea, which forced us out.

We went back to my apartment and I told Alex exactly what I'd been thinking about in Moritz's office. He barely lasted five minutes before he came in me, the urgency in his thrusting suggestive of an overlapping depravity, hinting perhaps at his own desires.

Then he lay me on my back and licked at my hole, my legs on his shoulders as he ate it like a cunt, long strong licks, frantic probings, his tongue lapping up his own cum as it spilled out of me. I stroked at my dick, holding his head in place, riding against his face, my fingers ensnared in his hair as he moaned obscenities inside me and splattered my stomach.

We called my roommate's dealer. We told ourselves we were more than justified in doing so, in *going on holiday* again, and he arrived with his dog and an old transistor radio from the DDR and the day became the night and the night became the morning and I heard my roommate leave for his 8 a.m. lecture and knew by the slam he gave the front door that we had been very badly behaved throughout.

Exactly what we might have done I couldn't remember, though flashes of the dealer sitting naked in the kitchen feeding his dog my roommate's rollmops troubled my edges.

Sometimes it's like that, isn't it? Sometimes the details evaporate and what remains is the most anonymous of outlines, so that when you look back at the night before all you have is the roughest tracing, like white chalk drawn around a dead body on your floor, and you find yourself being asked how you could've slept through a murder, how well you knew the victim.

II

We began an intense period of writing and research. I felt flushed with a sense of purpose for the first time in months. I showed Alex *Taxi Driver, Opening Night, The Cabinet of Dr. Caligari*, movies he'd never seen. He played me Arthur Russell and Julius Eastman. I read to him, too, bits of *Pale Fire, The Great Gatsby* and *American Psycho*, which he seemed to think was a comedy, books I couldn't believe he had never before heard of.

We watched an endless string of Romy Haag videos on YouTube, clips of her chatting to Nina Hagen about Buddhism and reincarnation, music promos with leather pants and waist-length wigs, old footage newly digitised from nightclubs where she lip-synched Bizet's 'Habanera' in layers of Belle Epoque tulle, snippets from her late-night chat show in the nineties, with special guests Take That and Chris Norman from Smokie, and of course the ineluctable fan montages of her and Bowie, slideshows of them smoking at parties soundtracked by 'Heroes'.

We were frequently up all night: either out dancing or smoking joints out of my bedroom window and storyboarding his career. He slept over more often than not, though besides some underwear and a copy of *Berlin Alexanderplatz,* most of his belongings remained at his place in Grunewald. And I cooked for him to the best of my abilities: scrambled eggs and fried chorizo, sometimes I seared a steak or a loin of venison. I don't think I ever saw him eat a vegetable; his diet was like Faust's, *not of earth*. Neither of us ate all that much really, we were usually too high. Toking on the dog-end of a joint Alex turned to me and said, 'You know, if I'm the new Bowie, then that makes you my Romy,' and my heart leapt in my breast.

We had been up until six with a bag of coke. It was early February maybe and I woke up shivering. I hadn't been asleep for long. The curtains were drawn and Alex's cigarette case sat open on my dresser catching the slither of pale sunlight that made it through. I grabbed for a fag, shaken with the cold and with the chill of expiring toxins, lit the smoke and cast about with my eyes, ill at ease in realising myself in the room alone. I held out hope that he was elsewhere in the apartment, shuffled to the kitchen wrapped in my duvet, to the bathroom, down the hall, cracked open my roommate's door even, but could not find him. He was gone, no note, no explanation. I hated it when he did that.

I went back to bed, aggrieved, intending to waste the day sulking, but though I tried, I couldn't get back to sleep. I was too wired, I wouldn't dream, I would only lie and fret over where he might be now and with whom. Some other girl, some older man? I knew that it would drive me mad if I speculated on it for too long, so I took a shower instead and decided to get a jump on the day, accepting that, as with a cat, Alex would only come back if I put him out of my mind.

There was a letter for me on the kitchen table. I recognised it as an upbraiding from the bank; I didn't open it. With just a little bit of patience these troubles would soon be behind us. The recording advance that Moritz offered was not life-changing, but it was significant. Still I was nervous that in spite of our signed contract he might have second thoughts, or that the funds might go astray, be seized by the German authorities as the profit of fraud or worse, that Alex might blow it all on shoes and smack. So, despite the quiet dread that

I was potentially committing heresy, I went out on Polly's advice to buy a pack of lucky green candles, a prayer to bring in prosperity.

It was at least an hour before I found anything suitable. I trawled two supermarkets, the €1 shop and a craft store, deploying the full breadth of my godawful German in the search. When I brought the candles back I couldn't find my candelabra, so I had to hunt about the apartment again, kitchen, bathroom, Carl's room, just as I had done when looking for Alex earlier, thinking it quite likely that he had moved it himself, opening every cupboard and shining a torch under and behind the beds and dressers, muttering in incremental frustration until I realised, with a short burst of hysteria, that I didn't actually own a candelabra.

I hooted to myself about that, the realisation breaking like a clap of thunder. 'Thank God nobody can see this scene!' I laughed. 'They'd *really* say I'm crazy!' I was delirious with sleep deprivation and, I recognised, very hungry, so I went out again, back to the supermarket to pick up a bunch of bananas.

From the grocery shop I decided to head over to Polly's house. I wanted to distract myself from all the nagging feelings I had swirling about me, plus I thought she'd find the candelabra story very funny. When I arrived, she wasn't at home. Callum told me she'd gone running, but he invited me in all the same. He never seemed quite as evil as Polly made him out to be, but then I've never been the best judge of character. He was wearing checked boxer shorts and a red hoodie, white socks with Adidas sliders, eating a bowl of cornflakes. He had a pair of emerald drop earrings in, and his lips were swollen, almost lasciviously overfull.

'Do you want a banana?' I asked.

'Oh yeah, ta,' he said. 'Do you want some coffee?'

He made me a cappuccino in the most painstaking fashion, weighing and grinding the beans, cooking the coffee in a magnificently rustic stovetop pot, frothing the milk to peaks with a tiny handheld whisk, really it was a beautiful thing to behold, and indeed to swallow. As he ate his banana he told me that he was starting to do drag and showed me a bunch of pictures of him all dolled up on his phone, once or twice scrolling back too far and pulling up images of himself naked and flexing, or gazing up at the camera and lapping at substantial pink tool.

'Whoops,' he said without blushing, 'didn't mean to show you *that* much!'

As Polly's key turned in the lock, he tossed the earrings on the table and bolted from the room.

'Charli?' she said when she saw me. 'Bit early for a social call isn't it?' She was sweating from her run. Her workout gear, running shorts and neon sports bra, looked wildly at odds with her patrician face, as strange as seeing a nun on the beach, and it was hard not to stare.

'I'm taking your advice,' I replied, 'all of it, I'm getting up with the sun.'

She sized me up and frowned. 'Yes, well, that only works if you've been to bed in the first place, dear.'

'Well,' I declared, 'I'm here now, and I brought bananas.'

She said, 'Yes, I see that. Did Callum let you in?'

'Hmmm?' I quizzed. 'Oh your roommate, yes.'

She saw the earrings on the table and her brows snapped together in irritation. 'The little shit.'

Polly went into the kitchen to make herself a glass of green juice. I followed her and said, 'I have the most extraordinary news! Alexander Geist is now officially a recording artist.' She flicked me a look of misgiving, and dropped down into the fridge. Someone more astute might've taken the hint, instead I explained the strategy that Moritz at Arial Records had laid out, as best as I could remember it. I told her that he found acts he thought had mainstream potential, polished them up, helped generate a little A/B tested hype and worked on their brand positioning, then, when the time was right, he sold the contract to the *big boys*. Polly continued shredding her spinach, not really paying a great deal of attention to me. It was all a little convoluted, I suppose.

'*He gets me high, he crashes my car into the night sky,*' I sang. 'You know that song? It's by the Mud Club Kidz.'

'Yes', Polly made a face, 'I hate it. They're forever playing it at the gym, it's awful.'

'I know,' I agreed. 'It's garbage, but they've got fifteen million streams on YouTube now and Moritz just got them signed to Sony. He thinks he can do the same for Alexander. It's all one big racket, do you see?'

She flicked on the blender; I covered my ears until it was over.

In the street below I watched an old woman pushing a shopping trolley full of empty bottles towards the supermarket, considered the absurdity of life, thought of Albert Camus saying that the stupidest way to die is a car crash, then dying in a car crash himself. Alex would've said the KGB were to blame. Polly poured herself a large glass of doleful, iron-rich sludge, she offered me some, I declined, she said that the whole situation sounded bizarre.

I followed her back into the living room and she asked me why, if they were any good, Sony or whoever didn't just sign the acts directly. I sighed, 'Oh, lover, you're being very twentieth-century in your thinking here.'

I told her that fans today didn't want to be told what to listen to by a record label, they didn't want to be marketed to, they wanted to be involved with an artist from the ground up, to watch them grow, to take the journey with them, to be a part of the climb. 'They're invested in authenticity,' I said, ever so sagely.

She snorted that the whole thing sounded about as authentic as a Happy Meal and I groaned in frustration. 'That's not the point Polly! You don't have to *be* authentic, you just have to *seem* authentic. We're looking for organic market buy-in here,' I said. 'Product. It's all just product.'

'No,' she shook her head, 'now you've lost me entirely.'

At this point I caught sight of myself in one of her mirrors on the living room wall, shaped like an ample pair of tits. There was a cock-shaped twin somewhere, though it might well have been broken at the last party. I saw myself underscoring key points very vigorously with a banana. My pallor was cadaverous and my eyes blood-shot, my hair was pointing in all four cardinal directions at once. I thought, *Well, that explains why nobody wanted to help me find those candles.*

Polly finished her smoothie and set down the glass. The sounds of a mother chastising her child in Turkish broke in through the window. I gazed into the mirror, pawing at my hair where it stood on end. 'I need to take a shower now,' Polly said. 'I think that you should go home and get some sleep. You look like hell.'

So I traipsed back home, speculatively shamed by the thought of running into anybody I might know in my degraded state, keeping my head down and the collar of my coat up high, the sun had come out in full hibernal drag. In the apartment I heard someone rattling around in the kitchen which I thought must surely signify Carl's infuriated return. I prepared myself to repent, only to face the most startling sight when I opened the kitchen door: Alexander wrangling with armfuls of glorious white calla lilies.

12

Alexander was looking petulant. He said, 'Well, where did you go?'

'Where did *you* go?' I asked.

'To the florist,' he said. 'Obviously. I was in the mood for luxury.'

I quietly totted up the cost of such a volume of flowers, told him that we didn't have anything suitable to put them in, they deserved fine crystal and hand-painted earthenware. I wanted to chide him but the lilies were too beautiful. So far he had marshalled an old spaghetti jar, a cafetière and a two-litre thermos. He was cutting the stems to size; he said that Carl had told him to use whatever he could find in the pantry. This heartened me: if he had helped Alex with the flowers surely he couldn't be all that cross.

'Your roommate is very handsome,' he said, 'you never told me this.' He kept his eyes on the lilies.

I coloured. 'He didn't seem upset?'

'Oh, no,' he said, 'he was *very* upset. You kept him awake all night being so loud, and then your mother called here at six hours and woke him up again.'

'Fuck,' I groaned.

'Yes,' he said, 'you should go to the booth and call her.'

We hadn't spoken since our quarrel after Christmas. She'd been leaving messages on the answerphone ever since to prove her contrition, chipping steadily away, if not at my resolve, then at my roommate's patience. I felt unwell, suddenly dehydrated, agitated, but I couldn't get to the sink because it was full of lilies. A panic came upon me that I had gone too far now, that Carl might well kick me out.

Alex worked at his floristry. He said, 'Don't worry, he won't,' replying to a fear which I hadn't yet verbalised, 'he is really not unkind.'

I blinked in confusion, in surprise. 'Sometimes,' I began, 'it's honestly like . . .'

He shook his head. 'No, no,' he said, 'I know you now, that is all.' He slid another lily into the thermos. 'I know where your thoughts they are going.'

An image came into my mind – I wondered if Alexander saw it too. Twin satellites whirling through space together, bouncing information between themselves and then back to the Earth below, a weather report for Malibu, the BBC World Service, GPS, a heat map of Shanghai, telecommunications, radio, the internet. I made a note to call my mother after dinner.

We took the flowers through to my room. I placed the tall pasta jar on the coffee table, and Alex put the flask on the dresser. The blooming cafetière could just about be made to fit on the bedside table. The room, lately so ripe with squalor, now august, was soaked in the majesty of a February afternoon, precious and rare, already scented with the piquant attar of lilies. My boudoir was dressed like a chapel for the Feast of St Anthony, and I felt humbled.

Alex sat on the bed and lit a Sobranie, a gyre of blue combustion rising from the amber tip and into the atmosphere. He wore pink socks; he looked like a prince-bishop enthroned. I sat in the spare cube of sunlight at his feet and caressed them as he smoked. His face devastated me. I said, 'I'm sorry I disappeared like that this morning, it was thoughtless.'

I took his foot in my hands and pressed the flat of my thumbs into his sole, up under his toes, along the ball of his foot, kneading through the delicate odourless fuchsia-pink cotton with quiet diligence, though he hardly seemed to register my touch. He yawned and stretched his left arm out behind him on the bed, leaning his weight back and dragging on his cigarette, only slowly letting his head drop over his shoulder, exhaling smoke and discreet pleasure.

I tugged at his sock with my forefinger, looping it over the elastic and stripping the foot bare, lifted it right to my lips and kissed the arch, my tongue long and slow, dragging up from heel to toe, my nose searching, hoping to find where he smelled the worst. I heard a brief hiss: he had dropped the cigarette butt into an old bottle of Sterni; then came the beloved whine of his zipper coming down, like dry boots on wet gravel.

I lapped at his foot, threading my tongue between his toes, bejewelling his sole with my saliva. When I looked up I saw that his cock was standing bolt upright through his fly, he was observing the sap already oozing, paying me practically no attention, he gave me only a cool stare of no concern. I kissed and I licked at his bare foot on my knees in reflection, in contemplation, in an adoration which he intentionally frustrated, pressing his other foot, still socked, down onto my cheek and with some cruelty, so that I overbalanced and sprawled backwards on the floor. Then he laughed, low and true, smearing the spit with which I had coated his sole, across my face.

In that position of perfected abjection, all I wanted was to touch myself, to make myself cum but I knew this was unthinkable. I existed to realise his desires now, if I existed at all. So, I took off his left sock and went at this foot with an even greater enthusiasm, wanting him to see how much it turned me on to receive his contempt, rising to my knees again, and shuffling like a penitent to swallow his cock, letting him buck up into my throat with such force that I choked and retched and had to squirm for air, his hands wrapped tightly through the length of my hair. 'Should I call your roommate in here?' he said. 'To see what a slut you really are?'

I shook my head, 'Please, no,' but in panting I gave myself away.

He unbuttoned his shirt lazily, allowing it to fall open over his pale, hairless torso, skinny as a Sphinx cat. I heard a neighbour call out 'Mahlzeit.' I felt for the button on his pants, fiddled it, unfastened it, tugged his trousers down his legs in order to start tonguing at his balls. The whole length of his body was milky and perfectly smooth, even his armpits were bare, not depilated but naturally clean; besides a curt triangle of short, vivid pubic hair he was as glabrous as a porn star. It came to my mind that maybe this total lack of body hair explained his invariable scentlessness, that inodorous rebuttal which allowed him to evade my ever knowing him fully. The thought made me suddenly and inexplicably angry.

I took ahold of him behind the knees and forced his legs up and apart so that he fell onto his back with his arse exposed and in my face, too shocked to express the alarm he surely felt at being so denuded. I started eating his hole with greed and ambition and he responded with immediate shudders of transparent delight, which not even the half-hearted struggle he played out on my shoulders could obscure. I pushed my tongue inside him until my frenulum strained and scraped on my teeth and Alex started gasping, then I toyed with him, sliding my middle finger inside him up to the second knuckle. I slipped a second finger inside him effortlessly, watched him from between his legs as he writhed on the bed. He whimpered, and I silently scorned him.

Without warning he took hold of a handful of my hair and dragged me almost viciously back towards his cock, started skull-fucking me with merciless vigour, until spit and mucus poured out of my mouth and nose, glazing his dick and matting his pubes, pooling in my palm as I groped under his balls, fingers still deep inside his arsehole. He laced his fingers tighter through my hair, pulling me back and up, forcing me to meet his eye, handling me as though I were the decapitated head of a traitor. 'Do you think you are going to fuck me?' he said. 'You think that?' He laughed and spat in my open mouth.

'Slut,' he ridiculed, and began to fuck my face again.

My heart was banging wildly against my ribs and in my ears, I can't ever remember being so afraid or so turned on in my life. He dragged me up onto the bed and pushed me flat on my back, one hand around my throat, the other stroking the length of his cock which was harder and throbbing more violently than I'd ever seen before. He craned himself astride me planting his feet aside my ears, squatting, rubbing his hole in my face, his balls slapping hard against my cheeks with every downward stroke of his shaft. I let my tongue snake out again to lap at his glossy pink hole, to show him the full extent of my willingness to submit, letting him ride my face as he jerked his dick closer to orgasm. I felt the waves of ecstasy inside him, they were building inside me too. As if I could jockey his pleasure to a climax myself, I found myself willing him to cum, expecting that his release would be mine too, though as he edged on the precipice he suddenly seemed struck by misplaced timidity and looked down at me now in pathos, now in concern.

I saw that what I had to do was make myself an object more completely: my personhood, my subjectivity shook his confidence. So I started to moan in rhythm with his strokes, lashing at his balls and at his arse with my tired tongue, begging him for his load. I was an instrument of gratification, nothing more. All my most graphic mumbles were crushed and muffled by the rise and fall of his slick junk smacking my face, but the intent reverberated up through his chakras, up along his spine. He arched his back like a showgirl, threw his head high and over his shoulder and started to groan, 'Yes, ah fuck I am going to . . .'

I whined, 'Cum for me. Shoot it in my fucking face. I am a slut. Fucking shoot it on me,' and he did.

He soaked my face, it sprayed over my shoulder and into my hair, thick and viscous, into the folds of my ear, trickling into my mouth, the taste acrid and familiar, bitter and mephitic like sweet chestnut in summer, and I thought, *Finally! I have the smell of him.*

Afterwards we showered together and Alex took pictures of me naked, posing like a cheesecake pin-up with shaving foam on my nipples. Then he rolled us a joint and searched for an episode of *Disclosed* on the internet, a reality show about the lives of alien abductees. His love for this kind of rubbish did not gel with his character at all and I often found myself watching him watching them, the subjects of these exploitative pseudo-docs, puzzling where his interest lay. He didn't find them funny, he was never scandalised by even the most ridiculous or offensive episodes; rather he almost seemed to be studying them, as if TV shows were the only window into reality he had.

Onscreen a lady in a lime mohair sweater and beige leggings fiddled with her scrunchie and told the camera this was not her first, not her second, no, *not even* her third experience, that she had in fact more than ten *encounters* so far with extraterrestrials, and these were just the ones she remembered.

I asked Alex, 'Do you think it's true? If there really are aliens out there how come I've never seen one?'

He shrugged. 'Maybe you are looking at one right now.'

I almost laughed but I caught myself – he had no sense of humour on this topic. I realised how heavy my body felt, how slowly time was passing by for me, crawling, a light ringing in my ears, my mind fading to a blank. I caught a panic rising in my throat, it climbed up my gullet and stuck in my candyfloss mouth, I could not swallow it back down, for a minute couldn't move my legs. Alex's eyes looked stranger than ever, sinister, reptilian, and I could not complete a thought for myself. It took me forever, a horrid little eternity of shallow breaths and forehead sweats, to recognise that I wasn't actually being abducted by aliens, I was just really, really high.

'Fuck,' I gasped, 'I am so stoned.'

'Uh-huh,' he said, 'me too. Isn't it the best?'

13

They have me sequestered away in here like a Da Vinci in a Swiss bank vault. They probably think they can wear me down with solitude, but I've always been able to make my own fun so the joke's on them. When I was a kid, late at night, inspired by seeing the little mouse from Tom and Jerry *eat mouldy cheddar before bed, I would sneak blue cheese from the fridge. I too had wild nightmares. Watching myself being cut in half by St Teresa, frozen with fear and unable to scream; gorgonzola was my gateway drug. My two halves would set off independently in different directions and I wouldn't know anymore which half was really me. See? I could have fun in an empty house. I won't crack in isolation.*

I know the doctors are trying to coerce me into saying it, but I never will. I know they plan to keep me in here until I give up and accept their version of events, they are trying to brainwash me completely. They want me to shoulder the blame you see, to take the fall. They've been paid off by Rick and Moritz. God it's so corrupt. It's no wonder I'm not allowed a television! This will be all over the news and they don't want me to see how they've manipulated the truth because they know I'll contest the story and that will cause them a real big headache. I was Alexander's right-hand man, lying to me is like lying to your dentist about how much Coca-Cola you drink, it won't wash. I'll sue them, I won't stop until this hospital is bankrupt, I'll be such a thorn in their side, Heaven help me. I'll never say it.

I had a radio, briefly, but it was too upsetting, all the lies. The nurse took it away and brought me a Walkman so that I could listen to the cassette I came in clutching. Probably somebody died listening to Doris

Day on this very device, Que sera, sera, *who can say? Naturally I've asked where my handbag is, so that I might pray the rosary in remembrance of the previous owner, but this perfectly ordinary line of questioning only inspires a shrug and the word 'Kaputt.' Fuck, they're such villains, I should never have come here. An Austrian spa break would've been much more suitable.*

I have to get away. To find someone who will help me get my story down straight. I have to get away from the doctors. They want to make me into their very own Lee Harvey Oswald. They are such pigs. They want to trick me into saying it. They ask me, Where do you think he is, Charli? What do you think happened to him? *but I'm never going to say it, no matter how much they press me. If they want to hear those words, they're going to have to speak them themselves. I know that they're waiting for me to admit it before they let me go, but it doesn't matter, I won't say it. I pray at least it was quick and that he didn't suffer terribly; I know it but I'm never going to say it. Until I say it, it isn't true, I was his midwife and I'll be his coroner, I'm never going to say, 'Alexander is dead.'*

14

It was my responsibility to sift through the inbox twice a day, to sort out anything that might be urgent or interesting or important from the spam, the hustle and the periodic abuse. I compiled a list of tasks to be actioned, pulling phrases like *Find tailor who works in velvet* and *Study New German cinema* from the notebooks I filled during our late-night research sessions. I chose to think of it as secretarial work, which helped me find some silver-screen glamour in what was really a heap of menial tasks: researching studios, replying to Moritz, meeting the interchangeable requests from music journalists. I found it much more entertaining to picture myself as Marilyn Monroe in her sweater and scarf in *Monkey Business*, strutting out from behind her desk to flash Cary Grant her non-rip stockings. This is what my sixth-form counsellor would have called gender-affirming behaviour, what second-wave feminists think of as a grotesque parody of womanhood. Polly sighed when I told her, 'You can be awfully camp sometimes, Charli.'

I read his fan mail sometimes too, though we had decided that once identified as such these messages should be forwarded to Alex's personal email. He had vanished again and I was bored and lonely and couldn't resist the temptation to pry. People wrote some really obscene things, one guy said they'd seen him on-stage and wanted to suck him off in the bathroom after his next gig, one said he'd gladly drink his piss, another that he was masturbating right now. Others were thankfully more timid, wanting to ask if he'd sign a gig flyer, or if he'd listen to their demo on SoundCloud. Some were indecipherable, and some were actually very tender. One admirer said they'd seen a picture of Alex in the listings section of a gay magazine, they had taken it to their hairdresser to get the same style, and the boy they were crushing on had asked them out the very next week. I was so touched by this that I replied, in character, trying to mimic Alexander's tone.

Hello, lover, I wrote. *So good to hear that I am inspiring your love life! Thank you for your note. Love, Alex*

Almost immediately I received a reply saying *Oh my god! I can't believe it is it really you?* which freaked me out so much that I slammed the laptop shut in fright and threw it across the room and onto the bed. I was doubly anxious because I realised then that Alex would probably see this exchange and know that I'd been snooping, and maybe that's why I did it in fact, because although I wasn't worried about him in his absence, that's not to say I wasn't longing for him still.

He said he was going to visit the graveyard where Anita Berber was buried, but that was a week earlier, so either he'd fallen in alongside her or he'd scored again. I tried to bury my apprehension; my concern was unsexy. I was growing used to his truancy, accepting it as an aspect of his personality, as another quirk of our relationship.

Carl was in the kitchen listening to a podcast, the greasy spiel of hucksters who would have their listeners believe that the Holocaust wasn't real but the need for handguns was. I was hungry but not hungry enough to interrupt him. We had been avoiding each other since I walked in on him masturbating to a video of two trans girls spit roasting a businessman. He had stuck a few notes on my bedroom door since, reminders about the rent and that sort of thing, but I thought it was for the best just to pretend I hadn't seen them, and he was either too conflict averse or embarrassed to follow up. I stayed in my room, smoking with the window open, even though it was terribly cold, emailing Radio Eins to set up an interview for Alexander.

Eventually the cacophony of paranoia subsided and I heard Carl tumble down the hallway. I waited for the front door to close behind him and once the coast was clear I went to see if the falafel I'd picked up from the kiosk at the end of the street was still in the fridge. It wasn't. I gave up trying to work, went over to the Späti, bought a BiFi mini and called my mother from one of the phones there. She was on her best behaviour.

She had warmed to the idea of Alex. Though she wouldn't say his name and only referred to him as 'your new friend', she at least kept conversation at a terrestrial level. She said, 'Your father wants to know if he's anything like Mr Froggy?' She chortled wholesomely down the line, 'Do you remember Mr Froggy, eh?' I could hear my father in the background egging her on.

I groaned. 'Oh mother, really. Not this again.'

She teased me, 'Because I remember Mr Froggy. Oh I remember him alright! You couldn't go anywhere without him when you were little. You used to say, "Wait Mummy, Mr Froggy needs to put his wellies on." Honest to God, you were the only kid I ever knew who had to get their imaginary friend dressed for the day's activities.'

I sighed. 'I'm going to have to hang up if you keep on with this.'

'I'm only playing with you, love,' she said. 'You know that. It's a mother's prerogative to tease her baby girl. Anyways, when are you coming back to see us?'

She told me that she still had all of my Christmas presents wrapped up on top of the wardrobe. 'Julie got at the truffles but besides that they're in all intact. Any chance you'll be home to pick them up soon, or am I going to have to bring them to Berlin myself?'

The thought horrified me. 'Yes soon,' I squeaked, 'in summer probably, we can ah, go bowling. I've just been so, so busy you see.'

'With what?' she said.

'With my PhD, of course.' I banged my head on the wall of the booth. 'Mother you never listen.'

'Oh right yeah, you did say, I haven't forgotten,' she assured me. 'What's it about again?'

I explained Romy Haag's impact on the history of rock'n'roll, very briefly, just the highlights. 'She was a disco singer and she ran a cabaret in Berlin, she was a total pioneer. Red hair, very glamorous, she looked a bit like Rita Hayworth. She's a trailblazer of trans culture,' I said, 'she's still a big star here actually.'

'Oh, *her,*' my mother put it all together, 'right yeah, I do remember something in the papers about her, years ago it was, going out with David Bowie.'

I was astounded. 'Yes, that's her!'

'I always thought she'd made the whole thing up! But she never,' she laughed. 'Just goes to show you, doesn't it?'

Later I met up with Finley and Polly at Roses. They were both a little strained from a long week in the studio, working on their collaboration: a series of gorgeous little Frankensteins which she started and he finished.

Finley said, 'It's good to see you, girl. It's been forever.'

Polly quipped, 'I'm amazed you could drag yourself *all the way* over here. I thought you'd be busy with Alexander.'

'I have the evening off,' I said. 'For good behaviour.'

Roses was famous for its decor: the walls were alternately covered in pink faux fur and decoupaged with photos of Michael Jackson and Dolly Parton, the bar staff charged you according to their mood and how much they liked the look of your face. The first time I went I couldn't even buy myself a gin and tonic because the old goth behind the bar wouldn't take my order, she just kept saying, 'Are you real? You're not real,' until some helpful Australian stepped in and bought me my G&T. I think I jerked him off under the table later in the evening.

It was always horribly crowded in there and you had to watch your purse. Once someone tried to slide Alex's wallet out of his pocket in the backroom, only he caught the inept thief by his wrist and slammed him up against the ratty pink-fur walls calling him a *sneaky little bastard* and slapping his face. Polly looked around, disgruntled. 'I don't know why we come here,' she said, 'it's not even that cheap.'

We staked out a little space between the jukebox and a fish tank, tried to talk to each other over the Euro-pop playlist. A sleazy looking man came to ask Finley if he was Turkish and if he'd like to buy some ecstasy, then three French girls burst through and flashed their tits at us, perhaps as part of a hen-night treasure hunt, we weren't really sure. Callum pushed through the crowd and engulfed us all in a very moist hug. 'You guys! *You* guys!' he said again and again. 'Oh my God, *you guys*!'

He pulled a shoulder of vodka out of his shorts and topped up what was once a glass of cranberry juice, though it was now only tinged with the faintest pink, really just the ghost of a soft drink. 'You want some?' he yelled. Only Finley accepted.

The ecstasy dealer asked Polly if she was interested perhaps. She told him to piss off and he said that if she didn't want drugs maybe she wanted sex, because he had a nice big cock and he was single, which was clearly a lie. Callum caught the conversation and spun around, one hand on his hip, saying, 'I'll have sex with you, pal,' which prompted him to back off sharply, mumbling, 'Sorry, I am not gay, sorry but I'm not.' The look on his face however suggested it might be worth Callum's while to check back in with him a few drinks later.

I started to talk about Alex of course, though I struggled to make myself understood over the noise of the room and the jukebox selections: ABBA, Nina Hagen, Kylie Minogue. My friends seemed hard-pressed to maintain any interest in what I was saying, dodging random elbows and avoiding sloshing steins of beer.

I said, 'I suppose it's the not knowing that makes it so exciting, isn't it?'

'Hmm, yes, sure,' nodded Polly noncommittally.

'*Every human creature is constituted*,' I said, '*to be that profound secret and mystery to every other*, etc. etc.'

Finley looked confused. 'What?' he asked with a finger in his ear.

'Dickens,' I spoke up. 'Nobody knows anybody really, do they?'

The man with the ecstasy came back to talk to Polly. He brought her a plastic rose and begged her to tell him her name, she ignored him. Callum said, 'I can introduce you to her. If you give me a free pill, like.'

'You little shit,' Polly hissed, 'one of these days I swear to God. And *you*,' she said, turning to the dealer, 'Lass mich in Rühe du hässlich Arschloch,' and tossed a stranger's Cuba Libre in his face.

As it transpired the dealer was good friends with the bartender who marched us straight out with threats to call the police, which not even the boos of the drunkards in the back could insulate us from. I hurried Polly out and we made our way down the street with real hurry in the direction of the Moritzplatz U-Bahn station, just in case the bartender really did call the cops. Finley and Callum stayed behind.

'I can't call my father from another police station. I just can't,' she said. 'He'd never let me live it down.'

It should have been funny, but it wasn't.

I wanted to go somewhere else, Polly didn't. I suggested that we go to Enklave because it was only 1 a.m. 'Forget it,' she said, 'that place is a fire trap and the music is loathsome.' She was in a terrible mood.

'Well, I'm going,' I continued, 'because I know I'm not going to be able to sleep anyway.' This was a lie of course: it was late and I was tired, I could've easily turned in with Polly, only I did not want to wake up alone at 6 a.m. feeling for Alex.

'I think I'm going to empty the recycling bin onto Callum's bed,' she said, 'see how he likes that.'

'Yeah,' I nodded. 'That sounds fun too.'

15

I picked up a €4 bottle of vodka for the road and went on to Enklave alone. I knew that I shouldn't really go, but I didn't have the strength of character to take myself home. I swigged as I tottered on down, the most peculiar tombola of feelings rattling around and around within me: lust, exhaustion, inebriation, dejection, and as I walked, I recognised that I really was sore at Alexander. My emotions have always been on something of a time delay. I told myself that I deserved better than a man who yo-yoed in and out of my life for a quick fuck or a place to crash. I was really getting cross – vodka makes me moody – and giving him a real talking to in my head when I realised that I didn't know where I was going, I didn't have the address. Finley and Ryan had always taken me over.

It was a moonless March night and I didn't have a phone for guidance, but somehow I got there all the same, independent of my conscious mind, like a driverless car. I walked for a while towards Karstadt, my cynosure. I knew Enklave was around there somewhere, so I just wove about the streets for a while hoping to pick up the vibrations. Eventually I recognised the place from the sight of two boys in leather puppy masks scampering out from an *altbau* and into the night, chucking a glass bottle away behind them.

Enklave was in the basement of a residential building, totally illegal of course. It was the local speakeasy that the neighbours didn't know about, and the owners wanted to keep it that way. I had to ring a doorbell and wait in the street, even as it started to rain, until someone scurried out, finger on their lips, to escort me silently into a cellar, soundproofed with mattresses. It was, as Polly said, a total fire trap. It was something like being led into a cave to participate in the Dionysian mysteries – you never knew when or in what state you might emerge, only that once you were inside all bets were off. It was really just a hole in the ground, but always so well filled.

The soupy subterranean atmosphere hit me hard as soon as the cellar door peeled back. Most people were topless; everyone was dancing. I pushed right in. I stuffed my coat behind some pipes, tied my shirt around my waist, began to bop about in my bra, alone and unhindered. It had been too long since I'd gone out dancing last. Alex loved dancing too, he moved beautifully, but no, I did not want to think about him right now.

I took a good long slug from my bottle of vodka, bad form I know, but I hardly bothered to conceal it. I slid further into the crowd where I might be more fully lost, elbow to elbow with some androgynous twinks, shimmying through, palms open, to find myself a little strip at the heart of the action, boogying between a man who could've been that creep from Crystal Castles and two ripped dykes grinding together like the molars of a lazy student on results day. I was sloshed and quite delighted with myself, barely cognisant of the ditch I was driving into. This was the point of the exercise: distraction, pretermission. I was twirling around to what was possibly Aphex Twin, arms up in a showstopper V, giving it the full girl-gone-wild, gyrating murderously when I slammed right up against West, who was at least as far gone as I.

'Wow, Charli!' he shrieked. 'Charli, you look so fucking hot!' and he started kissing me.

And I kissed him back, instinctively and without restraint. I ran my fingers through his hair, dragging my nails over his scalp, squeezing at his plump, full arse, the two of us stumbling in a passion about the dance floor, then from the dance floor to a slimy wall where we went at it even harder. I pinned him to the brickwork, he smelled like booze and sweat, and he moaned in my ear above the belt of the music, 'Charli, Charli,' I felt his cock stiffen as the room revolved around me, he kissed me again.

'Fuck,' he slurred a hiss in my face, 'I've wanted to do that for so long.'

'I know,' I smiled, 'I know,' and groped his arse again.

The magenta probings of a cheap disco club light strobed across us, then off around the room and back again, making fifteen-second circles, and each time the light hit his beautiful face, that face seemed to flicker and change, now sweetened in drunken pleasure, now unfocused and unsteady, now ghoulish, now groaning, now boyish and shy. I took his zipper between my thumb and forefinger, tugged at it playfully, then began to slide it down. He looked a little startled but smirked. 'Wow!' he hiccupped. 'Somebody knows what she wants.'

Around us the party went on. Nobody paid the blindest bit of attention – we had this damp strip of wall to ourselves, and we made good use of it. West's head jammed between my breasts as I toyed with his dick through the fly of his jeans, proving to myself that I was a free woman, even in this unfree world. A bassline, a clear favourite, subzero and synthetic, set the crowd howling and brought their bodies ever closer together, the last of the wallflowers surging towards the scrum, cigarettes in hand, the bartender screaming 'Wahoooo' from behind his stopgap bar top, punching the air, out of time.

And somehow the disco lights seemed to increase in speed, wheeling around on a relentless orbit, the way a room spins about you when you rise from a chair too quickly, and I started to feel very strange. Gone were the slow shadows over

West's face; now the light whipped around ever quicker as we kissed, showing him by turns fiendish, frantic and ecstatic, now with the icy leering countenance of Alexander himself.

I flinched and West giggled. 'Wha? What's wrong?' And though I think it was his voice ringing over the synth pop, I wasn't sure whether it was his face.

I pulled back a little, panicked, shaking my head to clear my vision, with this catalogue of countenances continuously scrolling over the space marked *West*. Even when I held myself still and rigid my head spun on until I thought I might puke and West started asking, 'Are you alright? Charli, are you feeling OK?' Only while he did so he seemed to be looking out at me through Alex's eerie green eyes; they caught the purple of the strobe light each time it ran, glinting like jewels the baroque faithful once stuffed into the sockets of revered patrons and martyrs.

'I'm fine,' I lied, 'I think maybe I drank too much. I just need some air.'

Of course he offered to take me outside, said he'd take me home in a cab if I needed him to, 'just so you're OK, like,' and though I was grateful for his chivalry, I was too alarmed, too disturbed to accept. If I was cracking up again, I needed to be alone.

'Call me,' I said.

'I did!' he replied. 'Are you sure you're OK? It's no problem, I can take you home.'

I shrugged off his assistance and slithered away and up the stairs solo with his voice ringing in my ears: 'Charli, where are you going?' I was back at street level before I'd even finished buttoning my shirt up, and halfway home before I realised I'd left my coat behind.

I shouted out into the street, 'What the fuck are you doing to me?' Then, recognising there was no one to answer, I gave myself a slap in the face and said, 'You have got to get a grip, Charli, you have got to get a grip.'

I knew it was the alcohol, I knew there was nothing more to it than that, there couldn't be, but all the way home, as I shivered and cursed my own stupidity, I was awash with an inexplicable paranoia, enraged that I'd left my booze behind at the club, my mouth stale and dry. I was desperate for a glass of water, desperate to get into bed. Staggering on, I could sense what a hangover awaited me already, denouncing myself for my foolishness, hobbling home in a cold sweat cursing the knowledge that, unlike every other drug, in Germany you can only get paracetamol from a licensed pharmacist.

The street door to my building was, as always, unlocked and I flashed anew with rage, *doesn't anybody ever think about security?* I almost tripped on a baby buggy in the hall because the lights in the vestibule were still out. In darkness I made my way up the stairs, punching each of the dimmers I passed in drunken spite. I stopped to take off my heels halfway up and began to ascend a little quicker, a little quieter, unencumbered but still wracked with tension. Rounding onto the final landing I grasped for the bannister and stifled a shriek as I was met by a pair of green animal eyes, glowing luminescent in the darkness. The light came on overhead, apparently of its own accord, and revealed Alexander, sitting unperturbed in my doorway, stroking a glowering tabby cat.

'Fuck!' I panted. 'You frightened me.'

'Hello, lover,' he said.

I caught my breath. 'If you're looking for Anita Berber, she doesn't live here anymore.'

'Don't be like that,' he said.

I asked where he had been, and he raised his eyebrows in a rather derisory manner, regarding me, shoes in hand, bra on display. He said, 'I should ask *you* the same question.'

I didn't respond directly, just took out my keys and unlocked the door. 'And why do you have a cat?'

'Oh, I don't know,' he shrugged, 'she followed me.' As he spoke, he was scrutinising my composure, a wry smile forming on his lips, as if to let me know that he had worked out exactly where I'd been. We went inside.

From the finger of light running under his door, I could tell Carl was at home, dozing to talk radio. Alex bundled the cat to me so he could take off his shoes, those creepy cloven boots of his, but she did not take to me at all. In fact, she puffed herself up in my arms and issued a long, low, sustained hiss, showing off an unfortunate set of fangs. I promptly dropped the horrid creature to the floor and she bolted down the hallway, disappearing into the gloom, yowling blackly as she went.

'Don't worry,' said Alex, 'she is only a little bit shy.'

The lilies in my bedroom were all wilted now; the stench of their decay was pressing. I felt that I would surely throw up now. The room was an awful mess, clothes discarded on the floor, dirty dishes on the dresser, makeup and falafel wrappings strewn across the bed. If I had not been so drunk I would've felt much more ashamed. Alex hardly seemed to notice, simply picked through the quagmire in search of a clearing to sit down in, and lit a skinny pink fag.

He took a deep drag and his eyes fluttered in his head. The smoke poured out of his nostrils almost orgasmically and he said, 'This is my last cigarette, lover. Share it with me?'

I walked over, unsteady on my feet, took the pink Sobranie from his lips and brought it to my own mouth between pincered fingers. I inhaled and stared down at him, dead in the eye, holding my breath for the deepest rush, then exhaled deliberately into his face. He didn't flinch; rather he smiled as if to compliment me on my hostility, then he caught me by the wrist and pulled me closer, rubbing my free hand on his crotch. I squeezed, but tighter than he expected, and drew the exact look of surprise from him that I was hoping for, though it was only an instant before he replaced it with one of malevolent glee. He let his head drop back and I tightened my grip, I wanted to hurt him, but he seemed to delight in it, after all masochism is only sadism subverted. I thought to myself, *So this is who you are when nobody is watching.*

'Take off your clothes,' I said, pressing my face right into his, 'and get on the bed.'

He did so silently and without hesitation, standing to unbutton his shirt, letting it drop, pulling off his trousers and kicking them aside, tugging at his underwear and bending to wiggle out of his socks, laying himself out as instructed, naked on the bed.

'Good,' I said, feeling for a character whom I could inhabit here, 'good.'

I had no clue what I was going to do with him, but having him stripped and suppliant made me extremely aroused, his cock stood upright and throbbing, my mind crackled with power. Gaunt and nude and lour-eyed lying there, he looked just like Bowie on the cover of *Diamond Dogs*, and it was like all my erotic Christmases had come at once. In the hallway I heard my roommate padding down to the kitchen, the light switch flicking on. I put out the end of the cigarette in a scummy cup of cold tea and said, 'I want to try something.'

From amongst the detritus on the floor I plucked one of the pink ribbons, now admittedly a little grubby, which had decorated the parcel of sheets Alex had gifted me back when I first moved in. I took it and looped it around his left wrist, fastening it tight to the iron bedstead, relishing the suggestion of concern manifesting in his face as I did so, the flex of his dick only slightly less obtuse. I stood and turned out the overhead light and Alex sank into the relative dimness of the bedside lamp, though he kept his eyes fixed on me, and as I set about finding a second length with which to secure him further, I saw him twist his wrist against the ribbon, to test how tightly he was bound. From the floor I selected a slender leather belt, whiplike, wrapping the end tip around the fingers of my left hand, securing the buckle in my right, pulling it taut like a garrotte; in the gloam Alex's grin returned.

'I'm going to tie your wrists together now,' I said, commanding my voice to remain steady, 'and then I'm going to do whatever I want with you.'

From across the bedroom I swear I could hear his heart beat in his chest. 'Yes,' he panted, 'please.'

Then came the most godawful screeching from the kitchen and the sound of a tower of empty saucepans hitting the deck, my roommate screaming, 'Verdmammt fotze! Was zum Teufel!' dropping whatever he had been holding and running from the room.

'Shit,' I said, 'the cat.'

My bedroom door was thrown open with almost enough force to wrench it off its hinges, and in came Carl thundering at me, 'You are fucking crazy! Did you bring a fucking animal in here from the streets? You are a fucking crazy bitch!'

'I can explain,' I began, though of course I couldn't.

'No!' he said. 'This is too crazy, you are too crazy, I cannot live anymore with this. All of this telephone calls and sex parties and wild fucking animals!'

'Shit, no,' I stammered, 'I'm sorry, look I'll clean up the kitchen for you. I'll get rid of the cat.'

But he wasn't listening. 'I wanted a quiet house for study! For making work and you make this house into a crazy place, like a fucking bordello!'

I was staggered, speechless. Alex simply looked on, one hand tied back behind his head, watching the scene unfold. Carl seemed not to have noticed him, which was a relief.

I don't think his presence, naked and bound to my bed, would've helped my case any.

'Look,' I said, 'let's go in the kitchen and talk,' and I tried to guide him out of the room with my hand on his shoulder, only he pushed me back with sudden unsuspected force.

'Do not touch me! I am serious now please,' Carl rasped, and only now that I was close to him did I see how wildly dilated his pupils were, how red his eyes. 'It is not possible for me to live anymore with you. Verstehst du? You understand?'

'Yes,' I stuttered, 'I understand, I'll start looking –'

But he interrupted. 'I am moving to my girlfriend,' he said, 'you are too fucking crazy for me.'

For a second it was almost tender between us, I thought surely one of us would start to cry, or that we'd at last embrace each other. We hadn't known each other that well, or for that long, but in a way weren't we very similar? Two fuck-ups flunking? For a second I considered kissing him, I really had nothing to lose, and I had always wanted to know what he had in those skinny jeans of his, but then the cat pounced into the room and he screamed and ran down the hall. I guess he had a real phobia.

In the filth of my bed Alex had found a crushed carton of cigarettes, and with his free hand had managed to stick one in his mouth. It hung from his lip unlit, like the gimcrack arm of a scarecrow. He mumbled like Humphrey Bogart: 'Get me a light, would you, lover?'

In my state of shock I didn't even try to argue. I rooted for the lighter and lit his crooked smoke. 'That,' I said, 'was truly an awful scene.'

'No, no, no,' he said, shaking his head in wild animation. 'It's perfect, don't you think?' He took a deep drag and said, 'Now I can move in.'

16

Carl left with very little ceremony. He and his girlfriend bundled as much as they could carry out of the apartment and he was spirited away the very next day on a cloud of whispered bickering. I thought for sure he'd be back to pick up the rest of his junk: his furniture, his answerphone, his spice rack maybe; I didn't realise that he was definitively gone for a week or so, until Alex pointed out that he'd left his keys on the table.

Alexander was very easy to live with at first, not that he was officially living with me. The deal was that he would rent the empty room and use it as an atelier, because my place was so much more convenient than his out in Grunewald or wherever it was (I don't know, because I'd still never been asked over). Really I was delighted that he was around so much; his company disrupted my tendency towards isolation and paranoia. Even if I had been cross at how he overstuffed my apartment, which I wasn't, quite the reverse in fact, I couldn't have complained: he'd rather graciously coughed up the three months' worth of rent Carl had absconded without paying.

He spent most of his time quite innocently scribbling lyrics in notebooks, sketching out stage sets for tours he wanted to mount, replying to the more curious fan emails, the ones that really caught his attention, researching designers for merchandise, padding around in the nude, and smoking of course, always smoking. He liked to write provocative messages to Moritz. He never crossed the line into vulgarity, but the email exchanges were often more salacious than I thought they needed to be when I read back over them. Sometimes I would catch him unawares and just watch him silently from the doorway, from the floor, from my chair across the room, in action. He had the funniest habit of smelling his own armpits, he'd pause at the desk mid-task to drape an arm over his head, take a few quick casual sniffs, and smile to himself, assuaged. I thought it was charming. He still vanished intermittently for days at a time of course, and without explanation. I read somewhere that Ian Curtis did that all the time too, though now that Carl was gone he reappeared again sooner, and I was comforted by that.

Polly called in unannounced one afternoon, she rang the bell around two. Alex was still sleeping, he kept the strangest hours. I closed the bedroom door on him, he was unbearable if his sleep was broken, and showed Polly in, less amiable than I might have been. It had been pouring with rain all morning, I was tired. It was unusual for Polly to pop by without an invite and it made me feel anxious.

She held up her umbrella above her head in the doorway and waved it, warlike. The shaft was bent at an acute, comic angle. 'Some grubby old bastard called me a *sexy kleines Mädchen* on the U-Bahn platform this morning,' she said. 'I gave him such a smack.'

I took the brolly and her coat, the old Armani trench. It was a good four sizes too large for her but she wore it well, slung over a slimmer leather jacket and fastened with a patent green belt. The radiator in the kitchen was the only one that ever got really hot, so I draped her stuff over it whilst she slipped off her shoes in the hallway. I fiddled about for longer than was needed – I wasn't feeling awfully sociable. I heard Polly open the door to Carl's old room and step inside.

I followed behind her, she was poking about the place as if to test the absence. She found the cat on the bed where she was sleeping in a patch of heatless sunlight. I said that I hadn't named her yet, just called her Cat as they did in *Breakfast at Tiffany's.* I liked having the silly old thing around, she did sort of suit the place, she blended with the queer character of the apartment seamlessly. Even her sandy colourings worked with the patches of exposed plaster and the yellowed cartoons Carl had collaged all over the kitchen walls.

Polly said, 'So, he's really gone?'

I nodded soberly and said yes, it was a shame he'd left the way he did, eulogising, 'You know, for a straight boy, he was alright.'

'Was he straight?' Polly looked puzzled. 'Finley told me he fucked him at Berghain once. Just after he got back from California.'

I yawned. 'Well, Berlin straight.'

She asked if I was going to advertise the room, and I told her I wasn't. My plan was to use it as a studio space for Alexander, the project was a growing concern and there was nothing like enough space in my bedroom for the two of us. Polly gave me a look of stern concern. 'Right,' she said, 'sure,' and headed into the bathroom.

It was true; I wasn't delusional, I wasn't making it up. My room was stuffed full of Alex's things already, he'd been ferrying them over in the old Mercedes nightly ever since Carl had taken his curtain call. My room had begun to look like the lost and found at Paddington Station. All his flotsam and jetsam had arrived in chaotic waves, as though he were simply grabbing whatever was to hand each evening and dashing out the door before he lost the will to execute the move. There were shopping bags full of records, Bowie mainly, and a few creaseless books in totes (he wasn't much of a reader), framed artworks, posters and prints hurriedly taped together between sheets of cardboard, three large suitcases of clothes, golf umbrellas, ski boots and a frankly unnecessary amount of cosmetics. What seemed like a significant chunk of the record label's money had been sunk into serums and cleansers, high-end lipsticks and eyeshadows he must've bought at KaDeWe, because nowhere else in the city stocked them.

To compound the mess, we had started borrowing clothes from PR agencies, leveraging Alex's growing celebrity to call in suits and shoes and capes and hats for him to wear onstage and in photo shoots, so now they too lay around the place, layered over all the rest of it, green silk tuxedos draped like old expired gentlemen across trash bags stuffed with unwashed bed linens. I was surprised at how easy it had been to get three grand's worth of tailoring couriered over, all I had had to do was email over a few press quotes and a couple of links to the contacts I'd found online. Of course I embellished some of the testimonials which starstruck journalists had apparently given Alex, but I figured, correctly, that nobody was all that likely to check too closely. I also realised quite quickly that the curter the email the quicker the response, and I always signed off as 'Stella Guinness, Executive PA to Herr Geist.'

The main benefit of all of this was, for me personally, getting to watch Alex try on Saint Laurent smoking jackets and satin shirts from Dior. When it came to playing dress-up he was quite happy to let me style him – after all, hadn't I scored the swag? We had such fun trying it all on, imagining ourselves at the Grammys; it didn't matter that it all had to go back after a week, ten days at most, paradise on loan is still bliss. Once I had him strip and step naked into a pair of black Balenciaga biker boots so I could admire him whilst he stroked his cock in front of the mirror, then when he was hard and horny, I had him come over and fuck me on the bare wooden floor of the hall. I imagined Carl was watching us.

The toilet flushed, the cistern clattered like an aged spin dryer and Polly wandered back into the empty bedroom. I was startled, I'd forgotten she was there in the apartment with me. Shaking her hands dry, flicking little beads of water off, vexed, she asked, 'Why is it you have seven kinds of toothpaste in there, but no clean hand towel?'

I smiled apologetically. 'Sorry, it's pretty disorganised around here right now, as you can see.'

The two of us were at a loose end: she was avoiding the studio and I was killing time until Alex woke up. We rummaged about together through the abandoned miscellanea of the bedroom. Polly said that if there was anything of any value I should sell it at Mauerpark, but we didn't find anything worth more than a few euros. She doodled in dust on the shelves, peered in the empty wardrobe, and I picked up scraps of paper and, failing to decipher their inscriptions, screwed them up and threw them out. I discovered a pair of white underpants behind the radiator, fished them out and tossed them to her. 'Give these to Finley,' I said. 'One final token of Carl's love.'

Polly caught them and then sniffed them and recoiled in distaste. 'Yes,' she said, 'definitely straight,' and we both giggled like Girl Scouts.

I offered to make some tea. We wandered into the kitchen and Polly plonked herself down at the table. She picked up a small parcel that was sitting there unopened. 'Who's Stella Guinness?' she asked suspiciously.

'Me,' I smiled as brightly as I could and explained the set-up. 'Well, it was Alex's idea really.'

'Honestly, you're such a scam artist, Charli,' she said. 'And what a ridiculous name! It's so stupid it's almost offensive.'

I brewed the tea and Polly told me a long, muddled story about how Callum had been using her electric razor to trim his pubes and had jammed the blades, then blamed it on Benedict, the guy she was fucking. I don't know how she had made her way to such a topic. I was thinking about Alex asleep in the bedroom next door, how I wanted to take his cock in my mouth whilst he slept so I could feel it harden in my throat.

At some point I became aware that Polly had stopped talking and that it was my turn.

I said, 'Oh really?' and turned to the fridge to fish out the milk.

'Yes well,' she concluded, 'of course I knew it was Callum because Benny doesn't have any pubic hair. He waxes religiously. Arsehole and everything.'

She poured herself another cup of tea and I did the same, she stirred in her milk. 'Oh!' she started up again. 'I didn't tell you but I saw a whole wall of your posters up in Mitte last week.'

'My posters?' I queried.

She corrected herself. 'Well, your *project*,' she said. 'Don't be so pedantic. Anyway, they looked great.'

I was suddenly very excited; I wanted to wake Alex, he would be thrilled. 'Where exactly?' I quizzed, much enlivened.

'Close to Alexanderplatz,' she said, 'funnily enough. Yes, I'd say there were about twenty or so in a row and they all said *Who is Alexander Geist?* which did seem a little counter-intuitive to me. I mean, you're trying to introduce people to this new persona . . .'

'No, no,' I said, 'it's exactly the *right* question, it gets people wondering, it generates mystique.'

I tried to explain that in show business you have to use classic reverse psychology but then the doorbell rang. I guessed that it was probably another courier and decided they could leave it outside, whatever it was. I didn't have the patience to deal with any more dinner jackets just now. The bell rang again, and again, it made me a little tense and Polly asked, 'Shouldn't you answer that? It might be something important.'

I said, 'You don't think it's the landlord, do you? Fuck. Or the police?'

'No,' she assured me. 'Don't be so paranoid, Charli. I'm sure it's just another parcel that needs a signature. I'll bring it in, don't fret so, your eyelid is spasming.'

She opened the front door and from down the corridor I heard her chatting with whoever it was out there, whoever had been so insistently ringing the bell; it sounded like the voice of a woman, an older woman, impatient and bad tempered. Polly spoke surprisingly good German, I always forgot that. The two of them were involved in quite a brisk exchange out there; I tried to decipher what it was they were talking about from the kitchen doorway without much success. Clearly she wasn't from the post office, this woman, that much I could understand, though the rest of the conversation remained veiled to me, obscured by my own ineptitude and the muddy acoustics of the hallway.

The dialogue picked up pace: it sounded pretty spicy in parts, and peaked with this unknown woman loudly and vehemently demanding to speak to someone, I don't know who. *Sofort*, she kept repeating, *sofort*, right now, straight away.

'Ich kann dir nicht helfen,' I heard Polly say. Then came the sound of the front door not exactly slamming shut, but closing conclusively all the same.

She came back flushed and clearly a little discomfited. 'It was your neighbour, from upstairs,' she said. 'The Hausmeister's wife. She wanted to talk to Carl about the noises she hears late at night. She was awfully cross.'

'Yeah,' I snorted, 'sounded like it.'

Polly sat back down. 'She said, "Tell your roommate who thinks they're David Bowie to close the curtains or I'll call the police".'

'The cheeky bitch,' I exclaimed. 'The cheeky fucking bitch!'

Polly continued, 'She was insistent that I bring her in to speak to Carl. Said she didn't want to talk about it with foreigners. She actually tried to push her way in! She seems absolutely demented.'

Intrigued, I expect by all the commotion, the cat padded into the kitchen looking cautiously regal and wound herself around Polly's ankles. Polly wiggled her finger over the cat's face and the cat pawed at her with affection, play fighting. Polly told me that I should call her David, because she deserved some dignity, and besides she was a tom. I agreed without really paying much attention or returning her lovely smile. I was too peeved, muttering into the sad grey puddle at the bottom of my cup.

'I should've answered the door myself.' I was really riled. 'Next time I'll tell her exactly where she can stick it. I know enough German words to put *that* across.'

Polly said that Benedict had been kicked out of an apartment once for something trivial like overfilling the recycling bin, and that I should take more care around my neighbours because residents' rights are taken very seriously in Germany. 'I don't know what you've been getting up to here, Charli,' she said, 'but . . .'

'I haven't been getting up to anything,' I barked defensively. 'What do you mean? Why is everybody so interested in my fucking business all of a sudden?' I slammed the cup down a little too hard and it broke on the countertop. 'Since when am I the object of such fascination?'

Polly didn't try to match my pitch. Instead, she asked sincerely, 'Charli, should I be concerned?' Cold tea dribbled down the front of the kitchen cupboard.

Alex didn't rise until very late that evening, not until well after midnight, long after Polly had gone. He was in the habit of sleeping through the day and working through the night; he said it's how Prince wrote too, it wasn't because he was depressed. I was sorry though because I thought that maybe an impromptu hang would help Alex and Polly see different sides of each other. I said, 'It's too bad you missed her. I'd really like you to get to know her better.'

'I know her well enough, I think.' He pinched at his cheek. 'Would you get my gel mask, please. From the freezer? I feel puffy.'

He had a real talent for making me feel like a maid. I was unimpressed by this brush-off but he didn't clock my annoyance, or perhaps he hadn't the energy to give to it. I went to fetch the mask; I didn't want to argue with him, but I wasn't ready to let my pique drop. I asked him why we had so much toothpaste. 'It looks like you had a manic episode in the chemist,' I said, 'who needs *seven* tubes of toothpaste?'

He looked at me as though I were being extremely petty and explained that he had taken one of each of the most natural-looking tubes because he was pressed for time, wasn't able to read the ingredients before the store closed and needed to be sure he got something without fluoride. 'It is a dangerous drug, Charli,' he said. 'It calcifies the pineal eye, you know? It interferes with your dreams and your visions.'

I didn't quarrel with him; I knew from his pale expression that his spirits were low. 'Oh,' I said, 'of course.'

'You know I need a clear head,' he sighed, 'when there is such a lot of work.'

Moritz had booked a recording studio for the end of the month but Alex did not feel that his material was ready. Now that the vaporous fantasy of making his record was solidifying, he seemed almost afraid of the weight and the mass of the dream. I told him that he'd feel better once he got down to it, that nerves were only to be expected, but he paid me no mind, he didn't even dress.

I made him some fennel tea and he sat sipping it on the sofa, bundled nude under a big tartan blanket, notebook open on his lap, pencil limp between his idle fingers, watching the cat bat at one particular shoe which she seemed to find unspeakably evil. I noticed the blanket had a great big cigarette burn in it and that pained me, the same way it does to watch a flower die. It fell from his shoulders and revealed his torso, naked and emaciated. It was a heavy, melodramatic scene with shades of *let this cup pass from me*, though I doubt Christ wore a cooling gel mask in the Garden of Gethsemane. Looking at him that evening no one would have recognised him as being on the brink of stardom. He didn't want to talk, he didn't want to fuck, he was lost in his own secret, catastrophising.

I found the atmosphere a little suffocating so discreetly excused myself and went to finish rearranging Carl's empty room, sweeping the old tissues and odd socks from under the bed, collecting cups, tinkering with the answerphone which had been the source of so much strife, trying to puzzle out how to reset the outgoing message, wiping down the desktop and putting a new bulb in the lamp. At times like this I pictured myself as Céleste Albaret, the woman who kept house for Proust for the last ten years of his life. Service was a way to give my life meaning.

When the room was decent I felt restored and ready to turn in. I am a firm believer in going to bed in a good mood whenever possible, because I find it always sets the table for pleasant dreams. The time on the answerphone read 03.33, though I don't think it was accurate. I decided that I should ask Alex if he needed anything else before I went to bed.

I tiptoed down the hall so as not to disturb him if he were writing, into my lawless bedroom where I found him quite conscious but unaware of me, smiling at himself in the mirror. I watched from the doorway as he ran through a whole parade of grimaces, from tight sadistic little smirks to broad, full grins, trying each on, searching for the right fit. I loved looking at him, he was so elegant. He still wore the mask though it couldn't possibly be cold anymore. He didn't notice me until he had circled through all of his smiles a few times over, sneer, beam, simper, leer, until the cat, darting from the room and through my legs, brought my presence to his attention.

Without any expressed surprise, he turned towards me, captious, in calm reproach. 'Charli,' he said, 'you must not hang around in doorways like that staring at people. It is very sinister, you know?'

17

There was a nun in my doorway this morning, she reminded me of someone. I thought she might come in only she seems to be in some sort of mortal standoff with the nursing staff. I've seen them all talking in the corridor, the doctor explaining I don't know what with open palm gesticulations, my nurse standing immovable, arms folded across her chest, determined. I think maybe the good sister is trying to come in and offer me some spiritual guidance, which I'm very much in need of at this particular juncture. I want to ask her to pray with me for the repose of Alex's soul. The nurse must be a Lutheran, probably doesn't go in for any such popery. I'll ask if I can at least have a book then, since I haven't been allowed a single visitor.

It's a disgrace. They keep you in hospital full of God knows what medication, or worse they look at the inexplicable developments in your life, and try to explain it all away with psychology, like academics arguing that all of Hildegard von Bingen's visions of God were actually just migraines. Fiery light of exceeding brilliance came and permeated my whole brain, and inflamed my whole heart and my whole breast – *does that sound like a headache to you? Her visions started at the age of three, but she was smart enough to keep a lid on it until she was a respected Abbess. She wasn't ever asked to leave a Pizza Express for accusing the chef of serving human flesh.*

There are scenes that play on my eyelids, in my Kopfkino, *as they say in German, which are so extraordinary they almost seem like hallucinations, only I know they are real. The paparazzi swarm Alexander outside Martin-Gropius-Bau, an upright piano plays itself in the cafe at Dussmanns, West turns away from me in the hall, two swans entwined by their long slim necks float down the Spree frozen solid in a block of ice. I see these images with perfect lucidity, but I am not a saint so I do not know what they mean. This is the line then, between mystic and crackpot, seer and lunatic, the power to translate. The voice of God commanded Saint Hildegard 'Speak therefore of these wonders' and insisted that she make the world listen, and the world did listen, kings and queens and popes. But when I try to tell my nurse what I have seen, she simply scribbles in displeasure on my chart. When I tell her that it is not my face in the bathroom mirror, when I scream that the radio news is lying to me again, she can only shake her head dolefully and say, 'Ach! Such things are no good for you, try for sleep,' because I have fallen on the wrong side of the dividing line.*

18

By late spring Alexander was popping up everywhere, first on local radio in Berlin, then on television, in magazines and in newspapers. He went from playing gigs in nightclubs and bars to concert halls; Moritz said if he kept it up he'd be headlining stadiums by the autumn. He put together a band for Alex, keyboard, saxophone, drums, they worked out of a practice room up in Pankow. Sometimes we saw Blixa Bargeld there, he winked at me once, in the elevator, and I squealed. We were delirious, it was punishing, putting in eighteen-hour days as standard, barely eating, swigging Hinoki in the back of the car between writing sessions and press interviews, fittings and label meetings, rehearsing most nights until way past 1 a.m.

The band recorded Alexander's first single for Arial Records, and the track so impressed Moritz's label partners in the USA that they slipped us a little cryptic cash to shoot a video. Moritz said that this was 'very significant'. Alex was thrilled, he was so happy that he gave a €100 bill to a junkie in the doorway of Karstadt and promised to buy us front row seats the next time Romy Haag played in Berlin. You might chalk it up to sheer unfounded naivety, to youthful vigour, or to the fact that we were smoking top-notch heroin in the plush bathrooms of the recording studio, but all the same it really seemed that there was an undeniable buzz around the endeavour, and it made us feel sacrosanct, golden. Alex was ready now; he had it all in hand, he assured me.

The invitations to perform poured in all spring, and though Moritz advised me never to take the first offer, the second or third was usually too good to turn down. Where all of those performance fees went, I truly do not know. Perhaps into an offshore bank account, perhaps directly into the label's coffers, who can say? There was always so damn much to think about with each and every gig that I had to leave the banking to somebody else's attention. With the musicians and the costumes and the tour photographer it was neither a cheap nor an uncomplicated operation to run.

Alex played a show to launch a new flavour of Fanta, watermelon, I think; he performed at a billionaire's birthday party in the dining room of the TV tower; and he gave a full concert at the Deutsche Oper to mark their hundredth anniversary, a show which caused great anxiety because somebody mentioned in passing that a student had been shot dead there in the sixties, protesting the Shah of Iran's visit. Alex was always very sensitive to these sorts of things; at one point he refused to go on stage for fear of the student's angry ghost.

'Will this make me complicit?' he asked. 'In the murder? I do not want to attract a negative energy, not now.' He sounded not unlike my mother.

I was steaming a rail of pussy-bow blouses for the band and nodding sympathetically to signify I heard and understood and cared. I didn't know how to answer, but thankfully Moritz was on hand to assure him that it had all happened *outside* of the building, and that there was no way the bad vibes could affect him *inside*. They agreed that Alexander would do it in memory of the murdered student; really it was only a happy coincidence that the fee was as handsome as it was.

Moritz was such a smooth operator, he knew how to handle Alex better than just about anyone. I was very grateful for this on days when I couldn't get him to answer interview questions or even out of bed, though I was terribly jealous too. Sometimes I noticed him fuss Alex's hair, or touch his shoulder to calm him down, and it made me indignant.

I was always off to the side but waiting on hand should Alex need anything, should an interview go awry, should a band member turn up late or stoned and require discipline. I suppose I was something like his agent, only I didn't ever get my 20 per cent. Of course, I wasn't ever expecting a cut. I didn't have the experience or the connections to warrant such a thing. I was there to support someone I cared for, and anyway how likely was it that I'd ever again witness such a star being born? Alex seemed grateful, or at least reassured, to have me there. He hadn't ever asked me to take on so much responsibility, though he never tried to dissuade me either, and certainly he made good use of me. I felt contented and requisite, and despite all the lessons from history, I didn't ever see myself as just another Margaret Keane, a Baroness Elsa von Freytag-Loringhoven, or an Angie Bowie.

Whenever Alex had a night off I would shake down Moritz to find out what was happening where: if a movie was premiering, which Michelin-starred chef had an opening, where the most exciting private view was being held. We would go over direct from the rehearsal room, sometimes with the band in tow, as a way to flex, to test the limits of Alexander Geist's new star power. Increasingly his profile gave us carte blanche to crash almost any party in Berlin, all we had to do was call ahead from the studio to let the club or the restaurant know that he was coming over and there'd be a table waiting or an open bar. We were introduced by the staff as treasured guests, sometimes people stood up and applauded. I told Alex I'd seen this happen to the Queen Mother once when I had tea at the Ritz for my thirteenth birthday. He said, 'Yes, I like to be with the rich. They make me feel safe.'

This kind of attention follows you though, whether you want it to or not, it doesn't dissipate, it lives a long half-life and that can be hard to manage. Ever since I had known him, Alex had been working out at a very fancy gym on Hermannplatz, just across from Karstadt. He ran on the treadmill every day whilst watching reality TV, and took Pilates and yoga classes several times a week too; he was proud of his lithe form, he was building towards the stamina needed to complete a world tour. His growing popularity, however, meant that he could now only work out at 5 a.m., and still it was likely that someone would come up and ask him, 'Excuse me, but aren't you . . .' as he crunched through his reps. It was the same on the U-Bahn and in supermarkets, the ineluctable ectoplasm of fame. Seemingly everywhere we went people stared, though I suppose the sight of this wan figure waiting in line at the Lidl checkout in a crushed satin frock coat was somewhat unusual.

'I think we should start shopping at better places,' he said, disdainful as I bagged up our orange juice and ham, 'this is too degrading.' Who was it who said, 'If you're going to be rich and famous, make sure you're rich'? One of the Beatles maybe. I forget now.

I remember being with him one evening, drunk at a gallery where they were showing new works by Gerhard Richter. Nick Cave and Neil Gaiman were arguing about veganism just a few metres away, one of the original supermodels arrived with her toddler, photographers were going crazy over it all; Alex was perfectly at peace there. He looked at me and whispered playfully, 'Success.'

In these atmospheres he excelled, as if he had been created expressly for them, and when people came over to talk, as they freely and constantly did, he could, there in all that reflected glory, chat with the greatest ease and charm. It was palpable that Alexander Geist was a star in the making, all the papers said so, and people wanted in on the action. He shook hands with famous film directors and posed for pictures with soccer players and fashion designers, the restaurant owner or the club's publicist making the most incongruous of introductions with the intent of maximising publicity. He handled himself with such cursive grace, it was almost impossible to reconcile this Alexander with the other, his identical twin, who fell into such moods of despondent anxiety at home that I frequently had to slice his salami and feed it to him. Still, I was always glad to see him shine, happy to watch him radiate charisma and dazzle, at one with all the other stars of the immeasurable night sky.

I woke up early one morning in the midst of all this, very early, well before noon. I couldn't sleep, but Alex was dead to the world. I slipped out of bed and checked the inbox: lots of spam, one legal threat and a magazine journalist who had emailed to say the piece she'd written was on the shelves today. Her editor had liked it so much he'd made it the cover story. I thought about waking Alex but thought better of it: Moritz had come into rehearsal the night before and had kept him really late. I decided to let him sleep and surprise him over breakfast. I wrote back to the journalist, 'Amazing news! So so happy about this. Best, Stella x' then I rushed out to get a copy from the tobacconist in the basement of Karstadt. Whilst I was there I picked up a carton of Sobranies and a Cuban cigar; I went into the food hall and bought chorizo and speck, orange juice and a decent bottle of Sekt. Alexander was sure to be delighted.

When I got back the cat was in the bed but Alex himself was gone, he'd scribbled 'Had to see Moritz xxx' on a Post-it and stuck it to the bathroom mirror. It felt like an insult, though he couldn't possibly have meant to hurt me. He hadn't even known where I'd gone – really in writing the note he was proving himself more courteous than I, don't you think?

I was disappointed but of course I still I wanted to celebrate the moment, here was Alexander Geist's first magazine cover! I didn't know when he would be back, so I took the Sekt and the sausages over to see Polly and Finley at the studio. They had a small kitchen there: we could mark the occasion together. As Polly had done the makeup for the shoot, I decided I would gift her the magazine and pick up another copy later.

When I arrived Finley was priming a canvas with a small can of gesso and Polly was drinking tea. They were arguing about Jeff Koons. 'I just think he's crass,' Polly said, 'he's gauche.'

I showed them the magazine, gushing with pride. Alexander smouldering on the cover in a golden kimono, lounging across the green leather tabletop of a library desk at the Grimm-Zentrum. Inside, groomed like a prize-winning spaniel, he ran through the stacks in a leather jacket and riding pants, frothy, lurid, foppish. 'And, as requested,' I noted, 'your *Beauty by Trudy* credit is right there.'

Polly hopped up. 'Trudy! You know, I'd almost forgotten about her? I ought to start a scrapbook.'

Off from the side Finley chimed, 'You two literally are insane, you should hear yourselves . . .'

We put the Sekt in the fridge. Polly said it was too early to start drinking. They both needed to work, but I was welcome to hang out in the studio. I asked if I could smoke and Finley said it was fine as long as I stayed over by the window. It must've been the very tail end of April because the sky was bright blue but the radiator was still warm to the touch. I read the magazine article sitting on the window ledge. The journalist was clearly very taken with Alex, she called him 'a disco debutant beloved for his erotic moodiness' and 'Berlin's daring darling'. I wondered if maybe she had a little crush on him, the thought made me bristle.

The article was ten pages long, including a six-page picture portfolio, lustrous full-colour spreads; the band in a heap on the library floor, a portrait of Alex sitting at a desk, sober and immediate, his eyelids a little heavy, his lips the colour of a forbidden fruit, set in an attitude of hauteur. There were also a few casual snapshots tossed in to break up the text, black-and-white and off the cuff: Alex signing something for an admirer outside Café Grosz, Alex behind the wheel of his Mercedes, Alex at the studio with Moritz. It was a very thorough profile.

The writer asked about his musical influences, he listed Bowie, Arthur Russell, Sparks; she asked if he was looking forward to touring Europe over the summer, he said he couldn't wait. Rather provocatively she asked if he was aware that the lead singer of the Mud Club Kidz, Jason Viber, had called him a 'manufactured phoney' in a recent TV interview, and he replied that no, he hadn't known but that also, he didn't care. He quoted a line from F. Scott Fitzgerald, 'one of his favourite writers' he said. '*The best thing to be in life is a beautiful fool*,' adding dryly, 'and Jason is halfway there already, one day he may grow into his looks also.' It was funny, sure, but I knew he'd never even read that book, and this nettled me.

I heard Polly say, 'That's what I mean, he's crass. He bought himself a career with all the money he made in finance, but that doesn't make him *a baller*.'

Finley rebuffed her. 'Girl, I never said he was a baller. I said he was a realist, OK? He understands the market.'

'Good God,' she rolled her eyes. 'He makes sculptures of *balloon animals*.'

Further down, the article listed some of Alexander's recent achievements and illustrated his road to success with burbling praise from fans and the band and Moritz: he was 'on fire,' they exclaimed, 'a Gesamtkunstwerk', 'an indisputable artist'. The journalist probed Alex for info on the upcoming music video, but he remained tight-lipped; they discussed at some length his fascination with driving around the city at night. When she asked about his love life, he brushed off the question. 'I'm seeing a few people,' he said, 'but no one special.'

I felt my jaw tense up, my throat was very dry but my teacup was empty now. I wondered who these *few people* might be. Naturally my eyes returned to the picture of Alex and Moritz in the studio, sitting side by side at the mixing desk, not quite touching. Alex wore a white shirt unbuttoned to the sternum under a dark jacket and a small wry smile. Moritz had rolled up the sleeves of an expensive-looking sweatshirt. He held a cigarette, or a joint, between his long slim fingers. The two of them seemed to be quite openly sharing a secret. I hated myself because I wanted to be in that picture with them, on my knees before them. The sliver of dead space between them seemed to quiver with an appetite. *No one special?* I thought, *You bastard.*

Polly said, 'My mother knew him when we were kids. We had one of his basketballs. George stabbed it with a penknife though because she grounded him for smoking weed on Christmas Day.'

Finley guffawed. 'Shut up! Shut the fuck up!'

Polly chewed on her paintbrush. 'You know, George does look an awful lot like him. I always thought that was simply *too much* of a coincidence.'

'Oh my God!' Finley whooped. 'Girl, are you for real? Is your brother hot?'

I was broiling too steadily with resentment to follow the rest. I closed the magazine but did not leave it for Polly. The thought that she might read what Alex had said was too excruciating. I felt too ashamed.

19

I did not change the locks or throw Alex's records out of the window and onto the street or cut holes in his favourite jacket. I had decided to do nothing with my anger, nothing but wait. He didn't come back for another three days.

It's not that revenge didn't occur to me, didn't appeal to me, because it did, only I doubted that he would notice, or even care that much. He was so blasé about his belongings it was almost reckless, he left something behind almost every time we went out, a scarf, a lighter, his keys. He racked up close to €1,000 in unpaid penalty notices in a little over six months because he parked his old Mercedes so carelessly, across driveways, against the flow of traffic. The only object he had ever paid any real attention to was his cigarette case, and even that spent much of its time knocking about in my room, waiting for his return, so it could hardly be said that he cherished it. Besides, I was sure he had a double: he had at least two of everything, living his life like a tech bro with me as the mistress in his holiday home. He was equally negligent with his money: he never knew how much he had, and he never had much. He lost multiple credit cards, he seemed to shed small bills and coins everywhere he sat to rest, like a cat casting off her winter coat. Often when Alex was away I would collect all the loose change he spilled about the place and scoop it up into a spaghetti jar, just for something to do.

This time I gave the place a real thorough going over, found €87.60 in ones and fives and coinage, bringing my grand total to €350, which I spent, perhaps a little rashly, on a roll-neck cashmere sweater I had seen marked down at Prada. It was too warm out to wear it now, but I was playing the long game.

When I got back from my shopping trip there was a concatenation of messages on the answerphone from Moritz, growing incrementally in urgency.

I hadn't been at the fitting with the costume designer, I hadn't returned any of his emails. We were shooting the music video that weekend and though he couldn't *imagine* how something as momentous as this would've slipped my mind, he wanted to make sure I'd be there. 'Seriously,' he said, terse, fraying, 'call me back already. You're stressing us all the fuck out.'

One after another I erased all of his messages, excoriating him internally for his audacity and priming myself to call his wife, ultimately thinking better of it – I could strike harder. If I was no one special then I was under no obligation to return anyone's call, under no obligation to do anything other than read Henry James in my underwear, until such a time as I saw fit. This was how I would wait it out, pure, unhurried passive-aggression. *I don't know, Alex, why do you think I'm pissed off?*

The cat had warmed to me: I was after all the one feeding her. She came to sit on my lap and I swaddled her like a baby in my new sweater. I smoked a whole pack of Sobranies while I watched *Lost Highway*, and ate a jar of olives and drank porn star martini–flavoured energy drinks. The phone was quiet all through supper, but it rang again around midnight. I heard a new voice on the machine, it was Finley. He said, 'Hey, Charli, you there?'

I picked up and we chatted, he was stoned, he had a plus one for Gegen and asked if I'd like go. 'I invited Polly,' he told me, 'but she said she'd rather die.'

Gegen was the gateway to a seventy-two-hour weekend. It took place every second month at the KitKatClub: not the glitzy joint Isherwood frequented before the war, because that never actually existed, but an homage to it of sorts in the remains of another old factory in Kreuzberg. It was always an absolute free-for-all: 2,000 people in drag, leather, neon body paint, hard techno, hard drugs, it's where you went to forget your own existence and get fucked on the dance floor. I popped the tab on another can and arranged to meet Finley there around two.

On the door, a giant bug-eyed creature scoured the guest list for my name; she asked me to spell *Hughes* several times over but still she couldn't find it. She looked me up and down, from head to toe, and asked me if anyone had ever told me that I looked just like *Alexander Guest*. I lied and said 'No,' so she began elbowing her colleague demanding corroboration. 'Doesn't she though,' she said, 'doesn't she look like him? The singer.'

The colleague worked on her vape pen, disinterested. 'Yeah, I guess.'

It wasn't the first time someone had pointed out the resemblance of course, not even the fifth, though I couldn't really see it myself. The first few times I found it cute, but it quickly began to grate. I didn't relish being told that I looked like a man. Alex said that it was only natural: 'People are always attracted by their doppelgängers,' he had said, 'surely you know this?' I found that endearing I admit, and I agreed that maybe in the slant of our brow, the slimness of our nose, there was some suggestion of kinship.

'It's Geist,' I corrected, though it made me feel dumb, 'not Guest. He's my brother.'

'For real?' The girl with the clipboard's expression had changed completely, she looked at me in something like wonderment. She stamped the back of my hand and said, 'You should've told me girl, go straight in.'

The place was packed. Finley hadn't specified where, when he said to meet him *inside*. I pushed my way across one of the dance floors, then the other, but it was too dark to see anybody properly and too loud to call out. I walked back on myself through the smoking area and past the sofas full of boys in bikinis making out, but I didn't find him there either. I saw Ryan and Suzanne outside by the pool; they were heading inside to watch the live acts, a Greek performance artist and a Brazilian rapper. They told me they'd seen Finley earlier, downstairs looking for drugs. I ran into Callum too, dressed in a PVC singlet with a zip-through crotch and knee-high spike-heeled boots. He was so skinny he looked like one of those merrymaking skeletons you see gloating through medieval manuscripts. He hadn't seen Finley yet. 'I want to though,' he said, and ran a hand over his plasticky crotch, 'if you know what I mean.' I laughed mechanically and he offered me some ketamine. *In for a penny*, I thought.

He opened a tinfoil wrap out on the cracked melamine of a freestanding bar table, slid aside a heavy glass ashtray and racked up lines with the spine of his health insurance card. The crystals sparkled so blue, so pretty, it was hard to believe that it was horse tranquilliser that he was chopping up. 'Do *not* tell Polly,' I said, 'she'd be so mad.' Callum grinned demonically.

I promised him that when I found Finley I would tell him he was wanted. Callum put my hand on his crotch and said, 'Swear on my balls,' which I did, though it seemed a little meaningless: I wasn't at all invested in his junk. I wondered if he understood how oaths were supposed to work. I thanked him for the drugs, wiped my palms on my skirt and headed downstairs. 'Don't forget,' he said, 'you owe me.'

In the basement it felt 5 degrees cooler. Red bulbs illuminated a brick network of strange little rooms and forgotten concavities, a passage opening intermittently onto sudden gaping spaces where people had gathered in more intimate bunches to smoke and drink. A dedicated few danced to the music that came tumbling down the stairs from the DJ set; one huddle seemed to be pooling money together for a big purchase; another broke out in peppery laughter and Italian curse words, *Putana! Che due coglioni! Putana!* Two of the Swedish boys from Polly's dinner party, tall and naked, ran through the room shrieking playfully, one chasing the other with a brilliant blue slushy, throwing handfuls of it, great globs of icy liquid splashing over the shoulders and faces of the other partygoers. No anger, no shock, no bad vibes: in fact I saw someone lick a cerulean smear from the back of their hand and swallow it as the two disappeared again, perhaps hoping for the happiest trace of LSD.

I found an alcove for myself in the corner of the basement and lit a cigarette. I like to watch people, people who are unaware of my presence. Alexander called it 'a minor perversion' of mine. In the supermarket I often read the back of a box of cake mix with fostered absorption again and again, so as to cover my study of the other shoppers and their mindless little tics and bumblings. In libraries too I like to stand silent and watch the patrons read, just to satisfy my curiosity, observing human life from a short distance. Inconspicuously I soaked up the swelling party crowd, leant on the wall half concealed by shadow, and admired their effortless ability to be. I felt just a little woozy.

A heap had formed, catty-corner to my hidey hole, five or six bodies not quite static, wriggling like larvae in subtle pleasure. I could discern limbs, arched backs, wigs and bra straps, and just one face, puckered in joy, rising to the surface as if to gasp for air. They were fucking of course, but from my vantage point the scene looked like seventies arthouse: an outstretched arm, a flash of bush, the peachy sheen of sweat on the muscular globes of an arse, the back of a head rising and falling, painterly flesh and a blameless atmosphere. Weightless as I was all over, I stood holding the dusty wall. I watched the bodies on the floor and the people who stopped to look on with their cocks in their hands and the people who came to watch these voyeurs jerk off. I saw how an expression of pure pornography would intermittently play across that one appreciable face in the fuck pile, a countenance of lordly satisfaction that said, 'I did all this. This is my power.'

I remembered that I was looking for Finley, and gradually eased myself off the bricks. I went on instinct alone back upstairs towards the swimming pool, telling myself that I would surely find him there: all cats come to lap at the water's edge eventually. I moved against the flow of the crowd who were heading en masse towards the main space, towards the headline set, a much-anticipated performance, a Polish DJ, a Latvian bodybuilder who sucked his own dick on-stage, I don't know, I was floating. I think I saw Mrs Campbell-Bannerman and the Hausmeister's wife, the two of them deep in hurried conversation, I spotted Callum again but no Finley, saw the slushy kids wrapped up together in a beach towel. I put my head down and pressed on through them all, not quite unnoticed, and came out poolside.

It wasn't very much more than an ornamental pond for swingers, but I had great affection for that pool. On my first ever visit to Berlin I had watched Polly and Finley dive-bomb the silky water naked and thought *who needs the Chateau Marmont?* I didn't ever dip myself in though; I was a little squeamish, I suppose. I didn't see how any volume of chlorine could keep that water clean. I liked to sit at the side of the pool and chat.

Around me people smoked joints and stripped to their underwear. Someone slapped the face of a friend who had taken too much of something, repeatedly, to revive them. I knelt and imagined myself on the shores of a lake on Saturn's largest moon, Titan. I watched the ripples and the waves, the neon refractions of the bar lights in the glassy shimmer, the reflection of the night sky pouring in though the open cloister roof. I let my hands go as limp as an abandoned marionette and dangled my fingers in the pool. I traced the infinity symbol over and over, frothing up the water with little flurries of my digits, marvelling at how my hand grew in size below the surface. I could see the bottom of the pool, though I could not reach it, or rather I feared I would slip if I tried, and I knew this was very much to be avoided.

I caught my own image looking up at me and it made me laugh, so I brought my face closer then pulled back away, up and down a couple more times, as if I were doing push-ups poolside, just so that I could repeat the thrill of coming face to face with myself in this liquid mirror. It came to my mind how as a child of five or six I had seen someone staring up at me from the milky puddle at the bottom of my teacup and had frozen in fear. I remember somehow being aware that to scream and cry about it would be not only naughty but also dangerous, that if I stayed quiet there was a chance that the monster in the milk might not notice me. For years afterwards, I kept my eyes closed or averted whenever I drank from a cup, honouring this unspoken deal I had made with the devil.

I don't know when exactly I made the connection between the faces, but I must've been about ten. I seem to recall it was around the time my mother banned all television news in the house. Even into adolescence my reflection would startle me, and I would be scared again for a moment, not by the presence of a monster, but by the memory of how I had once been that little boy, and how I had been unable to ask for help. I would feel such relief when I realised that I was no longer him, that sweet, defenceless child. It was like waking from a nightmare to know that I didn't live in that reality anymore, not really. Yet still we were tied, he and I, and I was plagued with survivor's guilt, burdened with the remorse of having left that little boy there alone behind me.

An uncanny, artificial laughter rose up from the party as if from the past to mock me. Even against the absurdity of the situation I leant right out over my reflection, like Narcissus above his ruinous lily pond, balancing on my forearms, and spoke to the face in the water. The lips moved in symphony as I spoke. 'It's OK Charles,' I said. 'It's all OK now. It's me, your big sister.' The happy face below me wobbled about, a gentle expression of fraternal affection, and though a smile had come to my lips, an unexpected tear concurrently spilled from my eye.

A fleet shadow fell on the pool, a presence loomed behind me, a true voice in my ear, steady, refined and adult: 'Charli, dear, you're a bit too close to the edge there. Why don't you come and have a little sit down, with me?'

'Don't I know you?' I asked the semi-remembered face, and it said, 'Yes, dear, it's Hubert. Now come away from the edge, there's a good girl.'

Hubert, the name was only very vaguely familiar, the sound of it came to me on a gentle wave of Bach with a side of Kartoffelsalat. By degrees I realised it was that funny old fellow from the supper party, *Hubert*. He had been watching me for a while. I felt a little embarrassed, so I guess I was sobering up. I explained that I wasn't in any danger, that I'd only been talking to my former self. He guided me patiently by the arm, towards a row of grimy sun loungers, and said, 'Well, yes, it's always nice to see old friends, isn't it?'

Jamie was watching our slow return from the other side of the pool; for a moment I forgot how much I hated him. I gave him an innoxious smile, raised my hand in a wave. He looked back at me blankly. 'Charli,' he said, 'you look like shit.'

I was aware that half of my hair had come down about my shoulders. There was a great streak of lipstick and mascara across the back of my hand, I checked for my skirt to make sure I was still wearing it.

In the way of neutral small talk Hubert started in on a long story about going backstage at a Bowie concert, how the rest of the band called him 'Jonesy' and moaned that he made them visit museums whenever they went on tour. I was nodding and smiling and sipping slowly on a gin and tonic. I didn't want to seem impolite, but I knew that if I drank it too quickly I would spew, so I concentrated all of my remaining energy on keeping my eyes focused and my torso upright. I lit a cigarette to revitalise myself and tried to remember what I was doing there, but the thread had snapped. Hubert ramped towards a big finish. 'Bloody 'ell, Jonesy,' he said, 'we're in a bloody rock band we don't wanna go to a bloody art gallery!' He approximated a broad Yorkshire accent pretty well, I thought. I gave him the biggest grin I could offer. 'Yes,' I said, 'quite.'

Jamie looked me over in distaste. 'I saw your friend downstairs, the Turkish guy. He looked really messed up.'

'Oh?' I was confused. 'You mean Finley?' A sense of panic fluttering in the distance. 'Is he OK?' A sudden shock of sobriety.

'I dunno,' he smirked. 'He was like naked and vomiting so . . .' He took the glass from my hand: the drink must've been his.

I turned to Hubert to excuse myself. I mumbled, 'I think I should go,' and Jamie jumped back in, 'Yeah you *really* should scurry along now. West is with him and I know how much you *love* my sloppy seconds.'

An unanticipated flash of rage lit me up like a Chinese cracker. I squared up to him full of bent valour. 'One of these days Jamie,' I growled, 'so help me God . . .' The colour drained from his face.

I dropped my cigarette into his drink and it went out with a satisfying hiss. I gave Hubert a kiss on the cheek, then hurried off to find Finley.

20

Finley was sitting on the ledge of a bricked-up window. He was naked besides one sock; he looked tired but not at any risk of collapse. West was sitting with him, trying to keep his feet out of the puddle of puke on the floor. They both seemed pleased to see me. Finley said, 'Hey, girl, I was looking for you.' His knuckles were bloody; he'd been in a fight with the wall. I told him Callum wanted to see him and he said, 'Girl, how do you think I got so fucked up?'

West looked so calm and ingenuous beside him. I don't think they'd even kissed. I asked what he thought of the party, and he said that he didn't usually come, Gegen freaked him out because it was so huge and so unpredictable. 'There's shagging in one corner and then someone overdosing in the other,' he said. 'You know what I mean? It's so . . .' He stopped to consider the word. 'Disparate.'

'Yeah, true.' I thought of *Brighton Rock* and agreed that '*Good and evil lived in the same country*.' I said, 'A party is a lot like life.'

Finley looked at me sideways, dubious, he said, 'Girl, you are too much sometimes.'

I realised that I had either left my cigarettes upstairs or dropped them on my ramblings. West produced a pack from his bum bag and passed them over. 'Here you go,' he smiled, 'knock yourself out.' I offered one to Finley, he declined and said he needed to go home. I said I'd walk with him but he wanted to be alone.

I was a little worried; I asked him if he was angry with me. He rolled his eyes in exhaustion. 'Come on, seriously. I just wanna get home, jerk off and go to sleep, OK?'

West guffawed and I coloured a little. 'OK, OK, I get it,' I said, embarrassed, 'keep your sock on!' He laughed at last and I relaxed.

His clothes were upstairs in the cloakroom, his bike was locked up outside. He wrapped me in a bear hug. I told him he smelled terrible so he rubbed himself on me all the more. We said goodnight affably and made plans to have lunch at the studio next week. He toddled off down the brickwork corridor, his bare arse all covered in dust like powdered sugar on a doughnut. 'You know,' said West, 'I don't think I've ever met someone so completely uninhibited.'

'Yeah,' I nodded. 'He's the best.'

I thanked West for sitting with Finley; he said it was no problem, he'd just given him some lemon water and kept him talking, that's all, it was no big deal. He lit a cigarette for himself, it seemed indecent that someone so sweet would have such a vice, it was unnatural, like getting the flu in July. I wanted to tell him to put it out, to warn him against ruining himself, but of course that would've been ridiculous. He cleared his throat and we sat and smoked, watching clutches of revellers stagger about, swerving to avoid Finley's puke just in time. Somewhere above us it was dawn.

'I called you,' he said, 'a few times, but it always goes to voicemail. You have *the* strangest outgoing message.'

I nodded. 'Yeah, I can't figure out how to change it.'

We made small talk for a while longer. I said that I'd been busy with my PhD research; he was impressed and asked me if I'd secured funding yet. I admitted that I had not – I joked that at this rate I was going to have to turn to prostitution or start selling bottles of piss to pay my way. I said that I'd actually seen somebody offer €20 per litre online, and, level-headed, he nodded. 'To think I've been giving it away all these years for free.'

I was both tickled and scandalised. I demanded to know to whom he had been giving his piss so gratuitously, he gestured towards the bathroom with his thumb and said there was a guy on his knees at the urinals who asked so nicely that it seemed a shame to waste it.

I threw back my head, unrestrained, and hooted, 'You are having me on!'

'I'm not,' he insisted and, emboldened, moved closer. He dropped his voice to a burlesque whisper. 'He said it was "So gelb, sehr lecker." So yellow, very tasty.'

'Dehydrated?' I teased.

'No,' he said. 'It's my magnesium supplement, actually. It makes me piss fluorescent.'

I must've been coming down because all I could think of now was how nice it would be to take a hot bath. I recognised that I was feeling cold. I wanted to sink beneath huge ice caps of bubble bath, I wanted to feel the heat bring my veins to the surface, I wanted to rinse off the past six months. I looked into the pool of vomit at our feet and I said, 'Do you ever worry that you'll never get clean again?'

If he had such a concern he didn't show it, instead he leant forward and kissed me with a coyness that flowered into passion. My head filled with a rush of blood and my ears rang, I took in the mix of sweat and tobacco and perhaps patchouli on his skin. His tongue was lithe and muscular, and maybe I was still a little high after all, because behind my eyes I saw two snakes knotting together and I felt a sudden steely heat radiate from my body and I wondered how it would feel to ride his face. One strap of my slip dress had fallen down my shoulder, slightly exposing the chubby curve of my breast. I guided it back into place with two extended fingers, West surveying me like a thing of wonder.

'Cigarette for the road?' I said.

It was after 6 a.m. when we got back to my apartment. I made him take his shoes off before we even ascended the staircase, expounding on how my dictatorial neighbour already had it in for me, on account of all the noise she claimed I made at ungodly hours. 'She's the Hausmeister's wife,' I explained, 'she really could get me thrown out.'

As it was, the building was pin-drop still, and it wasn't until I turned my key in the lock that the thought occurred to me that Alex might himself be at home: he had keys after all, and a perverse sense of timing. I wavered on the doorstep, thinking that I might have to send West away, because there was a light on in the hallway. The weight of dread only lifted once I realised we were in fact home alone. There were no other signs of life besides the mournful squall of the poor forsaken cat.

West said, 'This is a nice place, do you have it all to yourself?'

'I do now,' I said.

I walked into the bathroom, tossing my jacket aside as I went.

West took himself for a glass of water. 'I'll be right with you,' I called, 'I just need to pee.'

I started to run the bath, poured in half a bottle of lime-flower foam, some deathly expensive stuff Alex had bought with money from his advance. I rooted through the laundry basket for the two freshest looking towels.

The bathroom light was over-bright and horribly unflattering, so I turned it off and lit a few tea lights instead, and a candle left over from Christmas. It smelled like cloves and ginger, and I hoped West wouldn't notice, or if he did that he'd laugh it off. He had a pretty good sense of humour, very good-natured, a good kisser too. All of a sudden I found myself feeling shy. *Get a grip*, I commanded, *you're just running a bath for some boy you picked up. You don't have to make such a big deal out of everything!* I sat on the toilet, not to piss, simply to collect my thoughts and watch the bubbles rising, great sheets of mist floating off the water and through the room.

Polly used to say that my love of baths was the singular thing about me which made her unsure if I really was a Bette or a Joan, since Crawford famously thought it was beyond disgusting to float in your own filth. 'Baths aside,' she mused, 'I'd say you were quite clearly a Joan: same libido, same temperament too.'

West appeared in the doorway holding two tumblers. 'Wow,' he said, acknowledging the foam and the flickering candles, 'are we filming a Celine Dion video in here or what?' He laughed at his own joke. 'I made you a drink.'

He passed me a glass and I took it timidly, saying thanks and tucking my hair behind my ear. He told me it was a highball. 'Well, sort of,' he smiled. 'You didn't have any seltzer so I used Mineralwasser, mit Gas. Cheers.'

'Cheers.' I clinked my glass against his, then sipped. 'You're extremely useful to have around.'

The bath was by now full: all there was for it was to strip. In the candlelight West looked preternaturally handsome, his hair a dirty sort of honeyed blonde with heavy roots, a sheen of perspiration on his forehead where the immense heat and the bath's steam made contact and settled. I could smell him. I took his chin in my hand and tilted his face up towards me, he swallowed hard and his eyelids fluttered. He said, 'What should I do? Tell me.'

'Undress,' I told him, 'slowly.'

He started by slipping his hockey jersey over his head. His torso was soft with a triangle of unruly hair flourishing on his sternum, his armpits bushy, studded with beads of sweat, and when he turned to hang his shirt over the towel rail his bronzed back looked to me like a long stretch of unblemished golden sand. He tugged at his belt and his cut-offs hit the linoleum floor, heavy with the weight of his wallet and his keys and his phone. He stood there in his underwear, gingham checked boxer shorts, meek and comestible, and said, 'Undies too?' and though one half of his face was in shadow I could tell that he was blushing, so I nodded. I was nervous too.

He tucked his thumbs under the somewhat slackened elastic of the waistband and slipped them down, his leisurely pace proving that he preserved some semblance of self-possession, this ludic striptease revealing first his downy stomach, then his exuberant pubes, then his stiff cock standing upright like a sentinel over his balls, which hung tight and high. He really was beautiful, like a halter-broken sun god, laid bare and panting under my scrutiny, somewhat ashamed, wildly aroused. For a split second his fingers wavered as if he wanted to cup his hands over his junk, following some urge for modesty, so I reached out and held his wrists to his side. His dick jerked, throbbing harder at the appraisal. 'Good boy,' I said.

When I drew my hands back, he held his position, even as I flicked at the spaghetti straps and my slip fell from me like a dream, into a pool of lilac satin at my feet. I wore no bra, just a pair of black cami knickers with a French lace trim, a gift from Alexander. West's eyes widened. I leant forward with his stare on me, caressing me, and ran my forefinger over the tip of his prick, slick with sap. Somewhat sadistically, with two fingers and my thumb, I massaged his cockhead, the precum sparing him some of the friction but not enough and he winced, sipping short breaths of air between his teeth. Then I turned to pick up my highball again and said, so casually as to almost come off as uninterested, 'Hop in then, before the water gets cold.'

He seemed gently unsure of himself, but all the same he obeyed, slipping into the water and beneath the bubbles like Helios descending into his golden cup. I sipped at my drink, unhurried, trying to extend the illusion of my indifference, though this pose was critically undermined by the traitorous silk of my French knickers. He looked like Leonardo DiCaprio circa 1996, like a ripe peach, like a boy-nymph, and canny, aware, he began to lather himself up like a lewd cherub in response. He had turned quite pink, where the candlelight caught him at least, and he made sure to maintain eye contact with me as he soaped his arms, his legs, between his toes. He said, 'Don't you want to get in with me? I can make room.'

His hymeneal tone was like coffee over ice cream to me; any remaining misgivings melted away, all indecision liquified. I stepped out of my knickers and into the bath, above him, naked, sure that I could master this, and he looked up at me like Falconetti's Joan of Arc adoring the Eucharist, eyes full of blissful wonderment, such a perfect moment almost killed me, and I wanted to keep it, extend it forever, incorrupt. I slipped into the water at the opposite end of the tub and lay with my head back on the tiled rim, hair scooped up, luxuriating in the warmth and the suds. He smiled at me, I think he must've been a little drunk by now too, and I thought, *Oh but there's such effortless romance to sharing a bath! I'm sorry to say it, but you're dead wrong on this one, Joan.*

In the candle glow West stretched out a leg alongside me, his left foot breaking the water at my shoulder, coming to rest amidst the bubbles on my chest. I felt the toes of his right foot brush my cock, accidentally, I thought, then he said, 'I heard you like it when boys put their feet in your face, is that right?'

He toyed with me under the water. I wiped a gem of sweat from my cheek, downplaying my arousal, though it only increased as he pressed his foot harder against me. Since I hadn't replied to even try and deny his claim, and because my face was burning scarlet with embarrassment, he smiled to himself and slid a little further under the water. He raised his foot high off my shoulder and let lime spume drizzle off his toes onto me, onto my hair, onto my lips, then brought his foot down onto my face, quivering as I ran my extended tongue along his sole. Below the waterline he rubbed over my balls with his toes and stroked at the length of my shaft. ‘Fuck, Charli,’ he pronounced, proud and alarmed, ‘you’re really hard.’

He sat up and bent himself double so that he could bring his mouth to my dick where it pierced the soapy finish of the water and curl his lips around the tip, gliding his tongue across it keen and agile. I bucked my hips up so he had more to play with and watched him struggle to swallow deeper, his nose and mouth submerging, his eyelashes skating on the silver like dragonflies. When he pulled his head back to gasp for a breath I pounced like a thing uncoiled, pressing him back into the water and kissing him with clear and full intent. A switch had flipped, all games cast aside. I had to let him know how badly I wanted him.

I cradled his face in my hands and he kissed at my palms like a pet. I knelt above him hard as hell and said, ‘Now tell me, tell me what you like.’ I waited on his response, propped up on one hand, the other finding its way around his throat, his eyes scanning me rapidly for a trace of aggression, fearing he might find it, scared that he would not.

‘I like it,’ he cleared his timid throat, ‘I like it when the girl takes charge.’

To show me he was serious, he revolved in the water below me, before me, to bring himself onto his belly, ass up amidst the foam, curving his back and pressing himself against me with my cock rubbing between the cheeks of his arse. I reached my arm beneath him to pull him closer, held him against me, he looked over his shoulder to kiss me, and I used my free hand to squeeze his balls and make him yelp. Tracing the length of his cock with my fingertips as it flexed, I wrapped my palm tight over his glans. ‘Charli,’ he lowed, ‘Charli.’

He wriggled free from my grip, not to escape but in order to come onto his knees, and leant forward against the wall so that his face and torso pressed up on the tiles. One forearm cushioned his brow, the other reached back, groping, squeezing his big round arse, splaying it for me, showing me what he wanted, how he wanted it. 'Fuck me, Charli,' he said, 'come on, fuck me.'

I felt entirely manipulated by him, like he was using me for his own pleasure, and this combination of sensations – of being at once reduced to an object of service whilst also licensed to use this waiting hole – was entirely too much. I spread his ass and stretched him wide open, exposing him completely, wanting him to burn with humiliation at being so abased, and I stuck my face right inside him, sliding my tongue up inside, making him grunt, his groans almost violent. Then once he was pliable with hot saliva I slid my dick deep in him and felt his body shudder and surrender, one hand flat and wide on the wall for support, scrabbling and in turns pounding at the tiles as I gave him long quick strokes, holding him up at times to prevent him from slipping and smashing his pretty face on the lip of the bathtub.

I hadn't fucked anyone like this since I was fifteen or so, since before I transitioned. I thought for sure that it would freak me out, throw me into some dysphoric tailspin, but quite the opposite, I felt like I was meeting myself around a new corner. He pushed away from the wall so that he could wank his cock, brought our torsos closer into contact so that my nipples grazed his shoulder blades, I took hold of a handful of his hair, he squeezed himself tighter around my dick and mewled.

'Fuck,' he gasped, 'I love feeling your tits on my back, Charli.'

'Oh yeah?' I hissed in his ear. 'Is that how you like to be used then?'

'Fuck, yes,' he begged, 'use me, Charli, please.'

Then there was no turning back and I found myself throwing my full weight into each lunge, my balls slapping loudly on his arse, weaving my fingers through his hair to tighten my hold, smacking his ass hard with the back of my free hand, so that he yelped, 'Fuck I'm going to cum.'

'Shit,' I gasped, 'me too.'

He moaned, 'Fucking shoot in me, Charli, fucking cum in me,' and I went off like a firework, spraying white hot light deep inside him. Then his rigid body bucked beneath me and his hole squeezed tight around me and I knew that he'd reached his own spasming conclusion at the same time as me, and really, truly, that felt like something wonderful.

I pulled out of him with as much delicacy as I could, but still caused him to suck a snivel of air in sharp, to grasp for my hip so as to decelerate my withdrawal. 'Shit,' I mumbled, 'sorry, was that too rough?' He shook his head contemplatively and dropped back into the now cooling water, reached again to kiss me, and said, 'Charli, that was so hot,' and I could only grin in complete agreement.

The sun's initial lucent orange had long bled out through the early morning, the sky in the Hoff outside had coloured a most delicate powder blue. I gave in to my pressing exhaustion, yawned, smug. West too admired the sky, seemed to regret the passing of the night into day, sighing softly, plaintively.

'We must be crazy,' he said. 'It's going on close to eight o'clock and my shift starts at nine. We must be *crazy*.'

'Crazy, yeah,' I repeated, abstracted, wrapping my arms around myself to ward off the inevitable chill, and riffed, '*Ain't none of us pure crazy and ain't none of us pure sane until the balance of us talks him that-a-way.*'

West said, 'Oh, Faulkner. Cool. You know he wrote that whilst he was working nights at a power plant?'

'No,' I replied, 'I didn't know that.'

'Sort of gives me hope,' he smiled, 'that I'll manage to write something decent myself one day.'

He stepped out of the tub with a sudden burst of motion, the water droplets racing down his back and into the crack of his arse brought to mind the toy cars I used to race with my cousin on his Scalextric set. He couldn't risk missing another shift at Pfeiffer's, he said: if he lost this job, there'd be one more poet in Berlin bumming cigarettes and sleeping on his friends' floors. He sighed. 'And I cannot be that guy.'

I watched as he dressed, sinking deeper into the dirty water to try and retain some heat and failing, wishing to high heaven that he'd change his mind, call in sick and stay with me. Of course I didn't ask that of him, how could I? It's in a man's DNA to leave, I knew that. I simply stifled my shivers whilst he slipped his clothes on and tamed his hair with Carl's old comb, rubbed a finger full of toothpaste over his cream-coloured fangs, and slapped at his face to draw a little healthy colour.

He leant over the bathtub and kissed me. He said, 'Meet me on Saturday? I'm reading at KW; I can put you on the list.'

'Sure.' I was touched. 'I'd love that.'

'Great,' he said, 'well, ciao for now, *lover*.'

He blew me a little kiss as he exited the bathroom. I heard him fumble about for his shoes in the corridor and rush to get them on. In my chilly reverie I even forgot to care about the Hausmeister's wife and all her threats. Barely audible, disappearing down the corridor, West lit a cigarette, took a drag and set off out. As he departed Alexander returned. I didn't hear them speak, couldn't decipher so much as the exchange of a hostile *Morgen* between them, but that neglected morning they passed by each other deep in the murk of the hallway, two railroads through my life, diverging.

PART THREE

Imagine Sisyphus Happy

I

Of course I recognised his footsteps passing by the bathroom door, the voice he put on to whisper to the cat in the kitchen, uncharacteristically kind. I knew he'd go straight to the fridge to look for salami and orange juice, and he did. I made no haste though to get up and greet him, rather I languished longer in the water, discolouring it with my pent-up piss, then, disgusted with myself, stood up to shower off. I found one of the towelling robes he had taken from the spa at his gym, wrapped myself up in it tightly, but left the evening's clothes behind me on the floor, as though I had a maid to clear it all away. I tidied my hair, cleaned my mascara where it had smudged, steeled myself in movie-villain glamour; I needed this arrogance, this crystalline insolence, in order to face him.

I had seen enough flashes of his anger to know that I didn't want to be on the receiving end of it. I knew how sharply he could snap and did not want to provoke, but I had been caught red-handed and now there was nothing for it but to face the music. Still I would not scuttle, I would not try to appease, I would not apologise for taking my life back into my own hands. I wanted it to be clear that morning that frankly I could take him or leave him. That was the conceit, anyway.

He was smoking, of course, he looked like hell, bone-thin and exhausted, bags under his eyes like bruises, his skin like paper, sweaty and dirty, he was clearly coming down off a long jag. The cat rubbed up on his legs incessantly and he rewarded it with distracted little pats on the head, chewing at his bottom lip, fag at his fingertips, looking like James Dean after a beating. For the first time ever I think I caught the smell of him, it was sour like sex, like milk left out too long on the countertop. I think that if I'd acted in that moment, if I'd asked for the key and shown him the door, then yes, I could have rid myself of him for good. Only I guess we weren't done with each other yet.

Armoured in my post-fuck felicity, emboldened by the sight of how pathetic he looked, I took a cigarette for myself, lit it, and with just a slash of cruelty I asked, 'So, how was the video shoot?'

And where I had expected aggression he returned only arid resignation. 'Not a huge success,' he said. 'We were, ah, a little underprepared.'

I scoffed, 'Underprepared like *high* or underprepared like *lazy*?' and then realised that maybe Alex wasn't the one spoiling for a fight.

He didn't reply, it was as though he hadn't heard, or I hadn't spoken. He looked past me, through me, and I couldn't bear it, even when I was stood right in front of him he could choose not to see me. I wanted to flick my cigarette at him, laugh at him, kick the cat away from his attentions, but of course I didn't. I just said, 'Sounds rough, Alex, sorry I couldn't be there. I've been *awfully* busy.'

This seemed to pique him just so. He threw me a look of definite contempt, though shaded with a world-weariness. 'Yes, Charli, I saw your visitor. Very cute. Well done. Brava.'

'Yeah, well,' I shot back, 'cuter than Moritz, that's for sure.'

Alex put out his cigarette on a saucer with a few quick dabs and said, 'What?', his face a twist of incomprehension before my meaning dawned on him. 'Oh, Charli,' he sighed, 'sometimes you are just so dumb, I could slap you.'

'Try it,' I bristled, but he didn't even rise from his seat.

Too spent to quarrel, he dropped his head in his hands and slurred into his palms, 'I'm sorry. I did not mean that. I'm sorry, I am tired.'

Was I disappointed then that we didn't come to blows? Maybe. I think perhaps a part of me was willing him to knock me sideways and fuck me on the kitchen floor, but then I'm a pretty lousy feminist, and maybe it's true what all those angry people say online, that women like me only exist to perpetuate sexist clichés. He did not boil over, he didn't raise a hand, didn't even raise his voice; I was the only one shouting. He said, 'I did not come to fight with you, Charli. I just want to talk.'

Now I laughed, spitefully. 'You have a nerve to want anything of me.'

'I know,' he said. 'But I have no one else.'

Was I flattered by this, to hear I was the only one he could turn to? That seems myopic. It's really no great honour to be the last resort, but you see, I've always been so susceptible to adulation, however faint, and even though this was real thin soup I admit that I was placated.

I flopped into a chair. 'Right, OK, so talk. Unburden yourself.' I sat down still surly but with the sirocco well and truly taken out of my sails.

The glass bottle he had been swigging from was smeared with lipstick, beads of toxic sweat dotted his slanted forehead. Intermittently he looked off to the side, over his shoulder, as if concerned that somebody was there, watching. When a clatter came out of a cupboard he shrieked in fright and I had to still him, saying, 'Alex, it's OK, it's just the cat, calm down now.' I made him a cup of tea, lemon and ginger, something soothing like that, because I'm British and what other resources do we have? Then I asked him to tell me what went wrong, and he did.

His storytelling was messy in parts, over-long. He stumbled and rambled and I struggled to fully understand though I think I got the broad strokes: the studio's lacklustre facilities, the greenhorn's failure to book any security, a runner being hit on the head by a falling light. It sounded shambolic and I did feel kind of guilty. The band had been late to shoot their segment, the makeup artist they hired didn't know that Alex had an allergy to certain kinds of eyelash glue, without an iron his suit looked so crumpled onscreen that they had to send someone out to find a one-hour dry-cleaning service and lost another hunk of time there. The ambitions they had to film a verse with Alex walking backwards, and another with him French kissing his reflection in a mirror, were lost; the more complicated drone shots had to go too, until in the end all that remained of our cherished storyboard was the image of Alex singing against a white wall whilst a movie projector ran images over his body. It was our homage to Pasolini screening *The Gospel According to St Matthew* on his own chest in Bologna, 1975.

'Eighteen hours straight on set,' he said, 'and it comes to nothing.'

I saw that it pained him to recount it all, but he had to expectorate somehow. It was pitiful, and I felt culpable. I goaded myself, *Would it have killed you to be there with him for a while?* I didn't need to go out. I could've surely spared the evening to steam his suit, to run out and grab some Brötchen and cold cuts, maybe talk him out of some of those unnecessary trips to the bathroom. What was it he had done anyway, to warrant me reneging on the help I'd freely offered him, the help he'd come to depend on?

I tried for a bright tone but it was unearned. 'Well, at least there's the tour,' I said, 'a European tour! That could be really exciting.'

He looked through me again, simply exasperated, and said, 'Oh, lover, you just don't understand.'

The tour as it stood would not involve limousines between stadiums, nights at the Bristol or costumes by Thierry Mugler: it was to be two weeks in the rehearsal room in Pankow, then a month travelling Europe by train, Lisbon to Warsaw, with seventeen shows in between. It was four weeks for which he was contracted, and furthermore for which he had already been paid under the terms of his advance, and the whole thing was arranged so that when he wasn't on-stage or travelling to the next gig, he'd be giving interviews on local TV and radio. He cringed at the thought of it, crushed by the promised workload.

I said, 'But Alex, this is what you wanted,' and though I was trying to put across some enthusiasm, my own lack of sleep made me clumsy with my words, indelicate in my tone.

He recoiled. 'I do not know what I want, I do not know at all! I've lost myself, Charli,' he faltered, 'I've ruined everything, haven't I?'

Perhaps it was only a harsh comedown, and maybe I should've shrugged it off and left it there, but seeing him laid so low made me want to be lower still, to kneel at his bedside and pray for his recovery. I forgot that I was ever even pissed with him. I took his hand and said, 'No, I don't believe that, I don't believe that at all. You're just getting started.'

'I am afraid, Charli,' he whimpered. 'I do not think I can do this.'

But I wouldn't hear it. 'Of course you can,' I said, newly alive with a messiah complex, 'you are more than capable. You just need to rest up and then get down to business, that's all.' Then I paused and added what only an idiot would: 'And I'll help you. You're going to be great. I'll help you. You're going to be a huge success, a big, big star.'

'Really?' he said. 'You will help me?' His eyes were even a little wet with tears as he contemplated his future. 'You really think I will make it?'

'Oh yes, lover,' I said with total assurance, 'I do.'

Even at his most despondent, his most diminished, he still gave off the most lugubrious glamour, like a Swiss hotel resort out of season. He needed only a spiritual lick of paint, and I was sure that I was the one who could bring the sun back into his life. I said, 'Remember, *God would never inspire you with desires which cannot be realised.*'

He sniffed. 'Is it *The Great Fitzgerald* again?'

I laughed. 'No, it's St Thérèse of Lisieux, but don't sweat it. Are you tired?'

He nodded, docile, yawned. 'Yes, I am.'

'I'll make up the bed in Carl's old room, the mattress is more comfortable in there,' I said. 'Funny. How long am I going to keep calling it that?'

He coughed and cleared his throat, bashful. 'And will you get in with me? I do not want to be alone.'

I did, of course I did. I had plentiful experience dealing with the aftermath of a bender, so at least I could offer him the comfort he needed. We went to bed, far too tired to even consider a fuck, but too wired with all the morning's emotion to doze right off. He held me, or perhaps it's more correct to say that he was holding on to me, and it was the most intimate contact of my life, him in his grandfather's pyjamas, me in my old Garfield T-shirt. He told me that when he was away from me he felt like one of the ladies he'd seen on reality television who'd had so much plastic surgery she could no longer recognise herself. He said, 'Do not leave me please.' We curled up combined, enmeshed in the way felled trees become involved with moss after a storm. I don't think any other body had ever fitted me so well, encircled me so perfectly. When we were in each other's arms that morning it was as though we were one body, with no dividing line, Roquentin declaring himself to be the root of the chestnut tree. We spooned, I pressed my knees up under him, I could feel each of his his vertebrae pressed to my chest. He asked, 'Did you really think I have been sleeping with Moritz?'

'Well, aren't you?' I asked.

He sounded scandalised. 'Charli! No! He is a married man.'

'Oh, I just thought that . . .' I giggled. 'I guess I do rush to conclusions sometimes.'

He puzzled it out, 'And is that why you were so angry with me?'

'Yes,' I said, 'I suppose so.'

In a very silly sorry childish voice he bleated, 'And all this time we could've been friends.'

I laughed. 'Very nice.'

He said, 'You are a strange girl, Charli, you know that? These paranoias of yours. Always thinking up such strange things.'

'Hush, now,' I said, squeezing him closer. 'I'm sleepy. Turn off the light.'

From under the curtain the brilliant blue of a Berlin summer day crowbarred at our body clocks. The temperature raced to thirty, but it made no difference: the two of us were too shattered now to know which way was up. As soon as I closed my eyes and stilled my lips I slipped off into sleep, and dreamt of that first night, meeting Alex in London, the bad ketamine trip, Sophia, the lost tapestry. I woke myself up laughing.

Alex murmured, 'What? What is it?'

'Nothing,' I said. 'Just a funny picture in my head that's all. Go back to sleep now.'

2

I have been allowed a can of Fanta today, since the doctors have decided it's unlikely to prove overstimulating. I had wanted a Coke but they all baulked at the idea of that, zu viel Koffein, *too much caffeine! Honestly the way they reacted you'd have thought I'd asked them to fetch me an eight ball. All the same I'm delighted because I love Fanta – it's delicious. I remember when I first got to Berlin there was a huge billboard advertising the stuff up over Oberbaumbrücke, it said* 'Deutschland brauche mehr Fantasie', *Germany needs more fantasy, and I nudged Alex and said, 'It is lucky we're here then, eh, lover?' I tried to explain that to the doctor but she didn't laugh, she only looked sad and bemused.*

I've been looking out for the nun but she has yet to reappear. I think the nurse has finally warmed to me though: she's asking me how I am, I'm saying 'Gut, danke' and she is smiling and telling me that she has an Uberraschung *for me, a surprise. When she hands me a battered old copy of* A Tale of Two Cities, *I am quite touched, I don't remember the last time anyone gave me a gift. I think I can find the energy to dip into it, slowly at first, yes I think I have the strength now to start reading again, I'm much less confused than I was.*

Before, if I had tried to read a book I'm quite sure I would've have started to believe that I was living in the book myself because the line between reality and reverie had become really quite blurred for me. But things are more stable now. I'd been starting to feel like that Mondrian which was hung upside down for seventy-five years, but now I'm right side up. I've stopped asking about Alex, and they've dialled down the drugs. I've agreed to do as I'm told because they only want what's best for me, and really I'm in no position to argue since my door is locked from the outside. I know because I tried the handle when the hack in the corridor went out for a fag. He seems to be growing bored of waiting to get any intel: they brought him in to ask me some questions but I refused to tell him anything. 'I'm not going to sell Alex out,' I said, 'I know how you people operate.' He's been stood in the corridor ever since, alternately glaring in at me and yawning and picking his nose.

The doctor said that I might be able to have visitors soon, if it wouldn't be too distressing for me. She said that I'd made a lot of progress and that she was happy, that I seemed so much calmer now. I smiled. Of course I'm just showing her what she wants to see, like a magic mirror, and if I've somehow got the upper hand now I'd like to keep it like that. She asked who I'd like to see. I wanted to say Polly, but I don't know where she is with her legal situation and I didn't want to risk getting her in trouble. I didn't say Finley because I was worried about the money. Instead I told the doctor to call my mother, and now she's flying over and I'm going to have to explain to her how I got here, although I hardly know what has gone on myself.

I sip my Fanta and feel a little sorry for myself, but then I'm quite sure that's part of the recovery process, isn't it? Have you ever visited anyone in hospital who wasn't wallowing in self-indulgence? I remember West used to call Fanta 'Hitler's Coke' because it was invented here during the war. Coca-Cola didn't want to seem un-American by selling Coke to the Nazis, but they also didn't want to lose their share of the soft drink market, so the Coca-Cola plants in Germany started making Fanta instead, from whey and apple cider leftovers. I ask the doctor if he has been in touch, if my friend West has called or tried to visit me. She shakes her head softly and says, 'No.'

'Of course not,' I say, 'how silly of me. Stella would never allow it. She watches over me like a hawk.'

3

Tour rehearsals began in earnest at the practice room in Pankow. I tried to make sure that Alex arrived fed, watered and punctual every day, shepherding him to the rehearsal room like the nanny of a Tory MP out canvassing. His Mercedes was off the road for a while after he'd clipped a lamp post, which made for a laborious daily journey on public transport. We'd buy sandwiches from one of the bakeries inside the station at Hermannplatz and go over the order of the day's business on the platform, Alex picking out the salami slices from between the bread and nodding along with my proposals. The journey took almost an hour but we used the time effectively, drafting emails and answering fan mail on the U-Bahn, compiling a comprehensive spreadsheet of all the tour dates, drawing scowls from crushed commuters by pulling out a laptop on the U8. If anyone approached us on the train to ask Alex if he was who they thought he was, I would laugh on his behalf and say, 'What? He doesn't look anything like him!', a trick we'd learned from a Bowie biography.

In the rehearsal room too I made myself useful. I helped set up the equipment before the band rolled in, took notes on the set list as it evolved and kept an eye on the door so practice wasn't interrupted by looky-loos or stoner rockers who'd wandered down the wrong corridor. It felt great to be back in the thick of it, I was very glad to be near him again. This time he seemed intent on keeping me close. Pointedly, he always took my request first when it came time to order lunch, and he often asked for my opinion when considering a lyrical substitution. When a question of logistics came up, when there was some conflict of interest between the label and the band over styling, say, or the running order, he deferred to me too. 'Ask Charli,' he'd say with a wink, 'she will know.' Considering how things had been between us only a few days prior, I felt like I was walking on air. I imagined this was how Boccaccio's Patient Griselda must've felt after her husband gave her back her children and told her it had all been a test – no marchioness could touch me now.

In this mode of magnanimity, I apologised to Moritz over all those unanswered messages, and he authorised me to book train travel on the label's credit card so that Alexander could concentrate on his personal preparations. I put him in first class of course; the band were supposed to travel with him, but Alex thought that it was pure extravagance for them not to travel standard. The cost of their tickets would only be added to his bill anyway, set against his advance, and what he owed the label. He wasn't in the business of furnishing other people with luxuries.

We struck upon the pretty ingenious plan of buying the band their standard class tickets with Alex's own money and claiming it back from Moritz against his debts. All perfectly reasonable, except for the fact that the tickets were, unbeknownst to Moritz and the band, fake. We had read on a backpacker forum that if you downloaded the attached template you could print your own Deutsche Bahn tickets which no one could distinguish from the real things, especially not conductors from other parts of Europe's overlapping rail network. All you had to do was print them on the right kind of paper, readily available in art supply stores, and put them in a glossy wallet which you could pick up from any train station office if you said you'd spilled coffee on your own. The band wouldn't lose out but Alex would have a cool two grand's worth of ticket stubs to present with his other expenses at the end of the tour. I thought it was very clever when he described it to me, and honestly it wasn't at all hard to manage. I printed all the tickets myself at the Späti, it took me about twenty minutes and cost €11.50. We kept the receipt and charged the label for *miscellaneous (stationery)*. I decided to give my mother a call whilst I was there in the Späti. It had been some time; I never did figure out how to get an international line from the phone in Carl's old room.

'Oh here she is,' my mother chuckled. 'The frigging prodigal daughter! Where've you been then, eh? Have you joined a convent or something, cut ties with the secular world?'

'No, no,' I said, 'just been busy. This tour. God it's a lot of work.'

She told me that she'd seen a movie that she thought I'd like, it had come up on her *Recommended for You* page, she couldn't remember the name of it but Cate Blanchett was in it, playing Bob Dylan. Julie had to go to the vet about her hind leg but other than that the dogs were doing well, she was considering training to be a certified energy healer, you could do it online for £29.50. I made the right noises throughout but I was elsewhere, daydreaming and scratching Alexander's name into the plexiglass with my front door key.

'Polly said you've been a bit stressed lately,' she said, 'and so I was wondering if . . .'

I was startled into attention. 'Why on earth have you been talking to Polly?'

'Well, if you gave me a more reliable phone number,' she said, 'I wouldn't have to, would I?'

'Honestly,' I contended, 'this is insufferable!'

'Insufferable,' she chortled, 'oh you do make me laugh, Charli Hughes! We're just looking out for you, love, that's all.' She said, 'Me and your dad are going to the Lakes for a week next month. Why don't you come with us? We're doing the Beatrix Potter trail, you always loved that when you were little.'

'Mother,' I was vexed by what seemed like wilful incomprehension, 'I'm responsible for a major European tour here, I can't just jet off whenever I fancy. The recording industry isn't all glitz and glamour, you know.'

She was suddenly very serious, she said, 'Charli, do you need me to come and fetch you, love? I will if you need me to.'

'No,' I said, 'no of course not. I'm not a child.' I hated it when she spoke to me like this, it made me feel inexcusably guilty. 'Listen,' I lied, 'I have to go now, my money's running out.'

She said, 'Alright love, well, then I won't keep you.' She tried to conclude with a joke but I didn't have the patience for it: 'Anyways, say hello to Mr Froggy next time you see him, eh?'

I hung up and went back to rehearsal.

Before the tour Alex was playing a gig at Berghain with Peaches, the last rockstar minted before the whole world went fully digital. He wasn't supporting her as I had at first inferred, rather they were co-headlining, which made it an even bigger deal since Peaches was, as my mother would say, 'A legend in her own lunchtime.' She would play her set, Alex would join her for a duet of 'Father Fucker' then take the stage for himself. Moritz had curated it as a symbolic passing-of-the torch moment.

We had decided that in contrast to her fluorescent trashthetic of inflatable tits and dresses made from decapitated Barbie dolls, Alex would go full matinée idol, hair in a wave, double-breasted navy suit, masses of white lilies at his feet. We brainstormed well into the night at the end of rehearsal, pulling up old movie clips, sketching madly, mocking up mood boards for the lighting: a single white spot on Alex, the band lit from behind so they appeared only in icy silhouette.

It was amazing how productive we were, even after eight hours in the practice room we still managed another four or five at home planning the live show. If we flagged we just did a little coke, or a little speed, whatever we had to hand, and if we felt uninspired we smoked a bit of dope which put us right back into the mood, into the dream zone where designs flowed like melted butter. That's how I came up with the idea that the band should play blindfolded, like the orchestra in *Sunset Boulevard*, which I thought was the most gorgeous and dazzling image, so perfectly suited to Alex's particular brand of glamour.

The nights grew longer and longer, the window for sleep almost entirely fogged over with opiate smoke. Any shut-eye we did catch was more of a shared poppy dream. We had long since disabled the smoke alarms, and we made ourselves a den in Carl's old room from bed linens and neckties, a secret shell, like one of Kurt Schwitters' *Merzbau,* to keep what we were smoking from the nostrils of my nosy neighbours. Most likely they never would have noticed, since heroin of the purity we were smoking doesn't actually smell of anything, but we were so deep in our delusions that we were quite consistently imagining new pitfalls for ourselves.

We watched a lot of campy eighties horror movies: *The Company of Wolves*, *The Lair of the White Worm, The Witches of Eastwick*. I don't know who chose them, I only remember the very unconvincing special effects and all the parochial sexual morality, and laughing at the sight of the devil, as played by Jack Nicholson, caught in the rain outside his girlfriend's house as he begged her to take him back. I thought that this was beyond ridiculous. Nicholson's Satan is a powerful being, he can take the form of a wolf, he can make people vomit up cherry pits – couldn't he arrange an umbrella for himself? Alex looked at me from the corner of his eye. 'Of course he can,' he said, 'he is merely manipulating her,' and I felt very naive.

Eventually there was no separation between the day and the night, the studio and my bedroom, it all began sloshing together. We entered a semi-permanent Halloween, the screen between this world and the next so thin as to be completely permeable. Everything tumbled together like the ingredients for a Victoria sponge, tossed into a bowl and creamed. We shuttled back and forth for a fortnight, rehearsal room-bedroom-rehearsal room-bedroom, smoking this and huffing that and honestly believing we were working furiously the whole time. The sex dropped off, of course, but everyone accepts that as a standard corollary of heroin use.

Sometimes I would wake up and find a stranger making coffee in the kitchen or asleep on the little sofa in my room. It's a miracle nothing of any real value went missing, just some underwear and a few teaspoons. I thought it was sort of funny, but Polly did not. One day she called in on her way home from the atelier and a man came staggering out of Carl's old room naked – she screamed blue murder. For a moment I was afraid she might wallop him. She said we'd arranged her dropping in, but I didn't remember it.

She told me that I needed to snap out of it and pull myself together, that it was time to get serious about what I was doing with my life: I had talents, I was wasting them. I said that I thought I was putting whatever skills I had to good use managing Alexander's career, that I found it very fulfilling and besides which I didn't have a choice, not really. I said, 'I'm in love with him, you see. I know it's silly, but there you go.'

Polly was full of scorn. 'This whole thing is honestly pathetic, you *do* realise that?' She fizzed with an upright anger. 'He's not even a real person! He's barely even a sketch of a person, he's like something out of a bad trip.'

Moritz fired her from the tour shortly after that: he sent her an email explaining rather frigidly that the label could only pay for her services as a makeup artist in town but not on the road. Alex said it was probably just a coincidence and that besides, I could do his makeup just as well as Polly, which was more or less true.

He had put together a concise playlist of his favourite Fleetwood Mac songs, not the hits but rather troublesome deep cuts from less popular albums. He was playing 'The Chain' and 'Tango in the Night' over and over. I asked him, several times throughout the early hours, if we could turn it off or at least listen to a slightly wider selection, but he refused, almost panicked at the idea. 'Just once more,' he said, 'one more time, please,' explaining to me that he was drawing an enchanted circle around us with the music of Fleetwood Mac, to keep in-fighting, psychosis, physical violence, all the troubles that had befallen them, at bay. It was, he said, sympathetic magic. He was so nervous about the tour that I didn't argue with him, just accepted my life as the little bird who hops into the crocodile's mouth to clean his teeth.

We listened to those same few songs again and again and again until I stopped hearing them, until the lyrics and melodies had disintegrated into stainless steel and white noise, until it was time to get ready to head out to the practice room again. Alex shaved, I showered, we each snorted a line of coke off the kitchen table, brushed our teeth, daubed over our dark circles with a little Shiseido and took the train back up to Pankow like perfect little commuters, barely even aware of how everyone stared at us as we fell asleep in our seats and snored way past our station.

We arrived at the rehearsal room very late, later than the musicians even, because we'd been struck with the idea of bringing snacks for everybody, and so had headed back into the city to the big Dunkin' Donuts at Alexanderplatz. We figured they'd have the best selection there, and they did. We got two of everything, forty-something fatty puffs iced in lurid greens and pinks and yellows, filled with jam and cream and chocolate paste, four boxes with which we staggered on and off the train and finally into the studio.

The radio was on and the band were lying around: the keyboardist on his back reading an article about Kate Moss's alleged use of body doubles in a big ad campaign, the saxophonist filing his nails and nodding along with the radio programme, only the drummer, damp with sweat, was active, counting onwards through his push-ups. 'Achtunddreisig,' he grunted, 'Neununddreisig, Vierzig.' I always thought he was very sexy.

'Shhh, Schatzi, please,' said the saxophonist, 'I can't hear the radio.'

Alex wandered around the room offering donuts like Eva Perón gifting basketballs in the Argentine slums. 'What is it you are listening to?' he said, curious and stately.

The saxophonist took a Boston cream. 'You, baby,' he said, 'we're listening to your interview on Radio Eins.'

Alexander sat down to listen to himself back, squinting at the battered old Grundig transistor 305, chewing on a cruller, a look of quiet curiosity on his face as his voice spilled out. It was on the whole uneventful, the questions were the same every time: *Why did you move to Berlin? Who is your biggest influence? How do you feel about being compared to David Bowie?* Alex always answered diligently, tried to give each reply the flavour of a new thought – different every night, and all that. He usually managed to press a little humour from the situation too, because he was naturally very arch, as when the presenter quizzed him rather gracelessly about his famously flamboyant on-stage appearance. She said, 'You are wearing makeup and boots with high heels, but also men's suits and ties. You do not look like a woman, no, but you also do not look like a man, so how do you decide? Do you wake up and say "Ah! Today I feel I will be a boy"?'

Alexander took the slightest of steadying breaths before he replied. 'No, lover,' he spoke, without colour, 'usually when I wake up, I feel like breakfast.'

The host laughed along, she thanked him for his time and reminded her audience that he would be playing at Berghain that weekend, ahead of a European tour. Then she faded up a track by Molly Nilsson, 'We're Never Coming Home', I think, and the saxophonist turned the radio down to a murmur. On the studio carpet Alex sighed. 'You know I have done so many of these things now and I never remember a single one. I am always thinking, "Are these *my* thoughts?" Isn't that so peculiar?'

The drummer yawned, he leant back in his chair and flexed his biceps behind his head; the keyboardist said, 'Shall we like, get on with this?'

The band took their equipment and began tuning up. Alexander took his place at the microphone stand, he flicked the cable so that the mic flex smoothed itself out, rotated his head on his spine, his neck cracked loudly. I smiled on with pride, my man, his band, ready to conquer the world – I was quite lost in adoration. I twirled my hair around my fingers absentmindedly. Alex looked over at me, caught me staring at him like a lovestruck teen, and I blushed. He returned my affection with a warm insistent smile of his own, it fell on me like sunlight through stained glass. He said, 'Charli, tidy up the doughnuts for me now, would you, please?'

4

Polly was making me up for the afterparty at Berghain. It seemed to be taking years, but that might've been because when we'd arrived to soundcheck, six hours before the gig, some bright spark, probably one of the band, had suggested we all take shrooms to kill the time and so everything was very slippery that night. Polly was in a bold mood: she'd given me a huge shark's mouth of red lipstick and two eye sockets of aquamarine shadow. She said she wanted to make me into Joan Crawford for the night, but really I looked more like PJ Harvey after her nervous breakdown. She'd painted her own face too: powdered it a rococo white and drawn on beauty spots with liquid eyeliner. The two of us looked deranged staring back at ourselves from the dressing room mirror and pulling ghoulish faces.

The hours before the show had been immensely complicated, we'd had whole ranks of people backstage. Moritz of course, and the promoters, journalists, security guards, the musicians and their guests, crew bustling in and out, agents, assistants, the club's management, all of them needing something signed or signed off, various shadowy industry bodies with Swiss accents whispering amongst themselves and swilling half the champagne from the rider. I remember Peaches coming into the dressing room for a photo call with Alexander, and the intercom counting us down to showtime every fifteen minutes, first in German and then in English, then a sudden flash of 'Hals-und Beinbruch!' from the assembled, and Moritz clapping Alex on the back, saying, 'We'll be out there – watching,' before they all disappeared towards the stage en masse, like the tide withdrawing before a tsunami. Then suddenly, silence.

I was worried that Finley was mad at me, I hadn't been able to secure a backstage pass for him, but Polly assured me that he was happy enough with his afterparty wristband. 'He's waiting downstairs,' she said. 'Him and the old man he's going about with.'

'Gerhard,' I clarified.

Polly narrowed her eyes. 'I think he's awfully controlling.'

'I like him. He's sweet,' I said, though I didn't really have anything to base this on.

I poured a little more tequila into Polly's glass; she knocked it back and shuddered. 'Well, at least the old bastard's generous,' she said. 'Finley told me he just bought him a Dyson hairdryer.'

I gasped. 'Oh l'amour!'

We headed out from the dressing room to find the party, but there wasn't anyone around to show us the way. Inadvertently we took a left instead of a right somewhere inside the concrete labyrinth and came down the wrong staircase, through the wrong door, and right out in the middle of a crowd of screaming fans who had congregated, waiting on a glimpse of Alexander. They surged at us before we could explain that we weren't who they thought we were; it was really frightening, people were pushing at us from all directions. I tripped and almost fell, Polly held me steady, I had visions of going the way of cousin Sebastian at the end of *Suddenly, Last Summer.* A pair of bouncers pulled us from the scrum and hustled us, quite forcefully in fact, into the VIP area. 'For your own personal safety,' said one. 'Have a good night,' said the other.

On the other side of the velvet rope things were marginally less crowded but no calmer. People came barrelling up on all sides, the music cacophonous, obscuring their intent, a blonde boy who looked like he should've been in bed already high-fiving me, and a punk passing me a joint. 'Vorsicht!' he yelled in my ear. 'It has much PCP.' I took just the one drag, returned the high-five and passed the punk his smoke back. 'Really cool,' he shouted, the R wobbling around as though his voice were playing on a degraded tape cassette, 'really cool.' I turned to Polly to ask if she wanted a drink, but she had disappeared.

I scanned the room; I couldn't see her. Perhaps she had found Finley, though I couldn't spot him either. I saw the band just across from me, huddled around Peaches, posing for pictures in front of a big purple paper backdrop tiled with the logos of the brands who had sponsored the event: BMW, IBM, Chivas Regal. Alex wasn't with them, he was probably hidden in a more exclusive corner of the club, one reserved for the people you see on magazine covers, their handlers and their dealers. The saxophonist saw me and waved me over, mouthing, 'Get in here!', but I declined with a quick little shake of my head and sank deeper into the party, pushing on to find my friends, or a drink, whichever came first.

Moritz crashed into me at full tilt, throwing both arms around me and sloshing €100 worth of champagne over me from a bottle he was carrying about by the neck. I could smell his body odour, the heavy bulge in his trousers pressed into me when we embraced. 'The guys at the label are fucking psyched about tonight!' he shouted into my ear. 'Here. You want some speed?'

I yelled back, 'Sure,' and he passed me a bomb, a little wrap of amphetamine tied up in cigarette paper, which I chucked in my mouth and washed down with a good long glug of his booze. I tried to be as pornographic about it as possible, letting the fizz spray up into my face; he stared at me sloppy and rubbed on my shoulder. 'Now that's rock and roll, man, that's rock and fucking roll!'

I grinned, pseudo-sheepish. 'Have you seen Alexander?'

Moritz scrunched up his face. 'Huh? What?'

I cupped my hand over his ear. 'Have you seen Alex?' I wanted to slide my hand up his open shirt, across his hairy chest.

He said, 'No. Not until next week. Unless the weather clears up.'

I struggled to parse out what he meant, he tugged at his nose as though he feared it was dribbling snot, then someone new caught his attention and he threw up his arms again, spilling more champagne. 'Martin!' he shouted. 'Holy shit, Martin, my man!' and staggered off in his direction.

I was alone again at the centre of the room, people danced around me, throwing back their heads, limbs moving in all directions at once. The DJ was playing stone-cold disco, and disco does that to people, they lose their shit. The punk with the laced joint was here again and this time I took greater advantage of what he offered. He gave me a blowback, hot honeyed smoke passed from his mouth to mine, and I felt pretty good for a while. I boogied with the best of them, the drugs and the champagne and all the tequila from the green room cascading through my system. I twirled around and around, all my onlookers mercifully blurred so I that couldn't read their expressions of concern.

I felt an awkward ache, the sudden urge to piss, thought I might very well puke, pushed my way towards the neon figures on the other side of the room which advertised the closest available bathroom. I felt like I was fighting my way through V-J Day in Times Square, my knees buckled, I thought I might fall again, and again an arm reached out to steady me, Polly I presumed, but when I looked up it was Alexander.

'Charli,' he said, 'I have been looking all over.'

'I just really need to pee,' I yelped, 'but I can't stand up. Isn't that silly?'

Instinctively I slung my arm around his shoulder so that I could lean my weight on him, and we stumbled together towards the bathroom. The crowd parted for him and the line for the cubicles disintegrated at his smile, all eyes glistened, all mouths fell softly open as he called out in gratitude, 'Thank you, thank you. We have a small emergency here.'

I hitched up my skirt, he dropped me onto the toilet seat like a sack of potatoes, and I let myself go. 'Too much tequila,' I hiccupped, 'and not enough sushi.'

He groaned. 'You must be more sensible with these things, Charli. You are not a little girl.'

'I know, I know,' I said, but I couldn't take him at all seriously. He doubled down on his scowl; I could see how I was trying his patience, only I was too far gone to be sedate. I said, 'Thank you for rescuing me, lover, you're my hero, thank you,' and then started to sing 'The Wind Beneath My Wings' to him, very loudly and very badly. I don't know the lyrics much beyond the title, so I petered out soon enough. Lighting a cigarette, he asked me directly, 'What did you think of the show?'

I felt embarrassed, not because I was sitting with my knickers around my ankles, pissing in front of him, that hardly registered as undignified at all, the ignominy came from being found out. 'Oh,' I swallowed, 'I missed it. I had to stay in the dressing room with Polly, she, ah, wasn't feeling so good.'

'Liar.' He screwed his eyes shut in disappointment. 'I just saw her and she is fine.'

I didn't reply, just rearranged my clothes, flushed the loo, and started up with Bette Midler again, improvising lyrics to steady my nerves. We came out of the cubicle and into another huddle of bystanders and they all applauded. At first I imagined that they were cheering my singing but then I realised they were actually lauding Alexander once more for his performance that night. He stood amongst the swell of admirers, one arm reluctantly holding me up, the other raised high in a wave, almost a salute. 'Thank you,' he smiled, 'you are all so very kind.'

Someone offered us a bottle of Courvoisier and I took a great big gulp. It burned. A wild-eyed kid of indeterminate gender, dark hair flowing around their shoulders, huge brown eyes barely open, crept out from the crowd and spoke as if for all of them. 'I love you,' they said, 'I know it sounds crazy but your music, your style, your whole . . .' they took a manic drunken breath, 'I just,' they said, 'I just, I just,' then promptly threw up all over Alexander's Balenciaga motorcycle boots.

A scream of 'Oh my God!' went up from amongst the onlookers, so chilling you'd have thought there'd been a stabbing, and Alex turned white, completely blanched either in fury or outrage, I couldn't tell, his face a rigid mask of censure.

'I'm sorry,' gabbled the poor sickly fan, 'I'm so so sorry, I'm just . . . I'm just so so sorry.'

'Please excuse me,' was all Alex said.

I laughed quite hysterically as he dragged me out, because it was very funny. 'You have the nicest fans,' I said, but he did not respond, his mood had truly soured. His expression had set like thunder, and as we went back across the dance floor he raised an arm high across his face in an unmistakable gesture of rebuttal, eye contact refused, cutting down dead anyone who tried to grab him or his attention. People were aghast as he pushed his way through his guests propping me up; I thought of James Stewart hauling a plastered Katharine Hepburn about in *The Philadelphia Story* and laughed louder. I was wildly energised but not at all in control of my body, I remember how my mind raced in circuits even as my legs continued to wobble away below me. I kept yelling out, 'Where are we going Alex?' and though he had told me repeatedly, 'Home, Charli, we are going home,' I forgot each time what it was he was saying, even as he spoke the words. 'You are embarrassing yourself.'

My memory of the ride back is of streaks of light flashing across my face from the street lamps outside the car window, an advertisement for something called Dr Oetker's pizza burger playing on the radio, Alex looking down on me, displeased. 'This was such a big show for me, you know?' He shook his head, grim and tense. 'Sometimes you are just so selfish.' A brief burst of rain of hit the windows, 'Fame' on the radio. I realised that I had left Polly behind at the club.

I must've been closer to sober by home, or at least under the impression that I was, because I offered to cook. 'Should I make some eggs?' I asked. 'It's almost breakfast time, are you hungry?'

Alex offered a curt and uncharitable no and went off to dig about for a fresh pack of cigarettes. I shouted out after him, my own temper shortened, 'Well, I'll scramble some for the cat, she'll like that,' but then I remembered my neighbour.

As it was there weren't any eggs so the cat had to make do with cornflakes. The kitchen was basically empty. I ate a few squares of cooking chocolate which Carl had left behind, but I wasn't all that hungry, not really, more agitated, restless, unquiet. I could hear Alex kicking aside papers and dishes, heard them skitter across the bedroom floor. I wondered whether I should go and help him look for his fags, at least try to be accommodating, but thought better of it. The cat was pawing at huge gritty lumps in his litter tray, I felt quite nauseated.

The phone rang. Against the solitude of the hour it seemed alarmingly loud, it caused me to jump up out of my seat and hit my head on the pan rack. I hurried down the hall, clutching my brow, to take it off the hook, reprimanding myself all the while, *It's no wonder the bloody neighbours hate you now is it?*

The phone stopped ringing before I reached it, even before that impossible outgoing message clicked on, so I surmised it must've been a wrong number. Only it rang again and I froze to the spot, not wanting to touch the horrid thing, feeling sure that someone was playing a prank on me, unwilling to give them the satisfaction of knowing they'd riled me. I was just standing there staring at the phone stupidly when Alex came in, cigarette at his lip, tugging at his tie.

'Who the fuck is this?' he barked, and I shrugged, 'No idea.'

Carl's phantom drone started up, the same indecipherable request for the caller to leave a message after the tone, some pun, I think, playing on the homonyms 'sauber' and 'zauber', 'clean' and 'magic'. I never did understand German humour. The recording finished, the punctuating beep shriller than ever, then a voice said, 'Hi, Charli, it's me.'

It took me a second to realise that it was West. He sounded pretty drunk, there was an inflection of sorrow behind his cheery words. 'I know you're super busy. Just wanted to say that I had a great time with you . . . in the bathtub. And I, er, hope you haven't forgotten about me.'

Alex rolled his eyes. 'Oh it is *that* idiot. Of course.'

West continued, he said, 'I was reading something today, and I don't know, it made me think of you. Here, let me find the page.' He coughed to clear his throat, for comic effect, and to cut through his palpable nerves; he began to recite a poem.

Shall I say, I have gone at dusk through narrow streets
And watched the smoke that rises from the pipes
Of lonely men in shirt-sleeves, leaning out of windows?

Alex was reddening in the face now, he said, 'What the hell is he talking about?'

It was something of a sophomore choice but West's sincerity moved me. I smiled to myself. 'It's Eliot.'

Alex growled, 'And who the fuck is that please? Another lover of yours?' I admit I was beginning to feel a little uncomfortable.

'No!' I said. 'Of course not. It's poetry, that's all.'

We stood still and West read on, stumbling once or twice, picking up his place a beat later:

Stretched on the floor, here beside you and me.
Should I, after tea and cakes and ices,
Have the strength to force the moment to its crisis?

I broke into a wider smile, and Alex lost his head.

'This is pathetic,' he snarled, '*he* is pathetic! Why have you not told him that you are through with him already?'

'You're being silly.' I was taken aback. 'We're just friends.'

He seized me by the shoulders. 'Tell him,' he said, his spit flecking my face. 'Pick up the phone and tell this dumb cunt you are through with him. It is over.'

I laughed involuntarily and he tightened his grip, bringing his face right into mine with a mean, violent sneer. 'Do not laugh at me, Charli, do not dare to laugh at me.'

My body went slack, my mind went blank. West went on talking to me through the machine. 'So, yeah, it made me think about you, you being a modernist lit kinda gal and all that. Sorry this is such a long message, shit, I'm pretty drunk.' He hiccupped, 'I stole a bottle of Sekt from the Kaisers at Kottbusser Tor. I brought it over to your place, but you weren't home so I drank it by myself.'

Alex pincered my jaw with his bony fingers, thumb up under my cheekbone, squeezing the flesh of my face into a salacious expression of fear. Sternly, calmly, with icy intention he said, 'Pick up the phone, Charli. Tell this little faggot to stop calling.'

I had no doubt that he was serious; I did as I was told. He let go of my jaw, I went and lifted the receiver, steadied myself to speak, but West cut in first.

'Charli!' he whooped. 'Charli, are you there? Fuck did I wake you up? Fuck, Charli, I'm sorry I didn't mean to I was just . . .'

Alex's breath was sour in my face. 'Tell him now or I will!'

'West?' I stuttered. 'Hello, West?'

'Charli,' he giggled, 'Charli, baby.'

I called up a dispassionate tone, I said, 'You have to stop calling me, West, I'm sorry but . . .'

'What's wrong?' he asked, afraid. 'Are you mad at me? Shit I'm sorry, I'm drunk, I didn't mean to . . .'

My puppet master pressed me, 'Say that you are not interested in him, you never were,' and I repeated, 'I'm not interested in you, West, I never was.'

'Tell him that he is a complete bore and a lousy fuck,' said Alex and I replicated his insults: 'You're a complete bore, West, and a lousy fuck.'

He must've been crying by then because his responses came slower, with great big intermissions of breath. 'Why are you saying this, Charli?'

'Tell him that if he ever calls you again, you'll call the police. Tell him he is a dumb cunt,' Alex said, and yes I repeated that too.

West didn't say anything more, just whimpered at the end of the line. I recognised that a single tear was tracking its way down my cheek. Alex grinned with pure malevolence and flicked his spent cigarette to the floor. 'Now say goodnight, Charli. It is time for bed.'

'Goodnight, West,' I said and hung up.

Alex seemed satisfied; he turned his attention to changing into his pyjamas for bed. He opened the window to let in some fresh cold air. 'Good girl,' he said, unbuttoning his shirt. 'I think a clean break is best, don't you?'

5

Night beats around my head, I listen to the blood in my ears and the sterile air brushing against my hair, my eyes wide open in the dark. I know this room so well I can see without light, my bedside tableau as clear to me as Mont Sainte-Victoire to the painter who has depicted her 200 times. What might he have made of my modest mess, Paul Cezanne? A Dickens novel, a Fanta can, the last vestiges of character.

The strangest memories return to you when all you have is slackened time and insomnia, when you're a very caged bird you really do dream of flight, it's true. Without the medication coming in at such high dosages I barely doze. I lie here through the night poking around inside my own skull, worrying the curved corners with my bony fingers, looking for those memories of freedom. When we first arrived in Berlin, he used to drive me around the city late at night in his old Mercedes. It was very romantic. He liked to have me sit in the back and to pretend that he was my chauffeur. He'd ask, 'Where to, madame?' and I would instruct him to drive me west, through Bergmannkiez and into Schöneberg by Bowie's old apartment on Hauptstrasse, then up through Charlottenburg, along Kurfürstendamm past KaDeWe and the ruins of the Kaiser Wilhelm Memorial Church. He'd order me to masturbate on the backseat, his eyes glinting perversity in the rearview mirror. A hoot. Two nurses are in the corridor, laughing. Wendy Carlos synthesises Beethoven's Ninth.

I've lost the power to dream. I'm trapped here like a wasp between windowpanes, condemned to a life fully awake and awake to an endless reality, a life without sleep, sleep without dreams, and the truth of it all pains me. In dreams we can at least invent new people, characters we recognise without ever having seen them before, everything moves with an inherent logic, just like at the ballet. But here I have only what I have, I'm lashed to these characters Here *and* Now, *the remaining agents: the newspaper man, the nurse, the nun, the threat of my mother's impending visit, and none of them can offer me relief.*

All these disordered scenes and stubborn characters, misremembered yet unwilling to bend to comfort or convenience; I am accompanied by an armchair sprouting legs, by Finley laying flowers for Frederick the Great, a young girl watches Napoleon riding through the Brandenburg Gate, Hubert is hurling the good china at my head. Some sequences remain intact but I can't knit them together into any sort of sense, there's no imagination left in me with which to try and make meaning and so self-soothe. Worse, now that I'm awake I daren't fabricate, for fear of falling into delusion, I can only lie here in the ruins of a life, mangled dates and feral narrative. It's lucky I'm not writing a novel, I suppose.

6

I didn't ever imagine that I'd wind up in service, as the PA-cum-tour manager for a celebrity, lugging cases on and off trains, buffering back the press, coughing up blandishments on demand. When I was a child, I thought that I'd become a scholar, maybe a biographer, but then Esther Williams always wanted to play straight roles and Susan Sontag wanted to be known as a novelist. Alexander himself said that he always thought he'd become an actor, not a singer, that it just sort of happened this way. Ultimately though, we're made by other people, aren't we? Not ourselves – we're manufactured by a wider world. 'The public is never wrong,' that's how Dietrich put it, and she ought to know. 'You will stretch out your hands and someone else will put your belt on you, and bring you where you do not want to go' – that's St John's take.

We criss-crossed the continent for a month, through farmlands, mountain ranges, thunderstorms. I travelled with the musicians in standard class, the three of them usually stoned, completely ignorant of the fact that they were travelling on fake tickets, myself the only one sweating whenever the conductor asked for our reservations. On shorter journeys we sat around a table playing cards and eating pretzels from the onboard catering menu; on overnight voyages we'd share a berth in the sleeper car. It wasn't at all unpleasant, in fact nearly all of the good memories I have of that tour come from hanging with the boys in the band, drinking the vodka we bought when the train stopped for a change of staff in some small town whose name we couldn't pronounce, playing charades, getting a bunkmate off when we thought the other the boys were sleeping.

Some of the trains we travelled on were quite shabby, some impossibly elegant. The points where we had to transfer between lines could actually be quite shocking: stepping off a Wi-Fi-enabled carriage with sliding doors, smart lights and heated seats, and onto another which had not been refurbished since the Wall came down felt like an abrupt refutation of linear time. The civil conviviality of the German Intercity Express trains, with their double decks and ample bathrooms, the coffee poured by moustachioed gentlemen wheeling trolleys down the Italian line, breakfast rolls dished out with a wink and enjoyed on a pleather couchette pulling into Kraków. I remember the dining car on a train through Hungary having tables laid with cloths and linen serviettes, waiters in blacks scribbling on notepads, serving goulash, red wine, plum cake on china. An unseasonable mid-summer snow fell as we journeyed, and for a moment there in the carriage a wave of mystic nostalgia came over me, like past-life regression.

Alexander travelled alone in a first-class cabin, like Dracula carted over the globe in his coffin of earth. From time to time the porter would appear with a note and summon one of us to his cabin, usually when he needed a hit of something. Being possessed of such a paranoiac personality he insisted that the band travel with the drugs divided evenly between them, so that if any one of them were to be caught, they wouldn't be in possession of too serious a quantity. It was an illogical scheme of course – obviously if the police found a stash of heroin, cocaine, LSD and speed on one of us they'd search us all – but the band really appreciated the gesture all the same. It made them feel he cared for them, I suppose, and I didn't have the heart to tell them.

When he called for me it was for pragmatic purposes: to strategise on our media campaign, to index what he would wear and when, to gather intelligence on the band themselves. He was keen to be kept abreast of any potential mutiny, he said he needed to conserve every drop of energy between shows but all the same he was unable to stomach the idea that he was missing out on a single happening. He wanted to know who said what about him, who kept a diary, who drank to excess, who was fucking who (that seemed to excite him).

Sometimes I would read to him, bits of JT LeRoy and Araki Yasusada. He liked to hear Chekhov too, although it was a strain on my eyes since he kept the blinds drawn on both the door and windows and would only allow the puny overhead reading light for illumination. Intermittently his face would appear in the darkness, lit up by his cigarette lighter as he started on another Sobranie, somehow outfoxing even the Deutsche Bahn smoke detection systems. 'Charli,' he'd say, 'don't stop. You read so beautifully, don't stop. A little more. Please?' Sometimes he was just like a little boy, sometimes as insufferable as a nineties supermodel, his mood, his attitude, his whole personality as changeable as a Roman hour.

It was a strange shuttling existence coated in low-level mania, growing ennui and occasional emissions of high-voltage drama, such as when the keyboardist threatened to quit because he walked in on Alexander fucking the drummer in his cabin. The poor thing had been under the misapprehension that he and Alex had some sort of thing going on, it would've been laughable if it wasn't so pathetic. It took me two hours of begging and pleading to keep him from getting off the train in Belgrade and taking his keyboard with him, which was nothing compared with the stress of being found out for the fake tickets and having to persuade the guard that it was all *just some big mistake* on the part of our travel agent, accidentally brushing my cleavage against him as I bent over to point out various justifying details on the phony slips.

Halfway through the tour Alex broke out into uncontrollable hysteria, convinced that one of the boys had deliberately given him scabies, and we had to send out all of our clothes to the cleaners the minute we arrived in Budapest in order to contain the outbreak. It cost €800 and for an entire day none of us had a single article of clothing to wear. Alex insisted we sit in our underwear on paper towels and wait in our rooms. We were lucky to be staying in a decent hotel that evening or else it could've been very uncomfortable. I ate a packet of Lotus biscuits and watched a far-right politician argue on live television for a new *Anschluss,* a reunion of the two halves of the old Empire, shivering slightly in my panties, bored and biding my time. As it turned out, nobody ever had scabies. Alex was simply allergic to the soap powder they used on the bed linens of the sleeper car.

We really never knew what to expect when we stepped off the train, if we'd be harassed by fraudulent customs officers or mobbed by a scrappy bunch of local groupies, if someone would meet us or if we'd be left to take care of ourselves, if we'd be staying at a flop-house or in a penthouse. The accommodations varied wildly depending on how much the local promoters cared for their charges, or rather how much they expected to make on the door, and Alex's moods on arrival were equally unforeseeable. There was no reliable metric with which to measure or predict: sometimes the ugliest, most rundown two-star B&B would inspire in him diabolic fits of glee, sometimes the best the city had to offer failed to satisfy.

He was most often pleased when the respect he believed was due to him was paid, say when the night manager of a cheap hotel asked him to sign a picture to be displayed alongside those of other notable guests, former tennis players and visiting Buddhist monks, or when the concierge sent up a bottle of mid-price fizz with a note declaring it *an honour to have him stay*. Alex loved anything free, he saw it as a sign of success. 'They give to rich people so much,' he smiled wanly, 'even though they do not need it. It is a little perverse, yes, but that is life. And after all I am Alexander Geist now.'

Our personal finances remained sickly. We couldn't ever access much in the way of hard cash, and in-room dining, though billable, was exorbitantly expensive, so usually I'd have to trek around whichever city we had arrived in looking for sliced meats and orange juice and bring them back to the hotel, blushing at the disgrace of lugging an Aldi carrier bag through the lobby. The band had a petty cash subsistence agreement with Moritz, so they took themselves out for vegan meatballs and 2-4-1 Harvey Wallbangers. Myself, I ate a lot of chocolate soy pudding because it came in little single-serve pods and didn't need to be refrigerated.

In Vienna the promoter was clearly expecting a really big return, because he put us all up at the Hotel Sacher. Alex called me room to room, his mood clearly elevated by the sheer opulence of the place, his voice creamy over the phone line. 'Come up and see me, would you, lover?'

I must've sighed loudly because Alex took on a more imploring tone. 'Come on, Charli, I have a bottle of champagne on ice up here,' he said, 'it is only Veuve Clicquot, but still.'

I went up to his suite with my notepad and the underwear I had washed for him by hand in the sink. The door was open, his suitcases turned out on the floor, every light in the place was on. 'In here,' he called, and I followed his voice towards the bathroom. I found him submerged in ivory soap bubbles, smoking in the tub, filling in the *New York Times* crossword. The radio was on too, a Bose balanced precariously on the lip of the bidet, playing the second movement of Vivaldi's 'Spring.'

Alex said, 'He used to live across the street, you know?'

'Who?' I asked.

'Vivaldi,' he scoffed. 'Silly.'

He dropped the newspaper onto the tiles and felt for his champagne glass. Finding it empty on the trestle table, he waved it in the air: 'Top me up, would you, lover?'

At that moment, he seemed to me ridiculous, hardly human, the composite of innumerable clapped-out clichés. It was just like Polly said, he wasn't a real person, he was an icing sugar phantom confected from art-school scrapbooks and Hollywood offcuts, and I thought *How easy it would be to knock the radio into the bathtub, to slip the downers from my pocket into his glass and leave him to drown*. The idea chilled me.

'Take a glass for yourself,' he insisted, 'and sit down. There is a fruit basket somewhere too, maybe under these towels?'

I poured for us both and took a fat blushing orange from the basket, I sat on the toilet to peel it. Alexander started on the speech he'd called me in to hear. 'I know I haven't been so very nice to you lately,' he began, 'and I am sorry for that.'

He gave me a long, flat talk, nothing I hadn't heard before, about how embarrassed he was, how ashamed he was to have been so unkind. He blamed it all on the burdens of fame, on the demands of being an artist, touring, constantly having to smile for the camera. He was exhausted he said, so completely overworked – could we just put all of the unpleasantness behind us? He was sure we could.

He smoked his Sobranies and drank more champagne, moved across the full colour wheel of emotions, now contrite and humble, now grandstanding and vainglorious, forlorn, courageous, resolute, a turgid symphony of sentiments, *hate me, love me, forgive me, don't leave me*. He told me he wouldn't blame me for being upset with him, of course, he knew he could be difficult from time to time, it was his creative temperament, all he asked for was a little understanding.

'Do you know how exhausting it is to be me?' He emptied a flask of Floris Limes into the bathtub. 'No, of course you do not. It is not possible.'

Though frankly I wanted to say *get a fucking grip, Alexander* and go back to my own room, I found myself instead nodding along in sympathy with his story, apathetic as if hypnotised. 'Of course, Alex,' I said, 'of course, we all know how hard you work.'

These were not the words I wanted to say, but they were the words I heard myself saying. I lived like the Costa Rican spider which, injected with the parasitoid wasp's mind-controlling venom, begins spinning a web in which to host the hymenopteric larvae.

He grinned like a perfect ghoul over the rim of the bath. 'I knew you would understand, lover, I knew it. I put a lot of pressure on you. I know this, of course. But I put so much more on me,' he said, '*so* much more.'

I nodded in silent empathy, tuned half in, half out, punch-drunk from the fizz and the fumes from Alex's bath, glossy with steam, staring at the telephone mounted on the wall, which suddenly rang. I was shocked, it was like a gun going off in my hand, I thought I'd made it ring with the power of my mind. Alex reached and took it from the cradle, twirling the cord around his fingers as a voice prattled away on the other end, someone obsequious, someone who wanted something from him, badly.

He hemmed and hawed noncommittally for a little while as if unable to make up his mind. It was a slow sadistic while before he broke out brightly: 'Alright then, if it means *so very much* to the hotel, I can make time. But send up another bottle of champagne, would you, please? And a teller of cold meats. Oh, and a citrus reamer. I have all of these oranges in my basket you see, but no way to drink them. Yes, yes. Ciao, ciao.'

He hung up, lit another fag and sighed, but dreamily. The hotel management wanted him to participate in a photo shoot on the roof that evening. A menswear magazine was running a piece to celebrate the hotel's 140th birthday and Alexander's participation would prove perfection. The magazine would cover the cost of his stay at the hotel, of course, and so he very readily agreed.

'You see? It never ends!' He was transparently delighted. 'Tell me, did we pack the astrakhan jacket – the one from Dior? Or did it go back already?'

'It's here,' I said, 'I saw it on your floor,' but he wasn't really listening.

He rose from the water. 'This is what it will be like from now on,' he said, he was pink as a prawn and half hard. 'I must work continually to make myself. I am the artist and I am the artwork both.' He pulled out the plug, the water drained away, he stood and contemplated. I brought him a towel, of course I did. He was most probably speeding out of his brain, he had let the cigarette butt drop into the sudsy fragranced liquid lapping his calves, he said: 'There was a very good line in this play you read for me on the train. Something, something, *I cannot find peace in myself . . .*'

'*I can't get any rest away from myself*,' I corrected, '*I feel as though I am devouring my own life*. Yes,' I said, 'Chekhov.'

He stepped out of the tub, nodding fervently. 'That's it, that is it! This is the feeling I am having right now. I must take everything inside me and give it up, to my audience, to *them*.' He looked around the room wild-eyed as if *they* were all in the bathroom with us, then turned to fix his gaze on me, startled by a new idea. 'You really should be my spokesperson, Charli, you know? You speak so much better for me.'

The champagne and the cold cuts arrived. Alex tipped the bellboy €50. I helped him into his clothes and brushed his hair, styled it in the parting he always wore, dressed it perhaps a little too heavily with pomade, but not bad. I applied his turquoise eyeshadow and cardinal lipstick just as Polly had shown me – a pretty good job overall, I was well practised now, and besides the magazine could always retouch the corners where I had fucked up. We drank the second bottle of champagne and danced around the coffee table to 'Young Americans', made out a little, ate wurst and Black Forest ham, then at midnight went up to the roof terrace as directed.

Alex posed beautifully against the Vienna skyline, the moon plump and pregnant behind him, the opera house below, a crisp and clear and uncreased night. The lamb fur collar of his coat flipped up to his cheekbones, a gaggle of French girls running in and out of the frame with reflector boards, hydrating mist and hairspray. I watched from the shadows. When Alexander was on, really on, he radiated something so luminous that it threw everything else in the surroundings into deep obscurity.

He never fumbled, threw his arms wide, brought his hands up to flank his face, grinned, scowled, glowered, cast off his coat, draped himself over the replica Second Empire sofa they'd heaved up seven floors especially for this moment. The camera flash turned him silver, made him immortal, placed him in the firmament. When they wrote up this article they'd run the name Alexander Geist alongside Rudolf Nureyev, Grace Kelly, Graham Greene, his name belonged with theirs now. Tomorrow we might pay the price for such exertion, but tonight he was the dauphin, heir to a limitless kingdom, and he was treated as such.

The concierge came on set at least three times with more champagne, with fruit juice, with cigarettes, announcing that there were flowers and truffles waiting back in the suite. An assistant pressed me with vouchers for the spa, with a fistful of sleeping pills, gifts for Alex; another bellboy arrived and presented me with a glossy chocolate cake in a big wooden box with brass hinges. He wore a maroon uniform studded with two rows of polished buttons and bowed very formally. 'With compliments of the hotel.' It was preposterous, an impossible situation. Over and over the same thought came to my mind: *Is this really my life?*

One of the French girls shrieked, she said could see a shooting star. We all turned but it was only a plane coming in to land at Flughafen Wien. It was late now, maybe coming on for 2 a.m., the photographer spoke, gruff but charmed, 'These are cool, man, really cool. Think you can give us a couple more?'

Alex beamed with unconcealed delight. 'Of course, lover,' he said. 'I am here all night.'

7

We travelled on. Everyone's read a rock star's account of life on the road, haven't they? The tour diary, I honestly don't know how any of them can claim to recall it all. Jayne County, Patti Smith, Kim Gordon, how did they maintain a clear enough head to keep a record? Perhaps they just made it all up. Certainly, my own recollections are in large part indistinct; the experience for me was one of relentless mundane chaos. Ultimately every dressing room looks the same, every groupie, every dealer. Sometimes my memory feels like nothing more than a 2 kg plum pudding, unassailably rich, densely monotonous, and I am forced to plough my way through it alone, occasionally striking a gold coin reminiscence.

Most of the shows were triumphant. I have to hand it to Alexander there: on-stage he was unsurpassable. His volatility and manipulation transmuted into incontrovertible magnetism; up there he wasn't paranoid or cruel, he was all charm. It was as if he had been invented for this very purpose. When the lights hit him, this silly, skinny caricature, his borrowed clothes and hijacked mannerisms became something quite extraordinary, and I couldn't help but love him.

Of course some people hated him for this very reason, they thought it dark-sided. In Warsaw, a planned TV appearance drew protests from a homophobic church group, a hundred or so people outside the studio waving placards. I had to change into one of Alex's suits and hang about the lobby of the TV station, loitering in plain sight in his fedora and shades with all those zealots banging on the doors whilst the real Alexander was escorted out the back. Since we're roughly the same height and build we got away with it. I did such a good job in fact that I was almost wounded when a brick came sailing through the safety glass. In Sofia his gig had to be cut short when someone threw a lit firework on-stage. As scary as it sounds, two disasters across seventeen cities isn't so bad, and honestly in most places we were received like Jesus entering Jerusalem. People really loved him; it was easy to be swept up in the folly of it all.

In Madrid we played for 1,500 people in an Art Deco dance hall and stayed in some crummy Novotel at the back of the train station, which might've felt degrading if it hadn't given us the opportunity to have breakfast with another guest, himself a musician. He had been billeted there by the festival booker too and shared with Alex, over hard-boiled eggs and underripe melon, his theory that swathes of 'Song of Solomon' had been borrowed from the Egyptian *Book of the Dead*. Alex just drew that sort of conversation out of people, like a mesmerist, and later, back in the room, I heard him talking to himself, reliving the conversation in front of the mirror. 'Breakfast with Brian Eno,' he chuckled, 'imagine!', practising his vocabulary of smiles. 'You are a star now Alex,' he said, repeating it over and over like a mantra, 'you are a star.'

We visited Porto to play in an old opera house and afterwards we were shuttled about for a week between a string of luxury golf resorts, performing smaller shows for semi-retired billionaires, substantial Portuguese vistas blurring by the windows of our air-conditioned minibus, the keyboardist puking into a Dunkin' Donuts bag all the way. In Zagreb a boy climbed on-stage to kiss Alex and Alex kissed him back, passionately; the whole place went up in screams, I watched it back the next day on the Czech news. In Zurich Alex had a migraine which laid him out flat for a day and a half and I had to stand in for him at soundcheck, not singing or anything of course, just saying 'One two, one two' into the mic for an indeterminable amount of time whilst the band tapped and honked behind me checking their levels and the technicians perfected the mix. I thought, *So this is what it's like to be up here, is it?* And though I didn't feel any different, the people around me all acted as if I were suddenly very important, and I understood how completely power has the potential to corrupt.

For the rest of the afternoon all I had to do was scowl or raise my hand and someone would scurry over to ask if there was anything they could help with. It was good fun, until Alexander descended of course, then I was simply *chopped liver*, but then, that's the life of a star, here today, gone tomorrow. I wasn't troubled, just slipped off to order his steak since he had to eat precisely four hours before each show. He was following the Mick Jagger diet at the time, if I remember correctly.

Rome was something of a *succès de scandal*; we rode into the Eternal City on a wave of notoriety and endlessly exaggerated rumours of on-stage sex, terrorist bombings narrowly thwarted and papal threats of excommunication. Alex was forced to give a last-minute press conference by the show's promoter to appease the concerns of the Italian media. He was irritated by this and so gave deliberately eccentric answers to even the most asinine of questions, which led the journalists to report that not only was he an unrepentant libertine, he was also a drug addict. In the end the controversy surrounding the concert was so great that we had to add a second show.

Those crowds were the most raucous I've ever seen; they came in as if spoiling for a fight. Every last one of them was drunk, half of them on speed, the rest seemingly rolling on molly, ready for the time of their lives. Most of them smoked cigarettes throughout too, which delighted Alex of course, and right at the end of the second show, during the encore, he climbed down into the front row to show his appreciation with more kisses. I never thought of him as naive, but that night he certainly got more than he bargained for. There was a surge of bodies towards him, people were pulling at his clothes, at his hair, grabbing at his crotch. When security pulled him out of the Roman mêlée he was panicked, his hair was all messed up and his pink Versace trousers were ripped across the arse. It really freaked him out. I thought it was a very encouraging sign myself, and told him he should take it as an expression of their devotion. 'They love you,' I said, 'there's nothing to be afraid of.'

'Love!' he spluttered. 'Love like this is dangerous. It was a fan who killed John Lennon!'

I stroked him. 'Come on now, that was a one-off.'

La Repubblica ran a very uncharitable review of the shows under the headline *Il giovane pretendente*, the young pretender, which the saxophonist translated for us with his secondary school Italian. There were a couple of unnecessary digs at Alex's 'capelli grassi' and his 'abiti sgargianti', his oily hair and garish clothes. All in all it amounted to a two-page screed warning the Italian public not to fall for 'questo ciarlatano, questo falso', this charlatan, this fake, this pale imitation of the greats. Alex was enraged, he threw a vase of flowers at the wall, then he broke out howling. 'How dare they? To say I control my voice like a pubescent boy! How dare they?'

I tried to reason with him but he would not hear it. He was particularly incensed that they had called him a David Bowie wannabe in print – he was very superstitious about the written word. 'Every artist imitates,' I said, 'you know that. *Even* Bowie, *especially* Bowie,' but it didn't cool him off. I had to snatch an ashtray shaped like the Colosseum out of his hand before he threw that too. He blinked at me in surprise, taken aback by my uncustomary assertiveness, I suppose, and sat himself down on the bed. I tossed him his cigarette case and he lit up. I picked a few of the surviving roses out from the mess of glass and bourbon pooled on the floor and began a little pep talk.

Bowie mimicked Anthony Newley's voice and Bob Dylan's lyrics, I explained, he wrote 'Life on Mars?' as a Frank Sinatra parody, he copied backing vocals from the Beatles and stole one of Romy Haag's cabaret acts for a music video. 'I mean, he took the name Ziggy from Iggy Pop, for goodness' sake.' I rehomed the flowers I had salvaged in a champagne bucket. 'So really it's an honour that they say you're a thief too,' I said, 'why don't you think about it like that?'

I had failed to convince him, I could tell; he didn't seem liable to break anything else, but he still furrowed his brow. 'I will never sing in this shithole country again,' he cursed. 'I will never speak another word.'

For the rest of our time in Italy he refused to say anything, on this he would not budge. He insisted that I cancel his remaining interviews and scribbled all further communications on sheets of hotel notepaper, at dinner he would only point to the menu and glower. At the train station as we prepared to board the sleeper to France we were ambushed by an unholy congress of young fans, would-be business associates and members of the press, and still he declined to talk.

A camera crew forced their way through the throng and, without any of the usual formalities, began firing questions at him as we traversed the concourse. Apparently we were live on television and the journalist, despite her courteous rolling English, was not pulling any punches. *Would he like to explain his recent behaviour on-stage? Did he care nothing for the morals of Italy's youth? Was he deliberately trying to corrupt them, to provoke some sort of cultural revolution?*

She followed us to the platform, the whole crowd did, it expanded as we moved towards the train, where we reached a stalemate in a carriage-side corral. The musicians held the crowd back, the interviewer continued to harangue Alex.

'Do you have anything you'd like to say to concerned parents?' He remained impassive behind his sunglasses, and only shrugged at each question. I felt we were in danger of magnifying the trouble we'd already caused, unnecessarily, so I turned and spoke to the journalist myself. 'Herr Geist is incredibly fatigued,' I said, 'he would like to share his gratitude with all of his Italian fans, with everyone who came to see the shows in Rome and Milan, and he is very excited to return again very soon.'

With startling fluency the interviewer translated what I'd said into Italian for the benefit of viewers at home, then pivoted back to English and asked me, 'And do you have an answer to the reports of drug-taking and Satanism at your concerts?'

Alex stood beside me, arms folded in front of his chest, mute. I spoke for him, quietly thrilled, reminded of course of that old clip of Andy Warhol silent at a museum gala, having Candy Darling answer all of the questions put to him.

'I think it's wonderful,' I said, 'what a stimulating culture you have in Italy! Now, I'm afraid that's all we have time for. We mustn't keep the train or the other passengers waiting any longer. Thank you so much for your time, everyone. Alexander is so grateful to you all, he really is. Thank you.'

The small crowd whistled and cheered and the television host signed off her report, negating the noise with a finger in her ear. We boarded the train and waved from the windows, grinning like waxworks as we pulled out of the station. Still people ran alongside us, jumping up to slap kisses on the glass. Alex smiled graciously but behind his shades he hissed, 'This whole country is lunatic.' My God it was a relief to arrive in France.

8

The French were gearing up for an election, so Alex was kept off the front pages for a few days by a legendary film actress who came out swinging for a far-right candidate, peppering her every interview with extremely inflammatory Islamophobia. The landscape here was very different.

In Lyon we had an unsettlingly calm time of it, in Strasbourg we drew a few celebrities backstage but none of them spoke English, so the evening was a bust and we were back at the hotel eating macarons before midnight. At least I was, Alex was only crumbling them between his fingers resentfully, mumbling about the excessive sugar. 'People do not admit it,' he said, 'but of course they are all very addicted.' Only in Nantes did we encounter any real action, with the touring cast of Disney's *Beauty and the Beast*, who were probably the most debauched bunch of Casanovas and speed freaks that I've ever met.

In Paris, our last stop, we were welcomed by a very sweet trans girl who was interning with the local promoter, a drug dealer and Polly, who was staying in the Faubourg for a week with an aunt. She looked tired and a little browbeaten, I could tell that she needed to talk and since there were practically a whole twelve hours before the gig, I begged off and went to traipse the city with her. The young intern had a big bunch of flowers for Alexander, the dealer had an envelope full of goodness knows what, he was distracted by all the attention, and I saw my chance to slip away. Only the drummer called out after me, 'Hey! What about sound check?'

'You'll figure it out,' I shouted back, 'it'll be the same as always.' I left Gare de l'Est at a pace, relieved to be rid of them all.

Polly was very familiar with the city: her father used to bring her over every spring when he gave his annual lecture at the American Library; her French was pretty polished, she even understood the Metro system. We travelled down to Le Bon Marché on the 4 because she needed to replace some makeup and look for some lingerie; she picked up a few silk scarves and a tuberose candle whilst we were there, but it was all rather joyless. She went plodding around the store perfectly moribund, shopping under obligation, remarking on how ugly the place was since the renovation and detailing exactly how rapidly her own life was falling apart. She had lost a portrait commission after arguing with her gallerist over his cut, and had broken up with Benny, her boyfriend, even though things had been going great guns. It had not been a beautiful summer for her.

'I came back from the florist last week and found him in bed with Callum,' she said, 'the wretched little twink.'

'No, really?' I asked, aghast. 'What did you do?'

'Well, obviously I was fucking furious,' she said, 'I started hitting them with the flowers. This big bunch of dahlias. I just broke it over their heads and kicked them both out into the street half naked.'

I suppressed a giggle. 'Oh, Polly that sounds awful.'

'It was,' she said, 'I honestly cannot believe this is where I find myself in life.'

She had a real flair for melodrama which was quite at odds with her glacial Protestant persona. She could be very maudlin when the situation called for it, and that afternoon, as the sales assistant measured her for a bra, she was so full of conspicuous emotion that the marmish attendant had to ask her to please stop groaning so heavily, as she was making an accurate measurement impossible.

She regarded her reflection contemptuously in the back of the dressing room door and said, 'Do you ever wish you had been born ugly? Instead of having to watch it all slip away?'

'Well, now you're just being silly,' I protested. 'You're a beautiful young woman with unfortunate taste in men, that's all. God knows I can relate.'

She sighed. 'I'm thirty today, did you know? Thirty and single and can't sell a painting.'

Fuck. I had forgotten. I said, 'Fuck! It's your birthday, of course.' I was mortified by my thoughtlessness.

'Ahem,' the sales assistant coughed, 'quatre-vingt-cinq B, madame. Your size.'

'*Mademoiselle*, s'il vous plait.' Polly corrected her, then turned to me. 'You see what I mean? Sometimes I think my grandfather had the right idea. He just took himself to bed, drank a litre of whiskey and tied a plastic bag over his head.'

I pinched my brow. 'This is getting far too morbid now,' I said, 'it's a birthday not a cancer diagnosis. Look, we're in Paris, come on, forget the bra. Let's get you a cake.'

'Yes, you're right,' she acceded, 'fuck it all. I can always go to KaDeWe when I'm back. Au revoir madame, je vous remercie pour votre aide.'

In lieu of a strawberry gateau, we bought six finger-sized eclairs for €35 from a patisserie Polly knew over by Place des Vosges. We walked with them towards Notre-Dame.

We sat just across the street from the cathedral on the deep stone window ledge of some abandoned hôtel particulier; a notice affixed to the old coach door declared that it must remain vacant, so as to speculate in value. It was a blazing hot day, the sun was directly over the parvis, leaving no shadow. A great snaking line of sightseers suffered for admission, a flock of nuns hustled out of the cathedral shielding their faces.

Polly finished peeling the fondant from an eclair. 'I saw you on television,' she said, 'on the news. You looked particularly demented. How's it all going?'

I offered my palms to the sky in that universal gesture of bewilderment. 'God, I haven't been able to think straight for a month, I think I'm going mad with it all.' I threw a thumbnail of pastry at a mangy-looking pigeon, which set it flapping in a flamenco of appreciation. 'You know, last night I found myself longing for London.'

Polly cocked an eyebrow. 'Charli, really. How could anyone *long for London*? That's like saying you miss having cold sores.'

I laughed and she filled me in on everything I'd missed since I'd been away from Berlin: Suzanne had scored a big record deal and was moving to Los Angeles; Ryan had been fired from the magazine over an article he wrote, naming the doctor accused of touching up all those patients; Jamie had ditched Hubert for someone significantly more solvent.

'Speaking of,' she said, 'look at this,' and took her phone from her purse to show me a photograph of Finley and Gerhard smiling over affogati at Caffè Florian, on Piazza San Marco in Venice. Finley was wearing a parka and a tartan scarf; he was recovering from a bout of tonsillitis which he'd caught on the flight. She said that he'd spent a night in hospital with a forty-two-degree fever, and that Gerhard had been so worried he moved them from their three-star pension over to the Gritti Palace out of an exaggerated sense of guilt. 'Wow,' I said, 'and I thought the hairdryer was impressive.'

A woman in a wedding dress marched past with her skirts bundled up and her high heels tucked under her arm, her groom hurried along beside her in a bow tie and a suit jacket at least a size too small. He was holding a parasol above her head; she was berating him in Chinese. A photographer followed behind lugging two hulking SLRs and a reflector board, sweating. Polly watched them go by with a superficial curiosity. 'Oh, and did I tell you?' she said. 'My mother's trying to set me up with my brother's school friend, Eddy. That's my other big news.'

'Your mother reads too much Joanna Trollope,' I said. 'You really should slip her a copy of *The Second Sex* for Christmas.'

'It's obscene,' Polly continued. 'I've known him since we were children. My mother says that I'm not getting any younger, the miserable bitch, and that in *her day* it was *perfectly normal* to marry a boy your brother brought home from boarding school.' She sighed heavily. 'You're very lucky to be an only child, you know, Charli. Very lucky.'

I don't know why I chose this particular moment, perhaps because I felt very close to her that afternoon, because we were sharing our vulnerabilities, because I had missed her, I guess. I said, 'I'm not actually. Not really.'

'Charli,' she was frowning again, 'I've met your whole family. Your mother calls me all the time, of course you're an only child.'

'No, I had a brother,' I said. 'He died in a car crash. Drove his little Mazda into the side of a fast-food truck.'

Polly's face twisted up in distaste. 'That's not *desperately* funny, Charli. I know I was being a little flippant about my grandfather and all, but he was very old and very ill . . .'

'No, no,' I said, 'I'm not joking. I really had a brother, and he really did die. I was only nine or ten, he was much older than me. I wasn't even allowed to go to the funeral.' I kicked away the pigeon, it was grossing me out now. 'You know, I honestly don't know why I'm telling you this, maybe it's all the sugar, but *I am* telling you, so there you are. Happy birthday Polly Grainger.' I toasted her with the butt of my eclair.

Her mouth hung slack. 'Oh, Charli, that's awful, that's so awful. Charli, I'm so sorry.'

'It's weird,' I cleared my throat, 'you're the first person I've ever told.'

She looked dazed. 'Your poor mother,' she said. 'Explains a lot though doesn't it?'

'Yes,' I bobbed my head. 'She really went to pieces. She started to colour her hair compulsively and then she gave away the television. She refuses to talk about it, about *him*, my brother, even now. She won't say his name.' A cloud briefly concealed the sun, something caught in my throat. 'And I'm totally forbidden from mentioning him,' I said, 'still. I get scared that she'll find out I've spoken of him and scold me. It's ridiculous, why do I pay attention? She's bananas.'

'Well, it's good that you've told me,' Polly took my hand. 'And I'm not going to tell anyone else, so don't worry. I can keep mum.' She broke the final eclair in half. 'Fuck, what a day.'

From where we were sitting we could see the Chinese bride and groom setting up for their pictures in front of the cathedral. They had asked a passerby to hold the veil so that it would seem to flow back from her head romantically, but the stranger had arranged it artlessly and so it looked like a sheet of mosquito netting. I felt desperately sad for a minute, I wanted to rush in and save the shot, only the space between us seemed too vast to cross.

'I had a photograph of him that I hid under my mattress,' I said, 'away from my mother. After he died, I used to stare at it and try to, I don't know, to summon him up, I suppose. I must've seen something of the sort on TV; the noughties were very witchy, if you remember. I had this whole ritual, wicked, I'm sure. I used to light scented candles in front of his picture and chant things like, "If you are out there, if you are able to, please haunt me." Silly really.'

I smoothed out my skirt, knocking chips of fondant from my lap. They disappeared amongst the cobblestones, the pigeon shuffled cautiously back over.

'Of course my mother went spare and accused me of worshipping the devil. She dragged me out to see Father Stephen in the middle of the night, it was mortifying. I had to clean all the statues in the church every morning before school for a month. Father Stephen said it was a meditation to bring my mind back to where it belonged, back to God.'

Polly sniffed, 'Deranged,' though I wasn't sure if she meant me, my mother, or the Church. 'Do you miss him?' she asked. 'Your brother?'

'The funny thing is,' I said, 'I can't remember much about him. Only that I was a little afraid of him.'

'Yes well, older brothers can be *awful* bastards.' She was fanning herself with the flattened cake box. 'I'm not surprised. Would you like to go into the cathedral and say a prayer? I'm sure they'll have a few Madonnas you can dust.'

I hadn't ever been inside Notre-Dame, only driven past the exterior slowly on a school coach trip. I was cowed before we even stepped over the hallowed threshold, the monstrous scale, all the saints and martyrs crowded above the doorway, the gargoyles leering down. Polly led us in through the worshippers' door, skipping the line. This was a trick she'd learned from her father – she called it *speedy boarding for the faithfully departing*. She was perfectly at ease there, just as she was everywhere. Someone told me that this was the truest mark of breeding, this ineffable sense of belonging, even here on the chequerboard floor of eternity with irritable security guards sailing by to scowl and shush. We shunted through the hushed crush of tourists, all holding their baseball caps and their babies, and slipped into a pew.

'Eddy's family are Catholics,' she whispered. 'I wonder if my mother knows *that*? She has a lifelong hatred of *papists*, it's almost a fixation with her. She takes great pride in being able to trace her family back to Cromwell's lot. The ghoul.'

'Oh really?' I said, though it was hard to pay attention to family gossip now we were inside the cathedral itself, with the weight of eight centuries of mystery and legend bearing down upon us.

'Yes,' she continued, 'the Campbell-Bannermans are real solid old Jacobites.'

'But I met some Campbell-Bannermans,' I exclaimed perhaps too loudly, 'in the Groucho before I left London.' I dropped my voice a little lower. 'Margaret and Archie.'

'Yes!' Polly spoke in hurried snatches. 'Eddy's parents, ancient family. No real money of course, they had to sell the estate to a golf course development. Some very good pictures though.'

It was cool and murky inside the cathedral: summer did not penetrate. Coins dropped into collection boxes, and every so often a camera flash pierced the reverential permadusk and the security guards would all bustle towards the photographer, irate. Chairs creaked and old men coughed, worn-out sightseers shuffled about yawning, the panes of stained glass illuminated, high above the altar, glowed like nightlights in a nursery.

'My brother was very sexy,' I spoke in a whisper. 'The first erotic dream I ever had was about him. Do you think that's perverted?'

'Charli, honestly.' She looked at me as a sheep disturbed with a mouthful of cud might. 'I jerked off Gerhard's dog for a dare. I hardly think I'm the measure of what is and isn't perversion.'

I said, 'Oh, I didn't know Gerhard had a dog.'

Polly sighed, all woebegone. 'You know, maybe my mother's right. Maybe I should marry Eddy. I think I'd quite suit being a Right Honourable. And we can always get a divorce, can't we? If he's a total bore.'

I shook my head. 'Not if you're a Catholic, dear, we've quite famously drawn a hard line under that.'

'Bastards,' she said. 'Oh well, he's gay as a meadow anyhow.'

Polly didn't come to the show that night, she was having dinner with her aunt. I arrived a little late to the venue, but luckily the gig went off without a hiccup. The tour was done, no drama in Paris at least. When Polly got back to Berlin the next day she found that someone had broken into her apartment overnight; her dressing table and all of her cosmetics were smashed on the floor, the intruder had written *I'm a huge bitch* across the bedroom wall with her favourite Guerlain lipstick. The whole place had been ransacked, she told me in a message, devastated and enraged.

9

The journalist is here with me again and the nurse is not happy about it. She is frowning, she is scowling, 'Es ist zu früh,' it is too early, 'Es ist noch zu früh,' though it's gone ten-thirty and myself I'm feeling quite robust. Powerful even. The scandal must've done wonders for my profile. After a suitable period of mourning, I'm going to use all the accrued media interest to tell the world the truth, you can be assured of that. I imagine Oprah will want the exclusive, or Michael Parkinson, maybe.

Sunlight is streaming in through my window and the whole room is honeyed and glowing and I feel sure that if I were to roll out of bed I would float. I am chewing gum, I am craving a cigarette, I am praying the Salve Regina quietly under my breath, musing on what first prompted Edith Sitwell to convert.

The journalist is talking to me, in English thank fuck, he's saying, 'Are you aware, ma'am, that there was a fatality in your collision?'

He speaks like a TV cop and I almost want to laugh but I can feel that this is serious, and so I reply with more courtly manners, 'Yes, I am aware.'

He is pouting like a bullfrog, expecting me to show more of a response, only I'm damned if I'm going to give this hack anything of myself. The nurse is asking him not to press me and I'm irritated now – why has she even allowed him in?

'And did you know the victim?' he asks; and I reply, 'Yes I knew him well, he was my lover.'

This surprises the journalist, he looks at the nurse, quite startled. He must've been expecting me to break down and cry, but I will not,

not here, not in front of him. I will grieve in my own time, I will weep at his graveside, but I will not make a spectacle of myself, not here, not now.

'Emre Ekmekci?' he says. 'Emre Ekmekci was your sexual partner?'

I am irked, I snap, 'No. Alexander Geist, the man who was in the car with me. He was my lover.'

I can feel emotions rising and I struggle to keep them down but I know I must endure. I look to the nurse, she takes my hand, I have been too harsh on her. She strikes me now as an angel of mercy and I wonder if this isn't what my mother meant when she told me to always look for my guardian in moments of trial.

The journalist tries again. 'Ma'am, you were the only person we recovered from the vehicle.'

I have the most nauseating rush of realisation. I see the ambulance crew, the fire brigade, the police, crowding around the car now, cutting away the metal, peeling back the bonnet like the lid on a can of sardines. I am barely conscious, I am almost gone, I can hear them saying, 'Wir werden sie verlieren,' we are going to lose her, I can't speak but I can feel their hands, I don't want them to touch me, I want them to help Alex. Thunder is striking my body, two plates sending unwarranted voltage to my heart, a face emerges through the dark. 'Kannst du mich hören? Do you hear me?' I can blink yes, I think, I can turn my head and when I do I see a body on a stretcher under a wet white sheet, being loaded into an ambulance. I cry out for Alexander.

'Ma'am,' the reporter says, 'please try to stay calm.'

I will remain dignified even now. I speak, and my voice holds steady: 'Is his body in the hospital morgue? Can't I at least say my goodbyes?'

The reporter's composure is starting to crack, he's on the cusp, he wants to tell me the truth, I can see that, but he can't bear the disgrace, he fails, he says, 'I'm afraid not ma'am, no.'

'What do you mean, no?' I am squeezing the nurse's hand and I am shouting now, 'What have you done with his body?'

'Ma'am,' he repeats, 'please stay calm.'

But I cannot because I know the truth. I pull myself upright in the bed. 'You graverobber,' I curse him, 'you necrophile creep! You've taken his body haven't you? Are you planning to sell his corpse as a holy relic? Or did you cut him open to harvest his organs, hey? You filthy illuminati bastards!'

I am reaching for a weapon but all I have is half a can of Fanta, I throw that all the same. The journalist shields his face but he is unable to hide his fear, he knows that I have found him out, he's panicked, I could unravel this whole satanic network of his. I'm yelling 'Resurrection man!' and he's shouting at the nurse and she's shouting right back, she's fixing a needle and I think, Yeah, knock him out, put him to sleep, hand him over to civil authorities.

I screech at the journalist and he backs away. I turn to the nurse in conspiratorial glee, only rather than dosing the journalist, she slips the syringe in me. And here comes that old familiar feeling, I am a cough drop dissolving on my own tongue, I am car crash, I am choking on clouds, I am an octopus now all jelly and mind.

The nurse is escorting this murderer from my room and leaving me in peace, I am trying to thank her but my brain is on parental leave, or the power of speech is. I am slipping backwards again, into a bathtub, West rises at one end with a bunch of golden tulips and Alex appears at the other asking me to light his cigarette. I say, 'I'm sorry,' I say, 'I'm sorry, I want you both to know that I'm sorry.' There's a ringing in my ears, the dial tone from a slim-line phone expanding into the lament of a singing bowl and I know I'm going under. 'I can make it better, I promise,' I hear myself say as I disappear from sensation. The three of us are together in a lagoon of lime-flower bubbles, but they are swimming away from me at speed and I am calling after them, 'Please! I can make things right. Please. If we could just try again.'

10

At first Alexander was indignant that I'd gone AWOL in Paris; he wouldn't let me into the dressing room, he blanked me at the hotel after the show. At the train station the next morning, concealed behind mirrored shades and picking raspberries off a tart, he gave a short lecture on *loyalty and inconstancy,* addressed to no one in particular. Silently we boarded the 12.47 p.m. back to Berlin, me and the musicians filing down the aisle behind him as sombre and bemused as schoolchildren following their headmistress into the Three Hours Devotion on Good Friday afternoon. None of us were invited into his cabin; he intended to spend the whole journey regenerating inside an obdurate shell of pique, alone with his cold cuts, sulking under a green tea sheet mask.

The band slept upright in their seats in second class, weighted down by the last of the Valium. I worked through the eight-hour journey in the restaurant car, filing invoices and replying to emails, fighting the patchy Wi-Fi service over great stretches of France.

One of the brands from whom we had borrowed clothes was threatening to prosecute if we didn't send the suits and the boots back immediately, but I didn't think they sounded all that serious. Fan mail was coming in far too frequently to answer, so I disregarded that too, sifting through the inbox in search of gig offers, free gifts, interview requests, anything actionable.

Moritz had written to Alex, numberless times: he was delighted with how well the tour had worked out. He had cleverly collated, reshaped and redistributed all of the press attention Alex had received, sending it back out into the world, reworked via two separate PR agencies, as proof positive that Alexander Geist was about to make the big time. I wondered if a legal drama might perhaps add a nice texture to these heady circumstances so I took a moment to reply to the fashion PR with a simple *LOL*, sure that would be infuriating enough for them to contact their lawyers.

Moritz had secured an invite for Alex to appear on a new late-night television show, his first time performing live on TV. Even more significantly his partner at the label, Rick, the real power behind the throne, was coming to the taping. I knew this was a big deal: the serious money guys were starting to sit up and take note now that Alex had campaigned so successfully across Europe. The wheels were finally in motion. The filming was scheduled for the day after we arrived back in Berlin, though, and the band were by now severely depleted in their energies. I knew that they would be quite exasperated by this new request, but I was confident we could get another day out of them with a little sweet talk and a gram of decent coke. As long as Alex himself didn't get spooked over us being in an inauspicious phase of the moon or somesuch, we were golden.

Moritz wrote, 'This is so exciting man, you have no fucking idea. Rick is coming in from LA especially to see you guys!!! He wants to meet with you personally and he ⋆never⋆ travels unless he's ready to do business =} If he likes what he sees this could really go over. So psyched for you! So pumped! =p =p'

Rick was a real walrus of a man. I googled him passing through Frankfurt, he looked as though he had been breastfed until the age of six, but not by his mother, by the help.

He wore cowboy hats with navy suit jackets, he posed for pictures with rappers, politicians and pliant former stars of the Mickey Mouse Club on the cream leather seats of private planes, made incommodious by his corpulence. Everything about him spoke of grotesque power and wealth. Moritz's personal ecstasy came through volubly in the email thread, directing Alex to have a drink with Rick after the show. *Treat him nice, OK?*

'I *know* you can do that for me =p' he wrote, with all the subtlety of a brick to the face. 'And this will all work out beautifully. He likes you and what Rick likes goes over. For real.'

So these were the deals we made then, the instances in which we closed our eyes and waited for it to be over? Moritz signed off, 'So so proud of you *lover* =} =} See you in Berlin!!!!'

I closed the laptop, rolled my eyes and said, 'What a pimp.'

The old man next to me asked, 'Wie bitte?' I hadn't realised I had been talking aloud.

'Ach nichts,' I said, 'Entschuldigung, es ist nicht. Schon gut.'

My neighbour was reading an article on the statue of Christ the Redeemer in Rio de Janeiro, it was in English. He read very slowly, a finger wavering beneath each sentence, I followed it. The writer said that the famed monument looked staggering at a remove, but when she had ascended the Corcovado Mountain to the base of the statue she had found the throngs of tourists, religious tchotchkes and sugar-crazed wasps very unsavoury. 'Don't get too close,' the journalist noted, 'icons are after all designed to be worshipped from below.' I ruminated on the truth of that sentiment. I didn't get to find out whether she had a better time elsewhere in Brazil because my elderly companion suddenly dropped the magazine into his lap, having all at once fallen asleep. It fell in on itself, dull and crumpled on his knee like the spent head of a hydrangea, and I didn't care to pick the story up. The old man started snoring softly, I excused my shoulder from under his head and decided to go and apologise to Alex the only way I knew how. Of course he was ready for me, a petulant princeling, waiting to be pandered to.

The very first thing Alexander did upon arrival in Berlin was to go and get his hair restyled. He didn't even go home first, his debut appearance on live television was the number one priority. He'd parked the old Mercedes at Hauptbahnhof at the start of the tour, and so he drove straight off from the station, the salon staying open late to accommodate this star in the making. I took a taxi with the band, dutifully delivering them to their doors, fussing over their luggage and instrument cases as they disembarked, keen for them to feel esteemed, appreciated. Only once I had dispatched them did I slump, alone in the backseat, exhausted but revelling in my temporary freedom, slipping the driver €50 so that he'd let me smoke in his cab.

When finally I made it home it was gone midnight and I saw that my doorway was full of floral bouquets, all rotting away, gift baskets and parcels from chocolatiers and cosmeticians with cards reading *Dear Alexander, we are so pleased to share with you our latest products handcrafted in Berlin;* the door itself was plastered in notes from the Hausmeister's wife complaining about the mess. I lugged the cases inside. The apartment smelled abhorrent but the cat was nowhere to be seen. The small window in the bathroom was open, dead leaves had blown in. The answerphone was blinking, brimming with messages, several from my mother of course, one from Carl's dentist asking him to come in for a check-up, one from Hubert inviting me to his birthday party, though I don't ever remember giving him my number, another from Finley clearly very high, asking me if I had any K, before remembering, 'Oh yeah, you're out of town, sorry girl.'

I didn't reply to any of them, I didn't have time, I had to find a ring Alex thought he'd left in my apartment, gold with an enamel inlay, inherited from his grandfather, the same grandpa whose pyjamas he always wore. He was insistent that he have it in time for the TV show because he said it brought him good luck. I don't usually go in for this kind of hocus-pocus, secular superstition gives me the creeps, and honestly I didn't really believe that Alex had any such grandfather either. He was however adamant that the success, the real, huge, life-changing success that was at his fingertips, was all down to just such ritual observances. He had visualised it he said, and it had manifested.

I worried that I had a headache coming on so I took a few Diazepam and nibbled on a chicken stock cube, then I got to searching. I looked everywhere for the damn thing, dug though all of the dirty clothes and broken records and empty fag boxes, I tore the place apart, emptied every cupboard, scrabbled around on my knees until I found it under the cooker, glittering like a pomegranate seed, on a model battlefield of broken farfalle and dry cat food. I retrieved it with the aid of a coat hanger and toyed with it for a while, admiring its tarnished flamboyance until I fell asleep right there on the kitchen floor, clutching the ring to my breast. Just conked out like a motorboat out of gasoline, dirty and sweaty and beat.

I spent the next day in fervent preparation for Alexander's TV appearance: in addition to the ring, he needed arnica balm, British *Vogue* and a fresh carton of Sobranies. I had prompted him to buy the fags before we left Paris but he was still in a brown study then. Now I was landed with the task and had to try five different tobacconists before I could find a single pack on sale. Once I had finally secured the goods and cracked a pack open, I discovered to my horror that they were just plain white fags, not the fanciful pastel smokes Alexander adored. I hurried to find another stockist, faced the same calamity, pleaded with the shopkeeper in my hashed German to explain how this misfortune had befallen us. Had the factories run out of their crayon-coloured inks? No. The tobacconist showed me a webpage on his phone. The European Union were outlawing the sale of all coloured cigarettes, believing that they made smoking too attractive.

Too attractive? I thought, *Too attractive? Will these bureaucrats never be happy until the world is entirely stripped of beauty?* I tossed the clerk his phone and hurried on. In the end I had to go as far out as Pankow to get what I needed; it was harder than buying smack. I finally found a few packs of the now illegal goods in a dusty old kiosk at the back of St George's, a spot I knew from scouting photo shoot locations, where thankfully the news of the new edict hadn't yet come through on the wireless. The Oma in the tattered shawl who worked the Lotto counter there said almost no one bought this brand, she hadn't sold a packet for about ten years. I told her I wanted to buy as many packs as she had, she cooed and sold me eighty polychromatic smokes which I hoped would at least see us through the weekend. I bounded back out into the street and threw myself into another cab. 'Pariser Platz,' I puffed, 'schnell bitte. I'm late for a TV show. Sehr schnell.'

At the television studio it was twilight already and there was again a crush of fans, this time with hand-drawn signs and teddy bears. They screamed and rushed at the cab when I pulled up, expecting me, I suppose, to be Alex. It was terrifying, it always was. I had to get the driver to circle the block and drop me off around the back so I could sneak in by a freight door, which made me later still. Thankfully the production team were expecting me and brought me upstairs quickly and with minimal fuss, leading me through the complex and up to Alexander's dressing room.

There was a security guard stationed outside the door, hulking and impassive, he didn't smile, he didn't speak, he simply nodded and opened the door so I could bundle in with my parcels. I remember that it was incredibly warm in there,

Alex was lying about in his high-cut underwear drinking sencha, propped up on his elbows looking like a lizard on a faux deco chaise, bathed in the green glow of a wall-mounted TV monitor.

'It's infernal in here,' I said. The curtains were drawn.

'Yes,' he replied without turning his head to me. 'I do not want to get sick. Not now.'

The dressing room was an attempt at sophistication, a corporate composite of natural wood surfaces and olive velvet furnishings, a dressing table illuminated by soft white LED light bulbs, a framed print of the *Ziggy Stardust* album cover, an ensuite bathroom behind an ochre door. I noted that Alex had eaten half the oranges from the fruit basket. He was watching the show rehearsal on the relay monitor, the host was cursing at an assistant and seemingly threatening to punch him. She was much smaller on-screen than I remembered, so I couldn't be sure, but she certainly looked familiar.

'Is that what's-her-name?' I asked. 'From the House of Sin? Cindy.'

Alexander nodded. 'Yes, lover. This is her show.'

I was staggered. 'Surely not.'

'She *is* the queen of the underground,' he snickered with camp contempt, watching her fume on-screen, 'everybody knows *that*.'

'The queen of the twenty-four-hour underground car park at Platz der Luftbrücke maybe,' I scorned. 'Who on earth would put her on television?'

He looked up at me for the first time now with a shrug. 'Product,' he said, 'it's all product.'

I dropped the balms and the smokes and the battered British *Vogue* onto the dangerously low coffee table beside his chaise and stared at the run-through on the TV monitor. I saw now that the set was a working recreation of Cindy's nightclub. I was quietly impressed. They'd replicated the design quite accurately, the deer skulls and the table football, even the gigantic image of Saddam Hussein, though I did think that was just a little too gauche, even for late night television. The weekly guests were hosted on a grimy leather sofa which looked to have been airlifted directly from the party; the audience entered through a metal gate meant to mimic the club's backstage cage, and for maximum authenticity, Cindy also sang the show's theme tune; she was croaking through a practice run when Alex finally muted the monitor.

'Show business,' he sighed. 'It is just one humiliation after another.'

'Well,' I rooted in my purse for his lucky charm. 'I have your ring,' I said, 'I found it under the cooker. You must've dropped it; you know it took me an age to dig it out. I was scrabbling about all over, I was on my hands and knees until the early hours.'

'Oh yes,' he looked at me sceptically. 'That.' His forehead creased a little. 'Put it somewhere, will you?'

I tried my best to mask my irritation by fiddling with the flowers on his dressing table, worrying the petals with my fingers as one might self-soothe by absentmindedly mussing the hair of an incurious child.

Alex read the tension in my shoulders. 'I do appreciate it, Charli,' he said, 'really,' and bestowed upon me his most colloidal grin. 'Let's not pout.'

I couldn't help but blush when he stripped my thoughts bare like that. I felt exposed and infantilised, like a puppy dog in need of house training. I busied myself filling his cigarette case with Sobranies. I think this is where I began to chafe, to strain at the leash. I took off my jacket, I was too hot, I was stifled.

Alex strode to the window, cracked it open a third, strained to see the comings and goings down below. 'Is there a *really* big crowd out there?' he asked. 'Waiting to see me. Like in Italy?'

I felt perverse, I shook my head and lied, 'No, no, hardly anyone. When I came in it was quite empty down there, I just walked straight in, no problem.'

I added a few drab invented details here about how they didn't even have a bag search in operation, said I hadn't seen any cameras or photographers either, even though I had; he'd learn the truth soon enough of course, but for a moment I had the rare advantage. His face fell: he claimed to hate it when people clamoured for him, but he hated it more so when they didn't. He could be such a conceited little shit, and I relished the chance to nettle him.

'I'm *sure* all of that nonsense was just a one-off,' I said, 'I don't think you should worry yourself about that happening again.'

He scowled and seemed ready to curse me for impugning his celebrity. There was a knock at the door, a runner in a headset popped in to say, 'Alexander, we'll need you in fifteen minutes, OK?'

He threw her the most alarming smile, completely untroubled by the fact that he was addressing her in only his underwear. 'Of course, lover,' he said, 'I am raring to go.' It startled me, every time, how he could transform like that at the drop of a hat, become whatever was demanded of him. He hung his hands off his hips like some spindly Raquel Welch, and said rather too blousily, 'I'll dress and I'll come straight down,' glowing under the runner's obvious disorientation. When the door closed and we were alone again he growled, 'Fuck, it is so annoying that I cannot even smoke in here.'

He moved towards the clothes rail to pick out his get-up, fingering lapels and silk ties unhurriedly. Lithe, hairless, lactescent, he was almost translucent, like raw fish, those big inexplicable eyes of his unwilling to share, advancing silently, with unpublished muscles flexing beneath the skin as he held various suits up against himself. The clothes were already ironed, perfectly creaseless, and I wondered who had taken care of that, certainly not Alex.

'A girl from wardrobe did it,' he said languidly. 'Beautiful little thing. Took it all away and pressed it with a steamer. So quick.'

I watched him step into a lemon-yellow Versace suit, listened as he described the show ahead. He was going to perform a new song at the top of the first half; he was very keen to know what I thought of it, he was sure I was going to love it. He wanted me to know that I had inspired it: he said it was very significant for him to dedicate a song like this, he almost never did so, and that though of course he wouldn't ever say as much in front of the cameras, naturally he didn't believe in diluting his mystique like that, I myself would know, and that's what mattered. I was touched of course.

After the commercial break he told me he would chat with Cindy and the other guests on the couch, he'd prepared a few salacious quips in case the conversation went slack. He was concerned about being overshadowed by the others. I couldn't see why though, one was a local Green Party politician and the other a voice actor who dubbed crappy American movies like *Babe: Pig in the City* and *2 Fast 2 Furious* into German, neither seemed likely to steal the show. All the same he planned to French kiss the keyboardist to ensure enough attention in tomorrow's papers, maybe cup his balls too, just to be sure.

'And Rick's here, you know?' he spoke smugly, as if this news would smart. 'He is in from Los Angeles. Just for me.'

'I know,' I said, unruffled, 'I know that,' though if my prescience surprised him, he continued on, unconcerned by it.

He zippered his fly, preoccupied. 'He's going to come back after the filming. We are going to have a drink with him. Let us accommodate him, yes? We will be very nice to him.'

'Well, yes,' I replied, 'of course.'

He looked at me in wry suspicion. 'So, no disappearing tonight then, Charli? No sulking?'

'I don't sulk,' I said, 'do I?'

An irritating *ping* announced the arrival of an SMS. The label had sent him a very flashy new phone, and although I hated the lousy spyware-riddled thing, Alex thought it was extremely propitious that they'd gifted him something so expensive. He loved being given things, he was like a child in that way, he didn't have to need a thing – or even want it – to be pleased by it. He looked at the screen. 'They are already outside,' he grinned. 'They are watching.'

'Who?' I asked. 'How many of them are there?'

He didn't answer, rather he said, 'This tie. I cannot get it just so.'

I travelled the stain-resistant carpet between us, took my place behind him, adroit in front of the cheval mirror, right arm reaching over his shoulder, left up under his ribs, fiddling with his failed four-in-hand, a wife preparing her man for a day in the office. I wanted to hold him now, to press his body to me, he let me, he received my embrace, placid at first, then quickly febrile, and I felt inspired to pull the knot tighter and tighter again against his throat. In giddy response he bucked back against me, pressed his arse to my crotch, a wicked smile shimmering before me in the glass. 'That's nice,' he whined. 'That's nice.' I choked him a little, just enough to bring the first flush of fear to his eyes, though he made no attempt to break my hold, and when I ran my hands down over his crotch he was hard as hell. I'm quite sure he would've turned to kiss me only there was another knock at the door, a voice from the hallway, his five-minute call.

Acknowledging the summons with a chirp of innocence, 'Coming,' he dawdled under my caress for only a second more, then peeled off, incited. I had provided him with the charge he required to go out and conquer. He was so clever like that: people willingly gave him what he needed, he didn't ever even have to ask. He pulled away and smoothed his hair, stashed the cigarette case in his jacket pocket. 'So. Wish me luck,' he said, and disappeared from the room.

II

I took an apple from the basket and poked around the dressing room, looking through the knick-knacks Alex displayed on his makeup table: an evil eye medallion a fan had given him in Lyon, a little plaster frog wearing a wicker sombrero and playing a tiny trumpet, a Polaroid he'd taken of the Pietà in Rome. His gold cigarette lighter, inlaid with an enamel panther, reclined on a bed of arid orange peel and smeared tissues, tossed in an unspeakable salad along with Carl's keys and a grubby fund of makeup, much of which was once mine. I unmuted the TV monitor and watched the show begin.

Cindy came out in front of the curtain in a gown of black sequins and vinyl high-heeled boots, trailing a whip behind her. She was shockingly comprehensible, she spoke clearly and in connected sentences, cracking her whip to punctuate what I think had been written as jokes. When it came time to announce her musical guest, she even managed to get the name right.

'Meine Damen und Herren,' she spoke magisterially, 'bitte begrüssen Sie das fabelhaft, Alexander Geist!' and the curtains parted, revealing the band to the studio audience of 500 and to the thousands beyond that watching at home. The boys were swirled in dry ice, keyboards, drums, sax, heads down, vamping the intro on an anticipatory loop, edging the audience. Then Alex walked out, threw his arms back like Christ on the cross, like Diana Ross, and the crowd went crazy.

'Hello, lover,' he hurrahed over it all, 'I am Alexander Geist! *You* are beautiful,' and the band dropped the beat.

This new number was the tune I'd watched him tinker with on and off for the past few months, a song called 'Malediction,' he delivered it in that familiar throaty register of his, only elevated by all these weeks of public practice. Though I'd heard him sing a thousand times before, sitting alone backstage his voice came to me brand new. He performed with such grace and intention, it was like a sad scene in Kabuki, and for perhaps the first time, I really believed in the words he sang.

Instead of grinding against the microphone stand or touching himself up, he offered himself to the screen tenderly, he stroked his own cheek as though it were his beloved's face, cupping his androgyne features with long slim fingers, like Clara Bow in that most famous portrait. He adapted himself expertly to the medium, to the intimacy of the camera's lovelorn gaze, perfect theurgist as he was. Perhaps Hildegard von Bingen was right, the soul is symphonic, music does bring us closer to God.

The band shimmered at the edges of the tableau, floating on clouds of celestial carbon dioxide like guardian angels vibrating in their matching white tuxedos, giving the whole performance such an ethereal quality. Yet something tugged at me, an amanuensis in the wild weeds of Alexander's lyrics: his words were somehow too familiar. I knew the scene he was describing before he described it. How? He sang of shoplifting, stealing a bottle of Sekt to share with a lover, and I thought I must be mistaken, but no, in the next verse he was incanting the story of a night spent in the bathtub trading favoured quotes from William Faulkner. West. I felt sick.

Slack with quiet shock, dumbfounded by the stolen content of this love song, I slumped back down in the chair. I was aware of an anger, but not within my chest, it was located somewhere outside of me, above me; it came to me like the sound of neighbours shifting heavy furniture across the floor at night, it was not mine but it distressed me. Helplessness banged in my ears, as horrible as a nested dream, the awful claustrophobia of recognising yourself asleep inside a nightmare, unable to shake yourself awake. I was ten again, watching from behind the bannister. I saw my father arrive home with two police officers, watched my mother flinch from his scrawny comfort. She staggered backwards, holding her hands up in front of her as if to say *don't shoot*. Before he had even said a word she knew. A tear pricked my cheek; on-screen the band played on.

At the final chorus a gentle, steady shower of silver glitter fell over Alex and the boys. When the song finished there was a moment of reverential stillness, broken by a single 'Wow', a lone voice sounding almost afraid, a foreshock ahead of the whole studio lighting up in applause. As promised, he seized the keyboardist and kissed him; it was so unexpected after such a sensitive performance, and before the cameras could cut away they'd beamed the scene into homes around the country to the delight of budding homosexuals and tabloid journalists everywhere.

I remained staring at the screen, my stomach churning. I could feel the apple rotting on my palm, could only hope West had not been watching. Cindy returned to the set to thank Alexander in the most demonstrable manner, and a disembodied voice insisted that we, the viewers at home, must not go away. Cindy embraced Alex, he kissed her on both cheeks. Silently they complimented each other to excess as the hidden voice excitedly informed us that she and he would return after the break for more unmissable conversation. They held a collaborative grin until someone off-camera called 'Cut!' then they broke apart as quickly as was polite.

There were no commercials on the television set backstage: this was not real life. Instead, a makeup artist appeared to powder the host and a brown bear in a leather harness, the show's mascot, brought out a tray of shots. The guests sat down together on the sofa, laughing and toasting until broadcast began again. When I muted the monitor they continued oblivious, mime acts, unaware that from here on out they were merely pulling faces, gesturing towards an absent language. Without the audio I couldn't tell who was who, which the politician and which the voice actor. Alexander sat between them and seemed to positively relish every word either of them said.

I studied him on the monitor, charm personified, pantomiming flirtation, winking, grinning as Cindy re-entered the shot. I shuddered at the ease of his duplicity. Soon he'd come back and tell me they were all halfwits, disgusting wannabes, he'd take them apart for me mercilessly, as a sign of our shared confidence. It was almost funny how I imagined myself insusceptible to such treachery, despite everything I had been shown. This intimate stranger, this unfaithful friend, this scorpion on my back, of course he would sting me, it was his nature.

'You crooked fuck,' I muttered under my breath, and tossed the browning apple aside. Sometimes a slight or an injury can animate you, you can quicken under torment, but I was only enervated, my cortisol had not risen, my heartbeat did not yet peak, I was not adrenalised by indignation, perhaps I was simply too comfortable in bondage. I turned the television monitor off, yes, it was almost too funny.

Before long he burst back into the dressing room, calling out in the highest spirits, and in spite of the plain and filthy look on my face he had the gall to ask me what I thought of his performance. When I told him he had no right to take moments from my personal life and put them into his idiotic pop songs he sighed as if exhausted by a child, he loosened his tie. 'Oh, lover,' he said, 'all great artists steal.'

'But not from the people they care about,' I felt my bottom lip quiver, steeled myself against tears. 'You can't steal from *me*.'

'And why not?' He shrugged. 'Why can't I?'

'Because you're hurting me, Alex,' I blurted it out. 'And because I love you.'

Silence like tinnitus rang in my ears, the echo of my revelation.

He tossed his tie over his shoulder, onto the floor. 'Of course you do,' he said, 'everyone does. I am Alexander Geist.'

His detachment was so profound, so complete, it left me without a corner to fight. His disinterest was total, and I could not speak. He kicked off his shoes and strolled barefoot into the ensuite, the snap of the lock on the bathroom door indicating absolutely that he considered the matter of no further interest.

Vacant, I turned the monitor back on again. A German rock music video was playing, puerile and commonplace, the show was over. I heard the shower hiss and turned the music up louder to smother the sound of my surrender, louder to cover the death rattle of my scant remaining dignity, raw-boned and stillborn, louder to keep the news of this latest capitulation from my own ears. In the din and in the shame a calm came over me, like those first five minutes after confession, and I caught myself quoting the Sermon on the Mount: 'Offer the wicked man no resistance.'

I imagine that if the timing of things were ever so slightly different, I would have found myself dutifully cleaning Alexander's makeup brushes again, and ordering him dinner once he'd finished in the shower, salami most likely, veal if they had it. I honestly believe I would have continued in the role of Patient Griselda for the rest of eternity, that I would have fully sanctioned all future abuse with my submission, if only the perfect opportunity for satisfaction had not presented itself to me with a rap on the door. Standing there in the hallway, all hair plugs and china-white teeth, was the man Alex had been waiting for his whole life. Yes, it was almost funny.

12

Rick wore a navy blazer, aviator shades and Persian green polo shirt. He smelled like a walk-in humidor; the security guard was nowhere to be seen now. He said, 'Hey, hey, hey!' and threw his arms open wide. 'Would you look at that? Pretty damn quick on the uptake, I like that. I like that.'

I gave him nothing, no hint of excitement, recognition or even confusion. I presented him with an uncorrupted slate of indifference. I doubt that anyone had ever shown him such disregard. Rammstein was blaring on the TV in the background, he spoke louder to cut through the racket: 'It's me baby. Rick from Los Angeles.'

'Sure,' I nodded, 'I know. I know who you are.' I zapped the music off, but I didn't smile or feign pleasure at meeting him. I wasn't trying to be polite, I was simply keeping an ear out for Alex.

Rick was perplexed. He asked, 'So, uh, can I come in?'

I shook my head. 'Not tonight,' I said, 'sorry.' I know you won't believe me but I didn't plan it this way.

His faced reddened, with embarrassment or anger I couldn't tell, but I enjoyed his confusion all the same. He blinked in disbelief. 'Didn't Moritz tell you I was coming?'

'Ja,' I yawned, 'he did.'

Rick bristled. 'So . . .'

'So,' I said, 'Alexander isn't entertaining tonight. He has a touch of the Black Death, terribly sorry.'

He smiled. 'Oh I geddit, you're funny! Moritz said you were a *real* character!'

I groaned. 'Please leave.'

He held out his hands, palms up, imploring, 'But it's me, baby. Rick from Los Angeles.'

'And I'm Charli from Alderley Edge,' I smiled, deliberately false, 'so nice to meet you, goodbye.'

I tried to close the door on him but he pressed his foot against the flaking paintwork. 'So you like to play games, eh baby?' He ran a lewd tongue over pristine dental work and pursed his lips. 'Well, I like to play too. What do you say we go inside and play nice together. Me and you, alright?'

His breath on my face sent a shiver of disgust through the length of my body. I took a slight step back and assessed him in silence. I left it a beat so that he could feel how ridiculous he was making himself, then suspired in pity.

'It's me, baby. Rick from Los Angeles,' he repeated, but this time only faintly, as if unsure of his lines. 'It's me.'

I felt for my forehead. 'All of this repetition is really giving me a headache,' I said, 'will you kindly fuck off now please, Rick from Los Angeles?'

That tore it. He was so riled up I thought he might try and grab me. He flashed with rage, pink as forced rhubarb, and hissed, 'Do you even *know* who you're talking to *here*?' In his ire he spoke with the most peculiar inflections: '*Do* you *know what you're* saying?'

'Oh yes, *baby*,' I beamed, 'I'm saying goodnight,' and with that I finally slammed the door in his face.

He kicked it of course, but only once, then thumped his way down the hall issuing *cunts*, *faggots* and *morons* until his dwindling insults were finally eaten up by the quietude of the soundproofed corridor. My heart was in my mouth; I could barely believe my own audacity. What I had done was so simple, so perfect.

I thought I felt a giggle rise up in my throat, but it was a fistful of nausea, and I had to steady my tremulous body with an arm against the wall. I was myself flushed a tell-tale shade, I knew, so I set about tidying up, collecting the discarded tie and the socks and shoes from the floor, looking to camouflage my sedition in good works.

Alex came out of the bathroom, wrapped in a huge white towel, he asked, 'Who was at the door?' quite ignorant.

'Hmmm? Oh no one,' I said, 'just a production runner. I asked them to bring you some orange juice and salami.'

He nodded imperially, glad to see me returned to my station and, content that the world was in balance again, he started us off on a new conversation. 'She is mad, you know?' he began. 'Cindy. She is totally crazy. She actually thinks we are all in her nightclub together. Insane.'

'Oh really?' I just smiled and left my dish to cool.

'Yes!' he exclaimed, rooting about his dressing table. 'She believes that we are all at her party. She is completely insane, she is in a pure delusion.'

He was tired, but he could not afford to flag, not tonight. He said it was crucial he be on top form now and pulled a little baggie of coke out from inside the cap of a hairspray canister. I think he mistook the apprehension on my face for the first nagging clouds of a telling-off, because he started on some looping story about how Freud wrote all of his most famous essays on cocaine. 'My old dealer explained me that,' he said tartly, 'and *he* studied psychoanalysis in Vienna for two years, so.'

I wanted to point out that since his dealer had ended up at the bottom of the Landwehr Canal, perhaps he wasn't the go-to guy for life advice, but I didn't, I just looked on as Alex racked up two lines on the coffee table. He knelt on the carpet, bowed his head low as though before the executioner's block, sealed off one nostril with a fingertip and ingested the bitter powder up along a tubular €50 bill. He raised himself up a little and indicated that I should come and participate, but I declined with a sweet smile and the claim of a headache, so he snorted the second line himself, back-to-back with the first.

'We don't want to leave any clues,' he grinned maniacally, paranoia already edging into his mind.

He was suddenly concerned about money: were the TV company paying him? Was it enough? Cindy was making a serious cash and he was, he insisted, a much bigger star. I assured him that Moritz had taken care of all that, offering him the same advice as always, telling him it would be quicker and easier if we either invoiced in his legal name or opened a bank account in his stage name, since the discrepancy between the two often caused weeks of delays.

'Ha! My legal name,' he pulled a face, 'I do not even remember what that is.'

We waited.

Keen to be found buoyant and glorious when his visitor arrived, Alex draped himself in a purple silk robe and positioned himself on the chaise, chattering on and on like a howler monkey about world tours, new cars, villas in Miami. He did another line to keep himself golden but as impatience crept in his soliloquy darkened. He lit a cigarette against the studio's prohibition and started to expound his theory on the assassination of Gianni Versace. He asked me if I knew they'd found a dead dove alongside the designer's body, the calling card of a mafia hit. I admitted that I did not know this detail, my own pose of innocence straining.

He went on, 'The police of course claim it was a coincidence, a fragment of bullet killed the bird. It was not an assassination, *they* say. But does that not sound strange to you? *So* obviously a murder.'

He pressed his palms as if in prayer, tapping his index fingers together, running his eyes around the room, asking himself privately, *where the hell are they?* beating back the tension with a fixed expression of cheer. Then his phone rang, and even though I had been waiting for it, I squeaked in fright. Alex regarded me derisively, with a look that said *get it together.* He picked up his phone and smiled broadly. 'Good. Let me get this.'

He didn't even have time for his *Hello, Lover* bit before Moritz started in, I could hear him down the line ragged with panic and angst. Battered in a cocaine daze, Alexander's face dropped, a whitewash of horror, his mouth hanging open, eyes wide in alarm. I watched him grapple with the reality of the situation, struggle to understand how this had happened, jam the phone between his ear and his shoulder and light another cigarette, aghast.

From where I stood, Moritz's words were indistinct but unmistakable, rapid and acid, he barely allowed Alex the time to nod and say, 'I see,' before he hung up, ending the conversation at fever pitch, as abruptly as he had begun it. Blanched and shaken, Alexander distractedly slipped the phone into the pocket of his dressing gown. 'There has been some confusion,' he mumbled, insentient, 'with Rick. The guy from the label.'

'Oh that's a shame,' I mocked quietly, and he looked up at me, but he didn't catch my intent.

'Moritz will talk to him,' he continued. 'We can fix this, he is a reasonable guy.'

'Quite,' I poured on the scorn, '*such* a reasonable guy,' until the truth finally dawned on him.

A look of incomprehension slowly crowded his face. 'You?' he gasped. 'You did this?'

I said nothing but my smirk spoke for me. 'You bitch,' he croaked, 'you crazy bitch.' He stubbed the cigarette out on a magazine.

I shone with spite. 'Well, now we're even.'

'Why?' His eyes begged for understanding, his breath grew ragged. I had half a hope that I was inducing cardiac arrest. He shook his head in cold amazement. 'After everything I've done for you?'

I guffawed like a maniac. 'For me? What have you *ever* done for me?'

This brought him to his feet directly. 'I have paid for your life, you, you cunt. I took you all around Europe. I *brought* you to Berlin in the first place!'

I resisted this entirely. 'No!' I said. 'No, all you've done is drag me around behind you, like a dog on a leash, none of *this* was any kind of act of generosity.' But he was too far gone to hear me.

'Where would you even be without me?' he railed, stabbing my chest with his finger to punctuate his wrath. 'Where would you be right now without *me*?'

'Ha!' I laughed right up into his face. 'Where would *you* be without *me*? You can't find your dick in your own pants, Alex, you're an idiot. You're an imbecile and you're a bully. You haven't ever done a thing for me, for anyone, ever.'

'OK, then!' he bawled. 'So fuck off then please,' and his spit flecked my face. He pushed me away, hard, and I stumbled against the wall. 'Why don't you go back to dancing for your friend Sophia Hope? Little Red Dress Tranny.'

I recoiled from the word, but only for a second. 'You're a black hole, Alex,' I said. 'You're a stupid selfish baby, and you sing like shit.'

His whole body flexed, he balled up his fist, I saw it happen, at once accelerated and dragging through time. I really thought he would lose it, really thought he would hit me now, but I warned him plainly, 'If you touch me Alex, I swear to God I'll kill you.'

He looked at me in outrage, as if I'd accused him of something unspeakable, then he fell back onto the sofa, collapsed, head in his hands. 'You cunt,' he whispered almost to himself now, 'you stupid cunt.'

'Goodbye Alex,' I said. 'I'm taking the keys. And please don't ever call me again, I won't answer.'

I backed away and out of the room, in case he should repent at the last minute, or throw his phone at my head, but he didn't even look up.

PART FOUR

Laugh Away the Dust

I

When I first opened my eyes I thought that I must be in a hotel room on tour, my surroundings too clean and spartan to be any place I'd ever lived. It was almost funny to realise the truth. I lay awhile alone, observing the small white cabinet next to my small white bed, trying to anchor myself in the present moment of my existence. The Dickens is gone, and the Walkman, the Fanta too unsurprisingly, the cabinet's flat roof is bare besides a paper beaker of water, also small, also white. I take up the cup and I lap at it slowly; it reminds me of the little cones they give you to sip spring water out of in spa towns, nobody ever wants more than a mouthful, it's always so warm and sulphurous.

There's an episode of Mysteries and Scandals *I remember, which opens in a spa town. Alexander loved that show. Agatha Christie had run away to hide out there in 1926 and nobody could find her for a full eleven days. The world's most famous lady author, vanished, and even with the entirety of the tabloid press out looking for her she remained hidden in plain sight: she'd checked in at a hotel under her husband's mistress's name. I sip again at the tepid water, and it's as if I see the truth of the situation all at once. I can't help but laugh!*

Oh Alex, *I say,* what an awful lot of effort to go to for a practical joke! *He's not dead, of course not, this is just a stunt, he's arranged it all with Moritz's help, how could I have been so blind? This has all been a giant hoax to get him a wave of free press, how stupid of me! He's taken a page out of the Florence Lawrence playbook, that's all. She faked her own death in a car accident too, and it made her the very first movie star known to the public by name.* Oh lover, *I say,* you really had me going there!

I'm sitting up now, rolling out of my bed at this revelation, right arm in a sling, unsteady on my feet, making my way to the door. It is open, it is unlocked, I am going out into the corridor. I know now how I can find him; I just need a few hours outside of the hospital, that's all it will take for me to track him down. How have I missed all of these clues? Alexander couldn't be dead. If he was dead then I would be too, and clearly I am here, up and walking, so call me Lazarus or let me be on my way! The hall is long and lithe and cool under my feet, nineteenth-century tiles, and not another soul in sight, the journalist on a smoke break, nurses changing shifts. I wish I could bid them goodbye in person but I'm sure they'll understand. I'm coming to an archway, there are stairs on the other side, my gown is teal and insubstantial, Alexander will die laughing when he gets a load of me in this. I'm praying he will forgive me for not having understood sooner, but the medication they give you in these places, it's quite unmanageable, you can barely remember your own name half the time, and so you find yourself hurling scrambled eggs and cans of soda around the room.

There's a hand on my shoulder, it is firm, not unkind, it is the journalist steering me back home. I say, 'Sorry about the Fanta, I got a little overheated I guess.'

His face is implacable, saurian, he grunts, 'You shouldn't be out of bed.'

I'm giggling. 'Don't worry, I know where he is. If you give me just an hour, I can bring Alexander here.'

The journalist is not replying now, he is simply leading me back down the corridor, I find myself thanking him, saying, 'Yes, yes, you're right, I should go back to get my coat. It's cold once you get out of bed.'

I feel as though I have been walking this hallway all my life, each step a country mile, I'm becoming more keenly aware of my situation, perhaps they don't want me to leave. I'm rattled and I'm trying to break away but I know I'm too weak to fight him so I start to plead. I'm saying, 'Look this has all been a terrible mix-up, don't you see? He's staying in a spa hotel under the name of Agatha Christie. Why aren't you listening? Why won't you believe me?'

The journalist is opening the door to my room now and bringing me inside, he pushes the button which calls the nurse and leverages me impartially back into my bunk. 'Please ma'am,' he is speaking in a voice worn through, 'don't get out of bed again.'

The nurse has arrived, she looks different, I'd say a decade younger, perhaps she's had an eyelid lift, maybe she gets a discount since she's on staff. I can tell that she wants to come right over and comfort me, only the journalist catches her first and insists, 'She is going to have to take some responsibility sooner or later,' as if the nurse were my mother, and I wonder when exactly my mother is due to arrive. The nurse is looking disappointed in me and now I'm starting to feel ashamed, if only they'd listen. I'm sobbing, 'Have you tried the Hotel Adlon! I implore you to call them!' but they are both simply walking away out of the room, exhausted, and I am back in my bed.

2

Polly found me, rambling in the streets between her place and mine. I just couldn't bring myself to go home so I went on, making loops about the neighbourhood, describing circles. I wandered until dawn mumbling again and again, 'I've fucked everything up, oh God, I've fucked it all up.'

It was 7 a.m. and Polly was out for a run. She asked me if I had been out all night, I told her that walking helps the brain tissue smooth out, helps you to narrativise, understand your recent past, connect it to your history. She offered to take me home, but I didn't want to go.

I couldn't face my cranky neighbours, the answering machine full of messages, all the rotting flowers and unreturned clothes, or the thought that Alex might be pacing outside my door, ashen and apologetic. That was the real kicker, the soft ache I felt when I pictured him waiting, smoking, head in hands, worried sick, *Where have you been all night, Charli? I was so afraid.* I suppose I knew that this would never happen of course, but as long as I stayed away the possibility, however slim, could not be denied. I would refuse him even this patently counterfeit opportunity for repentance; if I could keep in touch with the sting inside of me, then we were still connected.

Polly offered me a place to crash. She still hadn't found a new roommate, but too many mutual friends lived too close by, and so I went to stay with Finley instead. Gerhard had set him up in a new place, over in Charlottenburg, an investment he had said, though I was unsure if he meant Finley or the apartment. Either way Finley had finally been moved up off the studio floor, our very own Dame aux Camélias. Rumours swirled again that the ateliers were all being sold to make way for condominiums and the move seemed doubly fortuitous.

He was working on a painting called *Ghost Sex* when I arrived; it was complex, he asked if I would make him a pot of coffee, he didn't want to lose his flow. He didn't grill me, despite whatever Polly might've told him, and she always overdramatises. He just tossed me his spare keys, said I could stay as long as I'd like, as long as I let him work. He wasn't going to keep tabs on me.

It was a big place and he had plenty of space there, a huge lounge, a galley kitchen and the dining room where he painted, so it was easy enough for me to tuck myself away without disturbing the balance of things. Despite the Altbau grandeur of the place, the lovely high ceilings and pre-war plasterwork, it wasn't at all lavish. Gerhard had given him a few chairs and an old record player, along with some pans and an ironing board, but there was still plenty wanting, and so the place felt transitional, like a rehearsal room backstage at the theatre, with real life marked out by cardboard boxes and stacks of books, a banana plant denoting where an armchair might one day sit. I took the smaller bedroom, it had Bayern Munich sheets and an antique footstool as a nightstand, no wardrobe, but then I didn't bring much in the way of clothes.

It was Gerhard's expressed intention to supply the remaining furnishings over the months and years; he didn't intend to give Finley everything he needed up front and so make himself redundant. As the mood took him, he would pop by unannounced with a set of mother of pearl butter knives, or a lamp, though Finley refused him a set of keys so he would have to stand on the doorstep with his flea market finds, blushing scarlet in case one of the neighbours saw him and somehow worked out what was going on in there.

All of Finley's neighbours in the building were affluent and elderly, dowagers in court shoes and tinted lenses trailing little dogs, grandfathers with big pink noses and bad tempers, wheezing into the elevator. I never spoke to any of them, never even made eye contact; they seemed just as keen to avoid scrutiny as me, to evade ever being seen. I couldn't shake the relentless suspicion that something horrible had happened there during those twelve years no one wanted to talk about, really it was the perfect place to fall out of existence. Sometimes we would see a neighbour in the lobby and Finley would wave and call out, *Hey, girl, you look so cute today. Where'd you get them shoes, mama?* but just to torment them, he could've easily spoken to them in German. Still they remained as silent and impassive as masonry. Finley said they ignored us because we were *auslander* and queer, but then I never heard them talk to each other either. The only noise I really ever remember hearing in the building was the sound of shallow laboured breathing in the stairwell, a cyhyraeth, the groan greeting death, the woman across the hall huffing home with her groceries.

It was a discreet address, set back a little from the glare of modernity, from the tourists with roll-along suitcases, the street prostitutes with their fanny packs full of Viagra, and the black bloc protests, but just a fifteen-minute shuffle, at an arthritic pace, from both KaDeWe and the twenty-four-hour sex cinema, where Finley worked a few nights a week, to keep his independence. He said, 'Girl, one day I'm gonna be forty and Gerhard is gonna move some other boy in here and that's life.'

Finley painted every day; he was extremely diligent. He set to it straight after breakfast, and worked through until seven or eight, he ate cold leftovers for lunch so that he wouldn't have to break off for too long. He was quite in love with his work, enraptured by it. Like a widower he argued with the radio as he went, he sang along with spirituals streamed from Pentecostal services. He drank sauerkraut juice and manic amounts of coffee, nibbled squares of extremely dark chocolate, 90 per cent cacao, which he said helped him focus. Whilst he painted, I read his art history books and rolled joints and tried to put Alexander completely out of my mind. I stopped going online, I stopped picking up newspapers and reading magazines, the only music I played was a Stevie Nicks album from the early eighties called *Bella Donna* which a previous tenant had left behind. Sometimes it was the only thing I achieved all day, lining up the 12-inch on Gerhard's old record player and laying myself out like a corpse on the living room floor, frequently so stoned I didn't realise that the music was over and that the needle was now skating in dusty silence over the dead wax at the centre of the disk.

From the dining room, Finley's voice would enter my head disputing the political assessment of an interviewee on NPR, or singing 'Ezekiel Saw the Wheel', or talking to his paintings. Two or three times a day he'd stop working to masturbate. Often he'd ask me if I wanted to join him, and we'd go lie down in his bed and take turns picking videos until we both came. He liked clips of anonymous sex, public sex and gang bangs. I liked seeing college girls get fucked by their gym instructors. 'I've never really watched this kind of thing before,' he said, 'but I'm kind of getting into it.' I took a lot of baths too, read *Lives of the Artists*, slept until two every day. I would've called it a blissful summer, if I hadn't been so heartsick.

Finley told me he was in love with Claude, the letting agent who had shown him the apartment. They were conducting a clandestine affair and I was sworn to secrecy. 'I think he really likes me,' Finley told me as he wiped my cum out of his bellybutton with a sports sock, 'he thinks we should try and be monogamous. And, girl! He has the biggest cock I've ever seen.' Occasionally I had to cover for them if Gerhard turned up unexpectedly with a chair or a second-hand toaster whilst Finley was at it with Claude, but then lies and excuses have always come to me very easily. 'Tut mir leid, Finley ist nicht da. Finley hat er aus der gym gehen,' and so on, stringing together a flimsy explanation on the spur of the moment, smoothing out the telltale folds from the Persian carpet, my poor German the perfect screen.

Very occasionally I left the house, though I didn't ever go very far. Usually I'd just go and loiter in the U-Bahn station, or walk over to KaDeWe and sit upstairs eating macarons on the Feinschmeckeretage, because I could use Alexander's American Express there. The food hall was all yellow tiles and endless rows of marmalade, vitrines of choux and regiments of seafood assembled on ice. Polly used to deride it as an *Art Nouveau nightmare* but I loved the place, especially as it was unlikely I'd see anyone I knew. I couldn't bear the thought of bumping into a friend because inevitably such a meeting would force questions I did not want to answer.

I bought myself a few dresses, underwear, cosmetics, the things I needed to replace those I'd left behind in my apartment, because when I came to Finley, I came empty-handed. I put it all on Alexander's credit card; I thought of this as reparations. Somewhere down the line he would get the statement, and eventually he would realise he hadn't made those purchases, but he was honestly such a mess I doubted that would happen anytime soon. And when he did realise, well, then I hoped he would be forced to think of me and that it would hurt.

I was careful enough not to arouse suspicion too soon though. Besides, if I shopped too effectively then I'd run out of reasons to return, and I did like to be there. To be lost amongst the Nazi widows and the botoxed newsreaders, the sightseers from out of town and the bored housewives, it made me feel blissfully forgotten, a nobody, a ghost of a person, so I eked out my purchases and for the most part simply languished in the food hall, trying samples of cheese and reading the back of cereal boxes. I saw David Bowie in there late one afternoon, scrutinising the label on a jar of Marshmallow Fluff which he'd picked up in the American Food aisle. I floated down past him on the escalator, gasped and changed direction on the next floor. Naturally I got stuck behind a group of Italian tourists taking selfies on the moving stairway, and by the time I scrambled back up to the Fine Foods department he was gone. I expect he decided that the sugar content was way too high. Or maybe he thought it was overpriced, he always struck me as economically minded. I took a jar home for Finley – I thought it might remind him of his childhood in Nevada, though when I gave it to him he choked at the sight of the price. 'Girl, you are crazy,' he said. 'Twenty-four euros for this shit?'

I shrugged off the cost. '*Anyone who lives within their means suffers from a lack of imagination*. Oscar Wilde.'

Claude was lying naked on a mattress in the dining room, on the wall next to him hung Finley's unfinished portrait in which he lounged nude and covered in bugs under the words SATANIC PLUMBING. His dick really was enormous. He got to be very intimate with the dead space behind the washing machine that summer: every time the doorbell rang Finley would stash him away there like the corpse in *Rope* in case it was Gerhard. Most older men and sugar daddies are very rigid in their topsy-turvy sexual morality, and Gerhard was no different. That's not to say he was ungenerous, he could be extremely benevolent, it's simply that he was adamant his rights as a consumer be protected, he wanted to be assured he had the monopoly on Finley's attention.

He had quietly accepted that I was living in the apartment too but he didn't see me as any kind of threat, and, on top of gifting us endless useless bric-a-brac, he started taking us on day trips, out for what he called *real English tea*, to museums, to the opera. He dragged us about to all kinds of historical hot spots, often with very little notice, he'd just arrive at the door at 9 a.m. and haul us off on four hours' sleep, like a governess, for our betterment.

I think that Finley might've put the lean on him, told him to do something worthwhile with his time and money, expressly to try and get me out of my funk, and he'd agreed I suppose. We saw a lot of old palaces, Schloss Charlottenburg, Schloss Sanssouci, Schloss Schönhausen, hunting lodges and memorials for prince-electors of the Holy Roman Empire; we had lunch in lakeside beer gardens crawling with wasps, we watched *Die Zwillingsbrüder* and *La traviata*, evidence abundant that Gerhard had either a very droll sense of humour, or no self-awareness, I couldn't ever tell which. He took us with him as his guests when a selection of the celadon pottery he had acquired on the black market for a song in the seventies was unveiled at the Museum für Ostasiatische Kunst. Finley had strong-armed him into that too. Myself I quite enjoyed all the pretzels and the Sekt he plied us with, all the more because I couldn't understand more than 20 per cent of the conversation, and also I didn't have to go home and jerk him off afterwards.

In Mitte, at a remaining stretch of the Wall, he insisted we take pictures of the old graffitied slabs where they rose from the ground like 200 metres of greyed teeth, and at the Brandenburg Gate he told us a story of an old lady his grandmother had known when she was herself a young woman who had seen Napoleon riding into the city at the head of the conquering French army. Finley, translating at quite a clip, tossed me a look embossed with shock, and said, 'I don't even think he's making this shit up.' When we went out to Frederick the Great's palace in Potsdam, Gerhard grew desperately emotional, delivering an account of how poor gay Frederick's outraged father had forced the young king to watch the decapitation of his handsome soldier lover, which kind of killed the mood. It was close to 30 degrees, and there was no shade, but we all felt obliged and so stood around the King's grave, sombre in the long day's sunshine, trying to look respectful, whilst tourists from Japan laid out spuds and origami swans on the tombstone. Finley told me they call Frederick *the potato king*.

'But why?' I asked.

'Fuck knows, girl,' he said. 'Fuck knows.'

Despite being kept in salad spinners and Dolce & Gabbana underwear by his sugar daddy, Finley couldn't ever lay his hands on much cash, and all I had were the credit cards. We were like investors lacking in liquidity: all of our assets were tied up. We had our overheads covered but we still had to earn our pocket money, so, if Gerhard hadn't booked him and he wasn't meeting anyone at the porno kino, Finley would take me out on his nightly tours of the city's cat houses. I was never a very successful whore. Finley said that you have to make the guy feel really sexy, like you'd fuck him anyway, like the money was just an afterthought, a tip, a *hey, kid, buy yourself something nice*, but I couldn't ever make them believe it. As soon as a man in a bar offered me a drink, or a cigarette, or told me I looked beautiful, I found myself wanting to cry and had to excuse myself, take myself to the bathroom to patch up my makeup.

Newton was way too upmarket for us and we had no luck, The Wall was a perfect shithole, Bull wouldn't let me in on account of their *no women no drugs* policy, though Cindy was a regular there and everyone who ever stumbled out of that place was high as a kite. So, we frequented the more bohemian spots. I liked Kumpelnest a lot, because there were always scores of elderly working girls getting sauced on cherry wine in there, but Finley preferred Boy Bar because Isa Genzken was a regular and she was his favourite painter. She was always game for a laugh, and we saw her often, handing out banknotes to the hustlers, like Tallulah Bankhead before her, giving away her Cartier lighters in Manhattan's dilapidated knocking shops of yore. She would get magnificently drunk and occasionally start fights but they never threw her out; Finley said that she'd bought the owner a BMW, and so he let her do whatever she liked.

Some nights we went back to hotel rooms, or to cars or dark spots in the park. Occasionally we took men back to Finley's place for a three-way, which meant we could ask for more money. Other nights we'd strike out and go home very drunk, very high with less to our name than we'd started out with, but it didn't matter really, not to me at least. I didn't care that I wasted whatever I made, all I wanted was a distraction, some way to keep myself under local anaesthetic, awake but unfeeling, I never wanted to go to bed because sleep was the surest sign that tomorrow was on its way and I couldn't face the fact. Inevitably of course I would pass out somewhere, in a bar, on the train, at the kitchen table, and wake up to find a cigarette smoking between my fingers, though I never remembered having lit one.

3

I started on a juice fast because Cookie Mueller said they cured all physical ills, heartache, even drug addiction. I smoked all the weed Claude brought over but it never seemed to make me hungry; I got so thin I was sheer. My life was as bare as the linden trees in December, I just wandered around the apartment in my underwear, adjusting the spartan furniture, repeating, 'I've lost all of my leaves,' whispering it to myself so as not to disturb Finley's work. I made him his Turkish coffee and I cleaned the bathroom, arranged and rearranged his bookshelf. He told me the housework wasn't necessary, he said I should take some time for myself, but I really didn't feel like I had a self left. I read that Céleste Albaret ran a modest hotel after Proust's death, and like her, I was so used to being in servitude that it was the only thing I could find comfort in. Finley lost his temper with me because I tidied away his brushes and couldn't remember where to.

I found myself in front of the bathroom mirror quite crazed with the THC intake and lack of sleep, with my fist in my mouth stifling a scream. I was convinced that it was Alexander's face looking back at me from the glass. I knew it was time to call my mother. How long had it been? There was a slimline phone in the bathroom, just like in a smart hotel, and so I rang her up and told her everything. Well, a near approximation. 'I've made such a mess of it all,' I said, 'really, such a mess. I wish I'd never come here.'

She lamented, 'Oh love. If wishes were horses, then beggars would ride. That's what your nanny always used to say.'

I had the strangest feeling, I couldn't shake it, that I was outside of my own body, looking on at myself. Polly told me this was called depersonalisation, she said it was a condition which Yayoi Kusama suffered from too, so at least I was in good company. 'That's what all the polka dots and mirrors in her paintings are about,' she explained, 'she lives in a facility you know? She only leaves once a day, just to check her bank balance.'

I was running us a bath. Polly was over, as often, to take advantage of Finley's huge tub since she only had a shower in her apartment. Truthfully I sensed that she was growing somewhat resentful of his new situation, and though she tried to hide it they inevitably squabbled about something apparently unrelated. I suppose she must've missed having him in the studio.

When the bath was full we slid in. I had tipped a great big slug of foam in there and a chug of Floris Limes too; the water towered with bubbles that threatened to spill out onto the bathroom floor. Polly was describing how useless the police had been in dealing with her break-in, they still hadn't arrested anyone although she was positive it must've been Callum.

'Obviously it was a personal vendetta,' she said, 'they didn't take anything of value, not my laptop, not my shoes. Just a photograph of my mother in the garden with Eartha Kitt.'

Finley wandered into the bathroom, already unzipping his pants to pee. He said, 'Girl, what?'

I was just as surprised. 'Why have I never seen this picture?'

Polly was exasperated, we were missing the point of the story. 'I always kept it hidden,' she said. 'We look so alike, I can't bear it.'

Finley was pissing a healthy stream of clear liquid. 'You and Eartha Kitt? Girl, you two do not look alike.'

'My mother and I,' Polly groaned, and Finley dropped his pants. 'Oh,' he said, 'sure.'

He stripped off, casting his clothes about the floor and climbed into the bath, there was plenty of room for us all. He said, 'Your mom really did know everyone, hey?'

'For all the good it did her, the old bitch,' scowled Polly. 'The old Filofax is full of legends, but they're all dead now.'

She told us that whenever Eartha Kitt was in Dublin she would come for lunch at the family's house and keep them all waiting, Polly, her parents, and the family accountant, a strange addition, I thought, but maybe they were swingers.

As the salads started to wilt and the anxious lunch party faded with hunger and too much sparkling wine, the adults discussed who they might get today, which version of the star: Glamourpuss Eartha or Earth Mother Eartha? Would she come over from the Shelbourne in her diamonds, or in a sweatsuit? I thought I understood why Eartha might always be so late, if she knew she was going to be so thoroughly scrutinised even before she arrived. I said that I thought it was horrible that even her friends held her under a microscope, that of course she would section herself off a little, public and private, it seemed perfectly reasonable. 'After all,' I argued, 'we all have two bodies, don't we?'

Finley and Polly only looked at me blankly, so I expatiated, 'I read that in an Olivia Laing book. I'm not talking out of my hat.' No response. 'Forget it,' I said and flopped back into the bubbles.

The buzzer rang; Finley was sure it could only be Gerhard.

'Not Claude?' asked Polly wickedly.

Finley said, 'Nah, girl, I gave him a key,' which I thought was a savage stance to take, but also very pragmatic.

Polly offered to answer the door. She stepped out of the tub and daubed her nipples with bubbles, making her breasts look like French desserts. 'I'll go like this,' she said, 'make it worth his while coming all the way over.'

Finley hooted, 'Girl, you are crazy,' which only encouraged her.

When we were alone Finley asked me if I was feeling OK, asked what I'd been doing in the bathroom for the past three hours. 'Oh nothing.' I dribbled bubbles over my head. 'Well, I was speaking to my mother for a while. Telling her my woes.'

'Your mother?' he said. 'From in here?'

Polly returned victorious before I could answer him, saying that she'd given Gerhard some story about Finley going away for a few days to paint. 'I said I was home alone right now, but that I'd *just love it* if he came in to take a warm bubble bath with me. He turned the colour of Pepto Bismol! Honestly, you should've seen his face.'

Finley clapped his hand over his mouth, scandalised, Polly regaled us, hand on hip like a Sargent painting, dripping soap suds on the bathroom floor. 'I'd say I've bought you a full week of freedom there,' she concluded smartly, 'he won't be back in a hurry.'

'Thank fuck!' Finley exploded in relief. 'Seriously,' he said, 'I need him off my back so bad. Girl, he's here every five damn minutes, it's like being in jail.'

Polly slipped back into the tub. 'You know, you girls need a man about the house.' She squeezed between Finley and me. 'Perhaps I should stay over? I can't bear my apartment just now anyhow. I feel like I need to sage the whole place, have it exorcised.'

I laughed darkly. 'Well, if you find anyone capable . . .'

After a while Finley hopped out to call Claude with the good news and Polly stretched out to luxuriate in the extra space. I topped us up with more hot water and emptied the remainder of the bath essence into the tub. She looked at me, grave and critical. 'Take it easy, Charli, that stuff is bloody expensive.'

A memory throbbed painful like a blister on the back of my heel: the Hotel Sacher, Vivaldi playing on the radio, the *New York Times* soggy on the bathroom tiles. 'Yes,' I sighed, 'it was Alexander's favourite.'

She sank deeper into the water, rested her fingertips on her forehead as if fending off a migraine. 'Good God,' she said, 'can we *please* talk about something else?'

I nodded, ashamed. 'Of course.'

'I don't mean to be a bitch,' she said, 'but that whole *situation* is just such an ambient bummer.'

I wondered where she'd picked up that phrase, maybe it was one of Finley's: it sounded like something he'd title a painting. He came crashing back into the bathroom, still naked, his dick at half-mast, waving his phone, shouting, 'Oh shit, girl! Jamie got arrested!'

I gasped 'No? What for? And he's *such* a nice guy . . .'

He perched on the side of the bathtub. 'So, he's been making a new film . . .'

Polly groaned. 'Oh God, not another one! What is it this time?'

'The forgotten women of rock and roll.' Finley scrolled down on his phone. 'Wait, no, wait,' he corrected himself, 'it's the forgotten *trans* women of rock and roll.'

I almost shrieked, 'How is that possible? He's a *deeply* transphobic person.'

'Yeah well, girl, not so much, that's the thing.' Finley smirked. 'He kept pulling his dick out during the interviews. Isn't that sick?'

Later we took shrooms together and went over to the Gemäldegalerie to look at the Brueghels. I didn't feel anything for a while, until we came to the famous portrait of the two chained monkeys, at which point things got very intense, especially when Finley and Polly started to argue about the moral shortcomings of figurative painting. It was probably a bad idea to begin with: we were all a little too frayed for psychedelics in public. I was way too high to follow their discussion properly, I could barely follow them around the gallery, the floors had all turned to leek and potato soup. Still I was hardly surprised when Polly stormed out calling Finley a misogynist after he said that Correggio's *Leda and the Swan* made him horny.

He said that she, *as a painter*, should know that art and sex are the places where you don't have to bow to taboos, and she said that *as a woman* she was offended by all attempts to romanticise sexual violence. She left very angry, her face replaced with that of one of Brueghel's little red-haired apes. Finley was so turned on by the whole flagration of monkeys and drugs that he went to find Claude at the letting agency and left me to my own devices with just a limp little hug. He said, 'You don't mind do you, girl? I've seen this shit a hundred times.'

I spent some time alone in the gallery, more time than I realised, hours maybe stood in front of Fra Angelico's *Last Judgement*, trying to find myself amongst the saved, fearing that I was more likely crowded in with the damned. An attendant eventually showed me out, not because I was talking aloud again, but simply, she assured me in her schoolgirl English, because it was now *free evening*. I didn't understand but at least I had sobered up enough to make my way onwards without too much fear that the *Witch of Haarlem* would follow me out.

I walked for hours, right across the city, until the sky started to change colour and I was unsure anymore if it was dawn or twilight, autumn or spring, and I felt afraid. I wondered if it was time for me to end it now, to walk out into the road and wait for a car to hit me. I pinched at the back of my own hand viciously. 'Charli, for fuck's sake get a grip.'

Somewhere over near Treptower Park I saw a row of three posters advertising one of Alexander's concerts from a date gone by, block text over a picture taken on the roof of that hotel in Vienna, his head thrown back onanistically. It stopped me in my tracks. The posters had each been vandalised, and in the most juvenile way. Kids had drawn a moustache and tits on him in magic marker, scrawled 'Fotze' across the face of one, doodled a swastika on another. They had mocked him, degraded the power of his image like tomb robbers smashing a Pharaoh's nose to deprive him of his life force, but still the fucker lingered on. His eyes on the wall glimmered alive in the gleam of the moon; even defaced he was taunting me, the whole row of posters grinned at me in unison, they spoke to me, telling me to give up the pretence, saying I was his forever and I knew it.

'I don't love you, Alex,' I shouted out, 'I don't. You're dead to me. So fuck off, you're dead to me, alright?' The sound of my voice, ragged and shrill, scared me and I stumbled a little on an uneven paving stone. A startled fox scurried past, glowing like a flame where the streetlight caught her fur. A breeze stirred the posters and caused them to ripple, set them off chattering again. 'Charli,' they said, 'I am coming back for you.'

I stood, transfixed by the way they fluttered, staring at the posters as though he might really step down from the wall, materialise like a phantom in front of me. I stood there, steeled and expectant, but no such thing happened, of course it didn't, it couldn't; like Jung says, ghosts are merely our own shadows.

I took the train back to Finley's house but couldn't sleep. I woke up every hour or so from a dream that wouldn't quit: Alex was calling me to tell me he was ill and would die without one of my kidneys. In the dream it was my mother who was to perform the operation, only when it came to the incision she broke down in tears, saying, 'I can't, I can't lose you again.' I'd wake up, I'd punch through the night in terror, alert and afraid for just a minute or so, before sleep dragged me back under and the dream started over again.

I dreamt this awful scene four, maybe five times, before I finally lifted myself out of the bed and waddled, sweaty and fitful, into the dining room. I opened Finley's laptop and casually, as if I had no agenda, sieved through all the garbage Google has to offer at 5 a.m. I gravitated to Alexander's email server, found the password was unchanged and, gluttonous for punishment, combed through his unread mail. I wanted to find something truly agonising, something that would hurt me so deeply I'd cry myself back to sleep and swear to never even think of him again. These are the actions of a masochist, of a woman determined to suffer because she fears that one day the pain will be over and then her love will really, truly be lost.

I looked for emails in which he mocked and insulted me, which made it clear he had been fucking Moritz the whole time and laughing at me with every thrust, balls-deep into his boss, I searched for broken glass I could grind into the palms of my hands. Instead, what I found were hundreds of messages from all around Europe, from people writing to tell Alex that he meant the world to them, saying that he was brave and sexy and that he inspired them to *speak their truth*. I felt jealous, wildly jealous: didn't I deserve some of this adulation? And I felt angry because I had thrown my lot in for so long with such a bastard and I had nothing but a paranoid personality disorder to show for it. I mean even little old Céleste got her medal from the Legion of Honour eventually. Mostly though I felt insidiously horny and found myself with my hands in my underwear thinking of the last time he fucked me, on the sleeper train to Paris. Dawn saw me jerking off to his pictures, cumming hard over his memory, feeling quite worthless, pathetic once the sun had risen, my only consolation being the hollow promise that all pain does fade eventually, like the night itself.

4

It was late summer and I was on the train on my way over to Hubert's birthday party, alone. Finley was pressed into Gerhard's service at the sauna and Polly was waiting in for a curator. They'd see me later on, early evening perhaps, don't stress, they'd both acclimatised too well. Berliners will arrive whenever they feel like it, unbeholden to anything besides their own dividends. No one in Berlin cares enough about anything to ever be on time, and when they do arrive they'll bring their dog, their kids, their groceries, as if the whole world were their kitchen-diner. *So thoughtless*, I muttered, *such an infantile refusal to stand on ceremony*. I cradled a pineapple on my lap, a birthday gift for Hubert, and thanked God for the Japanese.

I pictured him waiting on his friends, sighing and staring into a trifle, wondering if and when they would ever show up, his face sparkling with joy at my prompt arrival, he became ever dearer to me. *They* would all join later, but *I* was intent on being on time. I'd made such an exhibition of myself in front of Hubert last time I saw him at the side of the pool, I wanted a chance to present a more respectable face. And besides, I really didn't know what to do with myself, I'm ashamed to admit that without Alex I had absolutely nothing to fill up the void in my skull.

A twin set of screens in the U-Bahn carriage looped the day's headlines, celebrity gossip, cartoon puns I could only half comprehend and ads for monthly travel passes. A gaspipe deal with Russia had upset everyone, but for different reasons, The Mud Club Kidz were set to play the Mercedes Benz Arena, the lady who invented the currywurst insists that she is still just a simple sausage lady, Germany's biggest baby born at 6.10 kg. I watched the news cycle around and around, restless, anxious, I suppose, sweating it out, waiting manic as always on something else, a picture of Alexander being bundled into a cab, drunk, receiving an award, grinning at an interviewer. What do you think? The train rumbled on towards the party.

In the midst of my own unhappiness Hubert became invested with a new, pathetic grace. I knew of course that he'd been ditched by Jamie and I was tender to the suggestion of his suffering. Sadness always proves extremely sensitising for me, everyone else's injuries, real or imagined, become magnified by it. For some people I know, personal pain obscures everything else, it's all they can see, but for my part anguish summons me to deliver and so, my heart bleeding for all the world, I bravely raise the gonfalon of my own dismay on someone else's battlefield. If I felt silly turning up to the party alone, I knew at least that I was called to do so, to endure this minor ignominy and arrive early as an envoy for all his tardy friends, to offer Hubert some succour. Perhaps we could even console each other, two heartbroken lovers joining together in a rousing chorus of 'You Don't Own Me', drinking ourselves under the birthday table. I'm a great party guest, everybody says that, and if Hubert didn't care for pineapple, well then I would blend the flesh for a salsa and fashion the fronds into a garnish.

I arrived at three on the nose; my host was extremely surprised. 'Charli,' he said, 'you're awfully early. I was still in the shower. Come up.'

He buzzed me in, and I explained that Polly and Finley would be along a little later. I spun a story about them both volunteering at a soup kitchen, but he didn't seem to think their late arrival needed any justification. He was dressed but still a little damp from his ablutions, he yawned. 'I've barely woken up myself, dear. I was up 'til all hours, baking. Coffee?'

As it was just the two of us, I offered him some help with laying out the buffet and he took me through to the kitchen. He'd prepared a dozen quiches, tarts and flans, bought great wheels of French cheese from KaDeWe and hard-boiled a mountain of eggs. He now set about decanting great jars of olives and cornichons into frosted glass bowls whilst the coffee pot chortled, assigning me the task of stacking meatballs into pyramids.

I shuttled back and forth from the kitchen to the dining room, ferrying the foodstuffs through until the table looked like a Dutch still life, creaking under the weight of its own abundance. 'It's awfully good of you to help,' he said, 'as you see, I'm on my own here just now.' In his mustard tweed jacket and moss slacks, short and suave, he reminded me of an off-duty jockey.

He took me off on a tour of the house. His apartment was in the same building as Gerhard's, it was smaller, *but not small.* Hubert made a joke about the frequency with which people confused the two of them. 'Same age, same height, same house you see. The only way anyone can tell us apart is by square meterage.'

'That's funny,' I said. 'You know people would often confuse me and Alexander, too? Or they would think I was his sister. Although I don't think we look *that* much alike, not really.'

Hubert looked at me aporetically, his eyes drifted from left to right as clouds do across blustery skies, following a thought. He didn't reply.

I chewed a nail. 'They do say that people often fall for their doppelgänger though, don't they?'

One room opened onto another in a circular manner, just like Tegel, the doughnut-shaped airport which the French had built to get past Stalin's blockade. Each chamber was crammed with forty years of flea market finds. Although he wasn't rich, Hubert had grown up around wealthy people and had acquired that haut bourgeois eye for relics of quality. His home was full of busts and books and antique clocks, crammed to bursting with treasures, like an emperor's tomb. We walked through the lounge, the sunroom, the study where he worked on translations of art historical texts, over rugs and parquet and newspaper turned the colour of marmalade, patching odd holes in the bedroom carpet. Wind chimes and papier-mâché parrots enlivened the ceilings, Japanese lanterns and Italian brass floor lamps shedding dulled brilliance about the place, discreet, diffuse light, the clocks ticking all out of time with one another. Empty of guests the place was oddly discarnate, like a building site on a Sunday morning.

He had a can of baked beans, matte black and stencilled with a golden art deco motif. He said he'd bought it at Biba. 'My dear, I was *obsessed* with the place,' he tittered. 'Mother was quite horrified, she thought it awfully vulgar, but to me it was *divine*.' I began to think maybe he was a little batty. From a bookcase he produced a Bible, standard edition, hardly the sort of thing you'd gravitate towards considering the wider context, only this one was special because the flyleaf had been signed by John Paul I. 'Quite unusual to have a pope autograph something, you know?' he remarked. 'And, my dear, he really studied it well before he signed, I tell you. Had to make sure it wasn't *Venus in Furs,* I suppose.' In the lounge hung a framed poster of Romy Haag from '77/'78. I mentioned I was a fan and he said, 'Oh really? I could introduce you if you like,' an offer I smiled at but shrugged off as more chatter from a fantasist.

In the dining room I admired his porcelain, cups and plates and serving dishes stored in neat stacks, prize pieces facing out from the shelves of a primeval Welsh dresser. He said, 'Of course Gerhard's collection is a lot more impressive, but mine has the greater nostalgic value. Most of it was my great-aunt's; it survived the Dresden bombing, you know?' I thought about my father and his world of souvenir paper plates and I felt extremely morose.

We stood as if contemplating a Malevich abstract, or our own mortality, and I noticed there were a few gaps in Hubert's display. I asked if he had gifted some ceramics to a museum too.

'Oh no,' he sighed. 'No. That was Jamie.'

I was naturally shocked. 'He broke them on propose?'

'Threw them at me,' he replied, strangely unmoved. 'Of course, at first I thought he was just playing: artistic temperament, you know? But when he started with the Meissen, my dear, that's when I knew it was over.'

I shifted my weight from one foot to the other. 'Yes, I heard you two had ah, parted ways. I'm sorry about that.'

But he spurned my condolences. 'No you're not,' he said.

'No,' I laughed, 'I'm not. I can't say I liked him all that much. What happened?'

'Oh nothing,' he shrugged, 'Jamie came to Berlin to make films and I couldn't help him anymore. I never had any cash to offer of course, and he burned through all my connections such as they are, expeditiously.'

I said, 'Oh, but that seems so mercenary. Are people really like that?', though of course I well knew they were.

He busied himself pulling kitschy serviettes from a drawer in the dresser, folding them into triangles, stuffing them into pint glasses, and as he went he explained to me how he held no grudge against Jamie, how every artist comes to Berlin with a dream and must *realise it or die in the attempt*. 'Careless of what they are destroying,' he said, 'or whom.'

'Right,' I nodded, aware that my bottom lip was quivering a little, as it does whenever I hear Elvis sing 'How Great Thou Art'. I said 'Yes, right, I see.'

Hubert's own eyes twinkled with dew. 'It's a sad story. Such hubris,' he consoled himself with a gherkin.

I hated Jamie and his shitty films and the inscrutable axe he had to grind with me, but I found Hubert's good-natured desolation deeply moving, and there in front of the piles of pies and pickles, comestibles laid out like a wedding banquet for guests who might never come, I spilled out all my own feelings, like so much salad dressing. I told him how I too had been exploited by my own foolish obsession, that the dreams which had brought me to Berlin had come to nothing because I'd squandered my time and energy on someone who only ever saw me as a means to an end, as a way to get things done. I said, 'We're twinned in sorrow, you and I,' drunk on pompous heartbreak. 'Tell me, is this how people survived plagues and wars? Every day the same yet every day somehow worse?' I asked him. 'You're a historian, you must know.'

I was swollen with these emotions, but my friends rolled their eyes at the first mention of Alexander's name, I had no way to disperse these feelings until Hubert's birthday pathos overran me. I found myself sobbing into a stiff cotton napkin, it scuffed my cheek each time I wiped at the great green stream of snot. Hubert looked on at me, horrified.

'I'm sorry,' I said, still snivelling, 'I don't want to ruin your special day. God but I just feel like the Bishop of Lindisfarne, dragging St Oswald's head around with me everywhere I go, if you know what I mean? And it's too much,' I sobbed. 'It's all too much. I'm sorry.'

Hubert patted me on the back rather timidly. 'There, there now,' and assured me politely, 'That's quite alright, my dear,' though when I raised my mucous-streaked face to his, he looked at me as if assailed by the smell of blocked drains.

A dam had burst within me. I took a rather extended digression away from the subject of my former relationship, veering off through the undergrowth of astrology, literary criticism and party circuit gossip; only eventually did I come back to the topic, festooned with little sprigs of stargazing and Hemingway. 'He's not all bad,' I babbled. 'He's very funny and he's pretty good in the sack too, only we're too similar I suppose. We're both Geminis, you see, so we'll probably make up anyway and all of this silliness will have been for nothing.'

Hubert said, 'Quite,' and looked about the room as if hoping to find a hidden camera and discover to his relief that this was nothing but an elaborate birthday prank, potentially to be televised. He poured me a glass of whiskey, poured one for himself and knocked it back like a tequila shot, I followed suit and he poured us another.

'Do you think I've been a fool?' I queried him. 'If he had secrets that's only because I never asked him to share. Artistic temperament, like you say. Joe Orton was *forever* disappearing off, wasn't he? To find inspiration. And what about Agatha Christie? What has Alex ever done to me, really? Nothing that I haven't done myself.'

'Yes,' Hubert spoke with increasing anxiety, finger in his collar, 'yes, I suppose you're right.'

'And he did try to call and apologise,' I said. 'He rang me up on one of the phones at the bureau de change, of all places. Finley says it was just the ketamine, but *I'm sure* it was him calling. One knows doesn't one?' I continued. 'When one is bound to another one simply knows.'

'Quite,' he said again, at an utter loss.

I was giving him all this unasked for, and his lack of comprehension made me think of my mother's almost permanent state of confusion in the weeks following my brother's death, no longer aware of the time, still sitting up at the kitchen table as I came tip-toeing down the stairs seeking Coco Pops, towel around her shoulders, plastic bag on her head trying out a new hair colour. How she'd see me arrive, as if coming on set, and begin talking to me a mile a minute, sharing the fruits of last night's reasoning, playacting that I was a grown-up too and not a traumatised child, as an actress might use an amenable cleaning lady to run lines with. 'It'll all be OK now that I'm a blonde again,' she'd say, and though I couldn't validate her proclamations, somehow my hearing them made them more real for her. Hubert looked at me that day the way I'd looked at her then, wanting to be warm but not knowing how. I saw myself at nine or ten peering out from his weather-worn face, a child's eyes puzzling in an old man's countenance. I saw myself looking out at myself, made as if to stroke that peachy cheek, caught myself only just in time, hand hanging awkward in mid-air.

The buzzer blurted out, honking, yowling. I have never seen a person look so relieved to have a door to answer. Hubert scrambled to the intercom and practically begged his guest to hurry straight up to the third floor. I followed him to the hall. 'Do you think I should call him?' I pleaded for advice. 'Do you think I've blown the whole thing out of proportion?' I must've seemed completely out of my mind.

'Well, yes,' he said, puzzled as to how he'd become so entangled, 'I suppose you could,' and he set the front door ajar.

The sound of footsteps filtered in from the hallway as the first few guests climbed the stairs and I asked if I might use his phone. He told me it was in the bedroom then turned to welcome the new arrivals with the cheer, 'My dear, I am *so* happy to see you,' reading more truly as *thank fuck you're here.*

I went to the bedroom, found the phone and lifted the handset. The line hummed flirtatiously as if sizing me up. I dialled the number, I knew it by heart, my fingers stumbling with enthusiasm. My heart playing prestissimo to the moment's larghetto, the cream receiver weighed heavy in my hand; he probably wouldn't answer, he might be busy, perhaps still in bed.

Hubert's telephone looked at least thirty years old, and there seemed a decade between each burbling peal. I paced and the phone line chirped amiably in my ear, waiting patiently beside me for an answer, like a courtesan's faithful pet parrot. I hadn't even considered what I might actually want to say, I had so many conflicting emotions, *I love you Alex, you're a cunt, stop harassing me, I need to talk to you, we can work this out, I'm leaving for London tomorrow*, and here I was on the precipice of having to articulate it all. I started to compose my argument, or rather to try out the mouthfeel of these various propositions, speaking them out loud as a warm-up, as the phone rang on. *I want to tell you this, no, I need to tell you this no, no, I have to tell you this,* I was so caught up in my preparatory grandstanding that I didn't notice that I was talking to an answerphone, until the machine told me, *Die Frist für Ihre Nachricht ist abgelaufen*, the time limit for my message had expired.

First I laughed at the situation, the romantic comedy of it all. I felt just like Sandra Dee at her dressing table, caught in another adorably zany scenario, then I caught sight of myself in the mirror, red-eyed, pin thin and snot-streaked and started bawling again. I threw myself on the bed and smashed my head under a pillow. 'Idiot, idiot, idiot,' I shrieked, 'you stupid fucking idiot,' the soft underside of Hubert's pillow absorbing my sobs.

The buzzer rang out once more in the hall and Hubert squawked away in German to whoever was out there waiting. The time had come, the whole place was filling up. A bottle popped and a whoop went up in the kitchen, plates rattled and cutlery tinkled on the porcelain.

I was safe, secreted away in here for now, but soon enough someone would discover me on their way to do a bump in the bathroom. I couldn't face the humiliation of being found blubbering on Hubert's bed, I had to get a hold of myself, I needed to salvage something of my life. I'd been avoiding almost everyone I knew for weeks, I couldn't re-emerge in further disgrace, that would be the final defeat. I decided then to try and dry my eyes and feign a smile, to mingle for a while, have a drink, act human, and if I couldn't stick it until Finley or Polly arrived, then I'd fake a headache and bow out early, prematurely but with grace.

I rooted about in Hubert's drawers for a hanky, did what I could to restore my mascara, gave myself a spritz from one of the atomisers on his dressing table. It smelled like psychedelic cat's piss, but then beggars can't be choosers. I took a moment to steel myself, ran my fingers through my hair in front of the mirror and tried on my biggest grin. It was close enough to convincing. I'd tell them all I'd just spoken to Alex and he was in the best of moods and so happy to hear from me, no one would doubt it. Again the buzzer, Hubert invited yet more guests up, and I imagined that I was backstage at the opera, that he was giving the beginner's call. Shoulders back and head high, if they didn't look too closely they would never know.

I came out of the bedroom with as regal a manner as I could summon, ready to follow the voices back towards the kitchen. I graced the hallway, grinning benignly, welcoming guests, offering to take their coats. Then West walked in with a big bunch of yellow tulips and I dropped the jacket I was holding. He saw me and his cheeks flushed scarlet. I wouldn't have blamed him for spitting in my face, but he didn't, he wouldn't, he was better than us. He tucked his head down, hunched himself over the flowers. 'Hey,' I said, very humbly, contrite, but he walked straight on.

An unsociable snicker played in my ear though I stood alone in the hall, burning with shame and suddenly chilled, as though sunstruck. I crouched to collect the jacket I had dropped, but rather than hang it up I slipped it on and without further thought, I left. Outside the sky was as fresh and purple as a day-old bruise. I tumbled out into the street, scurried along through the city all the way back home.

5

We've had real trouble with the lights: they all go out suddenly, every few hours or so. The nurse said it's due to a cable being damaged during the renovation of the laser eye clinic, but of course I know it's down to the television trucks outside – they're putting too much pressure on the grid. In the afternoon it's a bit of a bore but when it happens at night it's wonderfully dramatic, only the bedside lamp stays on, floating like an angel above my little cabinet full of nothing.

They are trying me with a television set, not the news, of course – they're afraid that will set me off screaming. Rather they've put on the channel which shows classic films. It was the movies of Elizabeth Taylor last night and today we have a Fassbinder marathon, which I have to say is a stroke of luck. There are far too many commercial breaks though, they come in and fragment the narrative and it's hard for me to tell if this member of the Red Army Faction is genuine in her adoration of the Tropicana orange juice she's pouring for her children, or if this lesbian fashion designer really does need me to send €5 a month to help fight malaria in Kenya. Intermittently Sophia Hope appears advertising the new Hyundai, which feels like a prophecy, and I tell the room, 'I went to art school with her,' only there's no one to listen. Just now Dirk Bogarde is hiring a man to play his doppelgänger, though they look nothing alike. I'm not sure if it's supposed to be a joke.

The nurse hovers nearby though she's very cross with me after my break for freedom. I suppose I can hardly blame her now, can I? She has been so patient with me, I only came in for a rhinoplasty consultation and yet they've kept me here in relative comfort for days, soda and eggs on the house. As for the journalist, who knows? Sometimes I see him outside in the corridor but he keeps his distance now, no more attempts to grill me for the gossip columns, though I have let it be known that once my cast is off I'll gladly pose for a picture.

The nurse is talking. 'You have a visitor, will I show her in?' she says, and I can hardly believe how much her English has improved, maybe she's using Duolingo on the commute? The door is open, out goes the nurse and in comes a bride of Christ: the nun I once saw peeping in on me earlier in my stay. 'Sister,' I say, 'thank you for coming to see me. Please take a seat, I have an awful lot to unburden myself of.' The nun frowns, perhaps I am being too familiar. 'Forgive me, sister,' I say, 'if I am speaking out of turn.'

'Charli, love,' she says, 'it's me.'

I'm surprised to recognise the voice, and the concern in her eyes like soft-boiled eggs. 'Mother?' I say. 'Have you taken holy orders?'

'Stop being silly, now,' she shakes her head. She is not angry, she reaches for my face. 'You've got yourself into a right pickle here, haven't you?' Her index skates over my forehead and down along my bruised cheek bone. 'Just look at you.'

'I'm so glad you're here. Thank God! Finally someone who will listen. I've been asking for weeks but no one will tell me!'

She steels herself. She says, 'Tell you what love?'

'The truth,' I say, and I'm steadying myself now with an inhalation of breath: 'is David Bowie dead?'

'Bowie?' she exclaims. 'Of course not love, people like him don't die. What a funny thing to ask!'

She is relieved by the relative levity of the question, fearing much worse; she's squeezing my hand, pleased at her ability to answer without pain. With a brisk smile, she concludes, 'I saw him myself last week, getting off the London Eye.'

6

I surfaced about a week later. I thought Finley and Polly would be furious with me: not only had I left Hubert's party without any warning, I'd also failed to return to Finley's place. I hadn't intended to cause alarm, I just wanted to be alone for a while, back in my own apartment amongst my own things. Still I recognised that I had been irresponsible. When I finally did email them, I was careful to appear penitent, asking them to forgive me my misguided vanishing act, to let me make it up to them with some of Count Chipula's famous lentil soup. *I think I had some sort of panic attack*, I wrote, trying to propitiate, *I can explain better in person*. Neither of them seemed all that concerned, they wrote back simple messages of *Cool* and *See you there,* so to up the stakes I added the codicil, 'P.S. I have a big announcement.'

We arranged to meet at 11 p.m. but I was late because I got caught up watching a YouTube documentary on New York performance art in the 1980s. One particular clip held my attention, a curious discussion of Penny Arcade's mid-eighties on-stage impersonations of Margo Howard-Howard, the infamous crossdressing fraudster who had passed herself off in Manhattan as an English Dame. Arcade's performances were apparently so uproarious that no one would believe Margo was in fact a real person. Audiences and critics were convinced that she was some sort of alter ego, until Margo herself started showing up and shouting the punchlines from the crowd. Something about that clip spoke to me, the slipperiness, the impossibility, really, of being.

I took the train but ran from the station, for the last few blocks at least, so as to arrive looking sweaty and sheepish, a little out of breath. They were still in the street, they hadn't gone inside yet, and I thought at first that perhaps they were smoking, but as I got closer I realised that they were arguing, bickering over the Vetements leather shorts Finley was wearing. He said they were an investment; she said they were a betrayal of his politics. I said, 'Let's go inside.'

As always Count Chipula greeted us like long-lost friends. 'Guys guys guys, where you been? I miss you guys!' He grinned and showed us to the *table d'honneur*, wiping at a spot of grease with the tea towel he wore at his waist. 'I have new menus,' he said proudly, producing a pair of laminated cards from thin air. 'Look, see?' We nodded, smiled and thanked him. He slipped back behind his counter and Polly muttered, 'But it's the same old muck in a different font.'

We crowded over the menus to study what we already knew, Finley at my elbow, Polly opposite in a waspish mood. Besides the three of us, there were just two other customers, a pair of American girls, one in a baseball cap and one with a ponytail, deep in conversation, talking as if nobody else in there spoke English. One of them was telling the other, loudly, about how the marriage of Christie, a mutual friend from Christian college, had descended into unholy conflict.

She flipped her high pony and said, 'Oh sure, he slaps her around. Sure. Spends all their money on blow, but she just won't hear a word against him. She just says "Oh hun he's under a lot of pressure at work, ethical altruism, you know" yada yada.' Her friend in the baseball cap interjected with 'how awful' and 'no way' as appropriate, but seemed honestly more focused on double dipping her chips in the ketchup and mayo. She said, 'You should try this, it's really good. It's how Europeans eat French fries.' Her companion did so, taking up a fry as a singer snatches a breath when approaching the peak of an aria, before barreling on with the plight of their mutual. 'Sometimes love is like, really crazy.'

Polly plumped for the lentil soup, and I had ordered the same, though I really hate lentils. Finley asked for a veggie burger, *keine Tomate, zusätzliche Gurken,* inspired by the American girls. I poked at his chips. He said, 'There was this really hot Italian guy at the gym today, he kept looking over at me and rubbing his crotch. Made me so horny.'

'Some old toad did that to me in the elevator at Karstadt,' Polly said, 'I broke my handbag over his head, the handle came clean away.'

Finley paused with the burger at his lips. 'Girl, I think you have a problem with violence.'

I remembered my father telling me to eat soup from the outside in; I stirred clockwise, then anti-clockwise. There was a small fly drowning in it. The Yanks were still pawing over the sufferings of Christie. The girl with the ponytail said, 'But I guess that's love, right? I mean, sometimes it hurts.' She sighed, ran a finger around the circumference of her empty plate and nodded gravely. 'Like, it says right there in 1 Corinthians, *philosophy itself cannot explain the crucifixion.*'

'Yeah,' the girl in the cap agreed, 'dead ass.'

Her friend fiddled with her hair tie pensively. 'We should pray on it,' she said, and slurped the last globules of her Coke. 'You think they have dessert here?'

I closed my eyes against the intensity of Chipula's strip lights, conversation continued around me. Polly refuting Finley's accusation, Chipula calling 'Hello, my friend' to some stoned kid who'd stumbled through the doorway, the American girls asking a phone *How do I say 'Do you have dessert' in German?* Finley making the counterclaim, 'Well, girl, you fucked Callum up pretty bad.'

Polly exclaimed, 'He started it, the little shit! He stood there grinning at me all afternoon . . .'

One of the American girls was giggling. 'Nachtisch, *nach-titcsh*? That sounds so dirty.'

Finley elbowed me. 'Girl, you should've seen it, it was crazy.'

Polly continued, '. . . And he then came right up to me *in front of everyone* to ask if I was thinking about *redecorating* the apartment.'

'Seen what?' I asked, eyes still closed.

'Polly fucking destroying Callum,' he said, a little gruff, 'at Hubert's party. Are you doing smack again or what? Girl, I literally just said that.'

I sat up straight, opened my eyes. 'Of course not, no, it's just *so* bright in here.'

Polly was really rattled, she said, 'He practically admitted it, Charli!'

'And then *blam!*' Finley wailed. 'She just popped him right on the nose. There was blood everywhere, you should've seen it. We had to bail before they called the cops.'

I smiled awkwardly, I didn't know how to feel. 'Yeah,' I said, 'too bad I left early.'

Chipula served the Yanks their *sütlaç*, Turkish rice pudding, as requested; they accepted it with an awkward shared smile. The girl in the baseball cap whispered, 'That literally looks like puke.' Her friend blushed and sniggered, 'You're awful. You're so bad.'

Finley took out his phone and showed me a selfie from Callum's feed: he was posed to elicit both sympathy and sexual attention, his face swollen, his eye blackened, little strips of surgical tape spanning his nose. It was captioned, *Healing, Learning, Life Hurts.*

Finley whistled through his teeth, sickened, impressed. 'Yeah, you really fucked him up, he's never gonna get in your face again.'

I saw the picture and grimaced in agreement. '*Wherefore the injury we do to a man should be of a sort to leave no fear of reprisals.* Yikes.'

Finley said, 'Huh?'

'Machiavelli,' I sighed.

Polly rolled her eyes. 'Oh for God's sake, Charli, must you always witter on like a character from a bloody Donna Tartt novel? Can't you take a day off?'

Finley lingered considering the photo of Callum's bruised and swollen face, he chewed on his lip. 'I'd still fuck him.'

Polly's parents were apoplectic about the whole thing. They'd imagined her stay in Berlin would last a year or two at most, that she'd paint a little and learn German, meet an investment banker at a social function, then come home and get on with life. This was the new century's equivalent to her mother's eighteen months as au pair to an Austrian baroness, only after close to four years there was no engagement, only an ongoing drain on the family finances, whispers of orgies, break-ins, and now this threat of legal action from her ex-roommate.

'They make it all sound *so* dramatic,' she said.

For her birthday Polly's mother had sent her an enamel bracelet and the stark news that she was a grown woman now and they would no longer support her financially. If she wanted to live so wantonly, she could do it on her own dime. 'They've given me six months to straighten myself out and come home,' she scowled, 'or they're cutting me off.'

Finley laughed quietly, but not kindly. Polly was not amused, she screwed up her face. 'It's fine for you with your sugar daddy!'

'Whatever,' he shot back, 'girl, you've had a sugar daddy your whole life.'

They started squabbling again and I put my head in my hands, Chipula whistled along with 'Livin' on a Prayer'. 'Guys,' I said, 'come on, don't,' but they didn't hear. The American girls were craning their necks to hear us now; they were as indiscreet as eavesdroppers as they were in conversation. I felt embarrassed, I looked up and said, 'Well, what about Eddy Campbell-Bannerman? I thought he was your intended?'

'Girl, he's gay as hell,' Finley snarked, 'have you seen his pictures?'

'I *know* that,' I said, 'but, I thought you were going to come to some kind of *arrangement* and become his lavender bride and . . .'

'Yes, well,' she sighed, 'poor Eddy's been committed unfortunately, dear thing. *His* miserable family put him in a facility.'

Finley was open-mouthed with outrage. 'Do British people still do that? Send you to a psychiatric hospital if you're gay?'

Polly brushed him off. 'Oh honestly,' she said, 'no. He took too much acid and started shouting about being the Second Coming of Christ. Made a big scene at St John Bread and Wine, and they shipped him off to the funny farm the same night.'

'Yeah,' I nodded. 'Yeah. Jesus is still a quite common experience for people with grandiose delusions. Napoleon too actually, and Michael Jackson. When I was in hospital,' I spoke without shame, 'I met the Duke of Wellington, he was quite harmless really, just wore a bucket on his head and insisted that ABBA owed him five million dollars in royalties for using his life story without permission.'

Finley and Polly were not paying any attention, they were debating the propriety of the term *funny farm,* or rather he was telling her that it was an outdated, offensive term which stigmatised people, and she was telling him to stop mansplaining. She said she'd grown rather fond of Eddy, that they'd been texting incessantly for the past few weeks. She was sorry about it all, in a way.

'Anyway his friend Sam just moved here from London,' she said, 'and she's going to move into the studio with me. Maybe Eddy'll come too once he's out of hospital.'

'Is Sam a painter too?' I asked.

'Oh I don't know,' Polly shrugged. 'Her grandmother left her a tonne of money and so she's coming to Berlin to find herself. Yawn. That's what Thailand is for.'

A late summer storm had broken, flashes of lightning ripping the indigo night sky apart, a hush came over the restaurant, the sublime power of heaven to quiet – even the Yanks had quit yakking. Chipula's radio played 'I Drove All Night', another fat fly sat still and noiseless on the corner of our table, as if observing a minute's silence on Remembrance Sunday, then picked itself up and flew headlong into Polly's mouth. She didn't notice.

Finley jerked upright in his seat and dropped his fork onto the table. 'Fuck,' he said, 'girl, I totally forgot! I met that disco singer you love, the one you were going to write your paper on.'

'What?' I gasped. 'Romy Haag? Where?'

'At Hubert's party,' he said, 'she was there too. She and him are super close.'

Polly shook her head. 'No, no, that wasn't Romy Haag, that was Romy *Schneider*.'

He scorned, 'Girl, Romy Schneider's dead. It was *definitely* Romy Haag.'

'Are you sure?' she pressed him. 'I think you've got it confused. I know Hubert is good friends with Romy Kermer, it was probably her.'

'Who the fuck is that?' he asked.

'I can't believe this,' I whimpered, 'I can't believe I missed my chance.'

Polly said, 'Oh you know. She's the ice skater from the seventies. Hubert's always talking about how he sewed the leotard she wore when she won silver at the Olympics.'

'No, I'm sure it was Romy *Haag*,' Finley pursed his lips. 'Unless she said *Joni* Haag?'

I gave up, I drifted, I vaporised. Finley and Polly continued to quibble over who had in fact been at the party, but I was no longer present. I felt as though I were only a movie camera, decreasing my focal length, zooming out from the situation, panning across the restaurant, its glass vitrine of chopped salads and raw meats. On the counter a pristine white till, a plaster pig frolicking on plastic grass and a repurposed pickle jar, mouth open to receive *Trinkgeld*. I glided over the menu on the far wall, handwritten in impossible cursive, sweeping by the mural of Bob Marley hulaing with an alien on a tropical beach, and came to rest my lens on the plate-glass window, on our reflections overlaid against passersby running through the streets in the rain, streaks of colour from their jackets, shrieks of strange pleasure. I dropped my head on the table and all the cutlery jumped. Again there was silence.

Polly broke it, she asked me, 'So what was it you wanted to tell us, Charli?'

I didn't raise my head, I just said, 'Huh?'

And she prompted me, 'Didn't you have some news to share? Isn't that why we're here?'

I sat upright. 'Yes, right, yes of course.' I improvised, 'I'm going back to London. I spoke to a new PhD supervisor and ah, well, she's really keen to have me in the department, and ah, I think I've learned what I need to learn here.'

'Thank God,' said Polly, 'I thought you were going to say you were starting up with Alexander again. I honestly don't think I could've coped.'

Finley was more encouraging. 'Cool girl, yeah. You should totally go back to school. I think it'd be really good for you to do that.'

'We ought to toast to that,' Polly looked around. 'Fuck, I wish we could get a drink here, but Chipula keeps halal. We should go to Roses.'

Finley raised an index to me in question. 'But like, can you still work the door at Piggy on Sunday? Filip was going to do it but he's trying to quit G, so . . .'

I didn't remember him ever asking me this favour, but I agreed to keep my commitment all the same. 'Sure,' I said, 'for you, lover, anything.'

Polly waved to Chipula to make up the bill, as if this were The Ivy. She frowned. 'I cannot believe that party is *still* going. Didn't they find someone dead in the darkroom?'

We rose to pay, and Finley said, 'Yeah but that was weeks ago. People move on.'

Chipula gave us each a lollipop, which was sweet, and as we left I heard the American girl with the ponytail exclaim, 'Oh my God, Lindsay, did you get all that? Berlin is literally insane.'

The other girl said, quite deadpan, 'I know, right?'

'Christie is going to be so fucking jealous,' giggled her friend.

We walked over to Roses as Polly had suggested. The rain had passed but autumn still hung in the air. Polly said she hated the turn of the seasons because Germans always used it as an excuse for every small cold and headache and for cancelling plans; I said I hated it because it made me feel like death was outside my door. We said we'd go in for one quiet drink, Finley had to head back early anyway since Gerhard had started calling him at 1 a.m. every evening to check he was home alone. Claude knew the score, so he didn't cause any problems, though it was difficult Finley said, to explain the set-up to the guy he met whilst donating blood: it really put a kink in their romance.

Inside, the bar was almost totally abandoned, just one lonely dancer twirling solo to Tina Turner. Polly complained that it was a sorry situation when Roses was empty at midnight on a Thursday. The fun fur on the walls was matted and pressed, the tawdry disco lights looked absurd running over an empty dance floor, the bar staff were ever less inclined to serve anyone with any haste. They ignored us and chatted to each other instead, whilst 'Private Dancer' inexplicably played inexplicably three times in a row.

Eventually we got our Cuba Libres, Finley started eyeing up the lonesome dancer, Polly said, 'Gosh, do you remember the last time the three of us were in here?'

'When Callum tried to sell you for a pill?' I suggested.

'No!' she chastised me. 'When Finley and I came to meet you after a gig and we thought it'd be a laugh to arrive naked.'

'Oh yes,' I smiled, though I had no such recollection. 'How funny.'

Finley nudged me. 'Hey, do you think that guy over there is checking me out?'

'Probably not,' Polly intercepted. 'He's probably just looking around and wondering where he went wrong in life.'

But Finley blanked her. He said, 'I'm gonna go and say hey,' and stalked off across the vinyl floor, drink in hand, wicked smile primed.

'Honestly.' Polly's face was given over to pure resignation. 'It's like a vocation with him.'

We sipped our drinks, unsure really why we were there now. She said, 'I've never liked this place, but I keep coming back, I don't know why. One gets the strangest sense of déjà vu in here.'

I nodded. 'Yeah, it's like a bad dream, isn't it?'

I told her that lately I'd been feeling as though I'd woken up in a room in which all the furniture had been rearranged overnight whilst I slept. Everything was still there, somewhere, but it was all wrong, at sixes and sevens. I continued, 'I feel like a tour guide on one of those London City Sightseeing buses, going around and around to the same places, *Next stop St Paul's, Next stop Buckingham Palace,* day after day, and the longer it goes on the less sense it makes. Do you know what I mean?'

'Hardly,' she sighed, 'but then that's nothing new.' She knocked back the end of her drink. 'Let's go home,' she said.

I walked back along Kottbusser Damm alone and entirely out of season. I longed to take a holiday, for a big bag of dope to help me forget. When I got home the apartment was as quiet as the grave, but down the hallway Carl's bedroom light was on. I called out 'Hello' but received no response, and when I went to investigate, I found a cigarette burning in the ashtray by the bed. It was pink, a Sobranie freshly lit, glowing amongst the expired stubs of all the old joints, the golden filter tip stained crimson with lipstick. I held my breath, strained for any sound, but the room stayed silent, the apartment was still. I exhaled uneasily and caught the trace of laughter down the corridor and the sound of the front door closing behind a stranger.

7

There was another storm brewing, slowly building all weekend: the pressure made my head throb. I stayed home drinking powdered soup, watching out of the window in case the cat came back, preparing myself psychologically for the return to London. Now that I'd announced it, I had to act on it, at least until I could think up another plan of action. I started to pack, or rather I began to rifle through wreckage, it was all-consuming, overwhelming, I had no real exit strategy.

I initiated the organisation with real sincerity, once or twice each day, but I simply lacked the skills necessary to execute it. I was a little depressed I guess, and always angry, tired, anxious. I bit my nails and sat on the floor watching *The Real Life Vampires of Bulgaria*, videos about chemtrails and mind control, about how Randy Savage from the Village People, Marc Bolan from T-Rex, and Lisa Left Eye from TLC had each *unaccountably* died in a car crash, nodding along and thanking my mother for the wisdom she had shown in forbidding me to ever get behind the wheel.

An occasional burst of energy would overcome me, and every few hours I would rise up and set to again, dust the cobwebs off a windowsill with my hand, gather and stack plates jellied and fecund with mould, empty an ashtray and pull back the curtains, as if I had any workable intentions of facing the day. There were firecracker moments, whole hours when it seemed I might achieve something, that I might make a dent in this shambles; mostly though I did nothing, or nothing useful at any rate, simply wandered around the place in Alex's old suits, smoking all of the half-finished Sobranies that I found stubbed out on saucers in the corners of the room.

I picked up armfuls of laundry and put them on to wash in the machine, only to forget the task entirely and came back two days later to a drum full of musty, mildewing washing. I began sifting through the overwhelming coils of cabling and staggering heaps of shoes and magazines, only to find myself sidetracked by a record cover, previously unseen, and come to a halt, kneeling down to stare Edith Sitwell in the face and ruminate. I took endless breaks, sat in the kitchen cradling a single boot, reading aloud the captions from the cartoon strips Carl had plastered the kitchen walls with, trying to practise my German, but they danced about before my eyes after just a few minutes' study and made me feel like I was losing my mind, accomplishing nothing.

I could've made more effort, I suppose. I could've tried harder to separate out his junk from mine, to extricate myself and pack what little I owned into the suitcase I had arrived with, but to what end? Then what? I couldn't hope to be cured by a trip abroad, this was not a fever I was recovering from. I remembered a story about Bowie having his swimming pool in Los Angeles exorcised because he had become convinced that Satan had possessed it. I felt a flash of recognition, *Same dude, same,* wondered if I could hire a man with a van to take it all to the dump, decided I couldn't face that – this was a burden for myself alone, even if I could not shoulder it fully yet.

I fell back again into squalor, again into apathy. I watched another documentary series, a sequence about history's greatest unsolved disappearances: a pilot in Australia who vanished along with his plane, perhaps taken up by UFOs, Hitler's dietician who passed out of human records as the Soviets entered Berlin, the 5,000 Roman legionnaires who went missing all at once on campaign in Caledonia. Each episode was, to say the least, of questionable quality, but I took comfort in them, they seemed to suggest that I could myself simply vanish if need be, leave all this mess behind. I could get up and walk out of this place, right out of shot, out into the sea like Joan Crawford in the final frames of *Humoresque*. I didn't owe anything to anyone anymore. I came close to cancelling when it was time for me to go and help Finley on the door at Piggy, very close, only I couldn't think up a good enough excuse, and besides I was bored of my stay-at-home spiralling: it's not just the ghosts that get to Jack you know, it's the isolation.

I went in my spaghetti-strap dress, fully made up and wrapped in a winter coat. It was only September and the temperature was still above twenty, but I had the most urgent feeling that I must wear fur. My mother would've called it *a celestial direction*. I remembered those winter nights past when Polly and I would arrive to the party together after trudging through the snow, bundled up and availing ourselves of the bank next door with its twenty-four-hour foyer, stopping off to strip from our ungainly outer layers between the ATMs, stuffing our coats into totes so as to arrive camera-ready. I remembered seeing Suzanne play at the party before she blew up, and I thought of the night I introduced Alexander to the crowd for the first time, thought of what that had cost me, thought of how nervous I had been waiting for him to arrive, and again I almost cancelled.

I walked over alone and unhurried, stoic and as yet sober. The air was oppressively still, the promised storm hiding itself behind Karstadt's omnipotent facade. I showed up for duty an hour or so late, but it didn't seem to be a problem: the party was barely troubled by guests, the whole city felt like a graveyard that night. Finley said that it was probably the weird weather keeping people home: low barometric pressure triggers headaches. Plus a lot of gay boys were still on vacation in Greece, though I suspected the news of the corpse in the darkroom might've taken the bloom off the rose, somewhat.

He said, 'OK so it's five euros tonight girl, three if they leave their shirt at the door. The guest list is here,' he tapped his finger on a print-out of some five or six names. I nodded, he added, 'And girl, don't go downstairs tonight alright? I need you up here, OK?'

He sloped off back behind the DJ booth, stripped off his T-shirt, indifferent to but aware of how the old men smoking at their tables around the dance floor quickened in response to his fair demerara flesh. He played something in Spanish, 'A quién le importa', I think. His bare torso sailed above the CDJ decks but from the waist down he was lost, so that he appeared to be floating, like a poster advertising cologne, loosening on the breeze. The televisions spewed that inescapable stream of silent fuckings, the bartenders, bored, attended to clean glasses with chequered tea towels, eldritch men in the corners pressed against the walls, stood in the shadows where they formed, no more than twenty, uncanny and sparse.

To enliven the situation Finley jumped on the mic and announced that anyone who took off their shirt would get a shot. 'Free tequila!' he cheered. 'Free tequila if you show me your tits!'

He had a few takers: one or two pot-bellied leather daddies took up the challenge, and what's more stayed on their feet to shuffle about shirtless to Kylie Minogue once they'd shyly disrobed, but it wasn't quite enough to get the party started, and the room remained fundamentally lifeless, the atmosphere thin as that on Mars. An unhappy barback plonked a bottle of Sterni on the table next to me. I smiled. 'No thanks, I don't drink beer.' He shrugged and said, 'Whatever, bitch, it's free.' I took a swig so as not to appear ungracious.

A couple of French twinks timidly paid me their entrance fee. I couldn't break a twenty so I kept the change and waved them inside. They looked a little scared, but then no innocent ever came to this party, unless in the hopes of losing that innocence. Callum came too; he looked momentarily unwell at the sight of me but recovered his poise when I let him in for free. I figured Finley would be glad to see him, and that he'd likely have some K; besides, Polly had already settled her score with his face. Then Jamie arrived, looking atypically lecherous. 'Oh, Charli, hi,' he said, 'I didn't think I'd see you around here again.'

'Life is full of surprises,' I heard myself say. 'Does your parole officer know you're here?'

He grinned. 'You're so funny, I've always loved that about you. That British sense of humour.'

I widened the smile until my face ached with malice, and allowed myself the discreet pleasure of making him pay, even though Finley had written his name on the guest list. He pressed me of course, asking me to double-check, but I simply gave him my most insufferably saccharine twinkle. 'Yeah, sorry, no, it's eight euros tonight.'

For once he didn't seem to be spoiling for a fight, and my asinine attempts to get under his skin, to provoke him just enough, were wasted. He smiled back and handed over his money, casting about the hopeless party. 'I guess you guys do really need the cash,' he said. I think he was stoned.

I swept my arm out wide and gestured towards the dance floor. 'Thank you. You may go in now,' but he didn't shift.

'I think maybe you and me got off on the wrong foot,' he laughed. 'You're like the only person in Berlin I don't vibe with.'

I said, 'Oh really?', hoping that a new bunch of partygoers might dribble in and save me from this conversation, but nonsuch appeared. 'So,' he leant in, almost flirtatiously, 'how's it going with the band?'

'On hiatus,' I lied. 'But you know me. I've got so many other *really* exciting projects coming up.'

He nodded. 'Cool, cool. I was filming with Romy Haag today. You know her?'

'Of course,' I said, irked. 'Of course I know her, I'm writing a PhD on her.'

I had now apparently given him carte blanche to brag at length. I should have denied any knowledge of who she was, but it was too late, and besides, wasn't I unutterably fascinated?

He had been shooting with Romy all week, at her apartment no less. He'd been to her home and had had dinner with her and smoked joints with her and listened to choice cuts with her, from her record collection, on her pristine seventies turntable with its mother of pearl grill. He hadn't known who she was two weeks ago, he chortled, and now they were practically the best of friends, and it was utterly galling. He'd picked up a multipack of Diet Coke for her and taken it over. Just this afternoon they'd danced on her shag carpeting to 'Sound and Vision', and she had told him the real meaning of the lyrics to 'Breaking Glass'. That this scene, which I had imagined for myself again and again, had come to be inhabited by this unworthy turkey left me slack-jawed and disabled, unable even to muster the anger I felt rightfully entitled to. I couldn't stand to slap him, couldn't even seethe I was so staggered, could barely broil in resentment, could only ask, 'But how?' He didn't answer. Worse, I found myself pulling closer to him so as best to catch every word, inhaling deeply to see if I could catch a hint of her perfume on him, or even her second-hand smoke, clinging to this imposter's wardrobe.

He saw that he had me, he smiled self-satisfied. 'It's crazy,' he said, 'that we're friends now. You know she dated Bowie for like four years? It's like wow, I can't even.'

'Yes. I know that,' I sniped to deflate him. '*Everybody* knows that.'

'So, did you know that he's sick then?' he said, casual as the angel of death. 'Like, *really* sick.'

I found his blithe proclamation infuriating, but told myself *just disregard this stoner idiot*. He was always so full of shit, why should I pay him any credence now? 'No he's not,' I countered. 'Of course he's not. We would've heard about it if he was.'

A man with a small scar on his cheek and cryptic grey eyes ambled in through the door as if into a country park, comfortable and confident. He wore jeans and a bomber jacket, under which I could tell underneath he was very lean. He had olive skin and a moustache which was so dark it looked like a disguise. He handed over his €5 with a sweet smile, flashing a slightly crooked set of teeth, and headed into the party, intentions clear as day.

Jamie blabbed on, 'That's why he's not touring anymore. My friend Lindsay went to school with this other girl called Christie, and her dad is his lawyer's business partner, so . . . I don't think he has long left, honestly. Romy's keeping quiet.'

The wheels of disaster turned in my head, I itched to choke him. Finley played one of Sophia's singles. Remixed by a Swedish techno DJ, it had been a big hit in the gay clubs that summer, and in drug stores too: whenever I had to go in and buy arnica for Alex I would inevitably hear it. I scanned the club and spotted the handsome scarred stranger heading towards the darkroom. He turned back to look at me over his shoulder, grey eyes glinting, a bold invitation so early in the game. I remember clearly the overwhelming urge I felt to follow him below.

Jamie continued, oblivious. 'Lou Reed had a trans girlfriend too you know?' he said. 'And Bryan Ferry.'

I stood up, intent on deserting my post, but he caught me by the wrist and arrested my step, not aggressively, rather he was almost imploring me. He said, 'Charli, these are the women who have been written out of our cultural history.'

'Yeah,' I scowled, 'no shit.'

I had to hand it to him, he always found a new way to be awful. Every time we saw each other he took his natural insufferability to the next level, gave it a brand new spin. I released myself from his sticky grip, picked up my purse, said, 'I'm going now, great chatting,' and headed off on the path of the grey-eyed stranger.

Again he caught me, this time his hand on my shoulder, almost seductively. 'Don't go downstairs,' he pressed, 'stay. I wanna tell you about the movie. Maybe we can work together.'

'I'm awfully busy just now, Jamie,' I said, extracting myself from his grasp again. 'Lots of amazing projects . . .'

'Come on,' he cooed, a ridiculous half-baked coquette, pouting. 'What? Are you pissed with me or something?'

'Chill the fuck out,' I pushed him away. 'I'll be back. Get a grip. Watch the desk. Fuck.'

I took a circuitous route, avoiding the DJ booth so that Finley wouldn't spot me sneaking off, and when he did turn towards me I took a beat to buy a pack of fags from the vending machine with Jamie's €8 to throw him off the scent. Two guys in basketball vests came out of the bathroom swiping at their noses. They stopped at the table between me and the cigarette machine I was fumbling with to pick up a copy of a magazine and a handful of free condoms and lube. In the doorway above my head two muscle jocks with bleached mullets sized each other up on the television screen, licking their thin lips, shot reverse shot, slathered in Vaseline live from a pasteboard gym sometime around 1987, the year of *Never Let Me Down*, Bowie's worst ever album. I suddenly felt very out of place there in that crumbling temple of masculinity without Polly. She was a good friend and she was a great dancer, I was sorry she had stayed home to rewatch *Now, Voyager*.

I forged on alone, moved towards the stairs descending into the dark, a red-faced gentleman in a tank top and stone-wash jeans came up gesticulating wildly and trying to shunt me back in the other direction. 'Geh nicht nach unten, Fräulein,' he was saying, 'Geh nicht nach unten,' telling me not to go downstairs, that women weren't allowed, or some such bullshit. I gave him such an almighty shove that he stumbled backwards, cursing me, 'Du verrückte Fotze! Du bist verrückt!', and I sank into the underworld below.

8

My mother is sobbing at my bedside. 'It's all my fault,' she is saying, 'this all my fault.' I'm not listening, not really, I'm watching the shadows pulse up the wall, thrown by the police cars below. The sirens silent now, the strobes rotating still, blue lights neutralised by the beatific smile of the tubes overhead, colourless against the unending fluorescent glow of the hospital, we are forever bathed in margarine, suspended in casino time, time unchanging. 'Look at you, you're so skinny,' my mother says, 'this is all my fault.'

I have all but forgotten why she's here, but she is, and she has a copy of Woman's Own *in her lap. Eva Longoria is strutting on the cover, she has a new husband, a pop of neon green celebrates* Fifty gorgeous summer shirts for £5 or less!, *another bears the legend* True Life Stories: I cut his penis off!'

The room is still, it must be late, it's dark outside, night creeps in under the lowered blinds, inching along the margins where the canvas fails to meet the sill, the curtains have been dropped too hastily. There is a big bunch of cut tulips on the table beside my bed, wrapped in cellophane and belted at the waist with a rustic knot of reed and twine, little green feet standing in a big glass bulb of water, yellow heads slanted sad and rigid against the wall. My mother can see that I'm puzzling them. 'A friend brought them in for you,' she's saying, 'Wes, I think they said his name was,' she dabs her eyes.

Outside no nurse, now no nun, just the reporter's face glancing scornfully through the little pane in the door, dishonoured against the glass, I have him. He peels away embarrassed that I have caught him out again. I say, 'It is so annoying that I cannot even smoke in here.'

My mother is alarmed, she snaps up abruptly, flying around a hairpin bend from sorrow to ire. 'Don't tell me you've started up with that an' all!' I'm cursing myself, assuring her that I am only joking. 'Of course not, no of course not,' I'm blushing, 'I'm not an idiot.'

I'm forced to think about where I would be now if I had made different choices, I'm following a crack across the ceiling, how have I not yet noticed this fissure? It bisects the room, one third, two thirds, a grey wobble across the untroubled plaster, a schoolchild's attempt to divide the page without a ruler. I'm looking on at myself, at the life I am living in an adjacent reality, similar but not the same, where I am preparing for my wedding day. Over there I am the wife of a poet and I have a full, ripe life to contemplate, here I have only Alexander's funeral to attend. But I will not lament, I will remain proud, I will not give in to regret. 'It is love, not reason, that is stronger than death,' *I'm saying a prayer to Thomas Mann to thank him for teaching me that.*

My mother is reminiscing, and I don't know why, about the old George Henry Lee department store in Liverpool, the taste of heavily varnished wood remembered on my tongue, dulled brass and the phantoms of grandeur. 'Wasn't it a lovely place to shop?' I'm waiting for the appropriate moment to ask when we can leave and go home, she's telling me the story of a Saturday afternoon twenty-five years ago, of the terrible fright I gave her when I disappeared from my buggy whilst she was browsing soft furnishings. 'Turns out, your brother had put you in the lift and sent you down to the basement,' she's smiling to herself, 'he could be such a little shit sometimes. Oh, I could've strangled him.' I have no memory of this.

'You two always loved going into department stores. "The big shops," you called them.' She's crossing and uncrossing her legs, trying to find a way to sit comfortably, but she cannot. 'You were funny kids.'

I'm choked, I can't recall the last time she spoke about my brother, surely not since his funeral. I want to tell her that I'm sorry, I want to say 'I miss him too,' I want to offer some comfort, but when I turn to her to talk I catch the reporter staring in again, his eyes in the glass behind her, and I hiss, 'I wish that hack would just fuck off.'

She asks, 'Who, love?'

'Him!' I'm explaining, accusing with a belligerent pointer finger. 'The journalist. He's been hanging around trying for a scoop the whole time I've been in here. It's obscene.'

My mother is perplexed, she's looking over her shoulder, bemused. 'Charli, love, he's not a reporter. He's a police officer.' Her voice is only forcibly made calm and clear. 'This is serious love, someone died in that accident.'

I refute this. 'Don't tell me you didn't see the TV news crews outside?' I'm exasperated. 'They all want the exclusive on Alexander. He's famous all over Europe. You read the magazines, you *know that.'*

She's regarding me with a nescient fear. 'You have to stop acting like this now, Charli,' her voice quivers and swoops down, quietened by shame. 'You have to stop it. You can't carry on like this. They found a cat in your freezer for God's sake. You have to stop it.'

Somewhere down the corridor a doctor bids his colleagues goodnight, outside, the wailing of an alarm. I'm suddenly weak and desperate to be compliant. 'I don't like talking about all this, can we just go home? I think I'd feel better at home.'

My mother smiles weakly. 'It's not that simple. It's serious this time, love.'

The whole room is flickering like a row of candles before the bye-altar assaulted by a breeze, the lights are blinking in silent panic, and in an instant we're lost to a new wave of blackness. I'm muttering, 'Bloody news trucks. I told you. Idiots.'

My mother is weeping in the darkness, otherwise the room is quiet. The strobing on the ceiling is blue again now, she repeats, 'This is all my fault. This is all my fault,' again and again but I am not listening. I am remembering another night, lying on my back in Görlitzer Park, stoned, searching the evening sky for signs of life on other planets. Alexander beside me insists, 'There must be, there has to be.' I'm asking my mother, 'Did you really see him?'

She's sniffling. 'What love?'

I rephrase: 'Did you really tell me that you saw him, or did I invent that for myself too?'

She reaches through the darkness for the bedside lamp. It sits above the tulips and comes on with a pop, giving out a feeble yellow throw, casting me in half shadow, illuminating my mother, arresting her tears. 'I did and all, you know,' she laughs, and blows her nose hard. I can hear her rustle for another tissue. 'Tell me,' I implore.

She's lost in the murk, only the tips of her shoes and her fingers on her knees are visible to me. Her voice is bronzed, she's telling me the tale. 'Well, we couldn't get a direct flight over here, you see, so we had to take a train to London, and we decided to stay overnight because there was an offer on. I quite fancied going on the London Eye, because well, I never have, so we went down there the next morning to see about tickets. Anyway, your dad was looking at the board to see how much it would cost like, and I saw this tall fella getting out of one of the pods, or whatever they call them, with his wife and this beautiful little girl, well, probably a teenager really. He had this black baseball cap on and sunglasses, even though it wasn't all that warm out and I thought that's odd, *but then people do dress different in London, don't they? He had this really powerful angel aura about him, and I felt like I should talk to him but your dad was moaning about the cost of it all, saying that there were better things he could think of to do with forty quid, so I decided to mind my own business. Anyway, this fella and his family walked right past me, and you know that feeling? Like when someone walks over your grave? Well, that's what it felt like, when he came past. I didn't even think about it, I just turned right round and stared like, and then he turned back too like he knew me, and he took off his sunglasses and smiled. And that's when I realised – when I saw his eyes. Oh, Charli, I could've fainted! I mean, I thought I was seeing things, only your dad was stood right next to me and he saw the whole thing too. He went white as a sheet, I've never seen anything like it, he had to put his hand up on the information board and he said, 'Fucking Hell Maggie, I don't believe it. That was David Bowie.'*

9

The smell of the darkroom is so specific: amyl nitrate, cigarette smoke and damp. Everything below swims in a purple half-light. I was looking for the man I had followed downstairs. I didn't want to seem too keen, and rather than plunge right in behind him I stopped on the decomposing sofa to peel open my cigarettes. I checked my purse, but alas no lighter. Illuminated from above by a neon sign, a flattering pink glow powdered my skin and allowed me perfect legibility. Should my intended come this way, he would have no trouble finding me. I waited, unsure of how much time had passed.

I poked about further inside my bag for a box of matches, I thought I might've perhaps squirrelled some away in there, with my lipstick and keys and the greying business cards foisted on me by forgotten bodies from the music biz. But no luck, I struck out, the cigarette stuck in the corner of my eager mouth, impotent, comic. It was only a little busier in the darkroom than it was on the dance floor, a few skeletal gentlemen stalked the place, careful not to make eye contact with me in case I took this as an invitation to converse. I watched them make the rounds again and again as if in the hope of finding some new possibility this time around, though whenever I tried to stop one of these lonely hunters to ask for a light, they passed me right by, as though I simply did not exist. None of them would so much as look at me, let alone light my smoke. I began to feel like a gorgon in the demi-darkness, the Medusa of the darkroom with all these fags scurrying by across this desolate landscape, desperate to avoid my death-dealing gaze. And no sign of my man. So I stood up and stalked into the murk, let myself be swallowed up by the Cimmerian shade. I acquiesced to the will of the maze, everything would be revealed at the appropriate hour.

I made my way deeper into the artificial night, through soft moans and past amorphous conjugations of flesh, sinister as a Francis Bacon portrait. Puddles of amber light collecting on the floor, spilled by bulbs in sconces on the brickwork walls at the edges of the chamber. Ahead of me I heard laughter, one lone voice in the dark, tinkling and somehow familiar, it came and it went. I navigated the men leaning against subdividing plywood walls, huffing poppers and squeezing at their bulges, occasional fingertips making contact with the small of my back as I passed, the murk now granting me a paradoxical visibility. And no sign of my man.

On I went now and came to a wooden bench adorned with empty half-pint glasses and beer bottles, as though it were a ceremonial altar, a lost wallet, a discarded wedge of tissue, a tin ashtray choked full of butts, some still smoking. I poked about in the litter and found a yellow plastic Zippo on the floor, but it was spent and had no flame to give and so I pressed on. The alcove in the farthest corner was uninhabited tonight, the TV set in there wasn't showing the usual skin flicks but rather, at Finley's insistence, video art. His hope was that, along with the free tequila shots, these ten-minute loops of ants swarming crucifixes and sugar cubes melting in oil would help win back the party's popularity, but nobody came to this place for a righteous education.

I caught the laugh again, it seemed once more to originate just ahead of me, only by now I'd reached the far wall of the basement so it could only have been an echo rebounding. And still no sign of my man. I figured he must have found satisfaction elsewhere, or perhaps I'd misjudged his expression entirely, perhaps he hadn't meant to invite me down here at all, only to pass me a subtle sign of solidarity, *you are seen and you are valued*. God I hate men sometimes. I felt defeated: this was the end of the line then, I had taken my turn and now it was time to resume my post on the door. Maybe I'd even give Jamie the benefit of the doubt, at the very least he would have a lighter.

I retraced my steps through the labyrinth, over broken glass and cigarette ash, picking carefully through those few active bodies, only when I emerged back at the foot of the stairs I saw my man a few metres on, tall and lean, slipping back inside the catacombs. We had been travelling together in opposing loops, on separate circuits through this second midnight, perhaps even brushing past each other in purest ignorance. The thought thrilled me and I hurried behind him, back into the caliginous hole. The first room was dark, the second darker; I could barely tell if I was alone or surrounded on all sides, I trailed my fingernails over the chipboard partitions so as not to stumble. For a moment, I thought I had lost him again, I couldn't make out his shape even as my eyes adapted to this lower level of light, but then I saw his silhouette unmistakably, cutting across the room. I would've called out his name only I didn't know it.

The most compelling feeling came upon me: he was leading me on, away from the sparse interlopers. I followed him down the obscure hallway which runs behind the full length of the darkroom, and he made it feel like a strip that I had never walked before. Intermittent flashes of activity vented through doorways previously undiscovered, shadows and the sound of piss hitting concrete, the stranger striding on ahead, he knew where we were going. We rounded a corner, saw a slave on his knees attending to his master's boots, pushed on through a pair of heavy rubber curtains, ran a tight gauntlet, men pressing in on both sides of the corridor, closing in around whatever came by, and finally into an empty antechamber.

We were suddenly alone, together, my heart banging in my ears, his hot breath gracing my face, ten fingers at my waist climbing their way to my throat, nothing but lust swirling around us. He pressed me to the wall in the haste of desire, insistent, demanding, starved, kissing me and tearing at my dress. 'Endlich,' he said. 'At last'.

I was aware of somebody in the doorway looking on, and though I'm not a natural exhibitionist I was too far gone to care, I let him leer as my grey-eyed stranger slipped off my spaghetti straps and plunged his head between my breasts. My dress dropped and the stranger dropped with it, kissing my stomach and my thighs, yanking at my panties like a mad man, moaning, 'Oh my God yes, oh my fucking God, yes.'

Behind him in the doorway this voyeur loitered with intent, and the stranger on his knees, oblivious or only more aroused, started to work my stiffening cock with his anxious, zealous mouth. The wall damp against my back, right hand outstretched above me, the left forcing this unknown soldier to choke, I thought *so you like to watch do you?* and threw ferocious, libidinous glances towards the interloper, grinding my pelvis into the stranger's face.

I wondered if the man in the doorway would join us, if he would guide the head of my supplicant, use my cock to dominate him, I wanted him to, I could feel his gaze on me, and I wanted him to. I started to mewl pornographically, hoping to make it clear that his presence excited me. I didn't want to ask him to participate, that would be too polite, rather I wanted him to know it instinctively. The stranger's head worked frantically, he broke off only to huff his poppers, obscene and mindless, slobbering, spluttering, 'I fucking love your dick.' I paid him no attention; he was lost in his own world and I in mine – in the fantasy of being observed by unknown eyes. I stared ahead towards the shadow in the doorway, I gave it all to him, rolled down my bra to more fully expose my tits and purred loudly, 'You like that baby?' The stranger on his knees gasped, 'Yeah, oh fuck yeah,' though in truth I had not addressed the question to him.

I knew that this voyeur was taken in now, his arousal was palpable, I swear I could hear his breath in my ear, his voice telling me to cum. My knees began to shake, the stranger labouring nonstop, striving for perfection, forcing my final confession. With a full body spasm I groaned and gave way.

Then, there was stillness and darkness, with only the stranger's taxed pants spoiling the returning silence, *the hush in which something gathers or crouches*. As often, Henry James came to mind.

The voyeur reached into his pocket for a lighter and lit a cigarette, and in the momentary glow the fire gave his face I recognised what I suppose I'd already known, just who it was that had been watching.

'Alex?' I said, and the stranger, now dusting off his knees replied, 'No, Mark.'

I ignored him and pulled up my bra straps, watching the amber tip of the cigarette bob in the doorway, hauled up my dress with an increasing urgency, as if only now aware of my dishevelment. Yes, he was looking me over, I could feel it. He answered me smug and leisurely. 'Hello, lover,' he said, and took another long drag in the dark.

The man who had just made me cum stood up, perplexed, 'Who are you talking to?' but I was somewhere else now, moving towards the doorway, saying, 'Fuck, Alex? How long have you been here?'

'I cannot say,' he replied, 'it feels like forever.'

I had told myself many times that if I ever saw him again I would say nothing but *you're dead to me*, though in truth I was dead to myself. To see him now was like sliding into a warm bubble bath and I honestly did not care anymore that I might go under, never to see the surface again. I was kidding myself if I thought I deserved anything more.

'I can't believe it. Alex,' I gasped, hand to my sternum. 'Do you have a light?'

He laughed and it was the laugh I had been following all night, all summer, perhaps all my life. 'Sure,' he said and handed me his heavy cigarette lighter.

I felt for my purse and found my cigarettes, and said to my grey-eyed friend, 'Thank you, you can go now.'

Naturally he was disgruntled, he exclaimed, 'What?' I don't think he had pictured it playing out this way.

I said, 'It was a beautiful three minutes but now –'

He cut me off. 'You are one crazy bitch, you know that?'

'Yes Mark,' I sighed, 'I do know that.'

He kicked his way out of there, undoubtedly humiliated, but I was content in the knowledge that such disrespect would manifest usefully somewhere down the line in an ever-greater appetite for degradation. Alex watched him go and snorted wickedly. 'Oh lover, whatever happened to your beautiful English manners?'

I lit my Marlboro pensively. 'I think I lost them down the back of a sofa somewhere,' I said, 'what's your excuse?'

I felt that I should maintain a front, a pose of reserve, that I must not gush or squeal with joy, must not betray the immense relief of finding him again, and yet I knew that any such holding back was futile. He could always see right through my eggshell veneer, like those lucky art historians who X-rayed *An Old Man in Military Costume* and found another portrait beneath, Rembrandt's own face. A smile crept over mine.

'I did not think you would be so happy to see me,' he was smiling, shyly, I could tell, even in the gloom – it was in the tone of his voice. I flushed at the familiar feeling that he knew what I was thinking ahead of me. 'But I am,' I said, 'very happy.'

Of course it came to this, a Freudian might call it a repetition compulsion, the work of the death drive, a barely conscious desire to recreate the circumstances of one's own unhappiness. Myself I'm more of a Jungian, I'm an eternal optimist, this was a case of *try, try again.* Michael Jackson replaced Bubbles, his pet chimp, with a smaller more docile monkey, also called Bubbles, when the original grew too big and too aggressive; Damien Hirst has to install a new shark in the tank when the subject of *The Physical Impossibility of Death in the Mind of Someone Living* begins to rot; if a singer in a girl group gets too puffed up they switch her out for a new girl who looks just the same. Sometimes all you need is to take a moment and shuffle your deck.

I caught the hook from an old synth track playing upstairs, Throbbing Gristle maybe, 'United'. Somewhere in the darkness nearby, a man was choking on his own lust, flesh smacking flesh. I picked a piece of tobacco from my tongue, agitated, and took a breath, the bigger person. 'I wanted to apologise,' I said, 'if I caused you any trouble with the label, I'm sorry.'

'Ah,' he pouted, 'win some lose some.'

I had finished my cigarette already; I wondered if I should light up again so as not to lose the beat of this conversation. I had but one solitary desire: to get out of there and into the frangible madness of the world outside, to leave with Alex before he vanished again, to hold on to him for as long as I could, but I did not know how to put muscle on this fancy.

'I missed you, you know?' I said.

'I know,' Alex smiled, 'I tried to call you.'

I answered, 'Yes, sorry, I haven't been thinking straight. I've been confused.'

'And now?' he asked. 'Shall we take a drink together like old friends?'

'We can't,' I sighed, 'I'm supposed to be working.' It sounded like an excuse.

He considered this. 'I am sorry too. About the song, about my behaviour,' he bit his plump lip, 'about many things.'

'No, please,' I said, hurrying to assuage, 'I overreacted. And if you need me to, I can help you get things back on track. I have plenty of free time right now, and as you know I'm *very* organised and *incredibly* focused.' I was babbling. '*Use me but as your spaniel.*'

'What?' he said. 'I do not understand.'

'Shakespeare,' I went on, 'it doesn't matter. I want to be of service.'

'No, Charli,' he said, 'no more of this please. Things must be different.'

I pressed myself to him. 'But what if I liked it the way things were? What then?'

I thought, *why doesn't he get it? Why doesn't he just take me home? I don't want to be here, I want to leave, now with him, to be his again*, and again he answered my questions unvoiced. 'Then we should go to my place,' he flicked his spent cigarette to the floor, 'for a change. I have the car outside. We can leave anytime you want.'

I nodded frantically. 'Yes, alright then, yes.'

'Eager,' Alex chuckled. 'There's a bottle of Kräuterlikör in the glove compartment too, if you *really* want to party.'

'I do,' I whooped, 'I do!'

He tucked his hand inside his shirt, like a portrait of Napoleon, he said, 'We will go home to my wonderful big bed. That is something I have never shown you before.' A grin crawled over his face, my blush, he caught it. 'And in the morning we can have breakfast together, there is a patisserie just below my apartment, it is excellent. I will bring us croissants and marmalade. If you like we can go to the Brücke Museum after lunch, it is closed to the public right now, but I know the curator.' He paused to assess my reaction; he might've seen I was overwhelmed, he said, 'Or if you prefer we can visit the grave of Marlene Dietrich together? It is in a beautiful quiet cemetery, and it is not so far by car.'

'Oh Alex,' I was almost on the edge of tears, 'that sounds wonderful.'

'Come then,' he said and took my hand, 'it is getting late.'

I nodded. 'OK, but we're going to have to run straight out. Finley will be *so* pissed if he sees me leave.'

We headed out of the darkroom, up the stairs and back through the party. Finley was no longer at the decks, he was sat at a banquette straddling the lap of my man with the grey eyes, his leather shorts were on the floor next to him, I think he was getting fucked. A few men sat by, smoking and half-heartedly masturbating, the playlist giving out an uninspiring selection of Schlagermusik. Jamie was gone too and as we hustled out I grabbed the cash box for good measure. The coast was clear for a painless escape.

The sky was violent, the rain coming down in sheets, thunder and lightning roiling overhead: the storm had finally broken. We ran to the old Mercedes, howling like chimps, drenched to the skin by an almost tropical downpour, Alex twirling his suit jacket above his head like George Michael in a music video from the long dead past.

In the car we sheltered, waiting out the worst of the weather. I poked in the glove box for the booze and found the old Mary J. Blige tape, worn down, the kindest augury possible: we would be alright now. I sat in the front seat beside him, tonight he would be my lover, not my chauffeur.

A yellow streetlight poured through the waterfall on our windscreen, we sat side by side quietly, swigging at the herbal liquor. It tasted like my grandmother's cough drops, bitter and sticky and I laughed again at life. I said, 'Did you know that I had a brother called Alexander? I don't know if I ever told you that?'

He smiled. 'Of course, lover, it is all right there on your palm. Do not forget that we share the simian line.'

'*Two cuts lie parallel in the same flesh*!' I whispered. 'Anne Carson, you crafty old bitch!'

Alexander patted his pockets for the car keys. 'What?'

I reshaped my thoughts. 'I can't lose you again, Alex,' I said. 'I think I'd rather die.'

'Oh, Charli. Charli,' he said, and he took my hand and raised it to his lips and he kissed it, 'you crazy girl, I love you.' I blushed again, which seemed idiotic, and he smiled, very tenderly. 'Let us go home now.'

Alex started the engine, but I couldn't speak, so I slipped the tape into the deck and we pulled away from the kerb. The rain showed no sign of receding, still we couldn't very well sit out there all night. I took another deep slurp of the liquor and gave Alex the bottle, he took a big slug himself and passed it back, eyes on the road, shoulders hunched over the wheel trying to peer ahead through the deluge. The wipers worked overtime, squealing terribly. I felt I really should say something more, but words failed me. Above us lightning transformed the early hours into magnesium oxide and an almighty clap of thunder rocked the heavens, police headlights rushing towards us then squalling away behind.

We skimmed the west side of Tempelhofer Feld, past a huddle of screaming teens crowded in the doorway of Burger King at this unearthly hour, the giant blue U of the subway station at Paradestrasse rearing up out of nowhere. A taxi cut us up at the lights. 'Idiot,' cursed Alex, and swung a hard right.

I took another swig from the bottle and said the fatal words, 'I love you too, Alex.'

He looked at me then back to the road, then turned his head, 'Charli, do you really mean that?'

'In spite of myself,' I joked, 'yes, I do.'

Mary J. Blige was just finishing up 'I'm Goin' Down', I remember that. Alex's hands trembled reflexively on the steering wheel, his eyes fluttered, he turned and reached for my face, leant over to kiss me, then there was another flash of lightning, another roll of thunder, a white saloon car crossed in front of us and we drove straight into the side of it. We came to a violent end, brakes discordant, the sickening sound of something snapping, a wave of breaking glass, the car horn deafening, one solid impenetrable note blaring out into the night like a saxophone crushed. The rain was on the inside now, it ran in rivulets down my face, into my eyes, washing warm blood into my mouth. I looked to form words, to cry out for help, tried to reach for Alex but my arms were pinned to my side, I saw that my dress was torn open across the breast, my own flesh beneath the tear weeping scarlet. I thought, 'Oh! But now I'll never get to visit Dietrich's grave,' and the prospect made me heartsick, and that's all I can recall.

Acknowledgements

I want to thank my first and most cherished readers: Olivia Laing, Morgan M. Page and Torrey Peters. I'm forever grateful for the attention you gave to the early drafts of this book, and for your friendship.

Romy Haag, you are the diva of divas, I hope you know that. Sophie and Stevie, who saw it all, I love you. Sarah, you kept me looking cunty throughout – how can I ever repay the debt? Huge thanks due also to the little kid in the street who once said, "Hallo Geist!" and thus inspired this whole saga.

To Josey, Matthi, Mimzy, Paul, Ben, Greta, Malcolm, Snax, David, Fred, Nadia, Sam and the Crystal Tits, thank you for the ride of a lifetime. Molly Nilsson, Nadia Buyse, Mary Ocher, Easter, Planningtorock, SSION, Dan Bodan, Light Asylum and Dievondavon, your music defined my time in Berlin. Grammys for all of you.

To Paul and Allegra, thanks for giving this book a home. To Alicia, who acquired the title in the United States, and to Elizabeth, who saw me over the finishing line, thank you. Thanks to my dude Davey Davis for the introduction – I owe you. To everyone at Bloomsbury and Catapult: you're amazing, you have my endless admiration. And to Zoe and Olivia at United Agents for getting the ink on the page. Florian, I am beyond thrilled that you let me use one of your images on the UK cover. Thanks to Robin for the jacket photo and Peter Fingelton for the press shot.

Thank you also, Robert Chevara, Travis Jeppesen and Jake Arnott, for letting me weave your anecdotes into this book. I appreciate it, fellas!

To Boopie: You deserve everything I could ever possibly give you and more. I love being loved by you.

And finally I bow with the most profound gratitude to the Madonna de Montevergine in recognition of her glorious intercession, and to Saint Expedit, who made the (seemingly) impossible happen for me with this book.

LAUREN J. JOSEPH is a writer and performer. Her novel *At Certain Points We Touch* was chosen as one of *The Observer*'s debut novels of the year. Her other work includes the experimental prose volume *Everything Must Go* and the plays *Boy in a Dress* and *A Generous Lover*. Her recent nonfiction has appeared in *Granta*, *The Observer*, *Vittles*, *The Guardian*, *The Erotic Review*, and *Tate Etc*. *Lean Cat, Savage Cat* is Lauren's second novel.